Rules of Civility

RULES
OF
CIVILITY

Amor Towles

VIKING

VIKING
Published by the Penguin Group
Penguin Group (USA) Inc., 375 Hudson Street, New York, New York 10014, U.S.A. • Penguin Group (Canada), 90 Eglinton Avenue East, Suite 700, Toronto, Ontario, Canada M4P 2Y3 (a division of Pearson Penguin Canada Inc.) • Penguin Books Ltd, 80 Strand, London WC2R 0RL, England • Penguin Ireland, 25 St. Stephen's Green, Dublin 2, Ireland (a division of Penguin Books Ltd) • Penguin Books Australia Ltd, 250 Camberwell Road, Camberwell, Victoria 3124, Australia (a division of Pearson Australia Group Pty Ltd) • Penguin Books India Pvt Ltd, 11 Community Centre, Panchsheel Park, New Delhi—110 017, India • Penguin Group (NZ), 67 Apollo Drive, Rosedale, Auckland 0632, New Zealand (a division of Pearson New Zealand Ltd) • Penguin Books (South Africa) (Pty) Ltd, 24 Sturdee Avenue, Rosebank, Johannesburg 2196, South Africa

Penguin Books Ltd, Registered Offices: 80 Strand, London WC2R 0RL, England

First published in 2011 by Viking Penguin, a member of Penguin Group (USA) Inc.

10 9 8 7 6 5 4 3 2

Grateful acknowledgment is made for permission to reprint an excerpt from "Autumn in New York" by Vernon Duke. © Copyright 1934 by Kay Duke Music. Reprinted by permission of Boosey & Hawkes, Inc.

Photograph credits
Image copyright © The Metropolitan Museum of Art / Art Resource, NY
Page 11: The Metropolitan Museum of Art, Walker Evans Archive, 1994 (1994.253.622.5), © Walker Evans Archive, The Metropolitan Museum of Art • Page 57: The Metropolitan Museum of Art, Walker Evans Archive, 1994 (1994.253.612.3), © Walker Evans Archive, The Metropolitan Museum of Art • Page 147: The Metropolitan Museum of Art, Walker Evans Archive, 1994 (1994.253.514.1), © Walker Evans Archive, The Metropolitan Museum of Art • Page 249: The Metropolitan Museum of Art, Walker Evans Archive, 1994 (1994.253.606.3), © Walker Evans Archive, The Metropolitan Museum of Art • Page 313: The Metropolitan Museum of Art, Walker Evans Archive, 1971 (1971.646.18), © Walker Evans Archive, The Metropolitan Museum of Art

Publisher's Note
This is a work of fiction. Names, characters, places, and incidents either are the product of the author's imagination or are used fictitiously, and any resemblance to actual persons, living or dead, business establishments, events, or locales is entirely coincidental.

LIBRARY OF CONGRESS CATALOGING-IN-PUBLICATION DATA
Towles, Amor.
    Rules of civility : a novel / Amor Towles.
        p.   cm.
    ISBN 978-0-670-02269-4
    1. Young women—Fiction.   2. Upper class—New York (State)—New York—Fiction.   3. Nineteen thirties—Fiction.   4. Wall Street (New York, N.Y.)—Fiction.   5. New York (N.Y.)—Fiction.   I. Title.
    PS3620.O945R85 2011
    813'.6—dc22
    2011004118

Printed in the United States of America
Designed by Carla Bolte

FOR MAGGIE,
MY COMET

♦ ♦ ♦

Then saith he to his servants, The wedding is ready, but they which were bidden were not worthy. Go ye therefore into the highways, and as many as ye shall find, bid to the marriage. So those servants went out into the highways and gathered together all as many as they found, both bad and good: and the wedding was furnished with guests.

And when the king came in to see the guests, he saw there a man which had not on a wedding garment: And he saith unto him, Friend, how camest thou in hither not having a wedding garment? And he was speechless. Then said the king to the servants, Bind him hand and foot, and take him away, and cast him into outer darkness; there shall be weeping and gnashing of teeth. For many are called, but few are chosen.

—Matthew 22:8–14

Rules of Civility

Preface

On the night of October 4th, 1966, Val and I, both in late middle age, attended the opening of *Many Are Called* at the Museum of Modern Art—the first exhibit of the portraits taken by Walker Evans in the late 1930s on the New York City subways with a hidden camera.

It was what the social columnists liked to refer to as "a superlative affair." The men were in black tie, echoing the palette of the photographs, and the women wore brightly colored dresses hemmed at every length from the Achilles tendon to the top of the thigh. Champagne was being served off little round trays by young unemployed actors with flawless features and the grace of acrobats. Few of the guests were looking at the pictures. They were too busy enjoying themselves.

A drunken young socialite in pursuit of a waiter stumbled and nearly knocked me to the floor. She wasn't alone in her condition. At formal gatherings, somehow it had become acceptable, even stylish, to be drunk before eight.

But perhaps that wasn't so hard to understand. In the 1950s, America had picked up the globe by the heels and shaken the change from its pockets. Europe had become a poor cousin—all crests and no table settings. And the indistinguishable countries of Africa, Asia, and South America had just begun skittering across our schoolroom walls like salamanders in the sun. True, the Communists were out there, somewhere, but with Joe McCarthy in the grave and no one on the Moon, for the time being the Russians just skulked across the pages of spy novels.

So all of us were drunk to some degree. We launched ourselves into the evening like satellites and orbited the city two miles above the Earth, powered by failing foreign currencies and finely filtered spirits. We shouted over the dinner tables and slipped away into empty rooms with each other's spouses, carousing with all the enthusiasm and indiscretion of Greek gods. And in the morning, we woke at 6:30 on the dot, clear-headed and optimistic, ready to resume our places behind the stainless steel desks at the helm of the world.

The spotlight that night wasn't on the photographer. In his midsixties, withered by an indifference to food, unable to fill out his own tuxedo, Evans looked as sad and nondescript as a retiree from General Motors middle management. Occasionally, someone would interrupt his solitude to make a remark, but he spent whole quarters of an hour standing awkwardly in the corner like the ugliest girl at the dance.

No, all eyes were not on Evans. Instead, they were trained on a thin-haired young author who had just made a sensation by penning a history of his mother's infidelities. Flanked by his editor and a press agent, he was accepting compliments from a coterie of fans, looking like a sly newborn.

Val took in the fawning circle with a curious gaze. He could make $10,000 in a day by setting in motion the merger of a Swiss department store chain with an American missile manufacturer, but for the life of him, he couldn't figure how a tattletale could cause such a stir.

Always mindful of his surroundings, the press agent caught my eye and waved me over. I gave a quick wave back and took my husband's arm.

—Come on, sweetheart, I said. Let's look at the pictures.

We walked into the exhibition's less crowded second room and began working our way around the walls at an unhurried pace. Virtually all of the pictures were horizontal portraits of one or two subway riders seated directly across from the photographer.

Here was a sober young Harlemite in a gamely tilted bowler with a little French mustache.

Here was a four-eyed forty-year-old with a fur-collared coat and a wide-brimmed hat looking every bit the gangster's accountant.

Here were two single girls from the perfume counter at Macy's, solidly in their thirties, a little sour with the knowledge that their best years were behind them, riding with eyebrows plucked all the way to the Bronx.

Here a him; there a her.

Here the young; there the old.

Here the dapper; there the drab.

Though taken more than twenty-five years earlier, the photographs had never been shown publicly. Evans apparently had some sort of concern for his subjects' privacy. This may sound strange (or even a little self-important) when you consider that he had photographed them in such a public place. But seeing their faces lined along on the wall, you could understand Evans's reluctance. For, in fact, the pictures captured a certain naked humanity. Lost in thought, masked by the anonymity of their commute, unaware of the camera that was trained so directly upon them, many of these subjects had unknowingly allowed their inner selves to be seen.

Anyone who has ridden the subway twice a day to earn their bread knows how it goes: When you board, you exhibit the same persona you use with your colleagues and acquaintances. You've carried it through the turnstile and past the sliding doors, so that your fellow passengers can tell who you are—cocky or cautious, amorous or indifferent, loaded or on the dole. But you find yourself a seat and the train gets under way; it comes to one station and then another; people get off and others get on. And under the influence of the cradlelike rocking of the train, your carefully crafted persona begins to slip away. The superego dissolves as your mind begins to wander aimlessly over your cares and your dreams; or better yet, it drifts into an ambient hypnosis, where even cares and dreams recede and the peaceful silence of the cosmos pervades.

It happens to all of us. It's just a question of how many stops it takes. Two for some. Three for others. Sixty-eighth Street. Fifty-ninth. Fifty-first. Grand Central. What a relief it was, those few minutes with our guard let down and our gaze inexact, finding the one true solace that human isolation allows.

How satisfying this photographic survey must have seemed to the uninitiated. All the young attorneys and the junior bankers and the spunky society girls who were making their way through the galleries must have looked at the pictures and thought: *What a tour de force. What an artistic achievement. Here at last are the faces of humanity!*

But for those of us who were young at the time, the subjects looked like ghosts.

The 1930s . . .

What a grueling decade that was.

I was sixteen when the Depression began, just old enough to have had all my dreams and expectations duped by the effortless glamour of the twenties. It was as if America launched the Depression just to teach Manhattan a lesson.

After the Crash, you couldn't hear the bodies hitting the pavement, but there was a sort of communal gasp and then a stillness that fell over the city like snow. The lights flickered. The bands laid down their instruments and the crowds made quietly for the door.

Then the prevailing winds shifted from west to east, blowing the dust of the Okies all the way back to Forty-second Street. It came in billowing clouds and settled over the newspaper stands and park benches, shrouding the blessed and the damned just like the ashes in Pompeii. Suddenly, we had our own Joads—ill clothed and beleaguered, trudging along the alleyways past the oil drum fires, past the shanties and flophouses, under the spans of the bridges, moving slowly but methodically toward inner Californias which were just as abject and unredeeming as the real thing. Poverty and powerlessness. Hunger and hopelessness. At least until the omen of war began to brighten our step.

Yes, the hidden camera portraits of Walker Evans from 1938 to 1941 represented humanity, but a particular strain of humanity—a chastened one.

———

A few paces ahead of us, a young woman was enjoying the exhibit. She couldn't have been more than twenty-two. Every picture seemed to pleasantly surprise her—as if she was in the portrait gallery of a castle where all the faces seemed majestic and remote. Her skin was flushed with an ignorant beauty that filled me with envy.

The faces weren't remote for me. The chastened expressions, the unrequited stares, they were all too familiar. It was like that experience of walking into a hotel lobby in another city where the clothes and the mannerisms of the clientele are so similar to your own that you're just bound to run into someone you don't want to see.

And, in a way, that's what happened.

—It's Tinker Grey, I said, as Val was moving on to the next picture.

He came back to my side to take a second look at this portrait of a twenty-eight-year-old man, ill shaven, in a threadbare coat.

Twenty pounds underweight, he had almost lost the blush on his cheeks, and his face was visibly dirty. But his eyes were bright and alert and trained straight ahead with the slightest hint of a smile on his lips, as if it was he who was studying the photographer. As if it was he who was studying us. Staring across three decades, across a canyon of encounters, looking like a visitation. And looking every bit himself.

—Tinker Grey, repeated Val with vague recognition. I think my brother knew a Grey who was a banker. . . .

—Yes, I said. That's the one.

Val studied the picture more closely now, showing the polite interest that a distant connection who's fallen on hard times deserves. But a question or two must have presented itself regarding how well I knew the man.

—Extraordinary, Val said simply; and ever so slightly, he furrowed his brow.

By the summer that Val and I had begun seeing each other, we were still in our thirties and had missed little more than a decade of each other's adult lives; but that was time enough. It was time enough for whole lives to have been led and misled. It was time enough, as the poet said, to murder and create—or at least, to have warranted the dropping of a question on one's plate.

But Val counted few backward-looking habits as virtues; and in regards to the mysteries of my past, as in regards to so much else, he was a gentleman first.

Nonetheless, I made a concession.

—He was an acquaintance of mine as well, I said. In my circle of friends for a time. But I haven't heard his name since before the war.

Val's brow relaxed.

Perhaps he was comforted by the deceptive simplicity of these little facts. He eyed the picture with more measure and a brief shake of the head, which simultaneously gave the coincidence its due and affirmed how unfair the Depression had been.

—Extraordinary, he said again, though more sympathetically. He slipped his arm under mine and gently moved me on.

We spent the required minute in front of the next picture. Then the next and the next. But now the faces were passing by like the faces of strangers ascending an opposite escalator. I was barely taking them in.

Seeing Tinker's smile . . .

After all these years, I was unprepared for it. It made me feel sprung upon.

Maybe it was just complacency—that sweet unfounded complacency of a well-heeled Manhattan middle age—but walking through the doors of that museum, I would have testified under oath that my life had achieved a perfect equilibrium. It was a marriage of two minds, of two metropolitan spirits tilting as gently and inescapably toward the future as paper whites tilt toward the sun.

And yet, I found my thoughts reaching into the past. Turning their backs on all the hard-wrought perfections of the hour, they were searching for the sweet uncertainties of a bygone year and for all its chance encounters—encounters which in the moment had seemed so haphazard and effervescent but which with time took on some semblance of fate.

Yes, my thoughts turned to Tinker and to Eve—but they turned to Wallace Wolcott and Dicky Vanderwhile and to Anne Grandyn too. And to those turns of the kaleidoscope that gave color and shape to the passage of my 1938.

Standing at my husband's side, I found myself intent on keeping the memories of the year to myself.

It wasn't that any of them were so scandalous that they would have shocked Val or threatened the harmony of our marriage—on the contrary, if I had shared them Val would probably have been even more endeared to me. But I didn't *want* to share them. Because I didn't want to dilute them.

Above all else, I wanted to be alone. I wanted to step out of the glare of my own circumstances. I wanted to go get a drink in a hotel bar. Or better yet, take a taxi down to the Village for the first time in how many years. . . .

Yes, Tinker looked poor in that picture. He looked poor and hungry and without prospects. But he looked young and vibrant too; and strangely alive.

Suddenly, it was as if the faces on the wall were watching me. The ghosts on the subway, tired and alone, were studying my face, taking in those traces of compromise that give aging human features their unique sense of pathos.

Then Val surprised me.

—Let's go, he said.

I looked up and he smiled.

—Come on. We'll come back some morning when it isn't so busy.

—Okay.

It was crowded in the middle of the gallery so we kept to the periphery, walking past the pictures. The faces flickered by like the faces of prisoners looking through those little square openings in maximum security cells. They followed me with their gaze as if to say: *Where do you think you're going?* And then just before we reached the exit one of them stopped me in my tracks.

A wry smile formed on my face.

—What is it? asked Val.

—It's him again.

On the wall between two portraits of older women, there was a second portrait of Tinker. Tinker in a cashmere coat, clean shaven, a crisp Windsor knot poking over the collar of a custom-made shirt.

Val dragged me forward by the hand until we were a foot from the picture.

—You mean the same one from before?

—Yes.

—It couldn't be.

Val doubled back to the first portrait. Across the room I could see him studying the dirtier face with care, looking for distinguishing marks. He came back and took up his place a foot from the man in the cashmere coat.

—Incredible, he said. It's the very same fellow!

—Please step back from the art, a security guard said.

We stepped back.

—If you didn't know, you'd think they were two different men entirely.

—Yes, I said. You're right.

—Well, he certainly got back on his feet!

Val was suddenly in a good mood. The journey from threadbare to cashmere restored his natural sense of optimism.

—No, I said. This is the earlier picture.

—What's that?

—The other picture was after this one. It was 1939.

I pointed to the tag.

—This was taken in 1938.

You couldn't blame Val for making the mistake. It was natural to assume that this was the later picture—and not simply because it was hung later in the show. In the 1938 picture Tinker not only looked better off, he looked older too: His face was fuller, and it had a suggestion of pragmatic world-weariness, as if a string of successes had towed along an ugly truth or two. While the picture taken a year later looked more like the portrait of a peacetime twenty-year-old: vibrant and fearless and naïve.

Val felt embarrassed for Tinker.

—Oh, he said. I'm sorry.

He took my arm again and shook his head for Tinker as for us all.

—Riches to rags, he said, tenderly.

—No, I said. Not exactly.

NEW YORK CITY, 1969

WINTERTIME

CHAPTER ONE

The Old Long Since

It was the last night of 1937.

With no better plans or prospects, my roommate Eve had dragged me back to The Hotspot, a wishfully named nightclub in Greenwich Village that was four feet underground.

From a look around the club, you couldn't tell that it was New Year's Eve. There were no hats or streamers; no paper trumpets. At the back of the club, looming over a small empty dance floor, a jazz quartet was playing loved-me-and-left-me standards without a vocalist. The saxophonist, a mournful giant with skin as black as motor oil, had apparently lost his way in the labyrinth of one of his long, lonely solos. While the bass player, a coffee-and-cream mulatto with a small deferential mustache, was being careful not to hurry him. *Boom, boom, boom,* he went, at half the pace of a heartbeat.

The spare clientele were almost as downbeat as the band. No one was in their finery. There were a few couples here and there, but no romance. Anyone in love or money was around the corner at Café Society dancing to swing. In another twenty years all the world would be sitting in basement clubs like this one, listening to antisocial soloists explore their inner malaise; but on the last night of 1937, if you were watching a quartet it was because you couldn't afford to see the whole ensemble, or because you had no good reason to ring in the new year.

We found it all very comforting.

We didn't really understand what we were listening to, but we could tell that it had its advantages. It wasn't going to raise our hopes or spoil them. It had a semblance of rhythm and a surfeit of sincerity. It was just enough of an excuse to get us out of our room and we treated it accordingly, both of us wearing comfortable flats and a simple black dress. Though under her little number, I noted that Eve was wearing the best of her stolen lingerie.

Eve Ross . . .

Eve was one of those surprising beauties from the American Midwest.

In New York it becomes so easy to assume that the city's most alluring women have flown in from Paris or Milan. But they're just a minority. A much larger covey hails from the stalwart states that begin with the letter I—like Iowa and Indiana and Illinois. Bred with just the right amount of fresh air, roughhousing, and ignorance, these primitive blondes set out from the cornfields looking like starlight with limbs. Every morning in early spring one of them skips off her porch with a sandwich wrapped in cellophane ready to flag down the first Greyhound headed to Manhattan—this city where all things beautiful are welcomed and measured and, if not immediately adopted, then at least tried on for size.

One of the great advantages that the midwestern girls had was that you couldn't tell them apart. You can always tell a rich New York girl from a poor one. And you can tell a rich Boston girl from a poor one. After all, that's what accents and manners are there for. But to the native New Yorker, the midwestern girls all looked and sounded the same. Sure, the girls from the various classes were raised in different houses and went to different schools, but they shared enough midwestern humility that the gradations of their wealth and privilege were obscure to us. Or maybe their differences (readily apparent in Des Moines) were just dwarfed by the scale of our socioeconomic strata—that thousand-layered glacial formation that spans from an ash can on the Bowery to a penthouse in paradise. Either way, to us they *all* looked like hayseeds: unblemished, wide-eyed, and God-fearing, if not exactly free of sin.

Eve hailed from somewhere at the upper end of Indiana's economic scale. Her father was driven to the office in a company car and she ate biscuits for breakfast cut in the pantry by a Negro named Sadie. She had gone to a two-year finishing school and had spent a summer in Switzerland pretending to study French. But if you walked into a bar and met her for the first time, you wouldn't be able to tell if she was a corn-fed fortune hunter or a millionairess on a tear. All you could tell for sure was that she was a bona fide beauty. And that made the getting to know her so much less complicated.

She was indisputably a natural blonde. Her shoulder-length hair, which was sandy in summer, turned golden in the fall as if in sympathy with the wheat fields back home. She had fine features and blue eyes and pinpoint dimples so perfectly defined that it seemed like there must be a small steel cable fastened to the center of each inner cheek which grew taut when she smiled. True, she was only five foot five, but she knew how to dance in two-inch heels—and she knew how to kick them off as soon as she sat in your lap.

To her credit, Eve was making an honest go of it in New York. She had arrived in 1936 with enough of her father's money to get a single at Mrs. Martingale's boardinghouse and enough of his influence to land a job as a marketing assistant at the Pembroke Press—promoting all of the books that she'd avoided so assiduously in school.

Her second night at the boardinghouse, while taking a seat at the table she tipped her plate and her spaghetti plopped right in my lap. Mrs. Martingale said the best thing for the stain was to soak it in white wine. So she got a bottle of cooking Chablis from the kitchen and sent us off to the bathroom. We sprinkled a little of the wine on my skirt and drank the rest of it sitting on the floor with our backs to the door.

As soon as Eve got her first paycheck, she gave up her single and stopped drafting checks on her father's account. After a few months of Eve's self-reliance, Daddy sent along an envelope with fifty ten-dollar bills and a sweet note about how proud he was. She sent the money back like it was infected with TB.

—I'm willing to be under anything, she said, as long as it isn't somebody's thumb.

So together we pinched. We ate every scrap at the boardinghouse breakfast and starved ourselves at lunch. We shared our clothes with the girls on the floor. We cut each other's hair. On Friday nights, we let boys that we had no intention of kissing buy us drinks, and in exchange for dinner we kissed a few that we had no intention of kissing twice. On the occasional rainy Wednesday, when Bendel's was crowded with the wives of the well-to-do, Eve would put on her best skirt and jacket, ride the elevator to the second floor, and stuff silk stockings into her panties. And when we were late with the rent, she did her part: She stood at Mrs. Martingale's door and shed the unsalted tears of the Great Lakes.

◆ ◆ ◆

That New Year's, we started the evening with a plan of stretching three dollars as far as it would go. We weren't going to bother ourselves with boys. More than a few had had their chance with us in 1937, and we had no intention of squandering the last hours of the year on latecomers. We were going to perch in this low-rent bar where the music was taken seriously enough that two good-looking girls wouldn't be bothered and where the gin was cheap enough that we could each have one martini an hour. We intended to smoke a little more than polite society allowed. And once midnight had passed without ceremony, we were going to a Ukrainian diner on Second Avenue where the late night special was coffee, eggs, and toast for fifteen cents.

But a little after nine-thirty, we drank eleven o'clock's gin. And at ten, we drank the eggs and toast. We had four nickels between us and we hadn't had a bite to eat. It was time to start improvising.

Eve was busy making eyes at the bass player. It was a hobby of hers. She liked to bat her lashes at the musicians while they performed and ask them for cigarettes in between sets. This bass player was certainly attractive in an unusual way, as most Creoles are, but he was so enraptured by his own music that he was making eyes at the tin ceiling. It was going to take an act of God for Eve to get his attention. I tried to get her to make eyes at the bartender, but she wasn't in a mood to reason. She just lit a cigarette and threw the match over her shoulder for good luck. Pretty soon, I thought to myself, we were going to have to find ourselves a Good Samaritan or we'd be staring at the tin ceiling too.

And that's when he came into the club.

Eve saw him first. She was looking back from the stage to make some remark and she spied him over my shoulder. She gave me a kick in the shin and nodded in his direction. I shifted my chair.

He was terrific looking. An upright five foot ten, dressed in black tie with a coat draped over his arm, he had brown hair and royal blue eyes and a small star-shaped blush at the center of each cheek. You could just picture his forebear at the helm of the *Mayflower*—with a gaze trained brightly on the horizon and hair a little curly from the salt sea air.

—Dibs, said Eve.

From the vantage point of the doorway, he let his eyes adjust to the half-light and then surveyed the crowd. It was obvious that he had come to meet someone, and his expression registered the slightest disappointment once he realized that they weren't there. When he sat at the table next to us, he gave the room another going over and then, in a single motion, signaled the waitress and draped his coat over the back of a chair.

It was a beautiful coat. The color of the cashmere was similar to camel hair, only paler, like the color of the bass player's skin, and it was spotless, as if he had just come straight from the tailor's. It had to have cost five hundred dollars. Maybe more. Eve couldn't take her eyes off of it.

The waitress came over like a cat to the corner of a couch. For a second, I thought she was going to arch her back and exercise her claws on his shirt. When she took his order, she backed up a little and bent at the waist so that he could see down her blouse. He didn't seem to notice.

In a tone at once friendly and polite, showing the waitress a little more deference than she was due, he asked for a glass of scotch. Then he sat back and began to take in the scene. But as his gaze shifted from the bar to the band, out of the corner of his eye he saw Eve. She was still staring at the coat. He blushed. He'd been so preoccupied with looking over the room and signaling the waitress, he hadn't realized that the chair he'd draped his coat over was at our table.

—I'm so sorry, he said. How rude of me.

He stood up and reached over to retrieve it.

—No, no. Not at all, we said. No one's sitting there. It's fine.

He paused.

—Are you sure?

—As sure as the shore, said Eve.

The waitress reappeared with the scotch. When she turned to go he asked her to wait a moment and then offered to buy us a round—one last good turn in the old year, as he put it.

We could tell already that this one was as expensive, as finely made and as clean as his coat. He had that certain confidence in his bearing, that democratic interest in his surroundings, and that understated presumption of friendliness that are only found in young men who have been raised in the company of money and manners. It didn't occur to people like this that they might be unwelcome in a new environment—and as a result, they rarely were.

When a man on his own buys a round for two good-looking girls, you might expect him to make conversation no matter whom he's waiting for. But our smartly dressed Samaritan didn't make any with us. Having raised his glass once in our direction with a friendly nod, he began nursing his whiskey and turned his attention to the band.

After two songs, it began to make Eve fidget. She kept glancing over, expecting him to say something. Anything. Once, they made eye contact and he smiled politely. I could tell that when this song was over she was going to start a conversation of her own even if she had to knock her gin into his lap to do it. But she didn't get the chance.

When the song ended, for the first time in an hour the saxophonist spoke. In a deep-timbred, could've-been-a-preacher kind of voice he went into a long explanation about the next number. It was a new composition. It was dedicated to a Tin Pan Alley pianist named Silver Tooth Hawkins who died at thirty-two. It had something to do with Africa. It was called "Tincannibal."

With his tightly laced spats he tapped out a rhythm and the drummer brushed it up on the snare. The bass and piano players joined in. The saxophonist listened to his partners, nodding his head to the beat. He eased in with a perky little melody that sort of cantered within the corral of the tempo. Then he began to bray as if he'd been spooked and in a flash he was over the fence.

Our neighbor looked like a tourist getting directions from a gendarme. Happening to make eye contact with me, he made a bewildered face for my benefit. I laughed and he laughed back.

—Is there a melody in there? he asked.

I edged my chair a little closer, as if I hadn't quite heard him. I leaned at an angle five degrees less acute than the waitress had.

—What's that?

—I was wondering if there's a melody in there.

—It just went out for a smoke. It'll be back in a minute. But I take it that you don't come here for the music.

—Is it obvious? he asked with a sheepish smile. I'm actually looking for my brother. He's the jazz fan.

From across the table I could hear Eve's eyelashes flittering. A cashmere coat and a New Year's date with a sibling. What more did a girl need to know?

—Would you like to join us while you wait? she asked.

—Oh. I wouldn't want to impose.

(Now there was a word we didn't hear every day.)

—You wouldn't be *imposing*, Eve chastened.

We made a little room for him at the table and he slid up in his chair.

—Theodore Grey.

—Theodore! Eve exclaimed. Even Roosevelt went by Teddy.

Theodore laughed.

—My friends call me Tinker.

Couldn't you just have guessed it? How the WASPs loved to nickname their children after the workaday trades: Tinker. Cooper. Smithy. Maybe it was to hearken back to their seventeenth-century New England bootstraps—the manual trades that had made them stalwart and humble and virtuous in the eyes of their Lord. Or maybe it was just a way of politely understating their predestination to having it all.

—I'm Evelyn Ross, Evey said, taking her given name for a spin. And this is Katey Kontent.

—Katey Kontent! Wow! So are you?

—Not by a long shot.

Tinker raised his glass with a friendly smile.

—Then here's to it in 1938.

———

Tinker's brother never showed. Which worked out fine for us, because around eleven o'clock, Tinker signaled the waitress and ordered a bottle of bubbly.

—We aint got no bubbly here, Mister, she replied—decidedly colder now that he was at our table.

So he joined us in a round of gin.

Eve was in terrific form. She was telling tales about two girls in her high school who'd vied to be homecoming queen the way that Vanderbilt and Rockefeller vied to be the richest man in the world. One of the girls loosed a skunk in the house of the other the night of the senior dance. Her rival responded by dumping a load of manure on her front lawn the day of her sweet sixteen. The finale was a Sunday morning hair-pulling contest on the steps of Saint Mary's between their mothers. Father O'Connor, who should have known better, tried to intervene and got a little scripture of his own.

Tinker was laughing so hard you got the sense that he hadn't done it in a while. It was brightening all his God-given attributes like his smile and his eyes and the blushes on his cheeks.

—How about you, Katey? he asked after catching his breath. Where are you from?

—Katey grew up in Brooklyn, Eve volunteered—as if it was a bragging right.

—Really? What was that like?

—Well, I'm not sure we had a homecoming queen.

—You wouldn't have gone to homecoming if there was one, Eve said. Then she leaned toward Tinker confidentially.

—Katey's the hottest bookworm you'll ever meet. If you took all the books that she's read and piled them in a stack, you could climb to the Milky Way.

—The Milky Way!

—Maybe the Moon, I conceded.

Eve offered Tinker a cigarette and he declined. But the instant her cigarette touched her lips, he had a lighter at the ready. It was solid gold and engraved with his initials.

Eve leaned her head back, pursed her lips and shot a ray of smoke toward the ceiling.

—Now, what about you, Theodore?

—Well, I guess if you stacked all the books I've read, you could climb into a cab.

—No, said Eve. I mean: What *about* you?

Tinker answered relying on the ellipses of the elite: He was *from Massachusetts;* he went to *college in Providence;* and he worked for *a small firm on Wall Street*—that is, he was born in the Back Bay, attended Brown, and now worked at the bank that his grandfather founded. Usually, this sort of deflection was so transparently disingenuous it was irksome, but with Tinker it was as if he was genuinely afraid that the shadow of an Ivy League degree might spoil the fun. He concluded by saying he lived *uptown.*

—Where uptown? Eve asked "innocently."

—Two eleven Central Park West, he said, with a hint of embarrassment.

Two eleven Central Park West! The Beresford. Twenty-two stories of terraced apartments.

Under the table Eve kicked me again, but she had the good sense to change the subject. She asked him about his brother. What was he like? Was he older, younger? Shorter, taller?

Older and shorter, Henry Grey was a painter who lived in the West Village. When Eve asked what was the best word to describe him, after thinking a moment Tinker settled on *unwavering*—because his brother had always known who he was and what he wanted to do.

—Sounds exhausting, I said.

Tinker laughed.

—I guess it does, doesn't it.

—And maybe a little dull? Eve suggested.

—No. He's definitely not dull.

—Well, we'll stick to wavering.

At some point, Tinker excused himself. Five minutes went by, then ten. Eve and I both began to fidget. He didn't seem the sort to strand us with the check, but a quarter of an hour in a public john was a long time even for a girl. Then just as panic was setting in, he reappeared. His face was flush. The cold New Year's air emanated from the fabric of his tuxedo. He was grasping a bottle of champagne by the neck and grinning like a truant holding a fish by the tail.

—Success!

He popped the cork at the tin ceiling drawing discouraging stares from everyone but the bass player whose teeth peeked out from under his mustache as he nodded and gave us a *boom boom boom*!

Tinker poured the champagne into our empty glasses.

—We need some resolutions!

—We aint got no resolutions here, Mister.

—Better yet, said Eve. Why don't we make resolutions for each other?

—Capital! Tinker said. I'll go first. In 1938, the two of you . . .

He looked us up and down.

—Should try to be less shy.

We both laughed.

—Okay, said Tinker. Your turn.

Eve came back without hesitation.

—You should get out of your ruts.

She raised an eyebrow and then squinted as if she was offering him a challenge. For a moment he was taken aback. She had obviously struck a chord. He nodded his head slowly and then smiled.

—What a wonderful wish, he said, to wish for another.

As midnight approached, the sound of people cheering and cars honking became audible from the street, so we decided to join the party. Tinker overpaid in freshly minted bills. Eve snatched his scarf and wrapped it around her head like a turban. Then we stumbled through the tables into the night.

Outside, it was still snowing.

Eve and I got on either side of Tinker and took his arms. We leaned into his shoulders as if against the cold and marched him down Waverly toward the carousing in Washington Square. As we passed a stylish restaurant two middle-aged couples came out and climbed into a waiting car. When they drove away, the doorman caught Tinker's eye.

—Thanks again, Mr. Grey, he said.

Here, no doubt, was the well-tipped source of our bubbly.

—Thank *you*, Paul, said Tinker.

—Happy New Year, Paul, said Eve.

—Same to you, ma'am.

Powdered with snow, Washington Square looked as lovely as it could. The snow had dusted every tree and gate. The once tony brownstones that on summer days now lowered their gaze in misery were lost for the moment in sentimental memories. At No. 25, a curtain on the second floor was drawn back and the ghost of Edith Wharton looked out with shy envy. Sweet, insightful, unsexed, she watched the three of us pass wondering when the love that she had so artfully imagined would work up the courage to rap on her door. When would it present itself at an inconvenient hour, insist upon being admitted, brush past the butler and rush up the Puritan staircase urgently calling her name?

Never, I'm afraid.

As we approached the center of the park, the revelry by the fountain began to take shape: A crowd of collegiates had gathered to ring in the New Year with a half-priced ragtime band. All of the boys were in black tie and tails except for four freshmen who wore maroon sweaters emblazoned with Greek letters and who scrambled through the crowd filling glasses. A young woman who was insufficiently dressed was pretending to conduct the band which, due to indifference or inexperience, played the same song over and over.

The musicians were suddenly waved silent by a young man who leapt onto a park bench with a coxswain's megaphone in hand, looking as self-assured as the ringmaster in a circus for aristocrats.

—Ladies and gentlemen, he proclaimed. The turn of the year is nearly upon us.

With a flourish, he signaled one of his cohorts and an older man in a gray robe was foisted up onto the bench at his side. The foistee was wearing the cotton ball beard of a drama school Moses and holding a cardboard scythe. He appeared to be a little unsteady on his feet.

Unfurling a scroll that fell to the ground, the ringmaster began chastising the old man for the indignities of 1937: *The recession . . . The Hindenburg . . . The Lincoln Tunnel!* Then holding up his megaphone, he called on 1938 to present itself. From behind a bush an overweight fraternity brother appeared dressed in nothing but a diaper. He climbed on the bench and to the merriment of the crowd took a stab at flexing his muscles. At the same time, the beard on the old man became unhooked from an ear and you could see that he was gaunt and ill shaven. He must have been a bum that the collegiates had lured from an alley with the promise of money or wine. But whatever the enticement, its influence must have run its course, because he was suddenly looking around like a drifter in the hands of vigilantes.

With a salesman's enthusiasm, the ringmaster began gesturing to various parts of the New Year's physique, detailing its improvements: its flexible suspension, its streamlined chassis, its get-up-and-go.

—Come on, said Eve, skipping ahead with a laugh.

Tinker didn't seem so eager to join in the fun.

I took a pack of cigarettes from my coat pocket and he produced his lighter.

He took a step closer in order to block the wind with his shoulders.

As I exhaled a filament of smoke, Tinker looked overhead at the snowflakes whose slow descent was marked by the halo of the street lamps. Then he turned back toward the commotion and scanned the assembly with an almost mournful gaze.

—I can't tell whom you feel more sorry for, I said. The old year or the new.

He offered a tempered smile.

—Are those my only options?

Suddenly, one of the revelers at the edge of the crowd was hit squarely in the back by a snowball. When he and two of his fraternity brothers turned, one of them was hit in the pleats of his shirt.

Looking back, we could see that a boy no older than ten had launched the attack from behind the safety of a park bench. Wrapped in four layers of clothing, he looked like the fattest kid in the class. To his left and right were pyramids of snowballs reaching to his waist. He must have spent the whole day packing ammunition—like one who's received word of the redcoats' approach straight from the mouth of Paul Revere.

Dumbstruck, the three collegiates stared with open mouths. The kid took advantage of their cognitive delay by unloading three more well-aimed missiles in quick succession.

—Get that brat, one of them said without a hint of humor.

The three of them began scraping snowballs off the paving stones and returning fire.

I took out another cigarette, preparing to enjoy the show, but my attention was drawn back in the other direction by a rather startling development. On the bench beside the wino, the diaper-donning New Year had begun to sing "Auld Lang Syne" in a flawless falsetto. Pure and heartfelt, as disembodied as the plaint of an oboe drifting across the surface of a lake, his voice lent an eerie beauty to the night. Though one has to practically sing along with "Auld Lang Syne" by law, such was the otherworldliness of his performance that no one dared to sound a note.

When he had tapered out the final refrain with exquisite care, there was a moment of silence, then cheers. The ringmaster put a hand on the tenor's shoulder—recognizing a job well done. Then he took out his watch and raised his hand for silence.

—All right everyone. All right. Quiet now. Ready . . . ? Ten! Nine! Eight!

From the center of the crowd Eve waved excitedly in our direction.

I turned to take Tinker's arm—but he was gone.

To my left the walkways of the park were empty and to my right a lone silhouette, stocky and short, passed under a street lamp. So I turned back toward Waverly—and that's when I saw him. He was hunched behind the bench at the little boy's side fending off the attack of the fraternity brothers. Aided by the unexpected reinforcement, the boy looked more determined than ever. And Tinker, he had a smile on his face that could have lit every lamp at the North Pole.

◆　◆　◆

When Eve and I got home it was nearly two. Normally, the boarding-house locked its doors at midnight, but the curfew had been extended for the holiday. It was a liberty that few of the girls had made the most of. We found the living room empty and depressed. It had scatterings of virginal confetti and there were unfinished glasses of cider on every side table. Eve and I traded a self-satisfied gaze and went up to our room.

We were both quiet, letting the aura of our good fortune linger. Eve slipped her dress over her head and went off to the bathroom. The two of us shared a bed, and Eve was in the habit of turning it down as if we were in a hotel. Though it always seemed crazy to me, that unnecessary little preparation, for once, I turned the bed down for her. Then I took the cigar box from my underwear drawer so I could stow my unspent nickels before going to bed, just like I'd been taught.

But when I reached into my coat pocket for my change purse, I felt something heavy and smooth. A little mystified, I pulled the object out and found it was Tinker's lighter. Then I remembered having—in a somewhat Eve-like manner—taken it from his hand to light my second cigarette. It was just around the time that the New Year had begun to sing.

I sat down in my father's barley-brown easy chair—the only piece of furniture I owned. I flipped open the lighter's lid and turned the flint. The flame leapt and wavered, giving off its kerosene scent before I snapped it shut.

The lighter had a pleasant weight and a soft, worn look, polished by a thousand gentlemanly gestures. And the engraving of Tinker's initials, which was in a Tiffany font, was so finely done you could score your thumbnail along the stem of the letters unerringly. But it wasn't just marked with his monogram. Under his initials had been etched a sort of coda in the amateurish fashion of a drugstore jeweler, such that it read:

TGR

1910 – ?

CHAPTER TWO

The Sun, the Moon & the Stars

The following morning, we left Tinker an unsigned note with the doorman at the Beresford:

> *If you ever want to see your lighter alive, you'll meet us on the*
> *corner of 34th and Third at 6:42. And you'll come alone.*

I set the likelihood of his showing up at fifty percent. Eve set it at a hundred and ten. When he climbed out of the cab, we were waiting in trench coats in the shadows of the elevated. He was wearing a denim shirt and a shearling coat.

—Put em up, pardner, I said, and he did.

—How's it coming with those ruts? Eve prodded.

—Well, I woke at the usual hour. And after my usual squash match, I had my usual lunch. . . .

—Most people make a go of it until the second week of January.

—Maybe I'm a slow starter?

—Maybe you need help.

—Oh, I definitely need help.

We tied a navy blue kerchief over his eyes and led him west. A good sport, he didn't put his hands out like the newly blind. He submitted to our control and we steered him through the crowds.

27

It began to snow again. They were those large individual flakes that drift slowly toward the ground and occasionally perch in your hair.

—Is it snowing? he asked.

—No questions.

We crossed Park Avenue, Madison, Fifth. Our fellow New Yorkers brushed past showing seasoned indifference. When we crossed Sixth Avenue, we could see the twenty-foot-high marquee of the Capitol Theatre shining over Thirty-fourth Street. It looked like the bow of an ocean liner had crashed through the building's façade. The crowd from the early show was filtering into the cold. They were mirthful and at ease, exhibiting something of that tired self-satisfaction that's typical of the first night of the year. He could hear their voices.

—Where are we going, girls?

—Quiet, we cautioned, turning up an alley.

Large gray rats fearful of the snow scurried among the tobacco tins. Overhead the fire escapes crawled up the sides of the buildings like spiders. The only light came from a small red lamp over the theater's emergency exit. We passed it and took up our position behind a garbage bin.

I untied Tinker's blindfold holding a finger to my lips.

Eve reached into her blouse and produced an old black brassiere. She smiled brightly and winked. Then she slinked back down the alley to where the drop steps of the fire escape hung in the air. On the tips of her toes she hooked the end of the bra onto the bottom rung.

She came back and we waited.

6:50.

7:00.

7:10.

The emergency exit opened with a creak.

A middle-aged usher in a red uniform stepped outside, taking refuge from the feature he'd already seen a thousand times. In the snow, he looked like a wooden soldier from the *Nutcracker* who'd lost his hat. While easing the door shut, he put a program in the crack so that it wouldn't close completely. The snow fell through the fire escapes and settled on his fake epaulettes. Leaning against the door, he took a cigarette from behind his ear, lit it, and exhaled smoke with the smile of a well-fed philosopher.

It took him three drags to notice the bra. For a moment or two, he studied it from a safe distance; then he flicked his cigarette against the alley wall. He crossed over and tilted his head as if he wanted to read the label. He looked to his left and his right. He gingerly freed the garment from its snag and held it draped over his hands. Then he pressed it to his face.

We slipped through the exit making sure that the program went back in the door.

As usual, we ducked and crossed below the screen. We headed up the opposite aisle with the newsreel flickering behind us: Roosevelt and Hitler taking turns waving from long black convertibles. We went out into the lobby, up the stairs, back through the balcony door. In the dark, we made our way to the highest row.

Tinker and I began to giggle.

—Shhhh, said Eve.

When we had come onto the balcony, Tinker held open the door and Eve charged ahead. So we ended up sitting Eve on the inside, me in the middle, and Tinker on the aisle. When our eyes met, Eve gave me an irritated smirk, as if I had planned it that way.

—Do you do this often? Tinker whispered.

—Whenever we get the chance, said Eve.

—Sh! said a stranger, more emphatically, as the screen went black.

Throughout the theater, lighters flickered on and off like fireflies. Then the screen lit up and the feature began.

It was *A Day at the Races*. In typical Marx Brothers fashion, the stiff and sophisticated made early appearances, establishing a sense of decorum, which the audience politely abided. But at the entrance of Groucho, the crowd sat up in their seats and applauded—like he was a Shakespearean giant returning to the stage after a premature retirement.

As the first reel ran I produced a box of Jujubes and Eve brought out a pint of rye. When it was Tinker's turn to eat you had to shake the box to get his attention.

The pint made one circuit and then another. When it was empty,

Tinker produced a contribution of his own: a silver flask in a leather sheath. When it was in my hands, I could feel the TGR embossed on the leather.

The three of us began to get drunk and we laughed as if it was the funniest movie we had ever seen. When Groucho gave the old lady a physical, Tinker had to wipe the tears from his eyes.

At some point, I needed to go so badly that I couldn't put it off. I nudged out into the aisle and skipped down the stair to the girls' room. I peed without sitting on the seat and stiffed the matron at the door. By the time I got back I hadn't missed more than a scene, but Tinker was sitting in the middle now. It wasn't hard to imagine how that had happened.

I plunked down in his seat thinking if I wasn't careful, I was going to find a truckload of manure on *my* front lawn.

But if young women are well practiced in the arts of marginal revenge, the universe has its own sense of tit for tat. For as Eve giggled in Tinker's ear, I found myself in the embrace of his shearling coat. Its lining was as thick as on the hide of a sheep and it was still warm with the heat of his body. Snow had melted on the upturned collar and the musky smell of wet wool intermingled with a hint of shaving soap.

When I had first seen Tinker in the coat, it struck me as a bit of a pose—a born and raised New Englander dressed like the hero in a John Ford film. But the smell of the snow-wet wool made it seem more authentic. Suddenly, I could picture Tinker on the back of a horse somewhere: at the edge of the treeline under a towering sky . . . at his college roommate's ranch, perhaps . . . where they hunted deer with antique rifles and with dogs that were better bred than me.

When the movie was over, we went through the front doors with all the solid citizens. Eve began doing the Lindy like the Negroes in the movie's big dance number. I took her hand and we did it together in perfect synchronization. Tinker was clearly wowed—though he shouldn't have been. Learning dance steps was the sorry Saturday night pursuit of every boardinghouse girl in America.

We took Tinker's hand and he faked a few steps. Then Eve broke rank and skipped into the street to hail a cab. We piled in behind her.

—Where to? Tinker asked.

Without missing a beat Eve said Essex and Delancey.

Why, of course. She was taking us to Chernoff's.

Though the driver had heard Eve, Tinker repeated the directions.

—Essex and Delancey, driver.

The driver put the cab in gear and Broadway began slipping by the windows like a string of lights being pulled off a Christmas tree.

♦ ♦ ♦

Chernoff's was a former speakeasy run by a Ukrainian Jew who emigrated shortly before the Romanovs were shot in the snow. It was located under the kitchen of a kosher restaurant, and though it was popular with Russian gangsters it was also a gathering place for Russia's competing political émigrés. On any given night you could find the two factions encamped on either side of the club's insufficient dance floor. On the left were the goateed Trotskyites planning the downfall of capitalism and on the right were the sideburned tsarist distaff dwelling in dreams of the Hermitage. Like all the rest of the world's warring tribes, these two made their way to New York City and settled side by side. They dwelt in the same neighborhoods and the same narrow cafés, where they could keep a watchful eye on one another. In such close proximity, time slowly strengthened their sentiments while diluting their resolve.

We got out of the cab and headed up Essex on foot, walking past the well-lit window of the restaurant. Then we turned down the alley that led to the kitchen door.

—Another alley, Tinker said gamely.

We passed a garbage bin.

—Another bin!

At the end of the alley there were two bearded Jews in black mulling over modern times. They ignored us. Eve opened the door to the kitchen and we walked past two Chinamen at large sinks toiling in the steam. They ignored us too. Just past the boiling pots of winter cabbage, a set of narrow steps led down to a basement where there was a walk-in freezer. The brass latch on the heavy oaken door had been pulled so many times that it was a soft, luminescent gold, like the foot of a saint on a cathedral door. Eve pulled the latch and we stepped inside among the sawdust and ice blocks. At the back, a false door opened revealing a nightclub with a copper-topped bar and red leather banquettes.

As luck would have it, a party was just leaving and we were whisked into a small booth on the tsarist side of the dance floor. The waiters at Chernoff's never asked for your order. They just plopped down plates of pierogies and herring and tongue. In the middle of the table, they put shot glasses and an old wine bottle filled with vodka that, despite the repeal of the Twenty-first Amendment, was still distilled in a bathtub. Tinker poured three glasses.

—I swear I'm going to find me Jesus one of these days, Eve said, knocking hers back. Then she excused herself to the powder room.

On the stage a lone Cossack accompanied himself ably on the balalaika. It was an old song about a horse that returns from war without its rider. As it approaches the soldier's hometown, the horse recognizes the smell of the lindens, the brush of the daisies, the clang of the blacksmith's hammer. Though the lyrics were poorly translated, the Cossack performed with the sort of feeling that can only be captured by an expatriate. Even Tinker suddenly looked homesick—as if the song described a country that he too had been forced to leave behind.

When the song was over the crowd responded with heartfelt applause; but it was sober too, like the applause for a fine and unpretentious speech. The Cossack bowed once and retired from the stage.

After looking appreciatively around the room, Tinker observed that his brother would really love this place and that we should all come back together.

—You think we'd like him?

—I think you would especially. I bet you two would really hit it off.

Tinker became quiet, turning his empty shot glass in his hands. I wondered if he were lost in thoughts of his brother or still under the spell of the Cossack's song.

—You don't have any siblings, do you, he said setting his glass down.

The observation caught me off guard.

—Why? Do I seem spoiled?

—No! If anything the opposite. Maybe it's that you seem like you'd be comfortable being alone.

—Aren't you?

—Once I was, I think. But I've sort of lost the habit. Nowadays, if I'm in my apartment with nothing to do, I find myself wondering who's in town.

—Living in a henhouse, I've got the opposite problem. I've got to go out to be alone.

Tinker smiled and refilled my glass. For a moment, we were both quiet.

—Where do you go? he asked.

—Where do I go when?

—When you want to be alone.

At the side of the stage, a small orchestra had begun to assemble—taking their chairs and tuning their instruments, while having emerged from the back hall, Eve was working her way through the tables.

—Here she is, I said, standing up so that Eve could slip back into the banquette between us.

The food at Chernoff's was cold, the vodka medicinal and the service abrupt. But nobody came to Chernoff's for the food or the vodka or the service. They came for the show.

Shortly before ten, the orchestra began to play an intro with a distinctly Russian flavor. A spotlight shot through the smoke revealing a middle-aged couple stage right, she in the costume of a farm girl and he a new recruit. A cappella, the recruit turned to the farm girl and sang of how she should remember him: by his tender kisses and his footsteps in the night, by the autumn apples he had stolen from her grandfather's orchard. The recruit wore more rouge on his cheeks than the farm girl, and his jacket, which was missing a button, was a size too small.

No, she replied, I will not remember you by those things.

The recruit fell to his knees in despair and the farm girl pulled his head to her stomach, smearing her blouse red with his rouge. No, the girl sang, I will not remember you by those things but by the heartbeat you hear in my womb.

Given the miscast performers and the amateurish makeup, you could almost laugh at the production—if it weren't for the grown men crying in the front row.

When the duet ended, the performers bowed three times to boisterous applause, and then ceded the stage to a group of young dancers in
skimpy outfits and black sable hats. What commenced was a tribute to
Cole Porter. It began with "Anything Goes" and then ran through a
couple of refashioned hits including, "It's Delightful, It's Delicious, It's
Delancey."

Suddenly, the music stopped and the dancers froze. The lights went
out. The audience held its breath.

When the spotlight came on again, it revealed the dancers in a kick
line and the two middle-aged performers at center stage, he in a top hat
and she in a sequined dress. The male lead pointed his cane at the band:

—Hyit it!

And the whole ensemble finaléd with "I Gyet a Keek Out of You."

When I first dragged Eve to Chernoff's, she hated it. She didn't like
Delancey Street or the alleyway entrance or the Chinamen at the sink.
She didn't like the clientele—all facial hair and politics. She didn't even
like the show. But boy, it grew on her. She came to love the fusion of
glitter and sob stories. She loved the heartfelt has-beens who led the
numbers and the toothy hope-to-bes who made up the chorus. She loved
the sentimental revolutionaries and the counterrevolutionaries who shed
their tears side by side. She even learned a few of the songs well enough
to sing along when she'd had too much to drink. For Eve, I think an
evening at Chernoff's became a little like sending her daddy's money
home to Indiana.

And if Eve's intention had been to impress Tinker with a glimpse of
an unfamiliar New York, it was working. For as the rootless nostalgia
of the Cossack's song was swept aside to make room for Cole Porter's
carefree lyrical wit and the long legs, short skirts and untested dreams
of the dancers, Tinker looked like a kid without a ticket who's been
waved through the turnstiles on opening day.

When we decided to call it a night, Eve and I paid. Naturally, Tinker
objected, but we insisted.

—All right, he said stowing his billfold. But Friday night's on me.

—You're on, said Eve. What should we wear?

—Whatever you like.

—Nice, nicer or nicest?

Tinker smiled.

—Let's take a stab at nicest.

As Tinker and Eve waited at the table for our coats, I excused myself to take my turn in the powder room. It was crowded with the gangsters' dolled-up dates. Three deep at the sink, they had as much fake fur and makeup as the girls in the chorus and just as good a chance of making it to Hollywood.

On my way back, I bumped into old man Chernoff himself. He was standing at the end of the hallway watching the crowd.

—*Hello, Cinderella*, he said in Russian. *You're looking superlative.*

—*You've got bad lighting.*

—*I've got good eyes.*

He nodded toward our table, where Eve appeared to be convincing Tinker to join her in a shot.

—*Who's the young man? Yours or your friend's?*

—*A little bit of both, I guess.*

Chernoff smiled. He had two gold teeth.

—*That doesn't work for long, my slender one.*

—Says you.

—Says the sun, the moon and the stars.

CHAPTER THREE

The Quick Brown Fox

There were twenty-six red lights in the mahogany panel over Miss Markham's door, each one identified by a letter of the alphabet. That was one light and one letter for each girl in the Quiggin & Hale secretarial pool. I was Q.

The twenty-six of us sat in five rows of five with the lead secretary, Pamela Petus (aka G), positioned alone in front like the drum majorette in a dull parade. Under Miss Markham's direction, the twenty-six of us did all correspondence, contract preparation, document duplication, and dictation for the firm. When Miss Markham received a request from one of the partners, she would consult her schedule (pronounced *shed-ju-wul*), identify the girl best suited to the task and press the corresponding button.

To an outsider, it might seem sensible that if a partner had a good rapport with one of the girls, then he should be able to staff her on a project—whether it be the triplication of a purchase agreement or the cataloging of a wife's indiscretions in a divorce suit. But such an arrangement did not seem sensible to Miss Markham. From her standpoint, it was essential that each task be met with optimal skill. While all the girls were capable secretaries, there were those who excelled at shorthand and those who had an unerring eye for the misuse of the comma. There was one girl who could put a hostile client at ease with the tone of her voice and another who could make the younger partners sit up straight simply by the controlled manner in which she delivered a folded note to a senior partner midmeeting. If excellence is to be expected, Miss Markham liked to observe, you can't ask the wrestlers to throw the javelins.

Case in point: Charlotte Sykes, the new girl who sat to my left. Nineteen years old with black hopeful eyes and alert little ears, Charlotte had made the tactical error of typing 100 words a minute her first day on the job. If you couldn't type 75 words a minute you couldn't work at Quiggin & Hale. But Charlotte was typing a good 15 words per minute over the mean performance of the pool. At 100 wpm, that's 48,000 words a day, 240,000 words a week and 12 million words a year. As a new recruit, Charlotte was probably making $15 a week, or the equivalent of less than one ten-thousandth of a cent for every word she typed. That was the funny thing about typing faster than 75 words a minute at Quiggin & Hale—from there, the faster you were typing, the less per word you were being paid.

But that's not how Charlotte saw it. Like an adventuress trying to complete the first solo flight across the Hudson River, she hoped to type as fast as was humanly possible. And as a result, whenever a case surfaced requiring a few thousand pages of duplication, you could bet that the next light that clicked on over Miss Markham's door would be the one under the F.

Which is just to say, be careful when choosing what you're proud of—because the world has every intention of using it against you.

But on Wednesday, the fifth of January at 4:05 P.M., as I was transcribing a deposition, the light that clicked on was mine.

Slipcovering my typewriter (as we'd been taught to do for even the briefest of interruptions), I stood, smoothed my skirt, picked up a steno pad and crossed the pool to Miss Markham's office. It was a paneled room with the half door of a cabaret coat check. She had a small but ornate desk with a tooled leather top, the sort at which Napoleon must have sat when quilling directives from the field.

When I entered, she looked up briefly from her work.

—There is a call for you, Katherine. From a paralegal at Camden & Clay.

—Thank you.

—Keep in mind that you work for Quiggin & Hale, not for Camden & Clay. Don't let them slough their work off on you.

—Yes, Miss Markham.

—Oh, and Katherine, one more thing. I understand that there was a good deal of last-minute work on the Dixon Ticonderoga merger.

—Yes. Mr. Barnett said it was important that the transaction be completed before year-end. For tax reasons, I believe. And there were a few eleventh-hour emendations.

—Well. I don't like my girls working so late during Christmas week. Just the same, Mr. Barnett appreciated your seeing it through. As did I.

—Thank you, Miss Markham.

She released me with a wave of the pen.

Stepping back into the secretarial pool, I went to the little telephone table at the front of the room. The phone was made available to the girls should a partner or a counterparty need to communicate a revision. The law firm of Camden & Clay was one of the largest litigators in the city. Though they weren't directly involved in any of my matters, they tended to have a hand in everything.

I picked up the receiver.

—This is Katherine Kontent.

—Hey Sis!

I looked out over the pool where twenty-five of twenty-six typewriters were hard at work. They were clacking so loudly you could barely hear yourself think, which I suppose was the point. I lowered my voice anyway.

—Your hair better be on fire, friend. I've got a deposition due in an hour.

—How's it coming?

—I'm three misdirections and a whopper behind.

—What's the name of that bank where Tinker works?

—I don't know. Why?

—We don't have a plan for tomorrow night.

—He's taking us to some highbrow place, somewhere uptown. He's picking us up sometime around eight.

—Zowie. Someplace, somewhere, sometime. How'd you get all that?

I paused.

How *did* I get all that?

It was one hell of a question.

◆ ◆ ◆

On the corner of Broadway and Exchange Place across the street from Trinity Church there was a little diner with a soda pop clock on the wall and a hasher named Max who even cooked his oatmeal on the griddle. Polar in winter, oppressive in July and five blocks out of my way, it was one of my favorite spots in town—because I could always get the crooked little booth-for-two by the window.

Sitting in that seat, in the span of a sandwich you could pay witness to the pilgrimage of New York's devoted. Hailing from every corner of Europe, donned in every shade of gray, they turned their backs on the Statue of Liberty and marched instinctively up Broadway, leaning with pluck into a cautionary wind, gripping identical hats to identical hair-cuts, happy to count themselves among the indistinguishable. With over a millennia of heritage behind them, each with their own glimpse of empire and some pinnacle of human expression (a Sistine Chapel or *Götterdämmerung*), now they were satisfied to express their individuality through which Rogers they preferred at the Saturday matinee: Ginger or Roy or Buck. America may be the land of opportunity, but in New York it's the shot at conformity that pulls them through the door.

Or so I was thinking, when a man without a hat emerged from the crowd and rapped on the glass.

Trip of a heartbeat, it was Tinker Grey.

The tips of his ears were as red as an elf's and he was sporting a grin like he'd caught me in the act. Behind the glass, he began talking enthu-siastically—but inaudibly. I waved him in.

—So, is this it? he asked as he slid into the booth.

—Is this what?

—Is this where you go when you want to be alone!

—Oh, I laughed. Not exactly.

He snapped his fingers in mock disappointment. Then, announcing he was famished, he looked around the place with groundless appre-ciation. He picked up the menu and reviewed it for all of four seconds.

He was in the irrepressible good humor of one who's found a hundred-dollar bill on the ground and has yet to tell a soul.

When the waitress appeared I ordered a BLT; Tinker leapt straight into uncharted territory, ordering Max's eponymous sandwich which the menu defined as unparalleled, world famous *and* legendary. When Tinker asked if I'd ever had it, I told him I'd always found the description a little too long on adjectives and a little too short on specifics.

—So, do you work nearby? he asked, when the waitress retreated.

—Just a short walk.

. . .

—Didn't Eve say it was a law firm?

—That's right. It's an old Wall Street practice.

. . .

—Do you like it?

—It's a little stodgy, but I suppose that's predictable.

Tinker smiled.

—You're a little long on adjectives and short on specifics yourself.

—Emily Post says that talking about oneself isn't very polite.

—I'm sure Miss Post is perfectly correct, but that doesn't seem to stop the rest of us.

Fortune favoring the bold, Max's special sandwich turned out to be a grilled cheese stuffed with corn beef and coleslaw. Within ten minutes it was gone and a slice of cheesecake had been plopped down in its place.

—What a great spot! Tinker said for the fifth time.

—So what's it like being a banker? I asked as he attacked his dessert.

For starters, he confided, you could barely call it banking. He was really more of a broker. The bank served a group of wealthy families with large stakes in private companies controlling everything from steel plants to silver mines, and when they were seeking liquidity, his role was to help them find an appropriate buyer, discreetly.

—I'd be happy to buy any silver mine you've got, I said, taking out a cigarette.

—Next time, you'll be my first call.

Tinker reached across the table to give me a light and then set his lighter down on the table beside his plate. Exhaling, I pointed to it with my cigarette.

—So what's the story there?

—Oh, he said, sounding a little self-conscious. You mean the inscription?

He picked up the lighter and studied it for a moment.

—I bought it when I got my first big paycheck. You know, as sort of a gift to myself. A solid gold lighter engraved with my initials!

He shook his head with a wistful smile.

—When my brother saw it, he gave me hell. He didn't like that it was gold or that it was monogrammed. But what really ticked him off was my job. We'd get together for a beer in the Village and he'd rail against bankers and Wall Street and jab me with my plans of traveling the world. I kept telling him I was going to get around to that too. So finally, one night he took the lighter out into the street and had a vendor add the postscript.

—As a reminder to seize the day whenever you lit a girl's cigarette?

—Something like that.

—Well, your job doesn't sound so bad to me.

—No, he admitted. It's not *bad.* It's just . . .

Tinker looked out on Broadway, gathering his thoughts.

—I remember Mark Twain writing about an old man who piloted a barge—the kind that ferried people from a landing on one side of the river to a landing on the other.

—In *Life on the Mississippi?*

—I don't know. Maybe. Anyway—over thirty years, Twain figured this man had shuttled back and forth so often that he'd traveled the length of the river twenty times over, without leaving his county.

Tinker smiled and shook his head.

—That's what I feel like sometimes. Like half my clients are on their way to Alaska while the other half are on their way to the Everglades—and I'm the one going from riverbank to riverbank.

—Refill? the waitress asked, coffeepot in hand.

Tinker looked to me.

The girls at Quiggin & Hale had forty-five minutes for lunch and I was in the habit of being in front of my typewriter with a few minutes to spare. If I left right then, I could probably make it. I could thank Tinker for the lunch, jog up Nassau, and catch the elevator to the sixteenth floor. But what would the latitude be for a girl who was usually prompt? Five minutes? Ten? Fifteen if she broke a heel?

—Sure, I said.

The waitress filled our cups and we both leaned back, our knees knocking due to the narrowness of the booth. Tinker poured cream in his coffee and stirred it round and round and round. For a moment, we were both quiet.

—It's churches, I said.

He looked a little confused.

—What is?

—That's where I go when I want to be alone.

He sat upright again.

—Churches?

I pointed out the window toward Trinity. For over half a century, its steeple had been the highest point in Manhattan and a welcome sight to sailors. Now, you had to be in a diner across the street just to see it.

—Really! Tinker said.

—Does that surprise you?

—No. It's just that you don't strike me as the religious sort.

—I'm not. But I don't go during the services. I go in the off-hours.

—To Trinity?

—To all sorts. But I prefer the big old ones like Saint Patrick's and Saint Michael's.

—I think I've been in Saint Barth's for a wedding. But that's about it. I must have walked by Trinity a thousand times without stepping inside.

—That's what's amazing. At two in the afternoon there's nobody in any of them. There they sit with all that stone and mahogany and stained glass—and they're empty. I mean, they must have been crowded at one point, right?—for someone to have gone to all that trouble. There must have been lines outside the confessionals and weddings with girls dropping flower petals in the aisle.

—From baptisms to eulogies. . . .

—Exactly. But over time the congregation has been winnowed away. The newcomers set up their own churches and the big old ones just get left alone—like the elderly—with memories of their heyday. I find it very peaceful to be in their company.

Tinker was quiet for a moment. He looked up at Trinity where a pair of seagulls circled the steeple for old time's sake.

—That's really great, he said.

I toasted him with my coffee cup.

—It's something few people know about me.

He looked me in the eye.

—Tell me something that *no one* knows about you.

I laughed.

But he was serious.

—That no one knows? I said.

—Just one thing. I promise, I'll never tell a soul.

He crossed his heart to prove it.

—All right, I said, setting my coffee cup down. I keep perfect time.

—What do you mean?

I shrugged.

—I can count sixty seconds in sixty seconds. Minute in and minute out.

—I don't believe it.

I gestured with a thumb to the soda pop clock on the wall behind me.

—Just let me know when the second hand gets to twelve.

He looked over my shoulder and watched the clock.

—Okay, he said with a game smile. On your mark . . . Get set . . .

◆　◆　◆

Zowie, Eve had said later that afternoon. *Someplace, somewhere, sometime. How'd you get all that?*

In taking depositions, one thing you learn is that most people have respect for a direct and well-timed question. It's the one thing they're not prepared for. Sometimes, they show their cooperative intent (and buy some time) by repeating it back to their questioner: *How did I get all that?* they ask politely. Sometimes, they counter the boldness of the question with a touch of indignation: *How'd I get what?* Whatever the tactic, the seasoned attorney knows that when someone is stalling in this manner, there is fertile ground for further inquiry. So, the best response to a good question is something put simply without hesitation or inflection.

—He mentioned it when you were in the bathroom at Chernoff's, I said to Eve.

We exchanged a closing pleasantry and I returned to my desk. I removed the slipcover from my typewriter, found my place in the deposition and rattled away. In the second sentence of the third paragraph, I made my first typo of the afternoon. In transcribing a list of someone's chief concerns, for *chief* I typed *thief*. And let the record show that those two letters aren't even close to each other on the keyboard.

CHAPTER FOUR

Deus Ex Machina

On Friday night, as we were getting dressed, Eve wouldn't even chat about the weather.

My conscience having gotten the better of me, I'd fessed up. Sort of. In the course of conversation, I mentioned in an offhand manner that I'd run into Tinker downtown and that we'd had a cup of coffee.

—A cup of coffee, she said, equally offhand. How nice.

Then she clammed up.

I took a stab at complimenting her outfit: a yellow dress, six months out of season and all the sharper for it.

—Do you really like it? she asked.

—It looks great.

—You should try it on for size some time. Maybe you can have a cup of coffee with it.

I was opening my mouth, not sure of what to say, when one of the girls barged in.

—Sorry to interrupt, ladies, but Prince Charming's here. And he's brought his chariot.

At the door to our room, Eve took a last look in the mirror.

—I need another a minute, she said.

Then she went back into the bedroom and took off her dress, as if my compliment had put it out of style. Outside the window I could see that a cold drizzle was falling in vindication of her mood. I followed her down the stairs thinking: *We're in for it all right.*

———

In front of the boardinghouse Tinker was standing beside a Mercedes coupé as silver as mercury. If all the girls at Mrs. Martingale's saved a year's pay, we couldn't have afforded one.

Fran Pacelli, the five-foot-nine City College dropout from North Jersey who lived down the hall, whistled like a hard hat appreciating the hem of a skirt. Eve and I went down the steps.

Tinker was obviously in a good mood. He gave Eve a kiss on the cheek and a *You look terrific*. When he turned to me, he smiled and gave my hand a squeeze. He didn't offer me the kiss or the compliment, but Eve was watching and she could tell that she was the one who'd been short-changed.

He opened the passenger side door.

—It's a tight fit in back, I'm afraid.

—I'll take it, I said.

—That's mighty big of you, said Eve.

Beginning to sense that something was amiss, Tinker looked at Eve with a hint of concern. He put one hand on the car door and with the other gestured like a gentleman for her to get in. She didn't seem to notice. She was too busy looking at the car, sizing it up from hood to heel. Not like Fran had; more like a professional.

—I'll drive, she said, holding out her hand for the keys.

Tinker wasn't ready for that one.

—Do you know how to drive? he asked.

—*Do I know how to drive?* she said like a Southern belle. *Why, I been drivin my daddy's tractah since I was nyn yeahs old.*

She tugged the keys out of his hand and walked around the hood. As Tinker climbed in the passenger seat looking a little unsure, Eve made herself comfortable.

—Where to, Mac? she asked, putting the key in the ignition.

—Fifty-second Street.

Eve turned on the engine and ripped into reverse. She backed away from the curb at twenty miles an hour and screeched to a halt.

—Eve! Tinker said.

She looked at him and smiled sweetly, sympathetically. Then she put it in gear and roared across Seventeenth Street.

Within seconds it was clear that she was filled with the spirit of the Lord. When she swerved onto Sixth Avenue, Tinker almost grabbed the wheel. But as we zigzagged through traffic, she drove in one fluid motion, accelerating and decelerating in imperceptible increments like a shark cutting through water, timing each light to the second. So we both sat back, quiet and wide-eyed—like others who put themselves in the hands of a higher power.

Only as we turned onto Fifty-second Street did I realize that he was taking us to the 21 Club.

In a sense, Eve had cornered him into it. *Nice, nicer, nicest*—what was he supposed to say?

But just as Eve had wanted to impress Tinker by showing off the quasi-Russian demimonde that we semi-frequented, Tinker probably wanted to impress us by offering a glimpse of *his* New York. And from the look of things, he had a good shot at succeeding, whatever Eve's mood. In front of the restaurant, the exhaust of idling limousines spiraled from tailpipes like genies from a bottle. A valet in a top hat and topcoat opened the door of the car and another one opened the door to the restaurant, revealing a lobby full of Manhattanites waiting hip to hip.

At first glance, 21 didn't seem particularly elegant. The dark walls were decorated with framed drawings that could have been ripped from an illustrated weekly. The tabletops were scuffed and the silverware clunky like at a chophouse or a university dining hall. But there was no mistaking the elegance of the clientele. The men wore tailored suits and accented their breast pockets with untouched handkerchiefs. The women wore silk dresses in royal colors and chokers of pearls.

When we came before the coat-check girl, ever so slightly Eve turned her shoulders toward Tinker. Without missing a trick, he swung the coat off her back like a matador swinging his cape.

Eve was the youngest person in the restaurant not bussing a tray, and she was ready to make the most of it. Her last-minute dress was a red silk number with a scooped neckline, and she had apparently traded up to her best support bra—because the tops of her breasts could be seen from fifty feet in a fog. She had been careful not to spoil the impression with jewelry. In a small red lacquered box, she kept a pair of graduation-day diamonds. On her ears, the studs provided a nice little sparkle that complemented her dimples when she smiled. But she knew better than to wear them into a place like this—where one had nothing to gain from formality and everything to lose by comparison.

The maitre d', an Austrian who had plenty of reason to be harried and wasn't, welcomed Tinker by name.

—Mr. Grey. We've been expecting you. Please. Right this way.

He said the word *Please* as if it was a sentence unto itself.

He led us to a table on the main floor. It was the only empty one in the room and it was set for three. As if he could read minds, the maitre d' pulled the middle chair out and motioned for Eve to have a seat.

—Please, he said again.

Once we were seated, he held a hand in the air and three menus materialized like giant playing cards in the hands of a magician. He delivered them with ceremony.

—Enjoy.

The menu was the largest I had ever seen. It was almost a foot and a half high. I opened it expecting a cavalcade of choices, but there were only ten. Lobster tail. Beef Wellington. Prime rib. The items were hand-written in the generous script of a wedding invitation. There were no prices, at least not on my menu. I peeked at Eve, but she wouldn't peek back. She scanned her menu coolly and then laid it down.

—Let's have a round of martinis, she said.

—Capital! said Tinker.

He raised a hand and a white-jacketed waiter appeared where the maitre d' had been. He had all the fast-talking charm of a country club con artist.

—Good evening, Mr. Grey. Good evening, ladies. If I may be so bold, you're the best-looking table in the place. Surely, you're not ready to order? The weather is horrendous. May I bring an aperitif?

—Actually, Casper, we were just talking about having some martinis.

—Of course you were. Let me take these out of your way.

Casper tucked the menus under an elbow and within minutes, the drinks arrived.

Or rather, three empty glasses arrived. Each had a trio of olives skewered on a pin that was propped on the rim of the glass like an oar on the hull of a rowboat. Casper placed a napkin on top of a silver shaker and rattled it good. Then he carefully began to pour. First, he filled my glass to the brim. The liquor was so cold and pure it gave the impression of being more translucent than water. Next he filled Eve's glass. When he began filling Tinker's, the flow of alcohol from the shaker slowed noticeably. And then trickled. For a moment it seemed as if there wasn't going to be enough. But the gin kept trickling and the surface kept rising until with the very last drop Tinker's martini reached the brim. It was the sort of precision that gave one confidence.

—Friends, Casper observed, are the envy of the angels.

Before any of us noticed that the silver shaker was gone, Casper had produced a small scaffold topped with a plate of oysters.

—Compliments of the house, he said, and disappeared.

Eve clinked her water glass with a fork as if she was about to make a toast to the whole restaurant.

—A confession, she said.

Tinker and I looked up in anticipation.

—I was jealous today.

—Eve . . .

She put her hand up to silence me.

—Let me finish. When I learned that the two of you had your little coffee, cream & sugar—I admit it—I was green. And not a little bit peeved. In fact, I fully intended to spoil the evening to teach you both a lesson. But Casper is perfectly right: Friendship is the mostest.

She held up her drink and squinted.

—To getting out of ruts.

Within minutes, Eve was her perfect self: relaxed, buoyant, bright; inexplicable.

The couples at the tables around us were engaged in conversations they'd been having for years—about their jobs and their children and their summer houses—conversations that may have been rote but that reinforced their sense of shared expectations and experience. Shrewdly, Tinker swept that aside and launched a conversation more suitable to our situation—one grounded in the hypothetical.

What were you afraid of when you were a kid? he asked.
I said cats.
Tinker said heights.
Eve: Old age.

And just like that, we were off. In a way, it became a chummy sort of competition in which each of us tried to land the perfect answers—those that were surprising, diverting, revealing, but true. And Eve, ever under-estimateable, proved the runaway champ.

What did you always want that your parents never gave you?
Me: Spending money.
Tinker: A tree house.
Eve: A good licking.

If you could be anyone for a day, who would you be?
Me: Mata Hari.
Tinker: Natty Bumppo.
Eve: Darryl Zanuck.

If you could relive one year in your life, which one would it be?
Me: When I was eight and we lived above a bakery.
Tinker: When I was thirteen and my brother and I hiked the Adiron-
    dacks.
Eve: The upcoming one.

The oysters were consumed and the shells whisked away. Casper appeared with another round of martinis and then poured an extra one for the table.
—What shall we drink to this time? I asked.
—To being less shy, Tinker said.
Eve and I echoed the toast and raised the liquor to our lips.
—To being less shy? someone queried.
Standing with a hand on the back of my chair was a tall, elegant woman in her early fifties.

—That seems a nice ambition, she said. But better that one should aspire to returning one's phone calls first.

—I'm sorry, Tinker said a little embarrassed. I meant to call this afternoon.

She smiled winningly and waved a forgiving hand.

—Come on, Teddy. I'm only teasing. I can see that you've had the best of distractions.

She held her hand out to me.

—I'm Anne Grandyn—Tinker's godmother.

Tinker stood. He gestured to the two of us.

—This is Katherine Kontent and—

But Eve was already on her feet.

—Evelyn Ross, she said. It's so nice to meet you.

Mrs. Grandyn worked her way around the table to shake Eve's hand, insisting that she sit, and then continued on to Tinker. Barely marked by age, she had short blond hair and the refined features of a ballerina who had grown too tall for the ballet. She was wearing a black sleeveless dress that celebrated the slenderness of her arms. She wasn't wearing a choker of pearls, but she was wearing earrings—emerald studs the size of gumdrops. The stones were uncontestably glorious and happened to match the color of her eyes. From the way she carried herself, you could just tell that she swam with them. Coming out of the water, she would pick up a towel and dry her hair, not wondering for a moment whether the stones were in her ears or at the bottom of the sea.

Reaching Tinker, she offered her cheek and he gave her an awkward peck. When he sat down again she put a maternal hand on his shoulder.

—Katherine, Evelyn, mark my words. It's the same with godsons and nephews. When they first come to New York, you see them plenty. Like when the hamper's full or the pantry's bare. But once they get on their feet, if you want to invite them for tea, you have to hire a Pinkerton.

Eve and I laughed. Tinker mustered a sheepish grin. The appearance of his godmother was making him look sixteen.

—What a wonderful coincidence running into you here, Evelyn said.

—It is a small world, Mrs. Grandyn replied, a little wryly.

No doubt, she had taken Tinker here in the first place.

—Would you like to join us for a drink? Tinker asked.

—Thank you, dear, but I couldn't. I'm with Gertrude. She's trying to drag me onto the board of the museum. I'm going to need all my wits about me.

She turned to the two of us.

—If I leave it to Teddy, I'm sure that I will never see you again. So, accept my invitation for lunch someday—with or without him. I promise I won't bore you with too many stories of his youth.

—We wouldn't be bored, Mrs. Grandyn, Eve assured.

—Please, Mrs. Grandyn said, making the word a sentence just as the maitre d' had. Call me Anne.

As Mrs. Grandyn gave a graceful wave and returned to her table, Eve was aglow. But if Mrs. Grandyn's little visit had lit the candles on Eve's cake, for Tinker it had blown them out. Her unexpected appearance had changed the whole tenor of the outing. In the blink of an eye the caption had gone from *Man of means takes two girls to swanky spot* to *Young peacock shows off feathers in family's backyard.*

Eve was so rosy she couldn't see that the evening was on the verge of being spoiled.

—What a wonderful woman. Is she a friend of your mother's?

—What's that? Tinker asked. Oh. Yes. They grew up together.

He picked up his fork and turned it in his hands.

—Perhaps we should go ahead and order, Eve suggested.

—Do you want to get out of here? I asked Tinker.

—Could we?

—Absolutely.

Eve was plainly disappointed. She gave me that quick irritated glance. She opened her mouth ready to suggest we just have an appetizer. But Tinker's face was all lit up again.

—Right, she said, dumping her napkin on her plate. Let's beat it.

When we stood up from the table we were all feeling the good graces of the second martini. At the door, Tinker thanked the maitre d' and apologized in German for our having to rush. In a show of forgiveness,

Eve accepted my flapper's jacket from the coat-check girl, leaving me to don her fur-collared twenty-first birthday present.

Outside, the drizzle had stopped, the sky had cleared and the air was bracing. After a quick conference, we decided to head back to Chernoff's to see the second show.

—We may miss curfew, I noted, as I climbed in back.

—If we do, Eve asked turning to Tinker, can we bunk at your place?

—Of course.

Though the evening had started a little roughly, in the end our camaraderie had served us another good turn. Sitting in front, Eve reached back and placed a hand on my knee. Tinker dialed the radio to a swing tune. No one said anything as we turned onto Park Avenue and headed downtown.

At Fifty-first Street we passed Saint Bartholomew's, the great domed church built by the Vanderbilts. Conveniently, they had dropped it on a spot where every Sunday morning they could see Grand Central Station over the pastor's shoulder as they complimented his sermon. Like other royals of the gilded age, the Vanderbilts' roots reached back three generations to an indentured servant. Hailing from the town of De Bilt, he had sailed from Holland to New York in steerage, and when he stepped off the boat he was known simply as Jan from De Bilt—until Cornelius built his fortune and classed up the moniker.

But you don't have to own a railroad to shorten or lengthen your name.

Teddy to Tinker.

Eve to Evelyn.

Katya to Kate.

In New York City, these sorts of alterations come free of charge.

As the car crossed Forty-ninth Street, we could all feel the wheels slip a little beneath us. The road ahead shimmered with what looked like puddles but which, with the cessation of rain, had frozen into patches of ice. Tinker downshifted and regained control. He slowed to turn, thinking perhaps that Third Avenue would be better. And that's when the milk truck hit us. We never even saw it. It was coming down Park Avenue at fifty miles an hour loaded for deliveries. When we decelerated, it tried to stop, hit the ice and smashed us squarely from behind. The coupé launched like a rocket and vaulted across Forty-seventh Street into a cast-iron lamppost on the median.

When I came to, I found myself upside down, pinned between the gearshift and the dash. The air was cold. The driver-side door was thrown open and I could see Tinker lying by the curb. The passenger door was closed; but Eve was gone.

I untangled myself and crawled from the car. It hurt when I inhaled, as if I'd broken a rib. Tinker was standing now, stumbling toward Eve. Shot through the windshield, she was huddled on the ground.

Out of nowhere an ambulance appeared and there were two young men in white jackets with a stretcher, looking like something out of a newsreel on the Spanish civil war.

—She's alive, one said to the other.

They hoisted her onto the stretcher.

Her face was as raw as a cut of meat.

I couldn't help myself. I turned away.

Tinker couldn't help himself either. He fixed his eyes on Eve and wouldn't avert them until the doors of the surgery swung shut.

When he came out of the hospital, a line of taxis waited at the curb as if it was a hotel. He was surprised to find it already dark. He wondered what time it was.

The driver in the front cab nodded in his direction. He shook his head.

A woman in a fur coat came out of the hospital and jumped in the back of the taxi that he hadn't taken. As she closed the door she leaned forward to rattle off an address. The woman's cab pulled away and the other cabs advanced. For a moment, her urgency struck him as out of place. But then, just because we have good reasons to rush to a hospital doesn't mean we don't have good reasons to rush away again.

How many times had he jumped in the back of a cab and rattled off an address? Hundreds? Thousands?

—Would you like one?

A man had emerged from the hospital and taken up a position a few feet to his right. It was one of the surgeons—the chief specialist who had performed the reconstructive surgery. Poised and friendly, he couldn't have been more than forty-five years old. He must have been in between procedures because his smock was spotless. In his hand was a cigarette.

—Thanks, he said, accepting the offer for the first time in years.

An acquaintance had once remarked that if he ever quit smoking, he'd remember the last one better than all the rest. And it was true. It was on the platform of Providence Station, a few minutes before he'd boarded the train to New York. That was almost four years ago.

He put the cigarette to his lips and a hand in his pocket for his lighter, but the surgeon had beat him to it.

—Thanks, he said again, leaning toward the flame.

One of the nurses had mentioned to him that the surgeon had served in the war. He had been a young internist stationed near the front lines in France.

You could tell. It was in his bearing. He looked like a man who had gained confidence through exposure to a hostile environment; like one who no longer owed anything to anyone.

The surgeon eyed him thoughtfully.

—When was the last time you went home?

When was the last time I went home, he thought to himself.

The surgeon didn't wait for an answer.

—She may not come to for another three days. But when she does, she'll need you at your best. You should go home and get some sleep; have a good meal; pour yourself a drink. And don't worry. Your wife is in excellent hands.

—Thank you, he said.

A new taxi pulled up and took its place at the back of the line.

On Madison, there would be a line of taxis just like this one idling in front of the Carlyle. On Fifth Avenue, there would be another line in front of the Stanhope. In what city in the world were more taxis at your disposal? At every corner, at every awning they waited so that without a change of clothes or a second thought, without a word to anyone, you could be skirted away to Harlem or Cape Horn.

—. . . Though she's not my wife.

The surgeon took his cigarette from his mouth.

—Oh. I'm sorry. A nurse led me to believe . . .

—We're just friends.

—Why yes. Of course.

—We were in the accident together.

—I see.

—I was driving.

The surgeon said nothing.

A cab pulled away and the line of cabs advanced.

Oh—I'm sorry—Why yes—Of course—I see.

SPRINGTIME

CHAPTER FIVE

To Have & to Haven't

It was an evening in late March.

My new apartment was a studio in a six-story walk-up on Eleventh Street between First and Second avenues. It looked out into a narrow court where the laundry lines were pulleyed between the windowsills. Despite the season, gray sheets floated five stories above the frozen ground like drab, unimaginative ghosts.

Across the court an old man in his underwear wandered back and forth in front of his window with a skillet. He must have been a janitor or a watchman because he was always frying meat fully dressed in the mornings and eggs in his skivvies at night. I poured myself a taste of gin and turned my undivided attention to a worn pack of cards.

On something of a whim, I had spent fifteen cents on a primer for contract bridge and it had quickly earned its keep. Any given Saturday, I could play from reveille to taps. I would deal out the deck at my little kitchen table and move from chair to chair so that I could play each of the four positions in turn. I invented a partner in the north seat—an aristocratic Brit whose reckless bidding complemented my cautious inexperience. Nothing pleased him more than to raise my bid injudiciously, forcing me to play a doubled game in a minor suit.

As if in response, the personalities of East and West began to assert themselves: On my left sat an old rabbi who remembered every card and on my right a retired Chicago mobster who remembered little, sized up well, and occasionally slammed through sheer force of will.

—Two hearts? I opened tentatively, having counted my points with care.

—Two spades, said the rabbi with a hint of admonition.

—Six hearts! shouted my partner, still arranging his cards.

—Pass.

—Pass.

When the telephone rang, we all looked up in surprise.

—I'll get it, I said.

The phone was teetering on a stack of Tolstoy's novels.

I assumed the caller was the young accountant who'd tried so hard to make me laugh at Fanelli's. Against my better judgment, I had let him write down my number—GRamercy 1-0923, the first private line that I had ever had. But when I picked up the receiver, it was Tinker Grey.

—Hi Katey.

—Hello Tinker.

I hadn't heard from Tinker or Eve in almost two months.

—What are you up to? he asked.

Under the circumstances, it was a cowardly sort of question.

—Two games short of a rubber. What are you up to?

He didn't answer. For a moment, he didn't say anything.

—Do you think you could come by tonight?

—Tinker . . .

—Katey, I don't know what's going on between you and Eve. But the last few weeks have been a tough run. The doctors said it was going to get worse before it got better; I don't think I really believed them, but it has. I need to go to the office tonight and I don't think she should be alone.

Outside, it began to sleet. I could see gray splotches forming on the sheets. Someone should have reeled them in while they still had the chance.

—Sure, I said. I can come.

—Thanks, Katey.

—You don't need to thank me.

—All right.

I looked at my watch. At this hour the Broadway train ran intermittently.

—I'll be there in forty minutes.

—Why don't you take a cab? I'll leave the fare with the doorman.

I dropped the receiver in its cradle.

—Double, sighed the rabbi.

Pass.

Pass.

Pass.

◆ ◆ ◆

Those first few days after the crash, while Eve was still unconscious, Tinker led the vigil. A few of the girls from the boardinghouse took turns reading magazines in the waiting room, but Tinker rarely left her side. He had the doorman in his building deliver fresh clothes and he showered in the surgeon's locker.

On the third day, Eve's father arrived from Indiana. When he was at her bedside, you could tell that he was at a loss. Neither weeping nor praying came very naturally to him. He would have been better off if they had. Instead, he stared at his little girl's ravaged face and shook his head a few thousand times.

She came to on the fifth day. By the eighth she was more or less herself—or rather, a steely version of herself. She listened to the doctors with cold unaverting eyes. She adopted whatever technical language they used like *fracture* and *suture* and *ligature,* and she encouraged them to adopt her more descriptive terms like *hobbled* and *disfigured.* When she was nearly ready to leave the hospital, her father announced that he was taking her home to Indiana. She refused to go. Mr. Ross tried to reason with her; then he tried to plead. He said that she would regain her strength so much quicker at home; he pointed out that given the condition of her leg she wouldn't be able to climb the boardinghouse stairs; besides, her mother was expecting her. But Eve wasn't swayed; not by a word of it.

Tentatively, Tinker suggested to Mr. Ross that if Eve intended to convalesce in New York, she could do so in his apartment where there was an elevator, kitchen service, doormen, and an extra bedroom. Eve accepted Tinker's offer without a smile. If Mr. Ross thought the setup unacceptable, he didn't say so. He was beginning to understand that he no longer had a voice in his daughter's affairs.

The day before Eve was released, Mr. Ross went home to his wife empty-handed; but after kissing his daughter good-bye he signaled that he wanted to speak with me. I walked him to the elevator and there he thrust an envelope in my hand. He said it was something for me, to cover Eve's half of the rent for the rest of the year. I could tell from the thickness of the envelope that it was a lot of money. I tried to give it back to him, explaining that the boardinghouse was just going to stick me with another roommate. But Mr. Ross insisted. And then he disappeared behind the elevator doors. I watched the needle mark his descent to the lobby. Then I opened the envelope. It was fifty ten-dollar bills. It was probably the very same tens that Eve had sent back to him two years before, ensuring once and for all that these particular bills would never have to be spent by either of them.

I took the developments as a sign it was time to strike out on my own—especially since Mrs. Martingale had already warned me twice that if I didn't get all those boxes out of her basement, she was going to throw me out. So I used half of Mr. Ross's money to front six months' rent on a five-hundred-square-foot studio. The other half I stowed in the bottom of my uncle Roscoe's footlocker.

Eve intended to go straight from the hospital to Tinker's apartment, so it was my job to move her things. I packed them as best I could, folding the shirts and sweaters into perfect squares the way that she would. At Tinker's direction, I unpacked her bags in the master bedroom where I found the drawers and closets empty. Tinker had already moved his clothes to the maid's room at the other end of the hall.

The first week that Eve was in residence at the Beresford, I joined the two of them for dinner every night. We would sit in the little dining room off the kitchen and eat three-course meals that were prepared in the building's basement and served by jacketed staff. Seafood bisque followed by tenderloin and Brussels sprouts capped off with coffee and chocolate mousse.

When dinner was over, Eve was usually exhausted and I would help her to her room.

She would sit at the end of the bed and I would undress her. I would take off her right shoe and stocking. I would unzip her dress and pull it over her head being careful not to graze the little black stitches that tracked the side of her face. She would stare straight ahead, submissively. It took me three nights to realize that what she was staring at was the large mirror over the vanity. It was a stupid oversight. I apologized and said that I'd have Tinker remove the mirror. But she wouldn't let us touch it.

Once I had tucked her in, given her a kiss, and turned out the light, I would quietly close the door and return to the living room where Tinker anxiously awaited. We didn't have a drink. We didn't even sit down. In the few minutes before I went home, the two of us would whisper like parents about her progress: *She seems to be regaining her appetite. . . . Her color's coming back. . . . Her leg doesn't seem to be giving her so much discomfort. . . .* Self-soothing phrases pattering like raindrops on a tent.

But on the seventh night after Eve's release, when I tucked her in and gave her a kiss, she stopped me.

—Katey, she said. You know I'll love you till doomsday.

I sat on the bed beside her.

—The feeling's mutual.

—I know, she said.

I took her hand and squeezed it. She squeezed back.

—I think it would be better if you didn't come for a while.

—All right.

—You understand, don't you?

—Sure, I said.

Because I did understand. At least, I understood enough.

It wasn't about who had dibs now or who was sitting next to whom in the cinema. The game had changed; or rather, it wasn't a game at all anymore. It was a matter of making it through the night, which is often harder than it sounds, and always a very individual business.

◆ ◆ ◆

By the time the cab came to a stop on Central Park West, the sleet had turned to freezing rain. Pete, the night doorman, was there at the curb to meet me with an umbrella. He paid the cabbie two dollars for a one-dollar fare and gave me cover for the five feet between the cab and the canopy. Hamilton, the youngest of the elevator attendants, was on duty. From 'Lanta, Georgia, he brought a taste of plantation civility to New York that was either going to carry him far or get him in a world of trouble.

—Have you been travelin, Miss Katherin? he asked as we began our ascent.

—Only to the grocery store, Hamilton.

He gave a sweet little laugh to show that he knew better.

I liked his illusions too much to dispel them.

—Give my regards to Miss Evelyn and Mistah Tinkah, he said, as we slowed to a stop.

The door opened on a private foyer—a perfect example of Greek revival elegance with a parquet floor and white moldings and a preimpressionist still life hanging on the wall. Tinker was sitting on a side chair with his arms on his knees and his head lowered. He looked like he was back outside the emergency room. When I stepped off the elevator he was visibly relieved, as if he had begun to worry that I wasn't going to show.

He took both my hands in his. The features of his face had softened, as if he had put on the ten pounds that Eve had lost in the hospital.

—Katey! Thanks for coming. It's good to see you.

He was talking a little under his breath. It raised my antennae.

—Tinker. Does Eve know that I'm here?

—Yes, yes. Of course, he whispered. She's excited to see you. I just wanted to explain. She's been having a tough go of it lately. Especially at night. So I try to stay in as much as I can. She's just better when she . . . has company.

I took off my coat and laid it on the other side chair. It should have told me something about Tinker's state of mind that he hadn't asked me for it.

—I'm not sure how late I'm going to be. Can you stay until eleven?

—Sure.

—Twelve?

—I can stay as late as you need me to, Tinker.

He took my hands again and then let them go.

—Come on in. Eve! Katey's here!

We walked through the door into the living room.

If Tinker's foyer was classically decorated, it was something of a sleight of hand—because it was the only room in the apartment with furnishings from before the sinking of the *Titanic*. The living room—a grand square with terrace windows overlooking Central Park—looked like it had been airlifted right out of the Barcelona exposition at the 1929 World's Fair. It had three white couches and two black Mies van der Rohe chairs in tight formation around a glass-topped cocktail table, which was artfully arranged with a stack of novels, a brass ashtray and a deco-era miniature of an airplane. There was no satin, no velvet, no paisley—no rough textures or rounded edges. Just interlocking rectangles that reinforced a general sense of abstraction.

The machine for living, I think the French called it, and there was Eve lounging in the middle of the works. In a new white dress, she was reclining on one of the couches with one arm behind her head and the other at her side. It was a been-here-all-my-life sort of pose. With the lights of the city draped behind her and the martini glass on the carpet, she looked like an advertisement for being in a car wreck.

It was only when you got closer that you could see the damage. On the left side of her face there were two converging scars that cut all the way from her temple to her chin. What symmetry remained was spoiled by the slight droop at the edge of her mouth, as if she was the victim of a stroke. In the manner she was sitting, her left leg looked only slightly twisted, but peeking from under the hem of her dress you could see where the grafts had left her with the skin of a plucked chicken.

—Hey Evey.

—Hey Kate.

I leaned over to give her a kiss. Without hesitation she offered her right cheek, her reflexes having already adapted to her new condition. I sat on the opposite couch.

—How're you feeling? I asked.

—Better. How've you been?

—Same.

—Good for you. Would you like a drink? Tinker, sweetie, could you?

Tinker hadn't sat down. He was behind the empty couch leaning on its back with both arms.

—Of course, he said standing upright. What would you like, Katey? We were just having martinis. I'm happy to make you a fresh one.

—I'll take what's in the shaker.

—Are you sure?

—Why not.

Tinker came around the couch with a glass and reached for the plane that was on the cocktail table. The fuselage came up out of the wings— a witty piece of deco, teetering on the edge of fashion. Tinker plucked off the nose of the plane and filled my glass. He hesitated before putting the shaker back.

—Do you want some more, Eve?

—I'm all right. But why don't you stay and have one with Katey.

Tinker looked pained at the suggestion.

—I don't mind drinking alone, I said.

Tinker put the shaker back.

—I'll try not to be too late.

—Capital, said Eve.

Tinker gave Evey a kiss on the cheek. As he walked to the door she looked out over the city. The door closed. She didn't look back.

I took a sip of my martini. It was well diluted with the melted ice. You could barely taste the gin. It wasn't going to be much help.

—You look good, I said finally.

Eve eyed me patiently.

—Katey. You know I can't stand that sort of crap. Especially from you.

—I'm just saying that you look better than when I saw you last.

—It's the boys in the basement. Every day it's bacon with breakfast and soup with lunch. Canapés with cocktails and cake with coffee.

—I'm jealous.

—Sure. The Prodigal Son and all that. But pretty soon you feel like *you're* the fatted calf.

With some difficulty she sat upright. She reached out two fingers and picked up a small white pill that was almost invisible on the surface of the table.

—I'm gonna find me Jesus one of these days, she said, then she washed the medicine down with her tepid gin.

—Would you like another? she asked.

—If you're having one.

She leaned on the table to push herself up.

—I can get it, I said.

She gave a wry smile.

—The doctor encourages me to exercise.

Plucking the shaker off of its stand, she worked her way toward the bar. She dragged her left foot behind her the way a kid drags a suitcase down the street.

She picked up ice cubes with a set of tongs one by one and dropped them in the fuselage. She glugged out the gin inexactly and then measured the vermouth to the drop. There was a mirror over the bar and as she stirred the drink she studied her face with a certain grim satisfaction.

They say that vampires cast no reflection. Maybe the accident had made Eve some sort of haunting spirit with the opposite property: She was invisible to herself now except for on the surface of a mirror.

She capped the shaker and gave it a lazy toggle as she limped back to her seat. After filling her glass she shoved the shaker across the table toward me.

—How are you and Tinker getting along, I asked after filling my glass.

—I'm not up for small talk, Katey.

—Is that small talk?

—Small enough.

I gestured vaguely to the apartment.

—At least, it looks like he's taking good care of you.

—You break it, you've bought it. Right?

She took a fullmouthed swallow and then looked at me more directly.

—I don't suppose you'd just go home? I'm perfectly fine. And in fifteen minutes I'll be sound asleep.

By way of illustration, she waggled her glass.

—I've got nothing better to do, I said. I'll stick around long enough to help you to your room.

She waved a hand in the air as if to say: *Stay if you stay, go if you go.* She took another belt and lay back on the couch. I looked down into my glass.

—Why don't you read me something, she said. That's what Tinker would do.

—Would you like that?

—At first it drove me crazy. It was like he didn't have the courage to converse. But it's grown on me.

—All right. What do you want me to read?

—It doesn't matter.

There were eight books stacked on the cocktail table in descending order of size. With dust jackets designed in glossy evocative colors, they looked like a stack of neatly wrapped Christmas presents.

I picked up the book on top. None of the pages were dog-eared, so I started at the beginning.

> "Yes, of course, if it's fine tomorrow," said Mrs. Ramsay.
> "But you'll have to be up with the lark," she added.
>
> To her son these words conveyed an extraordinary joy,
> as if it were settled, the expedition were bound to take
> place, and the wonder to which he had looked forward,
> for years and years it seemed, was, after a night's darkness
> and a day's sail

—Oh stop, Eve said. It's dreadful. What is it?

—Virginia Woolf.

—Ugh. Tinker brought home all these novels by women as if that's what I needed to get me back on my feet. He's surrounded my bed with them. It's as if he's planning to brick me in. Isn't there *anything* else?

I tilted the stack and pulled a volume from the middle.

—Hemingway?

—Thank God. But skip ahead this time, would you Katey?

—How far?

—Anywhere but the beginning.

I turned randomly to page 104:

> The fourth man, the big one, came out of the bank door as
> he watched, holding a Thomson gun in front of him, and
> as he backed out of the door the siren in the bank rose in
> a long breath-holding shriek and Harry saw the gun muz-
> zle jump-jump-jump-jump and heard the bop-bop-bop-
> bop

—That's more like it, Eve said.

She arranged the pillow behind her head, lay back and closed her eyes.

I read twenty-five pages out loud. Eve fell asleep after ten. I suppose I could have stopped, but I was enjoying the book. Starting on page 104 made Hemingway's prose even more energetic than usual. Without the early chapters, *all* the incidents became sketches and *all* the dialogue innuendo. Bit characters stood on equal footing with the central subjects and positively bludgeoned them with disinterested common sense. The protagonists didn't fight back. They seemed relieved to be freed from the tyranny of their tale. It made me want to read all of Hemingway's books this way.

I emptied my drink and carefully set it down so as not to clink the stem against the glass of the table.

There was a white throw on the back of Eve's couch. I draped it over her as she breathed evenly. She didn't need to find Jesus anymore, I thought to myself; he had already come looking for her.

Over the bar hung four studies of gas stations by Stuart Davis. The only art in the room, they were painted in primary colors that contrasted nicely with the furniture. In front of the liquor bottles was another silver deco piece. This one had a little window and a dial you could turn that flipped ivory cards one over the other in the fashion of a railway station timetable. Each card had the recipe for a cocktail: Martini, Manhattan, Metropolitan—flit, flit, flit. Bamboo, Bennett, Between the Sheets—flit,

flit, flit, flit. Behind the bottle of gin there were four different kinds of scotch, not one of which I could afford. I poured a glass of the oldest and wandered down the back hall.

The first room on the right was the small dining room where we used to eat. Behind that was the kitchen, well outfitted and rarely used. There were untarnished copper pots on the stove and earthenware jars for FLOUR, SUGAR, COFFEE and TEA, all filled to the brim.

Beyond the kitchen was the maid's room. By all appearances, Tinker was still sleeping there. A sleeveless undershirt was on a chair and his razor was in the bathroom propped in a glass. Hanging over a small bookcase there was a rather primitive social realist painting. The image looked down on a freight dock where longshoremen were assembling for a protest. Two police cars had pulled up to the edge of the crowd. At the end of the dock you could just make out the words OPEN ALL NIGHT in blue neon. The painting was not without its virtues, but in the context of the apartment, I could see why it had been relegated to the maid's room. Victims of a similar exile, the bookcase was filled with hard-boiled detective novels.

I doubled back past the kitchen, past Eve's sleeping figure and went down the opposite hall. The first room on the left was a paneled study with a fireplace. It was half the size of my apartment.

On the desk there was another fanciful deco piece: a cigarette caddy in the shape of a race car. Each of these silver objects—the shaker, the cocktail catalog, the race car—fit nicely into the international style of the apartment. They were finely crafted like pieces of jewelry, but unmistakably masculine in purpose. And none of them were the sort of item a Tinker would buy for himself. They suggested the work of a hidden hand.

Between two bookends, there was a small selection of reference books: a thesaurus, a Latin grammar, a soon to be extremely outdated atlas. But there was also a slender volume without a title on the spine. It turned out to be a book of Washingtonia. The inscription on the first page indicated it was a present to Tinker from his mother on the occasion of his fourteenth birthday. The volume had all the famous speeches and letters arranged in chronological order, but it led off with an aspirational list composed by the founder in his teenage years:

Rules of Civility & Decent Behaviour in Company and Conversation

1st Every Action done in Company, ought to be with Some Sign of Respect, to those that are Present.

2nd When in Company, put not your Hands to any Part of the Body, not usually Discovered.

3rd Shew Nothing to your Friend that may affright him.

Etc.

Did I say et cetera? There were 110 of them! And over half were under-lined—one adolescent sharing another's enthusiasm for propriety across a chasm of 150 years. It was hard to decide which was sweeter—the fact that Tinker's mother had given it to him, or the fact that he kept it at hand.

The chair behind the desk was on a pivot. I spun around once and came to a stop. The drawers could all be locked, but none of them were. The lower drawers were empty. The upper side drawers were stuffed with the usual accessories. But sitting on top of a pile of papers in the center drawer was a letter from Eve's father.

> *Dear Mr. Gray* [sic],
>
> *I appreciate your candor in the hospital and I am prepared to take you at your word that you and Evelyn are not romantically involved. In part, that is why I must insist above your previous objections that I cover the costs of my daughter's stay in your apartment. I have enclosed a check for $1,000 and will follow it with others. Please do me the honor of cashing them.*
>
> *An act of generosity rarely ends a man's responsibilities toward another; it tends instead to begin them. Few understand this, but I have no doubt that you do.*
>
> *If things should develop between you and my daughter, I can only trust that you will not take advantage of her condition, her proximity or her indebtedness—that you will show the restraint that comes natural to gentlemen—until such a time as you are ready to do what is right.*
>
> *With Gratitude and Trust,*
> *Charles Everett Ross*

I folded the letter and returned it to the drawer with a heightened respect for Mr. Ross. In its stark factual prose, businessman to business-man, I think his letter could have stymied Don Juan. No wonder Tinker left it there—where Eve was sure to find it.

In the master bedroom, the drapes were open and the city glittered like a diamond necklace that knows exactly whom it's within the reach of. The bed had a blue and yellow cover that complemented a pair of upholstered chairs. If the whole apartment had been designed pitch perfect for a wealthy bachelor, here there was just enough color and comfort so that a woman who lucked into the room wouldn't feel herself on alien ground. It was the hidden hand again.

In the closet there were some new additions to Eve's wardrobe. They must have been bought by Tinker because they were not inexpensive and not Evey's style. As I ran my finger along the dresses, flitting through them like the cocktail recipes, a blue flapper's jacket caught my eye. It was mine. For a moment, I wondered how it had gotten there, since I was the one who had unpacked Evey's things. But then I remembered—Evey had been wearing it the night of the accident. Through a miracle of Civility & Decent Behaviour, it had been salvaged and cleaned. I hung it back in its place and closed the closet door.

In the bathroom Eve's medication sat on the sink. It was some sort of painkiller. I looked in the mirror wondering how I would bear up in her place.

Not so well, I reckoned.

When I went back to the living room, Eve was gone.

I went to the kitchen and the maid's room. I doubled back to the study. I began to worry that she had actually run from the apartment. But then I saw the living room curtain rise and fall and the white sil-houette of her dress on the terrace. I went out and joined her.

—Hey Katey.

If Eve suspected me of snooping, she didn't show it.

The sleet had stopped and the sky was starlit. The East Side apart-ment buildings glimmered across the park like houses on the opposite side of a cove.

—It's a little cold out here, I said.

—But worth it, right? It's funny. The skyline at night is so breathtaking and yet you could spend a whole lifetime in Manhattan and never see it. Like a mouse in a maze.

Eve was right, of course. Along whole avenues of the Lower East Side the sky was blotted out by elevated tracks and fire escapes and the telephone wires that had yet to be put underground. Most New Yorkers spent their lives somewhere between the fruit cart and the fifth floor. To see the city from a few hundred feet above the riffraff was pretty celestial. We gave the moment its due.

—Tinker doesn't like me out here, she said. He's convinced I'm going to jump.

—Would you?

I tried to put a hint of jest in the question, but it didn't come off.

She didn't seem particularly annoyed. She just dismissed the notion in four words.

—I'm a Catholic, Katey.

About a thousand feet off the ground three green lights entered our field of vision heading southward over the park.

—See those, Eve said pointing. I'll bet you a good night's sleep they circle the Empire State Building. The little planes always do. They just can't seem to help themselves.

As on those first nights out of the hospital, when Eve was ready I helped her back to her room; I helped take off her stockings and her dress; I tucked her in; I kissed her forehead.

She reached up, took my forehead in her hands and kissed me back.

—It was good to see you, Katey.

—Do you want me to turn out the light?

She eyed the bedside table.

—Look at this, she groaned. *Charlotte* Brontë. *Emily* Brontë. *Jane* Austen. Tinker's rehabilitation plan. But didn't they all die spinsters?

—I think Austen did.

—Well, the rest of them might as well have.

The remark caught me so off guard that I burst out laughing. Eve laughed too. She laughed so hard that her hair fell over her face. It was the first good laugh the two of us had had since the first week of the year.

When I turned out her light, Eve said that there was no point in my waiting for Tinker, that I should let myself out; and I almost did. But he had made me promise.

So I turned off the lights in the hall and most of the lights in the living room. I settled down on the couch with the white throw over my shoulders. I pulled a book from the middle of the pile and started reading. It was Pearl Buck's *Good Earth*. When it bogged me down on page 2, I turned to page 104 and started again. It didn't help.

My gaze settled on the pyramid of books. I considered the selection of titles for a moment. Then I carried the stack down the hall to the maid's room and swapped the lot for ten of the detective novels. When I put them on the living room table, there was no need to arrange their vertical order because they were all exactly the same size. Then I went to make myself some closed-kitchen eggs.

I cracked two eggs in a bowl and whisked them with grated cheese and herbs. I poured them into a pan of heated oil and covered them with a lid. Something about heating the oil and putting on the lid makes the eggs puff upon contact. And they brown without burning. It was the way my father used to prepare eggs for me when I was a girl, though we never ate them for breakfast. They tasted best, he used to say, when the kitchen was closed.

I was eating the last off my plate when I heard Tinker calling my name in hushed tones.

—I'm in the kitchen.

He came in with that relieved look.

—There you are, he said.

—Here I am.

He dropped into a chair. His hair was combed and his tie sported a crisp Windsor knot, but his turnout couldn't hide the fact that he was weary. With puffy eyes and depleted drive, he looked like a brand-new father who's been shocked into working extra hours by the arrival of twins.

—How'd it go? he asked, tentatively.

—Fine, Tinker. Evey's tougher than you think. She's going to be okay.

I almost went on to say that he should relax a little, give Evey some space, let nature take its course—But then, I wasn't the one who'd been driving the car.

—We have an office in Palm Beach, he said after a moment. I'm thinking of taking her down there for a few weeks. Some warm weather and new surroundings. What do you think?

—Sounds great.

—I just think she could use a change of pace.

—You look like you could use one yourself.

He offered a tired smile in response.

When I stood to clear, he followed the empty plate with the eyes of a well-behaved dog. So, I made him his own batch of closed-kitchen eggs. I whisked them and fried them, plated and served them. Earlier, I had seen an unopened bottle of cooking sherry in one of the cabinets. I pulled the cork and poured us each a glass. We sipped the sherry and drifted from topic to topic in unnecessarily hushed tones.

The notion of Florida brought mention of the Keys which brought memories to Tinker of reading *Treasure Island* as a boy and of digging with his brother for backyard doubloons; which brought memories to both of us of *Robinson Crusoe* and daydreams of being stranded; which got us on the track of what two belongings we'd want in our pockets when we were eventually shipwrecked alone: for Tinker (sensibly) a jackknife and a flint; for me (insensibly) a pack of cards and *Walden* by Thoreau—the only book in which infinity can be found on every other page.

And for the moment, we let ourselves imagine that we were still in Max's diner—with our knees knocking under the tabletop and seagulls circling the Trinity steeple and all the brightly colored possibilities dangled by the New Year still within our reach.

Old times, as my father used to say: If you're not careful, they'll gut you like a fish.

In the foyer, Tinker took both my hands in his again.

—It was good to see you, Katey.

—It was good to see you too.

As I stepped back, he didn't immediately let go. He looked as if he was wrestling with whether to say something. Instead, with Eve asleep at the end of the hall, he kissed me.

It wasn't a forceful kiss. It was an inquiry. All I had to do was lean a little forward and he would have wrapped his arms around me. But at this juncture, where would that have gotten anybody?

I freed my hands and put a palm on the smooth skin of his cheek, taking comfort in the well-counseled patience for that which bears all things, believes all things, hopes all things and, most importantly, endures them.

—You're a sweet one, Tinker Grey.

The elevator cables whooshed past as the car approached. I dropped my hand before Hamilton pulled back the elevator door. Tinker nodded and put his hands in his jacket pockets.

—Thanks for the eggs, he said.

—Don't make too much of it. It's the only thing I know how to cook.

Tinker smiled, showing a flash of his normal self. I got on the elevator.

—We didn't get a chance to talk about your new place, he said. Can I come by and see it? Maybe next week?

—That would be great.

Hamilton was waiting respectfully for the conversation to end.

—Okay, Hamilton, I said.

He closed the gate and pulled the lever, initiating our descent; and then he whistled a little tune to himself as he watched the floors pass.

After the Civil War the names of the founding fathers like Washington and Jefferson became plenty popular with his race. But here was the first Negro I'd ever met named after the death-by-dueling proponent of the central bank. When we reached the lobby, I stepped off the elevator and turned to ask him about that. But a bell rang and he gave a shrug. The great brass doors of the elevator quietly closed.

They were embossed with a dragon-crested shield inscribed with the motto of the Beresford: FRONTA NULLA FIDES. Place No Trust in Appearances.

I'll say.

Despite the fact that the groundhog had cast no shadow, winter laid siege on New York for another three weeks. The crocuses froze in Central Park; the songbirds, reaching the only sensible conclusion, doubled back to Brazil; and as for Mistah Tinkah, why the following Monday, he took Miss Evelyn to Palm Beach without so much as a word.

CHAPTER SIX

The Cruelest Month

One night in April, I was standing in the Wall Street stop of the IRT waiting to hoi polloi home. It had been twenty minutes since the previous train and the platform was crowded with hats and sighs and roughly folded afternoon editions. On the ground nearby was an overstuffed valise bound with string. But for the absence of children, it could have been a way station in a time of war.

A man who was squeezing past me knocked my elbow. He had brown hair and a cashmere coat. Like one out of keeping with the times, he turned to apologize. And for the briefest moment I thought it was Tinker.

But I should have known better.

Tinker Grey was nowhere near the Interborough Rapid Transit. At the end of their first week in Palm Beach, Eve had sent me a postcard from the Breakers Hotel where she and Tinker were holed up. *Sis, we miss you somethin' awful*—or so she wrote—and Tinker echoed the sentiment in the margin, wrapping little block letters around my address and up toward the stamp. On the picture, Eve had drawn an arrow pointing to their balcony overlooking the beach. She drew a sign stuck in the sand that read: NO JUMPING. The postscript read: *See you in a week.* But two weeks later, I got a postcard from the marina at Key West.

In the meantime, I took five thousand pages of dictation. I typed four hundred thousand words in language as gray as the weather. I sutured split infinitives and hoisted dangling modifiers and wore out the seat of my best flannel skirt. At night, alone at my kitchen table I ate peanut butter on toast, mastered the ruff and slough and waded into the novels of E. M. Forster just to see what all the fuss was about. In all, I saved fourteen dollars and fifty-seven cents.

My father would have been proud.

The gracious stranger maneuvered across the platform and took a position beside a mousy young woman who looked up at his approach and briefly met my gaze. It was Charlotte Sykes, the typing prodigy who sat to my left.

Charlotte had thick black eyebrows, but she also had delicate features and beautiful skin. She could have made a favorable impression on someone if she hadn't acted as though at any moment the city was going to step on her.

Tonight she was sporting a pillbox hat with a funereal chrysanthemum stitched to its crown. She lived somewhere on the Lower East Side and she seemed to be taking her cue from me as to how late one should work, because she often ended up on the platform a few minutes on my heels. Charlotte took a furtive look in my direction, obviously working up the courage to approach. Lest there be any doubt, I took *A Room with a View* from my purse and opened to Chapter VI. It is a lovely oddity of human nature that a person is more inclined to interrupt two people in conversation than one person alone with a book, even if it is a foolish romance:

> George had turned at the sound of her arrival. For a moment he contemplated her, as one who had fallen out of heaven. He saw radiant joy in her face, he saw the flowers beat against her dress

The beating of flowers was drowned out by the brakes of a train. The refugees on the platform gathered their possessions and readied themselves to fight for passage. I let them push their way around me. When the station was this crowded you were generally better off waiting for the next train.

Strategically positioned across the platform, rush hour conductors in little green caps acted like cops at the scene of an accident, broadening their shoulders and preparing to push people forward or back as necessary. The doors opened and the crowd surged. The blue-black chrysanthemum on Charlotte's hat bobbed ahead like flotsam on the sea.

—Make room in there, shouted the conductors, shoving high and low alike.

A moment later the train was gone, leaving a smattering of wiser folk behind. I turned the page secure in my solitude.

—Katherine!

—Charlotte . . .

At the last minute, she must have doubled back, like a Cherokee scout.

—I didn't know you took this train, she said disingenuously.

—Every day.

She blushed sensing that she'd been caught in a fib. The blush brought badly needed color to her cheeks. She should have fibbed more often.

—Where do you live? she asked.

—On Eleventh Street.

Her face brightened.

—*We're nearly neighbors!* I live on Ludlow. A few blocks east of Bowery.

—I know where Ludlow is.

She smiled apologetically.

—Of course.

Charlotte was holding a large document with both hands in front of her waist, the way a schoolgirl holds her textbooks. From the thickness of it you could tell it was the draft of a merger agreement or an offering plan. Whatever it was, she shouldn't have had it with her.

I let the silence grow awkward.

Though apparently not awkward enough.

—Did you grow up in the neighborhood? she asked.

—I grew up in Brighton Beach.

—Jeepers, she said.

She was about to ask what Brighton Beach was like or which subway ran there or if I'd ever been to Coney Island, but a train came to my rescue. There were still only a scattering of people on the platform so the conductors ignored us. They smoked cigarettes with worldly indifference like soldiers in between assaults.

Charlotte took the seat beside me. On the bench facing us, there was a middle-aged chambermaid disinclined to raise her eyes. She wore an old burgundy coat over her black and white uniform and a pair of practical shoes. Above her head hung a poster from the Department of Health discouraging the practice of sneezing without a handkerchief.

—How long have you worked for Miss Markham? Charlotte asked.

It was to Charlotte's credit that she said Miss Markham rather than Quiggin & Hale.

—Since 1934, I said.

—That must make you one of the senior girls!

—Not by a long shot.

We were quiet for a few seconds. I thought maybe she was finally getting the message. Instead she launched into a monologue.

—Isn't Miss Markham something else? I've never met anyone like her. She is just *so* impressive. Did you know that she speaks French? I heard her speaking it with one of the partners. I swear, she can see the draft of a letter once and remember it word for word.

Charlotte was suddenly chattering at twice her usual pace. I couldn't tell if it was nerves or an effort to say as much as possible before the train arrived at her stop.

— . . . But then all the people at Q&H are just *so* especially nice. Even the partners! I was in Mr. Quiggin's office just the other day to get some things signed. Have you been in his office? Why, of course you have. You know how he has that fish tank just filled with fish. Well, there was this one little fish that was the most amazing shade of blue and its nose was pressed against the glass. I couldn't take my eyes off it. Even though Miss Markham tells us not to let our eyes wander around the partners' offices. But when Mr. Quiggin finished he came right around his desk and told me the Latin names of each and every one of those fish!

As Charlotte was speeding along, the chambermaid across the aisle had raised her gaze. She was staring at Charlotte and listening as if she had stood in front of such a fish tank one day not long ago, when she too had had delicate features and beautiful skin, when her eyes were hopeful and wide and the world had seemed splendid and fair.

The train arrived at Canal Street and the doors opened. Charlotte was talking so fast she didn't notice.

—Isn't this your stop?

Charlotte jumped. She gave a sweet, mousy wave and disappeared.

It was only when the doors closed that I saw the merger agreement on the bench beside me. Clipped to the front was a note **FROM THE DESK OF THOMAS HARPER, ESQ**, with the name of a Camden & Clay attorney scrolled in Harper's prep school cursive. Presumably, he had sloughed off the delivery of this draft on Charlotte by applying a little schoolboy charm. It wouldn't have taken much. She was born to be charmed. Or intimidated. Either way, it showed a solid lack of judgment on both their parts. But if New York was a many-cogged machine, then lack of judgment was the grease that kept the gears turning smoothly for the rest of us. They'd both end up getting what they deserved one way or another. I lay the agreement back on the bench.

We were still stalled at the station. On the platform a few commuters had gathered in front of the closed doors looking hopefully through the glass like Mr. Quiggin's fish. I redirected my gaze across the aisle and found the chambermaid staring at me. With her doleful eyes, she looked down at the forgotten document. It wouldn't be the both of them who got what they deserved, she seemed to be saying. That charming boy with his fine enunciation and floppy bangs, they'll let him talk his way out of it. And little miss wide eyes, she'll pay the price for the both of them.

The doors opened again and the commuters piled on board.

—Shit, I said.

I grabbed the agreement and got an arm between the doors just before they closed.

—Come on, sweet stuff, said a conductor.

—Sweet your own stuff, I replied.

I headed up the east side stair and began working my way toward Ludlow looking among the wide-brimmed hats and the Brylcreemed hair for a bobbing black chrysanthemum. If I didn't catch her in five blocks, I told myself, this agreement was going to merge with an ash can.

I found her on the corner of Canal and Christie.

She was standing in front of Schotts & Sons—kosher purveyors of all things pickled. She wasn't shopping. She was talking to a diminutive old woman with black eyes in a familiarly funereal dress. The old woman had this evening's lox wrapped in yesterday's news.

—Excuse me.

Charlotte looked up. An expression of surprise turned to a girlish smile.

—Katherine!

She gestured to the old woman at her side.

—This is my grandmother.

(No kidding.)

—Nice to meet you, I said.

Charlotte said something to the old lady in Yiddish, presumably explaining that we worked together.

—You left this on the train, I said.

The smile left Charlotte's face. She took the document in hand.

—Oh. What an oversight. How can I thank you.

—Forget it.

She paused for a second and then gave in to that worst of compulsions:

—Mr. Harper has a meeting first thing tomorrow with an important client, but this revision needs to be at Camden & Clay by nine so he asked if on my way to the office I could—

—In addition to a Harvard degree, Mr. Harper has a trust fund.

Charlotte looked at me with bovine bewilderment.

—These will hold him in good stead should he ever be dismissed.

Charlotte's grandmother looked at my hands. Charlotte looked at my shoes.

In the summer the Schottses rolled their barrels of pickles and herring and watermelon rind right onto the sidewalk, sloshing a vinegary brine on the paving stones. Eight months later you could still smell it.

The old woman said something to Charlotte.

—My grandmother is asking if you would join us for dinner.

—I'm afraid I'm previously committed.

Charlotte translated, unnecessarily.

From Canal Street, I still had fifteen blocks to go, which was about ten too short to warrant another subway fare. So in the language of the neighborhood, I schlepped. At every intersection I looked to my left and right. Hester Street, Grand Street, Broome Street, Spring. Prince Street, First Street, Second Street, Third. Each block looked like a dead end from a different country. Tucked among the tenements you could see the shops of other Fathers & Sons selling the reformulated fare of *their* home countries—their sausages or cheeses, their smoked or salted fish wrapped in Italian or Ukrainian newsprint to be trundled home by their own unvanquishable grandmothers. Looking up, you could see the rows of two-room flats where three generations gathered nightly for a supper bracketed by religious devotions as saccharine and peculiar as their after-dinner liqueurs.

If Broadway was a river running from the top of Manhattan down to the Battery, undulating with traffic and commerce and lights, then the east-west streets were eddies where, leaflike, one could turn slow circles from the beginning to the ever shall be, world without end.

At Astor Place, I stopped to buy the evening edition of the *Times* at a curbside newsstand. The front page offered a modified map of Europe, graced with a gentle dotted line to reflect a shifting frontier. The old man behind the counter had the white overgrown eyebrows and kindhearted expression of an absentminded country uncle. It made you wonder what he was doing there.

—Nice night, he said, presumably referencing what little he could see of it reflected in the milliner's window.

—Yes, it is.

—Do you think it'll rain?

I looked over the East Side rooftops where the Evening Star shone as clear as the beacon of a plane.

—No, I said. Not tonight.

He smiled and looked relieved.

As I handed him a dollar, another customer approached and stopped a foot closer to me than was necessary. Before I had a chance to take him in, I noticed the newsman's eyebrows droop.

—Hey sister, the customer said. You have a smoke or somethin?

I turned and met his gaze. Well on his way from unemployed to unemployable, his hair was much longer now and he had a poorly groomed goatee, but he had the same presumptuous smile and the wandering eye that he had had when we were fourteen.

—No, I said. Sorry.

He gave a shake. Then he tilted his head.

—Hey. I know you, right?

—I don't think so.

—Sure, he said. I know you. Room 214. Sister Sally Salamone. I before E except after C . . .

He laughed at the thought of it.

—You've mistaken me for somebody else, I said.

—I aint mistaken, he said. And you aint somebody else.

—Here, I said, holding out my change.

He held up both hands in mild protest.

—I couldn't presuppose.

Then he laughed at his own word choice and walked off toward Second Avenue.

—That's the problem with being born in New York, the old newsman observed a little sadly. You've got no New York to run away to.

CHAPTER SEVEN

The Lonesome Chandeliers

—This is Katey Kontent.

—This is Clarence Darrow.

The typewriters at Quiggin & Hale steamed full speed ahead, but not so loudly that I couldn't hear the lilt back in Evey's voice.

—When did you get in town, Miss Darrow?

—Four score and seven hours ago.

—How was Key West?

—Droll.

—No need for jealousy on my end?

—Not a smidgen. Listen. We're having a few friends over tonight. We'd love it if you'd round out the table. Can we lure you away?

—From what?

—That's the spirit.

I arrived at the Beresford forty minutes late.

As embarrassing as it is to admit, I was late because I was having trouble deciding what to wear. When Eve and I lived at the boarding-house we shared our wardrobe with the other girls on the floor and we always looked smart on Saturday night. But when I moved out, I had something of a rude awakening—I discovered that all the fun clothes had been theirs. I apparently owned all the frumpy utilitarian numbers.

Scanning my closet, the clothes looked as drab as the sheets outside my window. I settled on a navy blue dress that was four years out of date and spent half an hour with a sewing kit shortening the hem.

Manning the elevator was a big-shouldered sort whom I didn't recognize.

—Hamilton isn't on tonight? I asked as we ascended.

—That boy's gone.

—That's too bad.

—Not for me, it aint. I wouldn't have no job if he still had it.

This time, it was Eve waiting for me in the foyer.

—Katey!

We kissed each other on the right cheeks and she took both of my hands in hers, just as Tinker liked to do. She stepped back and looked me over as if I was the one just returned from two months at the beach.

—You look great, she said.

—You're kidding, right? *You* look great. I look like Moby Dick.

Evey squinted and smiled.

And she did look great. In Florida, her hair had turned flaxen and she had cut it back to her jaw, accentuating the fineness of her features. The sardonic lethargy of March had been exorcised and a teasing glint had returned to her eye. She was also wearing a spectacular pair of diamond chandeliers. They cascaded from her earlobes to her neck and sparkled over the evenly tanned surface of her skin. There was no question about it: Tinker's Palm Beach prescription had been spot on.

Eve led the way into the living room. Tinker was standing beside one of the couches talking with another man about shares in a railroad. Eve interrupted him by taking his hand.

—Look who's here, she said.

He was looking good too. While in Florida, he had lost his nursemaid pounds and his hangdog demeanor. He had taken to entertaining without a tie and his tanned sternum showed through his open collar. Without quite letting go of Evey's hand he leaned forward and gave me a peck on the cheek. If he pecked to make a point, he needn't have. I had already gotten the lay of the land.

No one seemed particularly put out that I was late, but the price I paid was missing the drinks. About a minute after I was introduced, I was ushered into the dining room empty-handed. From the looks of the crowd, I had missed more than a round.

There were three other guests. Sitting to my left was the man that Tinker had been speaking to when I'd arrived: a stockbroker nicknamed Bucky who summered near Tinker as a boy. In the relapse of '37, apparently Bucky had had the good sense to cash out before his clients. Now he lived comfortably in Greenwich, Connecticut. He was a fine-looking charmer who, while nowhere near as smart as he sounded, was at least of better cheer than his wife. With her hair pulled back, Wyss (short for Wisteria!) seemed as prim and miserable as a schoolmarm. The state of Connecticut is one of our nation's smallest, but it wasn't small enough for her. In the afternoon, she probably climbed her colonial stair and looked out her second-story window toward Delaware with a bitter, envious gaze.

Seated directly across from me was a friend of Tinker's named Wallace Wolcott. Wallace, who had been a few years ahead of Tinker at St. George's, had the fair hair and solemn grace of a collegiate tennis star who never quite cared for the sport. For a moment, I wondered whether it was Eve's or Tinker's idea to invite him on my behalf. Maybe it was a shared plan, the sort of transparent conspiracy that good marriages are made of. Whosever idea, it was a misfire. Wallace, who had a slight speech impediment—a sort of dead stop in the middle of every remark—was obviously more interested in playing with his spoon than making eyes at me. All in all, one got the sense he'd rather be behind his desk at the family paper concern.

The party was suddenly talking about ducks.

On the way back to New York, the five of them had stopped over in South Carolina at the Wolcotts' hunting plantation and they were debating the finer points of mallard plumage. I let my mind wander until I became conscious that someone was asking me something. It was Bucky.

—What's that? I asked.

—Have you ever been hunting down south, Katey?

—I've never been hunting in any direction.

—It's good sport. You should join us next year.

I turned to Wallace.

—Do you shoot there every year?

—Most years. A few weekends in the . . . fall and spring.

—Then why do the ducks come back?

Everyone laughed but Wyss. She clarified on my behalf.

—They grow a field of corn and flood it. That's what attracts the birds. So in that sense, it's actually not that "sporting."

—Well, isn't that the way that Bucky attracted you?

For a moment, everyone laughed but Wyss. Then Wyss started laughing and everyone laughed but Bucky.

The soup was served. It was black bean with a spoonful of sherry. Maybe it was the sherry that Tinker and I had shared. If so, it was poetic justice for someone. But it was too soon to tell for whom.

—This is delicious, Tinker said to Eve, his first words in half an hour. What is it?

—Black bean and sherry. And don't worry. There's not a spot of cream in it.

Tinker gave an embarrassed smile.

—Tinker's been minding his nutrition, Eve explained.

—It's working, I said. You look terrific.

—I doubt that, he said.

—No, Eve said raising her glass to Tinker. Katey's right. You're positively glowing.

—That's because he shaves twice a day, said Bucky.

—No, said Wallace. It's the . . . exercise.

Eve pointed a finger at Wallace in agreement.

—In the Keys, she explained, there was an island a mile off the coast and Tinker would swim there and back twice a day.

—He was a . . . fish.

—That's nothing, Bucky said. One summer he swam across the Narragansett Bay.

The starlike blushes on Tinker's cheeks grew a shade redder.

—It's only a few miles, he said. It's not hard if you time the tides right.

—How about you, Katey, Bucky asked, taking another stab at it. Do you enjoy a good swim?

—I don't know how.

Everyone sat up in their seats.

—What's that?!

—You don't know how to swim?

—Not a stroke.

—Then what?

—I sink, I suppose. Like most things.

—Did you grow up in Kansas? asked Wyss without irony.

—I grew up in Brighton Beach.

More excitement.

—Splendid, said Bucky, as if I'd climbed the Matterhorn.

—Don't you want to learn? asked Wyss.

—I don't know how to shoot either. Between the two, I'd rather learn to shoot.

Laughter.

—Well that's well within your grasp, Bucky encouraged. There's really nothing to it.

—Obviously, I know how to pull a trigger, I said. What I want to learn is how to hit a bull's-eye.

—I'll teach you, said Bucky.

—No, said Tinker looking more at ease with the shift of attention. Wallace is your man.

Wallace had been drawing a circle on the linen with the tip of his dessert spoon.

—Is that right, Wallace?

— . . . Hardly.

—I've seen him shoot the center of a target at a hundred yards, Tinker said.

I raised my eyebrows.

—True or false?

—True, he said shyly. But to be fair, a . . . bull's-eye doesn't move.

When the bowls were cleared, I excused myself to go to the bathroom. A nice burgundy had been served with the soup and my head was beginning to turn on its spindle. There was a little washroom near the living room, but thumbing my nose at etiquette, I went down the hall to the master bath. From a quick look around the bedroom I could see that Eve was no longer sleeping alone.

I peed and flushed. Then, as I was standing at the sink washing my hands, Eve appeared. She winked at me in the mirror. She hoisted up her dress and sat on the toilet, just like old times. It made me regret having wanted to snoop.

—So, she said coyly, what do you think about Wallace?

—He seems grade A.

—And then some.

She flushed and pulled up her hose. She came over and took my place at the sink. There was a small ceramic cigarette box on the vanity. I lit one and sat on the john to smoke. I watched as she washed her hands. From where I was sitting you could see her scar. It still looked red and a little inflamed. But it wasn't getting much in her way anymore.

—Those are some earrings, I said.

She appreciated herself in the mirror.

—Aren't they, though.

—Tinker's treating you right.

She lit her own cigarette and tossed the match over her shoulder. Then she leaned against the wall, took a drag and smiled.

—He didn't give them to me.

—Then who?

—I found them in the bedside table.

—Gadzooks.

She took a drag and nodded with her eyebrows raised.

—Those have got to be worth over ten thousand dollars, I said.

—And then some.

—What were they doing there?

—No good to anyone.

I spread my legs and dropped my cigarette in the bowl.

—But here's the best part, she said. I've worn them every day since we got back from Palm Beach and he hasn't uttered the peep of a sheep.

I laughed. It was a great old Evey-sort-of-thing to say.

—Well, I guess they're yours now.

She tamped out her cigarette in the basin of her sink.

—You better believe it, Sis.

———

Two more bottles of burgundy were poured with the main course. They may as well have been poured over our heads. I don't think anyone tasted the tenderloin, or the lamb, or whatever it was.

Bucky, good and drunk, launched into a yarn for my benefit about how the five of them had gone to a casino in Tampa-Saint Pete. After they'd spent fifteen minutes around a roulette table, it became pretty clear that none of the boys intended to place a bet. (Presumably, they were afraid to lose the money that wasn't theirs in the first place.) So to teach them a lesson, Eve borrowed a hundred dollars from each and scattered chips across even, black, and her birthday. When nine red came up, she paid back the principal right there on the spot and stuffed the winnings in her brassiere.

When it comes to gambling, some feel nauseated when they win and others feel nauseated when they lose. Eve had a good stomach for both.

—Bucky dear, his wife warned, you're slurring your words.

—Slurring is the cursive of speech, I observed.

—Eckshactly, he said, elbowing me in the ribs.

Coffee in the living room was announced just in time.

Keeping an earlier promise, Eve took Wisteria on a tour of the apartment while Bucky cornered Wallace to secure a hunting invitation for the fall. So Tinker and I ended up in the living room alone. He sat down on one of the couches and I sat beside him. He put his elbows on his knees and clasped his hands. He looked back at the dining room as if he was hoping that a seventh guest would miraculously appear. He took his lighter from his pocket. He snapped the lid open and shut and then put it away again.

—It's good of you to come, he said at last.

—It's a dinner party, Tinker. Not a crisis.

—She looks better. Doesn't she?

—She looks great. I told you she'd be fine.

He smiled and nodded. Then he looked me in the eye, maybe for the first time all evening.

—The thing of it is, Katey—Eve and I are sort of making a go of it.

—I know, Tinker.

—I don't think we really set out—

—I think it's great.

—Really?

—Absolutely.

A neutral observer would probably have raised an eyebrow at my answer. There wasn't much jingle in my delivery, and one-word responses just have that way of not sounding very convincing. But the thing of it is, I meant it. Every one word of it.

For starters, you could hardly blame them. Balmy breezes, turquoise seas, Caribbean rum, these are well-established aphrodisiacs. But so too are proximity and necessity and the threat of despair. If, as was painfully apparent in March, Tinker and Eve had *both* lost something essential of themselves in that car crash, in Florida they had helped each other gain a bit of it back.

One of Newton's laws of physics is something about how bodies in motion will hew to their trajectory unless they meet an external force. I suppose, given the nature of the world, it was perfectly likely that some such force could present itself to set Tinker and Eve off their current course; but there was no way it was going to be me.

Bucky came stumbling into the room and collapsed in a chair. Even I was relieved to see him. Tinker took the opportunity to go over to the bar. When he came back with drinks that no one needed, he took a seat on the other couch. Bucky took a grateful swig and then vaulted back into the topic of railroad shares.

—So, you think it's in the realm, Tink? That we could get a piece of this Ashville Rail business.

—I don't see why not, Tink conceded. If it's the right thing for your clients.

—How about I come down to Forty Wall and we hash it out over lunch?

—Sure.

—This week?

—Oh, leave him alone, Bucky.

Wisteria had just come back with Eve.

—Don't be such a boor, she said.

—Come on, Wyss. He doesn't mind mixing a little business with pleasure. Do you, Tink?

—Of course not, said Tink politely.

—You see? Besides. He's got the whole concession. The world has no choice but to beat a path to his door.

Wyss glowered.

—Evelyn, Wallace interrupted adeptly, dinner was . . . delicious.

—Hear hear, was the chorus.

For the next few minutes, there was a thorough rehashing of the courses (That meat was delicious. The sauce was perfect. And ooh that chocolate mousse.) This was a social nicety that seemed more prevalent the higher you climbed the social ladder and the less your hostess cooked. Eve accepted the compliments with appropriate panache and a dismissive wave of the hand.

When the clock struck one we were all in the foyer. Eve and Tinker had their fingers intertwined, as much to shore each other up as to show affection.

—Lovely evening.

—Terrific time.

—Must do it again.

Even Wyss was encouraging an encore, God knows why.

When the elevator came it was the same man who had taken me up earlier.

—Ground floor, he announced once he'd pulled the caging shut, as if he had formerly worked in a department store.

—That's quite an apartment, Wyss remarked to Bucky.

—Like a phoenix from the ashes, he replied.

—How much do you think it cost?

No one answered her. Wallace was either too well raised or too disinterested. Bucky was too busy trying to bump his shoulder into mine unintentionally. I was too busy wondering when I received the invitation to the reprise, what reason I could give for not being able to attend.

◆ ◆ ◆

And yet . . .

When I was lying in bed later that night alone and alert, with the corridors of my walk-up unusually quiet, the person foremost on my mind was Eve.

For in the years preceding, if I had chanced onto the guest list of a dinner party like this one with all its temperate discord, and stayed out much too late for a school night, my one consolation would have been finding Eve, propped on her pillows, waiting to hear every last detail.

CHAPTER EIGHT

Abandon Every Hope

One night in mid-May, as I was crossing Seventh Street on my way home, a woman my age came around the corner and knocked me off my heels.

—Watch where you're going, she said.

Then she leaned over me to get a closer look.

—Bust my bosoms. Is that you, Kontent?

It was Fran Pacelli, the plum-chested City College dropout from down the hall at Mrs. Martingale's. I didn't know Fran that well, but she seemed a good enough sort. She liked to unsettle the prim at the boardinghouse by wandering the halls without a shirt on and asking loudly if they had any extra booze. One night I'd caught her climbing through a second-story window wearing nothing but high-heel shoes and a Dodgers uniform. Her father was in trucking, which in those days usually meant that he had run liquor in the twenties. From Fran's vocabulary, you might have suspected that she'd run a little liquor in the twenties too.

—What a lucky break! she said, pulling me to my feet. Bumping into you like this. You look great.

—Thanks, I said brushing off my skirt.

Fran looked around the street as if she was thinking something through.

—Uhm. . . . Where you headed? How about a drink? You look like you could use one.

—I thought you said I looked great.

—Sure.

She pointed back up Seventh Street.

—I know a cute little place right up here. I'll buy you a beer. We'll catch up. It'll be a gas.

The cute little place turned out to be an old Irish bar. Over the front door a sign read: GOOD ALE, RAW ONIONS, NO LADIES.

—I think that means us.

—Cmon, Fran said. Don't be such a Patsy.

Inside, the air was loud and smelled of spilled beer. Along the bar, the front lines of the Easter uprising sat shoulder to shoulder eating hard-boiled eggs and drinking stout. The floor was covered with sawdust and the tin ceiling was stained with the gaslight smoke of decades past. Most of the customers ignored us. The bartender gave us a sour look but didn't throw us out.

Fran took in the crowd with a glance. There were a few tables in the front that were empty but she shoved her way through the drinkers with a couple of excuse-me-mates. In the back, there was a cluttered little room hung with grainy photos of the Tammany crews—the boys who rounded up votes with billy clubs and cash. Without a word, Fran began moving toward the opposite corner. At the table nearest the coal stove three young men sat huddled over their beer. One of them, a tall, thin redhead, was wearing a jumpsuit with the words *Pacelli Trucking* stitched on the breast in a perversely feminine script. I was beginning to get the picture.

As we approached you could hear the three of them arguing above the din; or rather, you could hear one of them—the belligerent one with his back to us.

—Second of all, he was saying to the redhead, he's a fucking hack.

—A hack?

The redhead smiled, enjoying the tussle.

—That's right. He's got stamina. But he's got no finesse. No discipline.

The small man in between the combatants shifted in his seat uneasily. You could tell he was congenitally unsettled by confrontation. But he looked back and forth as if he couldn't afford to miss a word.

—Third of all, the belligerent one continued, he's more overrated than Joe Louis.

—Right, Hank.

—Fourth of all, fuck you.

—Fuck *me*? the redhead asked. In what orifice?

As Hank started to clarify, the redhead noticed us and gave a toothy grin.

—Peaches! What are you doin here?

—Grubb?! Fran exclaimed in disbelief. Well, I'll be damned! My friend Katey and I were in the neighborhood and just stopped in for a beer!

—What are the chances! said Grubb.

What are the chances? How about one hundred percent.

—Why don't you join us, he said. This is Hank. This is Johnny.

Grubb pulled a chair up at his side and hapless Johnny pulled up another. Hank didn't budge. He looked more inclined to throw us out than the bartender had.

—Fran, I said. I think I'll mosey along.

—Oh cmon, Katey. Have a beer. Then we'll mosey together.

She didn't wait for an answer. She went over to Grubb leaving me the seat next to Hank. Grubb poured beer from a pitcher into two glasses that looked like they'd already been used.

—Do you live around here? Fran asked Grubb.

—Do you mind? Hank said to Fran. We're in the middle of something.

—Oh, come on, Hank. Let it go.

—Let it go where?

—Hank. I get you think he's a hack. But he's the fucking precursor to cubism.

—Who says?

—Picasso says.

—I'm sorry, I said. Are you guys arguing about Cézanne?

Hank looked at me sourly.

—Who the fuck do you think we're arguing about?

—I thought you were arguing about boxing.

—That was an analogy, Hank said dismissively.

—Hank and Grubb are painters, Johnny said.

Fran squirmed with pleasure and gave me a wink.

—But Hank, Johnny ventured cautiously. Don't you think those land-scapes are nice? I mean the green and brown ones?

—No, he said.

—There's no accounting for taste, I said to Johnny.

Hank looked at me again, but more carefully. I couldn't tell if he was getting ready to contradict or hit me. Maybe he wasn't sure either. Before we found out, Grubb called to a man in the doorway.

—Hey Mark.

—Hey Grubb.

—You know these guys, right? Johnny Jerkins. Hank Grey.

The men nodded to each other soberly. No one bothered introducing us girls.

Mark sat down at a nearby table and Grubb joined him. I barely noticed when Fran followed, leaving me to fend for myself. I was too busy looking at Hank Grey. Unwavering Henry Grey. Older, shorter, he looked just like Tinker after two weeks without food, and a lifetime without manners.

—Have you seen his paintings? Johnny said, gesturing surreptitiously toward Mark. Grubb says they're a mess.

—He's wrong about that too, Hank said mournfully.

—What do you paint? I asked.

He considered me for a moment, trying to decide whether I deserved a reply.

—Real things, he said finally. Things of beauty.

—Still lifes?

—I don't paint bowls of oranges, if that's what you mean.

—Can't bowls of oranges be things of beauty?

—Not anymore they can't.

He reached across the table and picked up the box of Lucky Strikes that was sitting in front of Johnny.

—This is a thing of beauty, he said. The boat-hull red and howitzer green. The concentric circles. These are colors with purpose. Shapes with purpose.

He took one of the cigarettes from Johnny's pack without saying please.

—Hank painted that, Johnny said, pointing toward a canvas that was leaning against the coal scuttle.

You could tell from Johnny's voice that he admired Hank and not just as an artist. He seemed impressed with the whole program—as if Hank was carving out an important new persona for the American male.

But it wasn't hard to see where Hank was coming from. There was a new generation of painters trying to take Hemingway's ethos of the bullring and apply it to canvas; or if not to canvas, then at least to innocent bystanders. They were gloomy, arrogant, brutish, and most importantly, they were unafraid of death—whatever that means for a guy who spends his days in front of an easel. I doubt Johnny had any idea how fashionable Hank's attitude was becoming; or what sort of Brahmin bank account was propping up the rough indifference.

The painting, which was obviously by the same person who had painted the assembly of longshoremen in Tinker's apartment, showed the loading dock of a butchery. In the foreground were trucks parked in a row and in the background loomed a large neon sign in the shape of a steer that read **VITELLI'S**. While figurative, the colors and lines of the painting had been simplified in the style of Stuart Davis.

Very much in the style of Stuart Davis.

—Gansevoort Street? I asked.

—That's right, said Hank, a little impressed.

—Why did you decide to paint Vitelli's?

—Because he lives there, said Johnny.

—Because I couldn't get it out of my mind, corrected Hank. Neon signs are like sirens. You've got to tie yourself to the mast if you're gonna paint em. You know what I mean?

—Not really.

I looked at the picture.

—But I like it, I said.

He winced.

—It's not a decoration, sister. It's the world.

—Cézanne painted the world.

—All those fruits and ewers and drowsy dames. That wasn't the world. That was a bunch of guys wishing they were painters to the king.

—I'm sorry, but I'm pretty sure the painters who curried favor did history paintings and portraits. Still lifes were a more personal form.

Hank stared at me for a moment.

—Who sent you here?

—What?

—Were you the president of your debating society or something? All that may have been true a hundred years ago, or whatever, but after being soaked in admiration, one generation's genius is another's VD. Have you ever worked in a kitchen?

—Sure.

—Really? At summer camp? The dorm dining hall? Listen. In the army, if you draw KP, you might chop a hundred onions in half an hour. The oil gets so deep in your fingertips, for weeks you can smell it every time you take a shower. That's what Cézanne's oranges are now, and his landscapes too. The stink of onion in your fingertips. Okay?

—Okay.

—Yeah, okay.

I looked over at Fran thinking maybe it was time to go, but she had moved on to Grubb's lap.

Like most belligerent people, Hank was getting tiresome fast, so I had good reason to call it a night. But I couldn't stop wondering about Tinker's instincts. I mean, how should I take it that he thought Hank and I would hit it off? I decided to take it badly.

—So, I gather you're Tinker's brother.

I definitely knocked him off the rails with that one. You could tell it was a sensation he hadn't much experience with and didn't much like.

—How do *you* know Tinker?

—We're friends.

—Really?

—Is that surprising?

—Well, he was never much for *this* sort of back and forth.

—Maybe he's got better things to do.

—Oh, he's got better things to do, all right. And maybe he'd get around to doing them—if it weren't for that manipulative cunt.

—She's a friend of mine too.

—No accounting for taste. Right?

Hank reached over for another one of Johnny's cigarettes.

Where did this hack get off running down Evelyn Ross, I thought to myself. Let's throw *him* through a windshield and see how he holds up.

I couldn't resist observing:

—Didn't Stuart Davis paint a pack of Lucky Strikes?

—I don't know. Did he?

—Sure he did. Come to think of it, your paintings remind me a lot of his—what with the urban commercial imagery and primary colors and simplified lines.

—Nice. You should dissect frogs for a living.

—I've done that too. Doesn't your brother have some Stuart Davises in his apartment?

—Do you think Teddy knows the least thing about Stuart Davis? Fuck. He would have bought a tin drum if I told him to.

—Your brother doesn't seem to think so poorly of you.

—Yeah? Maybe he should.

—I bet you drew a lot of KP.

Hank laughed until he coughed. He picked up his glass and tilted it at me with his first smile of the evening.

—You got that right, sister.

When we all stood to go, it was Hank who covered the check. He took some wadded bills out of his pocket and tossed them on the table like they were candy wrappers. What about their colors and shapes? I wanted to ask. Didn't they have purpose? Weren't they things of beauty?

If only his trust officer could see him now.

◆   ◆   ◆

After the drink at that Irish bar, I figured I'd seen the last of Fran. But she got hold of my number and called one rainy Saturday. She apologized for having ditched me and said she wanted to make it up by treating me to the movies. She took me to a string of bars instead and we had a gay old time. When I got around to asking why she had bothered to track me down, she said it was because we were so simpatico.

We were about the same height with the same chestnut coloring and we were both raised in two-room apartments across a river from Manhattan. I guess on a rainy Saturday afternoon, that was simpatico enough. So we trooped around a bit and then one night in early June, she called to see if I wanted to go to the runarounds at Belmont.

My father abhorred wagering of any kind. He thought it the surest route to relying on the kindness of strangers. So I had never played penny-a-point canasta or bet a stick of gum on who could throw the first rock through the principal's window. I certainly had never been to a racetrack. I didn't know what she was talking about.

—The runarounds?

Apparently, on the Wednesday before the Belmont Stakes, the track was opened to the horses on the card so that the jockeys could give them a feel for the course. Fran said it was much more exciting than the race itself—a claim so unlikely that the runarounds seemed certain to be a bore.

—Sorry, I said. On Wednesdays I happen to work.

—That's the beauty of it. They open the track at daybreak so each of the horses can get a run in before it gets hot. We zip out on the train, watch a few ponies, and still punch the clock by nine. Trust me. I've done it a million times.

When Fran said that they opened the track at daybreak, I imagined this was a figure of speech and we would be heading out to Long Island some time after six. But it was no figure of speech. And this being early June, daybreak was closer to five. So she came knocking at 4:30 with her hair coiled in a tower on the top of her head.

We had to wait fifteen minutes for a train. It rattled into the station like it was coming from another century. The interior lights cast a half-hearted glow over the nocturnal flotsam in its care: the janitors, drunkards and dance-hall girls.

When we got to Belmont, the sun was just beginning to heft its way over the horizon as if it needed to defy gravity to do so. Fran was defying gravity too. She was perky, bright, annoying.

—Cmon, Patsy, she said. Hustle your bustle!

The sprawling race day parking lot was empty. As we crossed it, I could see Fran carefully scrutinizing the edifice of the track.

—Over here, she said without much confidence, heading toward the service gates.

I pointed toward the sign that said ENTRANCE.

—How about over here?

—Sure!

—Wait a second, Fran. Let me ask you something. Have you ever been here before? I mean ever once?

—Sure. Hundreds of times.

—Let me ask you something else. When you're speaking, are you ever not lying?

—Was that a double negative? I'm not too good with those. Now let me ask you something.

She pointed at her blouse.

—Does this look good on me?

Before I could answer, she tugged on her neckline to expose a little more cleavage.

At the main gate we passed the unmanned ticket booths, pushed through the turnstiles and headed up a narrow ramp into the open air. The stadium was eerie and still. A green mist hung over the track like you'd expect to see over the surface of a pond in New England. Scattered across the empty stands, the other early risers were huddled in groups of two to four.

It seemed unseasonably cold for June. A few feet from us a man in a quilted jacket was holding a cup of coffee.

—You didn't tell me it was going to be so cold, I said.

—You know what June is like.

—Not at 5:00 A.M. I don't. Everybody else has coffee, I added.

She slugged me in the shoulder.

—What a whiner you are.

Fran was scrutinizing again, this time the people in the middle of the stands. Off to our right a tall, thin man in a plaid shirt stood and waved. It was Grubb in the company of hapless Johnny.

When we got to Grubb's seat, he put his arm around Fran and looked at me.

—It's Katherine, right?

I was vaguely impressed that he knew my name.

—She's cold, Fran said. And mad she doesn't have coffee.

Grubb grinned. From inside a knapsack he produced a lap blanket that he tossed to me, a Thermos that he handed to Fran, and then like a hack magician he felt elaborately around the bag until he brought out a cinnamon donut perched upright on his fingertips. Which, as it turns out, is all it takes to secure a place in my affections.

Fran poured me a cup of coffee. I hunched over it with the blanket on my shoulders like a Civil War soldier.

Having come to the track with his parents when he was in shorts, the whole excursion to the runarounds was like a return to summer camp for Grubb, full of sweet nostalgia and youthful fun. He quickly gave us a lay of the land—the size of the track, the qualifying horses, the importance of Belmont versus Saratoga—then, lowering his voice he pointed toward the paddock.

—Here comes the first horse.

On cue the motley assembly rose.

The jockey wasn't wearing one of those brightly colored checkered outfits that helps the track pretend it's festive. He was wearing a brown jumpsuit like a diminutive garage mechanic. As he walked the horse from the paddock out onto the track, steam rose from the horse's nostrils. In the stillness, you could hear it whinny from five hundred feet. The jockey talked briefly to a man with a pipe (presumably the trainer) and then swung onto the horse's back. He cantered a little so that the horse could take in its surroundings, circled and positioned for a start. A hush fell. Without the shot of a gun, horse and rider took off.

The sound of the horse's hooves drifted up into the stands in muffled rhythm as clods of turf were kicked in the air. The jockey seemed to take the first lengths at an easy pace, holding his head about a foot above the horse's. But at the second turn he urged the animal on. He drew his elbows inward and squeezed his thighs around the horse's barrel. He tucked the side of his face against its neck so that he could whisper encouragements. The horse responded. Though it was getting farther away, you could tell it was running faster, thrusting its muzzle forward and drumming the ground with rhythmic precision. It turned the far corner and the beat of its hooves grew closer, louder, faster. Until it bolted through the imaginary finish line.

—That's Pasteurized, Grubb said. The favorite.

I looked around the stands. There were no cheers. No applause. The onlookers, most of them men, offered the favorite silent recognition.

They reviewed the time on their stopwatches and quietly conferred. A few shook their heads in appreciation or disappointment. I couldn't tell which.

And then Pasteurized was cantered off the track to make way for Cravat.

By the third horse, I was getting a feel for the runarounds. I could see why Grubb thought them more exciting than the Stakes. Though the stands were occupied by only a few hundred people (instead of fifty thousand), to a man they were aficionados.

Huddled at the rail—the innermost circle of the stadium—were the gamblers with unkempt hair who in refining their "systems" had lost it all: their savings, their homes, their families. With fevered eyes and rumpled jackets, looking like they'd slept under the stands, these inveterates leaned on the rail and watched the horses with an occasional licking of the lips.

In the lower stands sat the men and women raised on racing as a great entertainment. They were the same sort that you'd find in the bleachers at Dodger Stadium: the sort who knew the names of the players and all the relevant statistics. They were men and women who, like Grubb, had been brought to the track as children and who one day would bring their children, with a sense of loyalty to an idea that they might only otherwise display in a time of war. They had picnic baskets and racing sheets and formed fast friendships with whomever they happened to sit.

In the boxes above them sat the owners in the company of young women and other hangers-on. All of the owners were rich, of course, but the ones who came to the runarounds weren't the blue bloods or the dilettantes; they were the men who had earned every penny. One silver-haired magnate in a perfectly tailored suit leaned against the rail with both arms like an admiral at the helm. You could just tell that for him racing horses was no idle matter. It wasn't money in search of a distraction. It required all the discipline, commitment, and attention of running a railroad.

And above them all, above the gamblers and the fans and the millionaires, high in the thinner air of the upper stands, were the aged trainers—the ones past their prime. They sat watching the horses with the naked eye, without binoculars or stopwatches, having no need for either. They were measuring not just the speed of the horses, not just their start or their endurance, but their courage and carelessness too— knowing as precisely as one can what was going to happen come Saturday, without it ever occurring to them to place a bet and improve their meager lot.

The one thing for certain at Belmont was that on Wednesday at 5:00 A.M. there was no place for the common man. This was like the circles of Dante's *Inferno*—populated with men of varied sins, but also with the shrewdness and devotion of the damned. It was a living reminder of why no one bothers to read *Paradiso*. My father hated wagering, but he would have loved the runarounds.

—Come on, Peaches, Grubb said taking her arm. I see some old friends.

Grinning with outsized pride, Peaches handed me her binoculars. As they walked away, Johnny looked up hopefully. I ditched him, saying I wanted a closer look at the paddock.

When I got there, I turned Fran's binoculars back on the silver-haired admiral. There were two women in his box gossiping and drinking from aluminum cups. The absence of steam suggested that the cups were filled with liquor. One of them offered him a sip; he didn't deign a reply. He turned instead to confer with a young man who held a stopwatch and clipboard.

—You've got good taste.

I turned to find Tinker's godmother at my side. I was surprised that she had recognized me. Maybe a little flattered.

—That's Jake de Roscher, she said. He's worth about fifty million dollars, and self-made. I can introduce you, if you'd like.

I laughed.

—I think I'd be a little out of my depth.

—Probably, she conceded.

She was dressed in tan pants and a white shirt. Her sleeves were rolled up to the elbows. She obviously wasn't cold. It made me feel self-conscious about having the blanket over my shoulders. I tried to shed it casually.

—Do you have a horse in the race? I asked.

—No. But an old friend of mine owns Pasteurized.

(Naturally.)

—That's exciting, I said.

—Actually, the favorite rarely is. It's the long shots that are exciting.

—But I suppose it can't hurt your bank account if you own the favorite.

—Perhaps. But in general, investments that need their own food and shelter don't amount to much.

Tinker had implied at some point that Mrs. Grandyn's money had originally come from coal mines. Somehow that added up. She had a self-possession that could only be secured by the more immutable assets like land and oil and gold.

The next horse was on the track.

—Who's that? I asked.

—May I?

She held her hand out for my binoculars. Her hair was barretted back so there was no need to clear it from her face. She lifted the binoculars to her eyes like a hunter—turning the lenses directly on the horse, having no problem finding her mark.

—It's Jolly Tar, the Witherings' horse. Barry owns the paper in Louisville.

She lowered the binoculars but didn't hand them back. She looked at me for a moment and hesitated, the way some will when about to ask a sensitive question. Instead, she made a statement.

—I gather that Tinker and your friend are getting along. How long have they been living together? Is it eight months now?

—Closer to five.

—Ah.

—Do you disapprove?

—Certainly not in the Victorian sense. I have no illusions about the liberties of our times. In fact, if pressed, I would celebrate most of them.

—You said you didn't disapprove in the Victorian sense. Does that mean you disapprove in a different sense?

She smiled.

—I need to remind myself that you work at a law firm, Katherine.

How did she know that? I wondered.

—If I disapprove, she continued after weighing the question, it's actually on your friend's behalf. I don't see any advantage to her living with Tinker. In my day, a girl's opportunities were rather limited, so the sooner she secured an eligible husband the better. But today . . .

She gestured toward de Roscher's box.

—You see that thirty-year-old blonde next to Jake? That's his fiancée, Carrie Clapboard. Carrie moved all manner of heaven and earth to get into that chair. And soon she will happily oversee scullery maids and table settings and the reupholstering of antique chairs at three different houses; which is all well and good. But if I were your age, I wouldn't be trying to figure out how to get into Carrie's shoes—I'd be trying to figure out how to get into Jake's.

As Jolly Tar rounded the far turn, the next horse was ushered from the stables. We both looked down at the paddock. Anne didn't bother lifting the binoculars.

—Gentle Savage at fifty to one, she said. Now, there's your excitement.

CHAPTER NINE

The Scimitar, the Sifter & the Wooden Leg

When I came out of work on June 9, there was a brown Bentley parked at the curb.

No matter how much you think of yourself, no matter how long you've lived in Hollywood or Hyde Park, a brown Bentley is going to catch your eye. There couldn't be more than a few hundred of them in the world and every aspect is designed with envy in mind. The fenders rise over the wheels and drop to the running boards in the wide, lazy curve of an odalisque at rest, while the white walls of the tires look as improbably spotless as the spats on Fred Astaire. You can just tell that whoever is sitting in the backseat has the wherewithal to grant your wishes in threes.

This particular brown Bentley was the model in which the chauffeur rides in the open air. He looked like an Irish cop turned manservant. He was staring straight ahead and holding the wheel with big mitts stuffed into little gray gloves. The windows of the passenger compartment were tinted so that you couldn't see who was inside. As I watched the reflection of the masses drifting by, the window rolled down.

—Shiver me timbers, I said.

—Hey, Sis. Where you headed?

—I was just thinking of going down to the Battery to throw myself off the pier.

—Can it wait?

The chauffeur was suddenly at my side. He opened the rear door with surprising grace and adopted the posture of a midshipman at the head of a gangplank. Eve skooched across the seat. I saluted and climbed aboard.

The air in the car was sweet with the smell of leather and the hint of a new perfume. There was so much legroom that I almost slipped off the seat onto the floor.

—What does this rig turn into at midnight? I asked.

—An artichoke.

—I hate artichokes.

—I used to too. But they grow on you.

Eve leaned forward to push an ivory button on a chrome panel.

—Michael.

The chauffeur didn't turn his head. His voice crackled through the speaker as if he were a hundred miles at sea.

—Yes, Miss Ross.

—Could you take us to the Explorers Club.

—Of course, Miss Ross.

Evey sat back and I took her in. It was the first that we'd seen each other since the dinner party at the Beresford. She was wearing a silky blue dress with full-length sleeves and a low neckline. Her hair was as straight as if she'd ironed it. She pulled it behind her ears giving full visibility to the scar on her cheek. A thin white line suggestive of experiences that parlor girls only dream of, it had begun to look glamorous.

We both smiled.

—Happy birthday, Hotstuff, I said.

—Do I deserve it?

—Do you ever.

Here was the setup: For her birthday Tinker said she could rent out a ballroom. She told him that she didn't want a party. She didn't even want presents. All she wanted was to buy a new dress and have dinner for two at the Rainbow Room.

That should have been my first clue that something was in the works.

The car and driver weren't Tinker's. They were Wallace's. When Wallace heard about Eve's wishes, he had given her the car for the day as a present so that she could go from store to store. And she had made the most of it. In the morning, she had worked her way down Fifth Avenue on reconnaissance. Then after lunch, she circled back with Tinker's money and launched a full-fledged attack. She bought the blue dress at Bergdorf's, the new shoes at Bendel's and a bright red alligator clutch at Saks. She even paid for the lingerie. She was fully outfitted with an hour to spare so she'd come looking for me because she wanted to have a drink with an old friend before she turned twenty-five in the clouds over Rockefeller Center. And I was plenty glad she did.

Behind a panel in the passenger door there was a bar. It had two decanters, two tumblers and a sweet little ice bucket. Eve poured me a jigger of gin. She poured herself a double.

—Whoa, I said. Don't you think you should be pacing yourself?

—Don't worry. I've been practicing.

We clinked glasses. She took a mouthful of the gin and ice chips. She crunched the ice as she looked out the window reflecting on something. Without looking back she said:

—Doesn't New York just turn you inside out?

Located in a little townhouse off Fifth Avenue, the Explorers had been a second-rate naturalists and adventurers club that went bankrupt after the Crash. What little it possessed of value had been spirited away in the night by the well meaning to the Museum of Natural History. The rest—a misassembly of curios and keepsakes—had been left behind by the creditors to gather the dust it had deserved in the first place. In 1936, some bankers who had never been outside of New York bought the building and reopened the club as a high-end watering hole.

When we arrived, the street-level steak house was just filling up. We climbed the narrow staircase lined with old photographs of ships and snowy expeditions to the "library" on the second floor. The library had floor-to-ceiling bookshelves holding the club's carefully assembled collection of nineteenth-century naturalist texts that nobody would ever read. In the middle of the floor there were two old display cases, one with South American butterflies and the other with pistols from the Civil War. While all around in low leather chairs brokers, attorneys, and captains of industry mumbled sagely. The only other woman in the place was a young brunette with short-cropped hair sitting in the far corner under the moth-ridden head of a grizzly. Wearing a man's suit and a white-collared shirt, she was blowing smoke rings and wishing she was Gertrude Stein.

—Right this way, the host said.

As we walked, I could see that in her own way Eve had mastered her limp. Most women would have tried to make it disappear. They would have learned to walk like a geisha—taking small invisible steps with their hair turned up and their gaze turned down. But Eve didn't hide it at all. In her blue floor-length dress, she swung her left leg awkwardly in front of her like a man with a clubfoot. Her heels marked the wooden floor in rough syncopation.

The host showed us to a table right in the middle of the room. He put us front and center so that Eve's allure could be appreciated by all.

—What are we doing here? I asked when we sat.

—I like it here, she said looking around at the men with a discerning gaze. Women drive me crazy.

She smiled and patted my hand.

—Except for you, of course.

—What a relief.

A young Italian with hair parted in the middle appeared from behind a swinging door. Evey ordered champagne.

—So, I said. The Rainbow Room.

—I'm told it's pretty fab-dabulous. The fiftieth floor and all that. They say you can see the planes landing at Idlewild.

—Isn't Tinker afraid of heights?

—He doesn't have to look down.

The champagne arrived with unnecessary ceremony. The waiter placed a standing ice bucket at Eve's side and the host did the honors with the cork. Eve waved them off and filled the glasses herself.

—To New York, I said.

—To Manhattan, she corrected.

We drank.

—Any thoughts for Indiana? I asked.

—She's a sorry nag. I'm through with her.

—Does she know?

—I'm sure the feeling's mutual.

—I doubt it.

She smiled and refilled our glasses.

—Enough about all that. Tell *me* something, she prodded.

—What?

—Anything. Everything. How are the girls at Mrs. Martingale's?

—I haven't seen them in months.

This was a white lie, of course, since Fran and I had flapped around a bit. But there was no reason to tell that to Evey. She never liked Fran that much anyhow.

—That's right! she said. I'm so glad you've gotten your own place. How is it?

—It's pricier than the boardinghouse. But now I can burn my own oatmeal and plunge my own commode.

—There's no curfew. . . .

—Not that you'd know it by my bedtime.

—Oh, she said with mock concern. That sounded sad and lonely.

I picked up my empty glass and waved it at her.

—How are things at the Beresford?

—A little hectic, she said as she poured. We're about to have the bedroom remodeled.

—That sounds fancy.

—Not really. We're just sprucing things up a bit.

—Will you stay there during the renovation?

—As it happens, Tinker will be visiting clients in London. So I'll just take a room at the Plaza and push them to get the work done before he's back.

A birthday without presents . . . a business trip to London . . . a bedroom renovation . . . liberal use of the nominative plural . . . The whole picture was coming into focus. Here was a young girl drinking champagne in a brand-new dress headed for the Rainbow Room. Under the circumstances, you'd think she'd be giddy. But there was nothing giddy about Eve. Giddiness implies a certain element of surprise. A giddy girl can't tell what's happening next. She senses that it might be something marvelous, that it might happen at any moment, and this mix of mystery and anticipation lightens her head. But there weren't going to be any surprises for Eve. No unfamiliar gambits or sly combinations. She had drawn the squares and carved the pieces. The only thing she was leaving to chance was how big the stateroom on the boat was going to be.

Back at the 21 Club, when asked *If you could be any one person for the day, then who would you be?* Eve had answered Darryl Zanuck, the studio chief. Her answer had seemed so funny at the time. But sure enough, here she was floating over us on the arm of a crane, double-checking the set, the costumes, the choreography before cueing the sun to rise. And upon reflection, who could fault her for it?

A few tables away, two good-looking boors were getting loud. They were reminiscing about their misdeeds in the Ivy League and one of them unmistakably made use of the word *whore*. Even a few of the men had begun to stare.

Eve didn't look over her shoulder once. She couldn't be bothered. She had started talking about the renovation and just kept on talking—the way a colonel ignores the sound of mortar shells as the infantry ducks for cover.

The two drunkards suddenly stood. They reeled past us with bursts of laughter.

—Well, well, Eve said dryly. Terry Trumbull. Was that you making all that racket?

Terry came about like one of those little boats that children learn to sail in.

—Eve. What a great surprise. . . .

If it weren't for twenty years of private schooling he would have stammered it.

He gave Eve an awkward kiss and then looked inquiringly at me.

—This is my old friend, Kate, Eve said.

—Pleasure to meet you, Kate. Are you from Indianapolis?

—No, I said. I'm from New York.

—Really! Which part of town?

—She's not your type either, Terry.

He turned to Eve looking like he was about to parry, but then thought better of it. He was sobering up.

—Give my best to Tinker, he said.

As he retreated, Eve watched him go.

—What's his story, I asked.

—He's a friend of Tinker's from the Union Club. A few weekends ago, we all went to a party at their house in Westport. After dinner, while his wife was playing Mozart on the piano (God help me), Terry told one of the serving girls he needed to show her something in the pantry. By the time I showed up, he had her cornered by the bread box and was trying to take a bite out of her neck. I had to fend him off with a potato masher.

—He's lucky it wasn't a knife.

—A stabbing would have done him good.

I smiled at the thought of it.

—Well, the serving girl sure lucked out that you showed up when you did.

Eve blinked like she'd been thinking of something else.

—What's that?

—I say the girl was lucky you were there.

Eve looked at me a little surprised.

—Luck had nothing to do with it, Sis. I *followed* the bastard to the pantry.

Suddenly, I had an image of Eve prowling the halls of WASP New York, potato masher in hand, occasionally leaping from the shadows to put all manner of boorish behavior in its place.

—You know what? I said, with renewed conviction.

—What?

—You're the bestest.

When it was nearly eight and the champagne bottle was stuffed upside down in the ice bucket, I pointed out that Eve had better get going. She looked at the empty bottle a little forlornly.

—You're probably right, she said.

She reached for her new clutch and signaled the waiter in the same motion, the way that Tinker would have. She took out an envelope that was filled with brand-new twenty-dollar bills.

—No, I said. It's on me, birthday girl.

—Okay. But on the twenty-fourth, I get to return the favor.

—That would be great.

She stood up and for a moment I could see her in all her glory. With the dress falling gracefully from her shoulders and the red clutch in her hand she looked like a full-length portrait by John Singer Sargent.

—Till doomsday, she reminded me.

—Till doomsday.

As I was waiting for the waiter to bring the check, I wandered over to the display cases in the middle of the room. To someone with knowledge of such things, perhaps the gun case was an impressive showing of rare firearms. But to the inexperienced eye it just seemed shabby. The guns looked like they'd been dug up from the banks of the Mississippi while at the bottom of the case Civil War bullets sat in a pile like deer droppings.

The butterfly display was easier on the eyes, but it too evidenced a certain amateurishness. The insects were pinned on the felt in such a way that you could only see the topside of their wings. But if you know anything about butterflies, you know that the two sides of their wings can be dramatically different. If the top is an opalescent blue, the underside can be a brownish gray with ocher spots. The sharp contrast provides butterflies with a material evolutionary advantage, because when their wings are open they can attract a mate, while when their wings are closed they can disappear on the trunk of a tree.

It's a bit of a cliché to refer to someone as a chameleon: a person who can change his colors from environment to environment. In fact, not one in a million can do that. But there are tens of thousands of butterflies: men and women like Eve with two dramatically different colorings—one which serves to attract and the other which serves to camouflage—and which can be switched at the instant with a flit of the wings.

By the time the check came, the champagne was catching up with me.

I gathered my bag and set my sights on the door.

The brunette in the suit walked past me toward the bathrooms. She gave me the cold unfriendly stare of an old enemy at an unpopular peace. Wasn't that just perfect, I thought. How little imagination and courage we show in our hatreds. If we earn fifty cents an hour, we admire the rich and pity the poor, and we reserve the full force of our venom for those who make a penny more or a penny less. That's why there isn't a revolution every ten years. I stuck out my tongue at her retroactively and wove toward the door trying to look from behind like a movie star on a train.

At the top of the staircase, the steps suddenly looked narrow and steep. It was a little like the view from the top of a roller coaster. I had to take off my heels and cling to the banister.

As I descended with a shoulder to the wall, I realized that the photographs lining the stairwell were pictures of the *Endurance* frozen in the Antarctic. I stopped to look at one of them more closely. In it, the riggings on the ship had been cleared of their sails. Food and other necessities had been unpacked onto the ice. I wagged a finger at Commander Shackleton reminding him that it was his own damn fault.

When I got down to the street I was about to turn across Sixty-ninth to head over to the Third Avenue el when I saw the brown Bentley at the curb. The door opened and the chauffeur got out.

—Miss Kontent.

I was confused, and it wasn't just the booze.

—It's Michael, right?

—Yes.

It struck me suddenly that Michael looked a lot like my father's older brother, Uncle Roscoe. He'd had big mitts too. And a cauliflower ear.

—Did you see Eve? I asked.

—Yes. She asked that I see you home.

—She sent you back for me?

—No, Miss. She wanted to walk.

Michael opened the back door. It looked dark and lonely inside. Being June, it was still light out and the air was temperate.

—Do you mind if I ride in front? I asked.

—That wouldn't do, Miss.

—I suppose not.

—To Eleventh Street?

—That's right.

—How would you like to go?

—What do you mean?

—We could take Second Avenue. Or we could circle through Central Park and then head downtown. Perhaps that would compensate for not riding in front.

I laughed.

—Wow. That's a heck of a suggestion, Michael. Let's do it.

We entered the park at Seventy-second Street and headed north toward Harlem. I rolled down both windows and the warm June air showed me undue affection. I kicked off my shoes and tucked my legs under my chassis. I watched the trees go by and by.

I didn't ride cabs very often, but when I did, the goal was the shortest distance between two points. The idea of taking the long route home had never come up, not once in twenty-six years. It was pretty fab-dabulous too.

◆ ◆ ◆

The next day, I got a call from Eve saying she'd have to cancel our date on the twenty-fourth. It seems that Tinker, taking Eve "by surprise," had shown up at the Rainbow Room with another ticket for the steamer to Europe. Tinker was going to see clients in London and then they were going to drop in on Bucky and Wyss who'd taken a house on the Riviera for the month of July.

About a week later, when I met Fran and Grubb for a hamburger that had been advertised as a steak, she gave me the following tidbit, torn from the social columns in the *Daily Mirror*:

> Word from the mid-Atlantic has reached us that heads came about on the Queen Vic when C. Vanderbilt, Jr.'s annual midcrossing black-tie scavenger hunt was won hands down by new-comers T. Grey, the ever so eligible NYC banker, and E. Ross, his more glamorous half. Striking the upperdecks dumb with amazement, Grey & Ross succeeded in securing among fifty designated treasures: a scimitar, a sifter and a wooden leg. Though the young scavengers would not reveal the secret of their success, observers say

they had the novel approach of canvassing the crew instead of the passengers. The prize? Five nights at Claridge's and a private tour of the National Gallery. Alert museum security to pat down this canny pair before they skedaddle.

CHAPTER TEN

The Tallest Building in Town

On the twenty-second of June, I spent the afternoon taking depositions for young Thomas Harper, Esq., in a room without windows or ventilation at an opposing firm on Sixty-second Street. The subject of the deposition—the line manager of a failing steel mill—was sweating like a laundress and repeating himself even when it made no sense to do so. The only questions that seemed to really get him talking were those that revolved around how bad things were. Do you know what it's like, he asked Harper, to spend twenty years trudging through a business, showing up every morning when your kids are asleep, watching every detail on the line with the tick of the clock, only to wake up one day and find it's all gone?

—No, said Harper flatly. But could I turn your attention to the events of January 1937.

When we finally finished, I had to go to Central Park to get some air. I picked up a sandwich at a corner deli and found a nice spot near a magnolia tree where I could eat in peace in the company of my old friend, Charles Dickens.

As I sat there in the park, I would occasionally look up from the pages of Pip's progress to watch the strolling-by of those whose expectations had already been met. And that's when I saw Anne Grandyn for the third time. After a moment's hesitation, I stuffed the book in my purse and went after her.

Predictably, she kept a purposeful pace. Emerging from the park at Fifty-ninth Street, she crossed against the traffic and skipped up the steps of the Plaza Hotel. I did the same. As a uniformed bellhop spun the revolving door, it occurred to me that it was probably an unwritten rule of polite society that one should never follow an acquaintance into a local hotel. Though couldn't she be meeting friends for a drink? As the door spun, I decided to rely on scientific method.

—Eeny, meany, miney, moe . . .

Inside, I took up a position in the shade of a potted palm. The lobby was a beehive of the well dressed, some arriving with luggage, some heading for the bar, others coming up the stairs from the shoeshine or salon. Under a chandelier that could have shamed an opera house an ambassador with a grand mustache made way for an eight-year-old girl and a pair of poodles.

—Excuse me.

A page in a little red hat was peeking around my tree.

—Are you Miss Kontent?

He handed me a small cream-colored envelope—the sort that announces your table at a dance or wedding reception. Inside was a calling card. It read simply: ANNE GRANDYN. On the back in a wide, easy script she had written: *Come and say hello. Suite 1801.*

Whoops.

As I walked onto the elevator I wondered whether she had noticed me in the lobby or back in Central Park. The elevator boy looked at me with a take-all-the-time-you-need attentiveness.

—Eighteenth floor? I asked.

—Sure thing.

Before the doors closed a pair of honeymooners joined us. Bright, rosy and young, they looked like they were ready to spend every last penny they had on room service. When they skipped down the hallway on twelve, I offered the elevator boy a friendly smirk.

—*Newlyweds*, I said.

—Not exactly, ma'am.

—Not exactly?

—Not exactly newly. Not exactly wed. Watch your step.

Suite 1801 was immediately opposite the elevator bank. After I pressed the brass button on the door frame, a step heavier than Anne's sounded within. The door opened, revealing a slim young man in a Prince of Wales suit. A little awkwardly, I held out the calling card. He took it in well-manicured fingers.

—Miss Kontent?

His pronunciation was as tailored as his suit. But it was also wrong. He pronounced it *Kon*-tent, as in the content of a book.

—It's Kon-*tent*, I said, like the state of being.

—My apologies, Miss Kon-*tent*. Do come in.

He gestured precisely to a spot a few steps inside of the door.

I found myself in the foyer of a bright sunlit suite. On one side of the central living room was a closed paneled door, which presumably led to a bedroom. In the foreground a blue and yellow couch and two club chairs were gathered around a cocktail table striking an effective balance between masculine and feminine styles. Beyond the sitting area stood a banker's desk with a vase of lilies on one corner and a black-shaded lamp on the other. I began to suspect that the perfect taste on display at Tinker's apartment was Anne's. She had just that combination of style and self-confidence that one needed in order to bring modern design into high society.

Anne was standing behind the desk, looking out the window over Central Park as she talked on the phone.

—Yes, yes. I understand exactly what you mean, David. I have no doubt that you had no expectation of my making use of the board seat. But as you can see, it is very much my intention *to* make use of it.

As Anne talked, her secretary handed back her calling card. She spun around and waved me toward the couch. When I sat down my purse tipped over beside me and Pip peeked out in wonder.

—Right. Right. That's fine David. We'll hash it out in Newport on the fifth.

Ringing off, she came over to the couch and sat beside me. She acted as if I had just dropped in unannounced.

—Katey! How nice to see you!

She gestured back toward the phone.

—I'm sorry about that. I inherited a bit of stock from my husband

and it gives me authority that I haven't quite earned—a fact which seems to displease everyone but me.

She explained she was expecting an acquaintance at any moment, but if the stars were aligned we might have time for a drink. She instructed her secretary, Bryce, to prepare some martinis and excused herself to the bedroom. Bryce went to a fine maple cabinet, which held a bachelor's bar. He plucked ice cubes from the bucket with a pair of silver tongs and mixed martinis, stirring the liquor with a long spoon, showing care not to clank the sides of the pitcher. He set two glasses on the table along with a dish of pickled onions. As he was about to pour, Anne came out of the bedroom.

—I'll get that, Bryce. Thank you. That will be all.

—Shall I complete the letter to Colonel Rutherford? he prodded.

—We'll talk about it tomorrow.

—Yes, Mrs. Grandyn.

The unusualness of a woman telling a man what to do with such blunt authority was only slightly diminished by the relative primness of Bryce's demeanor. He gave a formal nod to her and a perfunctory nod to me. She sat back on the couch.

—Let's to it! she said.

She leaned forward in one of her quick synchronized movements—resting an elbow on a knee, reaching for the pitcher. She poured.

—Onion? she asked.

—I'm more of an olive girl.

—I'll remember that.

She handed me my glass and plopped two onions in her own. She put her left arm over the back of the couch. I raised my glass to her, trying to look as at ease.

—Congratulations on Pasteurized.

—None are in order. I bet on the long shot, just as I promised.

She smiled at me and took a drink.

—So tell me: What brings you to this part of town on a Wednesday afternoon? I seem to remember that you were at Quiggin & Hale. Did you take a new job?

—No. I'm still with Quiggin.

—Oh, she said with a hint of disappointment.

—I was with one of the attorneys at a deposition a few blocks from here.

—That's where you get to ask pointed questions before the trial and your opponent has to answer them?

—That's right.

—Well, at least *that* sounds like fun.

—It really depends on the sorts of questions that are being asked.

—And who's asking them, I suspect.

She leaned forward to put her glass on the table. As she did so her blouse separated a little where the top button had come undone. I could see that she wasn't wearing a bra.

—Do you live here? I asked.

—No, no. It's just an office. But it's so much more convenient than having space in a professional building. I can have dinner sent up. I can shower and change before going out. It's easy for people from out of town to come and see me.

—The only person from out of town who's ever come to see me is the Fuller Brush man.

She laughed and picked up her drink again.

—Was it worth his trip?

—Not really.

As she held the glass to her lips, she studied me out of the corner of her eye. When she put the glass back on the table she offered rather casually:

—I gather Tinker and Eve have gone abroad.

—That's right. I think they're spending a few days in London and then heading to the Riviera.

—The Riviera! Well that should prove quite romantic. All that warm water and lavender. But then romance isn't everything, is it?

—I gather you're still unconvinced by their relationship.

—It's none of my business, of course. And they certainly seem to light up a room. In fact, they could probably light up Buckingham Palace. But if *deposed*, I'd have to admit, I've always imagined Tinker with someone who would challenge him a little more. Intellectually, I mean.

—Maybe Eve will surprise you.

—A surprise is what it would take.

The doorbell rang.

—Ah, she said. This must be my guest.

I asked if there was somewhere I could freshen up and she sent me to the bathroom adjoining her bedroom. Wallpapered in a William Morris style, it was petite but glorious. I put cold water on my face. On the marble counter her bra was folded neatly in a square. An emerald ring sat on top of it the way a crown sits on a coronation day pillow. When I came back out, Anne was standing near the couch with a tall ashen-haired gentleman. It was John Singleton, former senator of Delaware.

Outside the hotel, the top-hatted doorman was helping a dashing pair into a cab. When they pulled away, he turned and caught my eye. He doffed his cap politely and stood back at attention—not bothering to signal the next cab in line. He had been doing his job too long to make an amateurish mistake like that.

◆ ◆ ◆

When I got back to my apartment building, you could tell it was Wednesday because the blushing bride in 3B was running roughshod over her mother's Bolognese. When she had transcribed the recipe, she must have written two heads of garlic instead of two cloves, because we'd all be wearing her home cooking for the rest of the week.

Letting myself in, I stood for a second at the kitchen table and sorted through my mail. At first glance, the selection looked as measly as usual, but tucked between two bills I found an airmail envelope, robin's egg blue.

The handwriting was Tinker's.

After rummaging, I found some unfinished wine and sampled it straight from the bottle. It tingled on the tongue like Sunday communion. I poured a glass, sat at my table and lit a cigarette.

The stamps on the envelope were English. One was the head of a statesman engraved in purple and the others were motorcars engraved in blue. It seemed like every country in the world had stamps of statesmen and motorcars. Where were the stamps of the elevator boys and hapless housewives? Of the six-story walk-ups and soured wine? I tamped out my cigarette and opened the letter. It was written on the tissue favored by Europeans.

Brixham, England, June 17

Dear Kate,
    Every day since we sailed, one of us has remarked "Katey would love that!" Today it was my turn. . . .

In a nutshell, the letter described how Tinker and Eve, having decided to drive along the coast from Southampton to London, had ended up in a little fishing village. While Eve was resting in the hotel, Tinker went for a walk and at every turn saw the steeple of the old parish church, the tallest building in town. Eventually, he circled his way toward it.

    Inside, the walls were painted white—like in a whaling church in New England.
    In the first pew a mariner's widow sat reading the hymnal. While well in the back, a bald-headed man with the physique of a wrestler wept beside a basket of berries.
    Suddenly, a group of girls in uniform burst through the door laughing like gulls. The wrestler leapt up and chided them. They crossed themselves in the aisle and ran back outside as the bells overhead began to ring . . .

Really. Is there anything nice to be said about other people's vacations? I balled up the letter and threw it in the trash. Then I picked up *Great Expectations* and turned back to Chapter XX.

My father was never much one for whining. In the nineteen years I knew him, he hardly spoke of his turn in the Russian army, or of making ends meet with my mother, or of the day that she walked out on us. He certainly didn't complain about his health as it failed.

But one night near the end, as I was sitting at his bedside trying to entertain him with an anecdote about some nincompoop with whom I worked, out of the blue he shared a reflection which seemed such a non sequitur that I attributed it to delirium. Whatever setbacks he had faced in his life, he said, however daunting or dispiriting the unfolding of events, he always knew that he would make it through, as long as when he woke in the morning he was looking forward to his first cup of coffee. Only decades later would I realize that he had been giving me a piece of advice.

Uncompromising purpose and the search for eternal truth have an unquestionable sex appeal for the young and high-minded; but when a person loses the ability to take pleasure in the mundane—in the cigarette on the stoop or the gingersnap in the bath—she has probably put herself in unnecessary danger. What my father was trying to tell me, as he neared the conclusion of his own course, was that this risk should not be treated lightly: One must be prepared to fight for one's simple pleasures and to defend them against elegance and erudition and all manner of glamorous enticements.

In retrospect, my cup of coffee has been the works of Charles Dickens. Admittedly, there's something a little annoying about all those plucky underprivileged kids and the aptly named agents of villainy. But I've come to realize that however blue my circumstances, if after finishing a chapter of a Dickens novel I feel a miss-my-stop-on-the-train sort of compulsion to read on, then everything is probably going to be just fine.

Well, maybe I had read this particular fable one too many times. Or maybe I was just annoyed by the fact that even Pip was on his way to London. Whatever the cause, after reading two pages I closed the book and climbed into bed.

CHAPTER ELEVEN

La Belle Époque

At 5:45 on Friday the twenty-fourth, all the desks in the secretarial pool were empty but for mine. I was just finishing a countersuit to be typed in triplicate, getting ready to mope my way home, when out of the corner of my eye I saw Charlotte Sykes approaching from the washrooms. She had changed into high heels and a tangerine-colored blouse that clashed with all her best intentions. She was gripping her purse in both hands. Here it comes, I thought.

—Hey Katherine. Are you working late?

Ever since I'd salvaged Charlotte's merger agreement from the subway, she'd been inviting me out: lunch at a diner, Shabbos with the family, a cigarette in the stairwell. She had even invited me for a dip at one of the massive new public pools built by Robert Moses where denizens of the outer boroughs could clamber about like crabs in a pot. So far, I had fended her off with ready-made excuses, but I didn't know how much longer I could hold out.

—Rosie and I were just about to head over to Brannigan's for a drink.

Over Charlotte's shoulder I could see Rosie studying her nails. Fully figured with a penchant for forgetting to button the top button of her blouse, you could just tell that if Rosie couldn't romance her way to the top of the Empire State Building, she was prepared to climb it like King

Kong. But given the circumstances, maybe her presence wasn't all bad. She'd make it that much easier for me to extricate myself after a drink. And given my recent bout of self-pity, maybe a closer glimpse into the life of Charlotte Sykes was just what the doctor ordered.

—Sure, I said. Let me get my things.

I stood up and covered my typewriter. I picked up my purse. Then with a quiet but audible click, the red light over the Q came on.

Charlotte's expression was more baleful than mine. *Friday night at 5:45!* she seemed to be thinking. *What could she possibly want?* But that's not what I was thinking. I had been having a little trouble getting out of bed lately, and on two days in ten I had shuffled in at five past the hour.

—I'll meet you there, I said.

I stood, straightened my skirt and picked up my steno. When Miss Markham gave you an instruction, she expected you to take it down word for word, even if it was a reprimand. When I entered her office, she was finishing a letter. Without looking up, she gestured toward a chair and scribed away. I sat, straightened my skirt for the second time in as many minutes and in a show of deference flipped open my pad.

Miss Markham was probably in her early fifties, but she was not unattractive. She didn't wear reading glasses. Her chest was not without definition. And though she wore her hair in a bun, you could tell that it was surprisingly thick and long. At one point, she probably could have become the second wife of any senior partner at the firm.

She finished her letter with a professional flourish and returned the pen to its brass holder; it angled in the air like a spear that's hit its mark. She crossed her hands on the desk and looked me in the eye.

—Katherine. You won't be needing your steno.

I closed the pad and tucked it beside my right thigh as Miss Markham had taught us, thinking: *It's worse than I thought.*

—How long have you been with us?

—Almost four years.

—September 1934, if I recall?

—Yes. Monday the seventeenth.

Miss Markham smiled at the precision.

—I've asked you in to discuss your future here. As you may have heard, Pamela will be leaving us at summer's end.

—I hadn't heard.

—You don't gossip much with the other girls, do you Katherine?

—I'm not much one for gossip.

—To your credit. Nonetheless, you seem to get along well?

—It's not a difficult group with which to get along.

Another smile, this one for the appropriate placement of the preposition.

—I'm glad to hear that. We do make some effort to ensure a certain compatibility among the girls. At any rate, Pamela will be leaving. She is . . .

Miss Markham paused.

—With *chy-uld*.

She used two syllables to bring the word to life.

Such news may have merited celebration on the crowded blocks of Bed-Stuy where Pamela came of age, but it didn't merit celebration here. I tried to adopt the expression of one having just learned that her colleague has been caught with her hand in the till. Miss Markham went on.

—Your work is impeccable. Your knowledge of grammatical rule excellent. Your comportment with the partners exemplary.

—Thank you.

—Initially, it seemed as if your shorthand might not keep pace with your typing; but it has improved markedly.

—It was a goal of mine.

—A good one at that. I have noticed also that your knowledge of trust and estate law is beginning to approach that of some of the junior attorneys.

—I hope that doesn't strike you as presumptuous.

—Not in the least.

—I've found it helps me to serve the partners better if I understand the nature of their work.

—Just so.

Miss Markham paused again.

—Katherine, it is my judgment that you are *quintessentially* Quiggin. I have recommended that you be promoted to take Pamela's place as lead clerk.

(Pronounced *clark*.)

—As you know, the lead clerk is like the first violin in an orchestra. You will have more than your share of solos—or better said, you will have a more *appropriate* share of solos. But you will also have to serve as an exemplar. While I am the conductor of our little orchestra, I cannot have my eye on every girl at every hour and they will look to you for guidance. Needless to say, this advancement will come with the appropriate raise in pay, responsibilities, and professional status.

Miss Markham then paused and raised her eyebrows indicating that some comment from me was now welcome. So I thanked her with professional restraint and as she shook my hand, I thought to myself: *How quintessentially Quiggin; how nearly neighbor; how so simpatico.*

Leaving the office, I walked downtown to the South Ferry stop so that I wouldn't have to pass the storefront of Brannigan's. A smell of spoiled shellfish drifted inland from the harbor as if the New York oysters, knowing perfectly well that no one was going to eat them in a month without an R, had thrown themselves onshore.

As I was getting on the train a lanky bumpkin dressed in overalls knocked my purse out of my hands while running from one car to the next; and as I bent to pick it up, my skirt tore a seam. So when I got off at my stop, I bought a pint of rye and a candle to stick on the cork.

Luckily, I drank half the bottle's contents at my kitchen table before taking off my shoes and stockings, because when I stood to scramble an egg, I bumped the table and spilled the rest over a flawed finesse. Cursing Jesus the way my uncle Roscoe would have—in verse—I mopped up the mess and then plopped down in my father's easy chair.

What was your favorite day of the year? That was one of the beside-the-point questions that we posed to each other at the 21 Club back in January. The snowiest, Tinker had said. Any day that wasn't in Indiana, Eve had said. My answer? The summer solstice. June twenty-first. The longest day of the year.

It was a cute answer. At least, that's what I thought at the time. But on cooler reflection, it struck me that when you're asked your favorite day of the year, there's a certain hubris in giving *any* day in June as your answer. It suggests that the particulars of your life are so terrific, and your command over your station so secure, that all you could possibly hope for is additional daylight in which to celebrate your lot. But as the Greeks teach us, there is only one remedy for that sort of hubris. They called it *nemesis*. We call it getting what you deserve, or a finger in the eye, or comeuppance for short. And it comes with an appropriate raise in pay, responsibilities, and professional status.

There was a knock at the door.

I didn't even bother to ask who it was. I opened to find a Western Union kid bearing the first telegram of my life. It was posted from London:

HAPPY BDAY SIS STOP SORRY COULDN'T BE THERE STOP TURN THE TOWN UPSIDE DOWN FOR THE BOTH OF US STOP SEE YOU IN TWO WEEKS STOP

Two weeks? If the postcard from Palm Beach was any indication, I wouldn't be seeing Tinker and Eve till Thanksgiving.

I lit a cigarette and reread the telegram. Given the context, some might wonder if by **FOR THE BOTH OF US** Eve meant her and Tinker, or her and me. Instinct told me it was the latter. And maybe she was on to something.

I got up and pulled Uncle Roscoe's footlocker from under my bed. At the very bottom, buried under my birth certificate and a rabbit's foot and the only surviving picture of my mother, was the envelope that Mr. Ross had given me. I spilled the remaining ten-dollar bills onto my bedcover. Turn the town upside down, the oracle had said, and the very next day that's exactly what I intended to do.

♦   ♦   ♦

On the fifth floor of Bendel's there were more flowers than at a funeral.

I was standing in front of a rack of little black dresses. Cotton. Linen. Lace. Backless. Sleeveless. Black . . . black . . . black . . .

—Can I help you? someone asked for the fifth time since I'd entered the store.

I turned to find a woman in her midforties in a skirt suit and glasses standing at a respectful distance. She had lovely red hair tied back in a ponytail. It gave her the appearance of a starlet playing the part of a spinster.

—Do you have something a little more . . . *colorful*? I asked.

Mrs. O'Mara ushered me to a cushiony couch where she could ask me questions about my size, my coloring and my social schedule. Then she disappeared. When she returned she had two girls in tow, each with a selection of dresses flung over an arm. One by one Mrs. O'Mara introduced me to their virtues while I sipped coffee from a fine china cup. As I offered my impressions (too green, too long, too tepid) one of the girls took notes. It made me feel like I was an executive in the Bendel's boardroom signing off on the spring collection. There wasn't a hint in the air that money would soon be changing hands. Certainly not mine.

A professional saleswoman who knew her mark, Mrs. O'Mara saved the best for last: a white short-sleeved dress with baby blue polka dots and a matching hat.

—The dress is obviously fun, Mrs. O'Mara observed. But an educated, elegant fun.

—It's not too country?

—On the contrary. This dress was designed as fresh air for the city. For Rome, Paris, Milan. It's not for Connecticut. The country doesn't need a dress like this. We do.

Tilting my head, I betrayed a gleam of interest.

—Let's try it on, said Mrs. O'Mara.

It fit almost perfectly.

—Striking, she said.

—You think?

—I'm certain of it. And you don't have shoes on. It's one of the great tests of a dress. If it can look this elegant in bare feet, well then . . .

We were standing next to each other looking coolly in the mirror. I turned a little to one side lifting the heel of my right foot off the carpet. The hem shifted slightly around my knees. I tried to imagine myself barefoot on the Spanish Steps and almost succeeded.

—It's terrific, I admitted. But I can't help thinking how much better it would look on you, given the color of your hair.

—If I may be so bold, Miss Kontent, the color of my hair is available to you on the second floor.

◆　◆　◆

Two hours later, with the red hair of the Irish, I took a taxi to the West Village to La Belle Époque. It was still a few years before French restaurants would be in vogue, but La Belle Époque had become a favorite among the expatriates whenever they repatriated. It was a small restaurant with upholstered banquettes and still lifes on the wall depicting objects from a country kitchen in the manner of Chardin.

After taking my name the maitre d' asked if I would like a glass of champagne while I waited. It was only seven o'clock and less than half the tables were taken.

—Waiting for what? I asked.

—Are you not meeting someone?

—Not that I know of.

—*Excusez-moi, Mademoiselle.* Right this way.

He walked briskly into the dining room. At a table set for two he paused for a fraction of a second then continued to one of the banquettes with a view of the entire room. When he had me comfortable, he disappeared and returned with the promised champagne.

—To getting out of ruts, I toasted myself.

My new navy blue shoes were digging into my ankles. So under the veil of the tablecloth I kicked them off and exercised my toes. When I took a pack of cigarettes from my new blue clutch, a waiter leaned across the table with his stainless steel lighter and ignited a flame that was fully adequate to the task. I took my time sliding the cigarette out of its box while he remained as immobile as a statue. When I drew the first breath of smoke he stood up and closed the lighter with a satisfying snap.

—Would you like to see the menu while you wait? he asked.

—I'm not waiting for anyone, I said.

—*Pardon, Mademoiselle.*

He snapped a finger at a busboy who cleared the setting beside me. Then he presented the menu, cradling it in the crook of his arm so he could gesture to various dishes and remark on their virtues, much as Mrs. O'Mara had with the dresses. It all gave me confidence; if I intended to dig a hole in my savings, then at least I appeared to be on the right track.

The restaurant took its time coming to life. It filled a few tables. It served some cocktails and lit some cigarettes. It proceeded methodically and unrushed, secure in the knowledge that by nine o'clock it would feel like the center of the universe.

I took my time coming to life too. I sipped a second champagne and savored my canapés. I had another cigarette. When the waiter returned, I ordered a glass of white wine, asparagus gratin, and for the entrée, the specialty of the house: *poussin* stuffed with black truffle.

As the waiter sped away, I noticed for the second time that the old couple sitting in the opposite banquette was smiling at me. He was a stocky man with thinning hair dressed in a double-breasted suit and bow tie. He had milky eyes that seemed ready to tear at the slightest sentiment. A good three inches taller, she had on an elegant summer dress, curly hair and a genteel smile. She looked like the sort who at the turn of the century entertained the bishop for lunch and then was off to lead the suffrage march. She winked and sort of waved; I winked and sort of waved back.

The asparagus arrived with a touch of fanfare, presented tableside in a small copper pan. The individual spears were arranged in perfect order—each identical in length, no two overlapping. On top had been delicately scattered a mixture of buttered bread crumbs and fontina cheese which had been broiled to a crunchy, bubbling brown. The captain served the asparagus with a silver fork and spoon. Then he grated a touch of lemon peel over the plate.

—*Bon appétit.*

Indeed.

If my father had made a million dollars, he wouldn't have eaten at La Belle Époque. To him, restaurants were the ultimate expression of ungodly waste. For of all the luxuries that your money could buy, a restaurant left you the least to show for it. A fur coat could at least be worn in winter to fend off the cold, and a silver spoon could be melted down and sold to a jeweler. But a porterhouse steak? You chopped it, chewed it, swallowed it, wiped your lips and dropped your napkin on your plate. That was that. And asparagus? My father would sooner have carried a twenty-dollar bill to his grave than spent it on some glamorous weed coated in cheese.

But for me, dinner at a fine restaurant was the ultimate luxury. It was the very height of civilization. For what was civilization but the intellect's ascendancy out of the doldrums of necessity (shelter, sustenance and survival) into the ether of the finely superfluous (poetry, handbags and haute cuisine)? So removed from daily life was the whole experience that when all was rotten to the core, a fine dinner could revive the spirits. If and when I had twenty dollars left to my name, I was going to invest it right here in an elegant hour that couldn't be hocked.

When my waiter took away the asparagus plate, I realized that I shouldn't have had that second glass of champagne. I decided to visit the ladies' room and dampen my brow. I slipped my left foot into one of the navy blues, but as I felt around with my right foot I couldn't find the other shoe. I did a quick disorderly search. My eyes shifted back and forth around the room. With my toes I began a more systematic investigation moving in concentric circles as far as they could reach without changing my position. When that failed, I began to slouch.

—May I?

The bow-tied gentleman from across the room was standing in front of my table.

Before I said anything he eased down on his haunches. Then he stood back up with the shoe balanced on his palms. He leaned forward at the waist with the formality of the king's regent presenting the glass slipper and discreetly placed it behind the breadbasket. I whisked it off the table and dropped it on the floor.

—Thank you. That was rather inelegant of me.

—Not in the least.

He gestured back toward his table.

—Forgive my wife and I, if we were staring; but we think they're splendid.

—I'm sorry, they?

—Your dots.

At that moment my entrée arrived and the teary-eyed gentleman retreated to his table. I began methodically cutting away at my fowl. But within a few bites, I knew I couldn't finish it. The heady aroma of the truffles wafted off the plate and swirled my senses. If I took one more bite of that chicken, I was pretty sure that it was coming back up. When they took half of it away at my insistence, I was pretty sure it was coming up anyway.

I dumped an assortment of bills onto the tablecloth. In a rush to get fresh air I didn't wait for the table to be pulled far enough back and I toppled the glass of red wine that I didn't remember ordering. Out of the corner of my eye I could see soufflés being presented to the elderly couple. The suffragette gave a perplexed wave. At the door I made eye contact with a rabbit in one of the paintings. Like me, it was hanging by its feet from a hook.

Outside, I headed for the closest alley. I leaned against a brick wall and took a cautious breath. Even I could appreciate the poetic justice of it. If I got sick, from the heavens my father would be staring down at the pool of asparagus and truffle with glum satisfaction. There, he would say, is the ascendancy of your intellect.

Someone put a hand on my shoulder.

—Are you all right, dear?

It was the suffragette. From a polite distance her husband was watching through his teary eyes.

—I think I may have overdone it a little, I said.

—It's that awful chicken. They're so proud of it. But I find it positively repugnant. Do you think you need to be sick? You go right ahead, dear. I can hold your hat.

—I think I'm going to be okay now. Thank you.

—My name is Happy Doran; this is my husband, Bob.

—I'm Katherine Kontent.

—Kontent, said Mrs. Doran, as if she might recognize it.

Sensing that everything was going to be okay, Mr. Doran edged closer.

—Do you come to La Belle Époque often, he asked, as if we weren't standing in an alley.

—This is my first time.

—When you arrived, we assumed you were waiting for someone, he said. If we had known you were dining alone, we would have invited you to join us.

—Robert! said Mrs. Doran.

She turned to me.

—It is inconceivable to my husband that a young woman would *choose* to dine alone.

—Well, not *all* young women, said Mr. Doran.

Mrs. Doran laughed and gave him a scandalized look.

—You're terrible!

Then she turned back to me.

—The least you can let us do is take you home. We live on Eighty-fifth and Park. Where do you live?

At the end of the alley I saw something that looked very much like a Rolls-Royce slowing to a stop.

—Two eleven Central Park West, I said.

The Beresford.

A few minutes later, I was in the backseat of the Dorans' Rolls-Royce being driven up Eighth Avenue. Mr. Doran insisted that I sit in the middle. He had my hat carefully propped on his knees. Mrs. Doran had the driver turn on the radio and the three of us had a gay old time.

When Pete the doorman opened the car door, he gave me a confused look, but the Dorans didn't notice. There were kisses all around and promises to meet again. I waved as the Rolls pulled away from the curb. A little awkwardly, Pete cleared his throat.

—I'm sorry Miss Kontent, but I'm afraid that Mr. Grey and Miss Ross are in Europe.

—Yes, Pete. I know.

When I boarded the downtown train, it was crowded with faces of every color and clothes of every cut. Shuttling back and forth between Greenwich Village and Harlem with two stops in the theater district, the Broadway local on Saturday night was one of the city's most democratic. The buttoned-down were tucked snugly among the zoot-suited and the worse-for-wear.

At Columbus Circle, a lanky man in overalls boarded the train. With long arms and stubble on his chin, he looked like a past-his-prime pitcher from the farm leagues. It took me a moment to realize it was the same country type who had knocked the purse out of my hands the day before on the IRT. Rather than take an empty seat, he stood in the middle of the car.

The doors closed, the train got under way and he produced a little yellow book from his overall pocket. He opened it to a dog-eared page and began reading loudly in a voice that must have been uprooted from Appalachia. It took me a passage or two to realize that he was reading from the Sermon on the Mount.

> —And he opened his mouth, and taught them, saying, Blessed are the poor in spirit: for **theirs** is the kingdom of heaven. Blessed are they that mourn: for **they** shall be comforted.

To his credit, the preacher wasn't holding on to a strap. As the car rocked back and forth, he was keeping steady by gripping the sides of his righteous little book. One got the sense that he could read the Gospels all the way to Bay Ridge and back without losing his footing.

> —Blessed are the meek: for **they** shall inherit the earth.
> Blessed are the merciful: for **they** shall obtain mercy.
> Blessed are the pure in heart: for **they** shall see God.

The preacher was doing an admirable job. He was speaking clearly and with feeling. He captured the poetry of the King James version and he punched every *they* like his life depended on it, in celebration of this central paradox of Christianity—that the weak and weary would be the ones who would walk away with it all.

But on the Broadway local on a Saturday night, all you had to do was look around you to see that this guy didn't know what he was talking about.

◆ ◆ ◆

Shortly after my father died, my uncle Roscoe took me to dinner at his favorite tavern near the seaport. A stevedore, he was a bighearted lumbering sort, the kind of man who would have been better off at sea—that world without women or children or social graces, with plenty of work and unspoken codes of camaraderie. It certainly didn't come very naturally to him to take his newly orphaned nineteen-year-old niece for a meal; so I guess I'll never forget it.

By then I already had a job and a room at Mrs. Martingale's, so he didn't have to worry about me. He just wanted to make sure I was okay and see if I needed anything. Then he was happy to carve up his pork chop in silence. But I wouldn't let him.

I made him tell some of the tall tales from the old days like when he and my father stole the constable's dog and stuck him on the train to Siberia; or when they set out to see the traveling tightrope walkers and were found twenty miles from town, headed in the wrong direction; or when they arrived in New York in 1895 and went straight to see the Brooklyn Bridge. I had heard these stories time and again, of course, which was sort of the point. But then he told me one that I had never heard before, which was also from their first days in America.

By that point, New York already had its fair share of Russians. There were Ukrainians and Georgians and Muscovites. Jews and Gentiles. So in a few neighborhoods, the shop signs were in Russian and the ruble was as widely accepted as the dollar. On Second Avenue, Uncle Roscoe recalled, you could buy *vatrushka* every bit as good as what you'd find on the Nevsky Prospekt. But a few days after they arrived, having paid a month's rent, my father asked Roscoe for all the Russian currency he had left. He combined the bills with his own and then he burned them in a soup pot.

Uncle Roscoe smiled sentimentally at the memory of what my father had done. Looking back, he said he wasn't sure it made all that much sense, but it was a fine story nonetheless.

I guess that Sunday, I thought a lot about my father and my uncle Roscoe. I thought about them arriving on the freighter out of St. Petersburg in their early twenties without knowing a word of English and going straight to see the Brooklyn Bridge—the largest tightrope in the world. I thought about the meek and the merciful; about the blessed and the bold.

The next morning, I woke at the crack of dawn. I showered and dressed. I brushed my teeth. Then I went to the quintessential offices of Quiggin & Hale and quit.

*Entering the suite with the bookseller's bag in hand, he laid the room key qui-
etly on the front table. Down the hall he could see the bedroom door was still
closed, so he went into the large sunlit living room.*

*Hanging over the arm of the high-back chair was the half-read copy of the
previous day's* Herald. *On the coffee table was the bowl of fruit missing an
apple and the towering arrangement of flowers. All were precisely where they
had been in the smaller room on the second floor.*

*The previous night, after his meeting in the City, he had gone to a little spot
he liked in Kensington where Eve was to meet him for dinner. He had arrived
on time and ordered a whiskey and soda assuming she would be a few minutes
late. But near the bottom of his second glass, he began to worry. Could she have
gotten lost? Had she forgotten the name of the restaurant or the time they were
to meet? He considered going back to the hotel, but what if she was already en
route? As he was weighing what he should do, the hostess approached with the
phone.*

*It was Claridge's. For the first time in ten years, the manager explained
somberly, the hotel's lift had malfunctioned. Miss Ross had been trapped
between floors for thirty minutes. But she was unharmed and on her way.*

*Despite his assurances that it wasn't necessary, the manager insisted that
he and Eve be moved to a finer room.*

*When Eve arrived at the restaurant fifteen minutes later, she wasn't in the
least put out by the mishap. She had enjoyed herself immensely. Aside from
the elevator boy, who did top-notch impressions of Hollywood gangsters and
carried a flask of Irish whiskey on his hip, the only other passenger on the ill-
fated descent had been Lady Ramsay, the white-haired wife of a peer who,
when pressed, could do a few Hollywood impressions of her own.*

When they returned to the hotel after dinner, there was a handwritten note

waiting, inviting them to a party the next night at Lord & Lady Ramsay's residence on Grosvenor Square. Then the hotel manager ushered them to their new suite on the fifth floor.

All of their belongings had been expertly moved. The clothes had been hung in the paired closets in the same arrangement—jackets to the left, shirts to the right. His safety razor was standing in its glass on the sink. Even the casually laid items—like the little welcoming card from Anne that had accompanied the flowers—had been left purposefully askew, as if tossed on the table.

It was the sort of attention to detail that one might expect to find at the scene of a perfect crime.

He went to the bedroom and quietly opened the door.

The bed was empty.

Eve was in the window seat with a glamour magazine. She was mostly dressed, wearing a pair of light blue slacks and a spring shirt. Her hair hung loosely above her shoulders and her feet were bare. She was smoking a cigarette and tapping the ashes out the window.

—*Top of the morning, she said.*

He gave her a kiss.

—*Did you sleep well?*

—*Like lead.*

There was no tray on the bed or on the coffee table.

—*Have you had breakfast? he asked.*

She held up her cigarette.

—*You must be starving!*

He picked up the phone.

—*I know how to call room service, sweetie.*

He put the phone back in its cradle.

—*Already out and about? she asked.*

—*I didn't want to disturb you. I had breakfast downstairs and then went for a walk.*

—*What'd you buy?*

He didn't know what she was referring to.

She pointed.

He'd forgotten that he still had the bookseller's bag in his hand.

—*A Baedeker's, he said. I thought we might see some of the sights later.*

—I'm afraid the sights are going to have to get in line. I'm having my hair done at eleven. Nails at noon. And at four the hotel is sending up tea with an expert in royal etiquette!

Eve raised her eyebrows and gave a smile. A lesson in royal etiquette was just the sort of thing that appealed to her sense of humor. He must have looked like he was going to spoil the fun.

—You don't have to stick around, she said. Why don't you get a head start on the museums? Or better yet, why don't you go get yourself those shoes that Bucky was talking about? Didn't you say that if the meetings went well, you'd treat yourself to a pair?

It was true. He had said that to Bucky; and the meetings had gone well. After all, he had the whole concession and the world had no choice but to beat a path to his door.

As he rode the lift downstairs, he told himself that if the doorman didn't know the address of the shop, he wouldn't go. But, of course, the doorman knew exactly where the shop was; and in his tone he made it clear that for a Claridge's guest there was really no other shoemaker's address worth knowing.

The first time down St. James's, he walked right past the shop. He still wasn't accustomed to the British style of purveying. In New York, the Shoemaker to the King would have taken up a city block. It would have had a neon sign that blinked in three colors. Here, the shop was the width of a newspaper stand and cluttered. That was a mark in its favor.

But however humble the appearance, according to Bucky there was nothing more extravagant than a John Lobb shoe. The duke of Windsor got his shoes there. Errol Flynn and Charlie Chaplin got their shoes there. It was the very pinnacle of cobbling. The final say in the great winnowing of commerce. At John Lobb, they didn't just make shoes. They actually stuck your foot in plaster and kept the cast in storage so that whenever you wanted, they could make you another perfect pair.

A plaster cast, he thought to himself as he stared through the window—just like they made of a dead poet's face or of a dinosaur's bones.

A tall Brit in a white suit came out of the shop and lit a cigarette. Well bred, well educated, well dressed, he too seemed the product of a great winnowing.

In an instant, the Brit had gone through a similar calculus and nodded to him as an equal.

—*Lovely day,* the Brit said.

—*Yes,* he agreed and lingered for a moment, knowing instinctively that if he did, the Brit was bound to offer him a cigarette.

In St. James's Park, he sat on an old painted bench and savored the smoke. The tobacco was noticeably different from an American blend, a fact which was at once a disappointment and a pleasure.

While the park was sunlit and lovely, it was surprisingly empty. It must have been an in-between hour—in between the march to work and the break for lunch. He felt lucky to have happened there.

Across the lawn, a young mother chased her six-year-old out of a tulip row. Dozing on a neighboring bench, an old man was about to spill a bag of nuts on the ground as a council of squirrels gathered wisely at his feet. Over a cherry tree shedding the last of its blossoms passed a cloud in the shape of an Italian automobile.

When he put out his cigarette, it didn't seem right to toss it on the ground. So he wrapped the butt in his handkerchief and put it in his pocket. Then he opened the bookseller's bag, took out the book and started at the beginning:

> When I wrote the following pages, or rather the bulk of them, I lived alone, in the woods, a mile from any neighbor, in a house which I had built myself, on the shore of Walden Pond. . . .

SUMMERTIME

CHAPTER TWELVE

Twenty Pounds Ought & Six

Nathaniel Parish was a senior fiction editor at the Pembroke Press and something of a fixture. With a pitch-perfect ear for the nineteenth-century narrative sentence and a religious conviction that the novel should illuminate, he had been an early champion of the Russians and originated authoritative translations of Tolstoy and Dostoevsky into English. Some say that he traveled all the way to Yasnaya Polyana, Tolstoy's country homestead, just to discuss an ambiguous sentence in the closing paragraph of *Anna Karenina*. Parish had been a correspondent of Chekov's, a mentor of Wharton's, a friend to Santayana and James. But after the war, when editors like Martin Durk came to prominence by trumpeting the timely death of the novel, Parish opted for a reflective silence. He stopped taking on projects and watched with quiet reserve as his authors died off one by one—at peace with the notion that he would join them soon enough in that circle of Elysium reserved for plot and substance and the judicious use of the semicolon.

I had seen Parish a few times when I had gone to meet Evey after work. He had wispy eyebrows and hazel eyes; in summer he wore seersucker and in winter an old gray raincoat. Like other aging, awkward academic sorts, he had come to a point when young ladies gave him anxiety. When he left his office at lunch he would virtually run to the elevator. Eve and the other girls would torture him by blocking his way with their literary queries and tight-fitting sweaters. In self-defense, he would wave both arms and invent improbable excuses (*I'm late for a meeting with Steinbeck!*). Then he would go to the Gilded Lily, the long-in-tooth restaurant where every day he lunched alone.

That's where I found him, the day I quit my job. He had just taken his seat at his usual table. After perusing the menu unnecessarily, he ordered soup and half a sandwich. Then, before turning to the book that was sitting beside his plate, he did what any of us would do: He surveyed the restaurant with a relaxed smile, satisfied that his food was ordered, his hour was empty, and all was well with the world. That's when I approached him, a copy of *Vishniovy Sad* in hand.

—Excuse me, I asked. Are you Martin Durk?

—Certainly not!

The old editor's retort was so emphatic, it even caught *him* off guard. By way of apology, he added:

—Martin Durk is half my age.

—I'm so sorry. I'm meeting him for lunch, but I don't know what he looks like.

—Well, he's a few inches taller than I am with a full head of hair. But I'm afraid that he's in Paris.

—Paris? I said in distress.

—According to the society pages.

—But I'm here for an interview. . . .

I fumbled and dropped my book. Mr. Parish leaned out of his chair to retrieve it. When he handed it back, he studied me a little more closely.

—You read Russian? he asked.

—Yes.

—What do you think of the play?

—So far, I like it.

—You don't find it dated? What with all that fuss over the end of agrarian aristocracy? I should think it very old-fashioned to sympathize with the plight of the Ranevskayas.

—Oh, I think you're wrong. I think we all have some parcel of the past which is falling into disrepair or being sold off piece by piece. It's just that for most of us, it isn't an orchard; it's the way we've thought about something, or someone.

Mr. Parish smiled and handed me back the book.

—Young lady, Mr. Durk has no doubt done you a service by failing to keep his appointment. I'm afraid your sensibilities would be wasted on him.

—I guess I'll take that as a compliment.

—You most certainly should.

—I'm Katey.

—Nathaniel Parish.

(*Aghast.*)

—You must think me a fool. Going on about the meaning of a Chekov play. How mortifying.

He smiled.

—No. It was the pinnacle of my day.

As if on cue, a bowl of vichyssoise was put on the table. I looked down at the soup and gave it my best Oliver Twist.

◆ ◆ ◆

The next day, I went to work at the Pembroke Press as Nathaniel Parish's assistant. When he offered me the job, he immediately tried to dissuade me from taking it. He said I'd find Pembroke forty years behind the times. That he wouldn't have enough work for me to do. That the pay was terrible. A job as his assistant, he concluded, would be a cul de sac.

How good were his predictions?

Pembroke *was* forty years behind the times. On my first day on the job I could tell that the editors at Pembroke were nothing like their younger counterparts around town. Not only did they have manners, they thought them worth preserving. They treated the opening of a door for a lady or the hand-scripted regret the way an archaeologist treats a fragment of pottery—with all the loving care that we normally reserve for things that matter. Terrance Taylor definitely wouldn't have hailed a cab away from you in the rain; Beekman Canon wouldn't have let the elevator door close as you approached; and Mr. Parish would never have raised his fork before you raised yours—he would sooner have starved.

They certainly weren't the sorts to hound out the "boldest" new voices, elbow their way into contracts and then mount a Times Square soapbox to advertise their authors' artistic bravery. They were English public school professors who had misread the map in the tube and haplessly gotten off at the World of Commerce stop.

Mr. Parish *did not* have enough work for me to do. Mr. Parish still received plenty of unsolicited manuscripts, but his reputation having outlived his enthusiasm for new fiction, they were generally sent home in the company of a polite regret—an apology from Mr. Parish for not being quite as active as he once was and his personal encouragement for the artist to persevere. At this stage, Mr. Parish avoided meetings and administrative responsibilities of all kinds and his circle of serious correspondents had dwindled to a reassuring handful of septuagenarians who alone could decipher each other's faltering script. The phone rarely rang and he didn't drink coffee. To make matters worse, within days of my starting, the calendar turned to July. Apparently, come summer the writers stopped writing, editors stopped editing and publishers stopped publishing—allowing everyone to extend their weekends at their family enclaves by the sea. Mail piled up on the desks and the plants in the lobby began to look as wilted as the academic poets who would occasionally appear unannounced and wait Job-like for an audience.

Luckily, when I asked Mr. Parish where I could file his correspondence, he said I needn't bother, making an oblique reference to his system. When I insisted he elaborate, he sheepishly looked toward a cardboard box in the corner. It seems that for over thirty years whenever Mr. Parish finished reading an important letter, that's where it was filed. When the box was full, it was carted off to storage and replaced with an empty. This, I explained, was not a system. So, with Mr. Parish's consent, I pulled a few boxes from the turn of the century and began building chronological correspondence files alphabetized by author, subcategorized by theme.

Though he had a house on Cape Cod, Mr. Parish had avoided going there ever since his wife died in 1936. *It's really just a shack*, he would say, referencing that self-imposed simplicity favored by New England Protestants who respect everything about wealth other than its uses. But in his wife's absence, the hooked rugs, wicker chairs and rain-gray shingles that for so long had been symbolic of the perfectly understated summer retreat had suddenly revealed themselves to be inherently sorrow-making.

So as I sorted through his old correspondence, I would often find him peering over my shoulder. Occasionally, he would even pluck a letter from the pile and retreat with it to his office. There, with the door securely closed, in the quiet of the afternoon, he could revisit the faded sentiments of faded friends, undisturbed by all but the occasional thud of an ax in the distance.

The pay *was* terrible. Terrible, of course, is something of a relative term and Mr. Parish actually never quantified what *he* meant by terrible. Under the genteel circumstance of cold potato soup, I certainly hadn't pried.

So on my first Friday when I went down to payroll to pick up my check, I was still in the dark. Looking around, I took heart from the fact that the other girls were chirpy and well dressed. But when I opened the envelope, I discovered that my new weekly rate was half of what I'd made at Quiggin & Hale. Half!

Oh my God, I thought. *What have I done?*

I took another look at the girls around me who with blasé smiles had begun chattering about where they intended to weekend and it hit me: Of course they were blasé—they didn't need the paycheck! That's the difference between being a secretary and an assistant. A secretary exchanges her labor for a living wage. But an assistant comes from a fine home, attends Smith College, and lands her position when her mother happens to be seated beside the publisher in chief at a dinner party.

But while Mr. Parish had been right on these three accounts, he couldn't have been more wrong about the job being a cul de sac.

As I stood in the payroll department licking my wounds, Susie Vanderwhile asked if I wanted to join a few of the other assistants for a splash. *Sure,* I thought. *Why not? What better reason for a drink than looming penury?*

At Quiggin & Hale when you went out with the girls, you'd hoof around the corner to the local well, snipe about your day, speculate on interoffice pinching, and then head for the elevated insufficiently soused.

But when we walked out of the Pembroke Press, Susie hailed a cab. We all hopped in and headed to the St. Regis Hotel, where Susie's brother Dicky, a floppy-banged gregarious sort freshly out of college, was waiting in the King Cole bar. In company were two of Dicky's classmates from Princeton and a roommate from prep school.

—Halloo Sis!

—Hello Dicky. You know Helen. This is Jenny and Katey.

Dicky rattled off introductions like a machine gun.

—Jenny TJ. TJ Helen. Helen Wellie. Wellie Katey. Roberto Roberto.

No one seemed to notice that I was the oldest person by a few years. Dicky slapped his hands together.

—Right then. What'll it be?

G&Ts were ordered for all. Then Dicky ran off to roust up club chairs from around the bar. He pushed them up to our table, ramming them into each other like the bumper cars at Coney Island.

Within minutes there was some story about how Roberto, under the influence of Bacchus and in the bad graces of Poseidon, had gone astray in the fog off Fisher's Island. He had steered his father's Bertram right into a concrete bulkhead, smashing it to smithereens.

—I thought I was a quarter mile offshore, Roberto explained, because I could hear a bell buoy off the port bow.

—Rather sadly, said Dicky, the bell buoy turned out to be the supper bell on the McElroys' veranda.

As Dicky spoke, he made animated and democratic eye contact with all the girls and he punctuated the details of his story with assurances of shared familiarity:

You know how the fog is off Fisher's Isle.

You know how those Bertrams come about like a barge.

You know dinner at the McElroys': three grandames and twenty-two cousins gathered round a rib roast like cubs around the kill.

Yes, Dicky, we knew.

We knew the curmudgeonly old gent who stood behind the bar at Mory's in New Haven. We knew how dull was the crowd at Maidstone. We knew the Dobsons and the Robsons and *all* the Fenimores. We knew a jib from a jibe, and Palm Beach from Palm Springs. We knew the difference between a sole fork, a salad fork, and that special fork with the bent tines used for breaking the kernels of corn when it's served on the cob. We all knew each other *so* well. . . .

And therein lay the first of two unanticipated advantages of taking a job at the Pembroke Press: presumption. For a young woman the pay at Pembroke was so bad and the professional prospects so poor, it went without saying that you took the job because you could absolutely afford to do so.

—Who are you working with? one of the girls had asked in the cab.

—Nathaniel Parish.

—Oh! How terrific! How do you know him?

How did I know him? My father and he were at Harvard? Grandma and Mrs. Parish grew up summering in Kennebunkport? I spent the semester in Florence with his niece? Honey, you can take your pick.

Dicky was standing now. He took the imaginary steering wheel in hand. He screwed up his eyes and pointed to where the bell buoy tolled.

—You, Aeolus—to whom the king of men
And of the gods has lent the awesome power
To calm the rolling waves, or with the winds
Incite them—now stir your gales to fury;
Upend and sink their ships; or toss them with
their crews upon the open emerald seas!

He gave the Virgil in perfect meter, iamb for iamb. Although, one suspected that Dicky's ability to quote classical verse stemmed less from a love of literature than from a rote education in prep school which time had yet the time to erase.

Jenny applauded and Dicky bowed, knocking a glass of gin into Roberto's lap.

—*Mon Dieu*, Roberto! Be a little more fleet of foot, man!

—Fleet of foot? You've ruined another pair of my khaki trousers.

—Come now. You've a lifetime supply.

—Whatever the state of my supply, I demand an apology.

—Then you shall have one!

Dicky pointed a finger in the air. He adopted the appropriate expression of sober contrition. He opened his mouth.

—Pencey!

We all turned to see what a Pencey was. It was another Ivy Leaguer coming through the door with a girl on each arm.

—Dicky Vanderwhile! Good God. What next.

Yes, Dicky was a genuine mixer. He took relative pride and absolute joy in weaving together the strands of his life so that when he gave them a good tug all the friends of friends of friends would come tumbling through the door. He's the sort that New York City was made for. If you latched yourself onto the likes of Dicky Vanderwhile, pretty soon you'd know *everyone* in New York; or at least everyone white, wealthy and under the age of twenty-five.

When the clock struck ten, at Dicky's instigation we trundled over to the Yale Club so that we could get a hamburger before the grill closed. Gathered around the old wooden tables, as we drank flat beer from water glasses, there were more wild-eyed anecdotes and witty exchanges. There were more familiar faces, more rapid-fire introductions, more assumptions, presumptions, resumptions.

—Yes, yes. We've met before, one of the new arrivals said when Dicky introduced me. We danced a lick at Billy Ebersley's.

I had been wrong in thinking that no one had noticed my age. Dicky had noticed and, apparently, he found it enticing. He began to leer at me across the table conspiratorially when anyone had anything the least sophomoric to say. He clearly believed too many of the stories he'd heard from school chums about summer escapades with older sisters' friends. While Roberto and Wellie drew straws to see which of their father's accounts would be charged, Dicky took the opportunity to drag up a chair.

—Tell me, Miss Kontent, where can we find you on the average Friday night?

He gestured toward his sister and some of the other girls at the table.

—Not with this sorority, I suspect.

—On the average Friday night, you'd find me at home.

—At home, eh? Please be more precise with your adverbial phrases. If you say *at home* with this crowd, we'll assume that you're living with your parents. Wellie there wears candy-striped pajamas and Roberto has model airplanes hanging from the ceiling over his bed.

—So do I.

—The pajamas or the airplanes?

—Both.

—I'd love to see them. So where is this home, precisely, where one can find you in candy stripes on a Friday night?

—Is this where one can find you on the average Friday night, Dicky?

—What's that?!

Dicky looked around the room in shock. Then he waved a dismissive hand.

—Certainly not. It's a bore. Geriatrics and rush chairmen.

He looked me in the eye.

—What do you say we get out of here? Let's take a turn through the Village.

—I couldn't steal you away from your friends.

—Oh, they'll be all right without me.

Dicky put a hand on my knee, discreetly.

— . . . And I'll be all right without them.

—You'd better throttle back, Dicky. You're steering straight for a bulkhead.

Dicky took his hand off my knee with enthusiasm, nodding his head in agreement.

—Righto! Time should be our ally, not our enemy.

He stood up knocking over his chair. He pointed a finger in the air and proclaimed to no one in particular:

—Let the evening end as it began: with a sense of mystery!

♦ ♦ ♦

Unanticipated advantage #2?

When I arrived at work on July 7, Mr. Parish was in his office talking to a handsome stranger in a bespoke suit. In his midfifties, he looked like a leading man a few years past his prime. From the way the two conversed, you could tell that they knew each other well but maintained a certain self-imposed distance, like high priests from different orders of the same faith.

When the stranger left, Mr. Parish called me in.

—Katherine, my dear. Have a seat. Do you know the gentleman with whom I was just speaking?

—I don't.

—His name is Mason Tate. He actually worked for me as a younger man before he moved on to greener pastures; or rather, I should say, a *series* of greener pastures. At any rate, he works for Condé Nast now, where he is in the process of launching a new literary journal and he's looking for a few assistant editors. I think you should meet with him.

—I'm happy here, Mr. Parish.

—Yes, I know you are. And were it fifteen years ago, this would have been just the place for you. But it isn't any longer.

He patted the pile of rejection letters awaiting his signature.

—Mason is mercurial, but he is also very capable. Whether his journal succeeds or fails, a young woman with your intelligence will have the chance to learn a great deal at his side. And day to day, it is certain to be more dynamic than the offices of the Pembroke Press.

—I'll meet with him if you think I should.

By way of answer, Mr. Parish held out Mr. Tate's card.

Mason Tate's offices were on the twenty-fifth floor of the Condé Nast building, and from the looks of them you would have thought his forthcoming journal had been a success for years. A striking receptionist sat at a custom-made desk accented with freshly cut flowers. As I was led to Mr. Tate's office, we passed fifteen young men talking on telephones or hacking away at brand-new Smith Coronas. It looked like the best-dressed newsroom in America. Along the walls were atmospheric photographs taken in New York: Mrs. Astor in an enormous Easter hat; Douglas Fairbanks in the chauffeur's seat of a limousine; a well-heeled crowd kept waiting in the snow outside the Cotton Club.

Mr. Tate had a corner office with glass walls. The top of his desk was a piece of glass too, floating on a lazy stainless steel X. In front of his desk was a small sitting area with a couch and chair.

—Come in, he called.

His accent was patently aristocratic—part prep school, part Brit, part prude. He pointed a commanding finger at one of the chairs, reserving the couch for himself.

—I've heard good things about you, Miss Kontent.

—Thank you.

—What have you heard about me?

—Not very much.

—Excellent. Where were you raised?

—In New York.

—City? Or state?

—The city.

—Have you ever been to the Algonquin?

—The hotel?

—Yes.

—I haven't.

—Do you know where it is?

—West Forty-fourth Street?

—That's right. And Delmonico's? Have you dined there?

—Isn't it closed?

—In a manner of speaking. What did your father do?

—Mr. Tate, what is this all about?

—Come now. You can't be afraid to tell me how your father earned his living.

—I'll tell you what he did, if you tell me why you want to know.

—Fair enough.

—He worked in a machine shop.

—A proletarian.

—I suppose.

—Let me tell you why you're here. On January first, I will be launching a new magazine called *Gotham*. *Gotham* will be an illustrated weekly and its purpose will be to profile those who hope to shape Manhattan and, by extension, the world. It will be a sort of *Vogue* of the mind. What I am looking for is an assistant who can triage my phone calls, my correspondence, and my laundry, if need be.

—Mr. Tate, I was under the impression that you were looking for an editorial assistant for a literary journal.

—You were under that impression because that is what I told Nathan. If I had told him I was recruiting a lackey for my glamour magazine, he would never have recommended you to me.

—Or vice versa.

Mr. Tate narrowed his eyes. He pointed his commanding finger at my nose.

—Precisely. Come over here.

We walked to a drafting table by the window overlooking Bryant Park. On it were candid photographs of Zelda Fitzgerald, John Barrymore and one of the younger Rockefellers.

—Everyone has their virtues and vices, Miss Kontent. In rough terms, *Gotham* will cover the city's lights, its lovers, its letters, and its losers.

He gestured to the three photographs on the table.

—Can you tell me which of those categories these people would fall under?

—They're all of the above.

He gritted his teeth and smiled.

—Well said. Relative to your life with Nathan, working for me would be quite different: Your pay would double, your hours triple and your purpose quadruple. But there is one hitch—I already have an assistant.

—Do you really need two?

—Hardly. My expectation is to run you both ragged until January first and then let one of you go.

—I'll forward my résumé.

—For what?

—To apply.

—This isn't an interview, Miss Kontent. This is an offer. You may accept it by being here tomorrow at eight.

He went back around his desk.

—Mr. Tate.

—Yes?

—You haven't told me yet why you wanted to know my father's profession.

He looked up surprised.

—Isn't it obvious, Miss Kontent? I cannot abide debutantes.

◆　◆　◆

On the morning of Friday, July first, I had a low-paying job at a waning publisher and a dwindling circle of semi-acquaintances. On Friday, July eighth, I had one foot in the door of Condé Nast and the other in the door of the Knickerbocker Club—the professional and social circles that would define the next thirty years of my life.

That's how quickly New York City comes about—like a weather vane—or the head of a cobra. Time tells which.

CHAPTER THIRTEEN

The Hurlyburly

By the third Friday in July, this is what my life was like:

a.)

At 8:00 A.M., I am standing at attention in Mason Tate's office. On his desk are a bar of chocolate, a cup of coffee and a plate of smoked salmon.

To my right is Alley McKenna. A petite brunette with a sky-high IQ and cat's-eye glasses, Alley is wearing black pants, a black shirt and black high-heel shoes.

In most offices, the loosely buttoned blouse could take the ambitious girl from reasonably proficient to utterly indispensable in the turn of a calendar year, but not in Mason Tate's. From the first, he made it clear that his affinities lay in another hemisphere. So we could save the fluttering of our eyelashes for the boys at the ballpark. He barely even looks up from his papers as he rattles off Alley's instructions with aristocratic remove.

—Cancel my meeting with the mayor on Tuesday. Tell him I've been called to Alaska. Get me all the front covers of *Vogue*, *Vanity Fair* and *Time* for the last two years. If you can't find them downstairs, take a pair of scissors to the public library. My sister's birthday is August first. Get her something timid from Bendel's. She says she's a five; assume she's a six.

He pushes a pile of blue-lined copy in my direction.

—Kontent: Tell Mr. Morgan that he's on the right track, but he's a hundred sentences short and a thousand words too long. Tell Mr. Cabot yes, yes and no. Tell Mr. Spindler he's missed the point entirely. We still don't have a strong enough cover story for the first issue. Inform the lot of them that Saturday's been canceled. For lunch I'll take ham on seeded rye with Muenster and relish from the Greeks on Fifty-third.

In suitable unison: *Yes Sir.*

By 9:00 the phone is ringing.

>> *I need to meet with Mason immediately.*
>> *I wouldn't meet with Mr. Tate if he paid me.*
>> *My wife, who is ill, may contact Mr. Tate. I ask that he show the appropriate consideration for her well-being by encouraging her to return home to her children and the care of her physician.*
>> *I have some information on my husband that Mr. Tate may find interesting. It involves a harlot, a half a million dollars and a dog. I can be reached at the Carlyle under my maiden name.*
>> *My client, a citizen above reproach, has learned that his troubled wife is making delusional accusations. Please let Mr. Tate know that should his forthcoming periodical publish any of these sad and fantastic claims, my client is prepared to file suit not only against the publisher, but against Mr. Tate personally.*

How do you spell that? Where can you be reached? Until what hour? I'll give him the message.

—Ahem.

Jacob Weiser, Condé Nast's corporate comptroller, is standing at my desk. An honest, hardworking sort, he has one of those unfortunate mustaches made popular by the likes of Charlie Chaplin until the likes of Adolph Hitler put them out of fashion forever. You can tell from his expression that he doesn't like *Gotham*, not one little bit. He probably thinks the entire venture seedy and prurient. Which, of course, it is, though no more so than Manhattan, and no less glamorous.

—Good morning, Mr. Weiser. How can I help you?

—I need to see Tate.

—Yes. I spoke with your assistant. You're on his schedule for Tuesday.

—At 5:45. Was that some kind of joke?

—No, sir.

—I'll see him now.

—I'm afraid that's impossible.

Mr. Weiser points through the glass to where Mr. Tate is gingerly dipping a chocolate square in the remnants of his coffee.

—I'll see him now, thank you.

Mr. Weiser advances. It is plain that he would give his life to correct an imbalance in the company's accounts. But when he takes a step around my desk, I have no choice but to block his way. His face grows as red as a radish.

—Look here missy, he says, trying to constrain his temper, unsuccessfully.

—What's this all about?

Mr. Tate is suddenly standing between us, directing his question to me.

—Mr. Weiser would like to see you, I explain.

—I thought I was seeing him on Tuesday.

—You are scheduled to do so.

—What's the problem then?

Mr. Weiser pipes up:

—I've just received the most recent expense report on your staffing. You're thirty percent over budget!

Mr. Tate turns slowly on Mr. Weiser.

—As Miss Kontent has apparently made clear—*Jake*—I am not available right now. Come to think of it, I'm not available on Tuesday either. Miss Kontent, please meet with Mr. Weiser in my stead. Take note of his concerns and let him know that we will get back to him shortly.

Mr. Tate returned to his chocolate and Mr. Weiser to his adding machine somewhere in the recesses of the third floor.

Most executives expect their secretaries to show an appropriate level of deference; they expect them to be courteous and even-tempered to whomever they're talking. But not Mr. Tate. He encouraged Alley and me to be as imperious and impatient as he was. At first I thought this was an irrational extension of Tate's aristocratic belligerence and his Sun

King self-importance. But over time, I began to see the genius of it. By making the two of us as rude and demanding as he, Tate was solidifying our positions as his proxy.

—Hey, Alley says, sidling up to my desk. Get a load of this.

At reception there's a teenage messenger lugging a ten-pound edition of *Webster's Dictionary*. It's finished off in a pretty pink bow. The receptionist points to the middle of the bullpen.

Each of the journalists eyes the messenger coolly as he approaches their desk and smiles wryly once he's passed. Some of them stand to watch the show. At long last, he comes to a stop in front of Nicholas Fesindorf. When Fesindorf sees the dictionary, he goes more crimson than his BVDs. To make matters worse, the messenger begins to sing. It's a little ditty set to the tune of a Broadway love song. Though octavely unsure, the kid puts his heart into it:

Alas, 'tis true that words are queer
And yet my son, you need not fear.
For in this volume can be seen
All English words and what they mean.

Tate had directed Alley to get the dictionary and had written the verse. But the singing telegram and pink ribbon, those were Alley's personal touches.

◆　◆　◆

At six o'clock, Mr. Tate left the office to catch a train to the Hamptons. At 6:15 I caught Alley's eye. We covered our typewriters and put on our coats.

—Come on, she said as we walked toward the elevators. Let's cake it up.

My first day at *Gotham*, when I went to the washroom, Alley had followed me. Leaning over the sink was a girl from graphics. Alley told her to beat it. For a second I thought she was going to cut off my bangs and toss my purse in the toilet like the welcoming committee at my old high school. Alley squinted through her cat's-eye glasses and got right to the point.

She said that the two of us were like gladiators in a coliseum and Tate was the lion. When he came out of the cage, we could either circle him, or scatter and wait to be eaten. If we played our cards right, Tate wouldn't be able to tell which one of us he depended upon more. So she wanted to establish a few ground rules: When Tate asked where one of us was, the answer (day or night) was the ladies' room. When he asked us to double-check each other's work, we were allowed to spot one mistake. When we received a compliment on a project, we answered that we couldn't have done it without the help of the other. And when Tate left at night, we'd give him fifteen minutes to clear the building, then we'd take the elevator to the lobby arm in arm.

—If we don't fuck this up, she said, come Christmas we'll be running this circus. What do you say, Kate?

In a state of nature some animals, like the leopard, hunt alone; others, like hyena, hunt in packs. I wasn't one hundred percent convinced that Alley was a hyena. But I was pretty sure that she wasn't going to wind up as prey.

—I say all for one, and one for all.

On Friday night, some girls liked to go to the Oyster Bar in Grand Central and let the boys riding the express train to Greenwich buy them drinks. Alley liked to go to the automat, where she could sit by herself and eat two desserts and a bowl of soup—in that order. She loved the indifference of it all: the indifference of the staff; the indifference of the customers; the indifference of the food.

As Alley ate her frosting and then proceeded to eat mine, we had a good laugh over the dictionary gag, then we talked about Mason Tate and his hatred of all things purple (royalty, plums, fancy prose). When it was time to go, like an alcoholic Alley stood up and walked straight to the door without showing the slightest signs of having overdone it. In the street at 7:30, we congratulated each other on another Friday night without a date. But as soon as she had turned the corner, I went back inside the automat, found the bathroom and changed into the nicest dress I owned. . . .

b.)

—Isn't that a hedge?

That was Helen's query two hours later, as five of us picked our way through a flower bed in the dark.

After a quick round at the King Cole bar, Dicky Vanderwhile had driven us out to Oyster Bay on the promise of a wingding at Whileaway—the summer house of a childhood friend. When Roberto asked how Schuyler was doing, Dicky, always so quick to bring one up-to-date on the antics of another, was uncharacteristically vague. And when we saw a couple in their midthirties greeting guests at the door, Dicky suggested we not get bogged down in the lobby. He referenced a lovely garden gate and steered us toward the side of the house, where we quickly found ourselves ankle deep in chrysanthemums.

Stiletto heels sank in the soil at every step. I stopped to pull off my shoes. From the vantage point of the garden, the night seemed surprisingly still. There wasn't a trace of music or laughter. But through the well-lit windows of the kitchen, you could see a staff of ten arranging cold and hot hors d'oeuvres on platters destined to be whisked through swinging doors.

The privet that Helen had observed in the shadows now towered before us. Dicky ran his hands along it like one looking for the latch to the hidden door in a bookcase. In a neighboring yard a rocket whistled and popped.

Roberto, a little slow on the uptake, came to a congenial realization:

—Why Dicky, you old crasher. I'll wager you don't even know whose house this is.

Dicky stopped and pointed a finger in the air.

—It is more important to know when and where than whom or why.

Then, like a tropical explorer, he parted the hedge and poked his head through.

—Eureka.

The rest of us followed Dicky through the branches, emerging surprisingly unscathed onto the back lawn of the Hollingsworth mansion where the party was in full swing. It was unlike anything I had ever seen.

The back of the house stretched before us like an American Versailles. Through the gentle grid work of the French doors, chandeliers and candelabra cast a warm yellow glow. On a slate terrace that floated like a dock over a manicured lawn, a few hundred people mingled gracefully. They paused in their conversations just long enough to pluck a cocktail or a canapé from the circulating trays as music from a twenty-piece orchestra, invisible to the naked eye, drifted aimlessly toward the Sound.

Our little crew climbed over the terrace wall and followed Dicky to the bar. It was as large as what you'd find in a nightclub with all manner of whiskey and gin and brightly colored liqueurs. Lit from below, the bottles looked like the pipes of a supernatural organ.

When the bartender turned, Dicky smiled:

—Five juniper and tonics, my good man.

Then he leaned his back against the bar and took in the festivities with all the satisfaction of a host.

I saw now that Dicky had plucked a small bouquet of flowers from the cutting garden and stuffed them into the breast pocket of his tuxedo. Like Dicky himself, the corsage looked bright and reckless and a little out of place. Most of the men on the terrace had already lost their boyish attributes—the rosiness of their cheeks, the wispiness of their hair, the Puckish glint in their eye. The women, draped in sleeveless dresses that fell to the ground, had jewels and wore them with taste. All were engaged in conversations that looked effortless and intimate.

—I don't see anyone *I* know, said Helen.

Dicky nodded while nibbling on a celery stalk.

—That we are at the wrong party is not exactly out of the question.

—Well, where do you *think* we are? said Roberto.

—I had it on good authority that one of the Hollingsworth boys was throwing a fandango. I'm fairly certain that this is the Hollingsworths' and it is definitely a fandango.

—But?

—. . . Perhaps I should have asked which of the Hollingsworth boys was fandangoing.

—Schuyler is in Europe, isn't he? asked Helen, who without ever trusting in her own intelligence always seemed to have something sensible to say.

—So there you are, said Dicky. It's settled. The reason Sky neglected to invite us is that he is presently abroad.

He handed the gin and tonics around.

—Now then. Let's to the band.

From the neighbor's lawn another rocket whistled and then burst overhead in a small spray of sparks. I let the group get a few paces ahead. Then I veered off through the crowd.

Since first meeting Dicky at the King Cole bar, I had tagged along with his traveling circus a few nights. For a group freshly spilled from the country's finest schools, they were surprisingly aimless, but that didn't make them bad company. They didn't have much spending money or social status, but they were on the verge of having both. All they had to do was make it through the next five years without drowning at sea or being sentenced to jail and the mountain would come to Muhammad: dividend-paying shares and membership at the Racquet Club; a box at the opera and time to make use of it. Where for so many, New York was ultimately the sum of what they would never attain, for this crew New York was a city where the improbable would be made probable, the implausible plausible and the impossible possible. So if you wanted to keep your head on straight, you had to be willing to establish a little distance, now and then.

As a waiter passed, I traded in my gin for a glass of champagne.

All the French doors to the Hollingsworths' great room were open and guests were flowing in and out, instinctively maintaining a constant equilibrium between the terrace and the house. I wandered inside trying to size up the invited as Mason Tate would have. On the edge of a couch, four blondes sat in a row comparing notes like a conspiracy of crows on a telephone wire. By a table crowned with two cloved hams, a broad-shouldered young man ignored his date. While before a pyramid of oranges, lemons and limes a girl in full flamenco was making two men spill their gin with laughter. To the unpracticed eye they all looked of a piece—exhibiting a poise secured by the alchemy of wealth and station. But aspiration and envy, disloyalty and lust—these too were presumably on display, if only one knew where to look.

In the ballroom, the band was beginning to pick up the tempo. A few feet from the trumpet, Dicky was doing a jitterbug with an older woman at pace and a half. He had taken off his jacket and his shirttails were loose. One of the flowers that had been in his breast pocket was now cocked behind an ear. As I watched, I became aware of someone standing quietly beside me, in the manner of a well-trained servant. I emptied my glass and turned with my arm extended.

—. . . Katey?

Pause.

—Wallace!

He looked relieved that I had recognized him. Though given his pre-occupied demeanor at the Beresford, I was surprised that he had recognized *me*.

—How have . . . you been? he asked.

—All right, I guess. In a no-news-good-news sort of way.

—I'm so glad to . . . bump into you like this. I've been . . . meaning to call.

The song was winding to a close and I could see Dicky preparing for a big finish. He was going to tip the old lady like a teapot.

—It's a little loud in here, I said. Why don't we go outside.

On the patio, Wallace secured two glasses of champagne and handed me one. There was an awkward silence as we watched the goings-on.

—It's one heck of a shindig, I said at last.

—Oh, this is . . . nothing. The Hollingsworths have four boys. Over the course of the summer, each . . . gets to throw his own party. But Labor Day weekend, it's an all-out where . . . everyone is invited.

—I'm not sure I'm in that *everyone* group. I'm more in the no one group.

Wallace offered a smile that gave no credence to my claim.

—Let me know if you ever want to . . . trade places.

At first glance, Wallace had looked a little uncomfortable in his tuxedo, like one who's dressed in borrowed clothes. But on closer inspection, you could tell the tuxedo was custom-made, and his black pearl shirt studs looked like they'd been handed down a generation or two.

Another silence.

—You were saying something about meaning to give me a call? I prompted.

—Yes! Back in March I made you a promise. I've been meaning to . . . make good on it.

—Wallace, if you want to make good on a promise that old, it had better be a doozy.

—Wally Wolcott!

The interruption came from a business school classmate of Wallace's who was also in the paper business. When the conversation turned from mutual friends to the Anschluss and its effect on pulp prices, I figured it was a good opportunity to visit the powder room. I couldn't have been inside more than ten minutes; but by the time I got back, the paper manufacturer was gone and one of the blondes from the couch had taken his place.

This, I suppose, was to be expected. Wallace Wolcott had to be in the sights of every young socialite without a ring on her finger. Most of the able-bodied girls in town would know his net worth and the names of his sisters. The industrious ones knew the names of his hunting dogs too.

The blonde, who looked like she'd been thrown a cotillion or two, was wearing white ermine a few months out of season and close-fitting gloves that climbed all the way to her elbows. Drawing closer, I could tell that her diction was almost as good as her figure, but that didn't mean she was captive of a ladylike reserve. As Wallace was talking, she actually took a drink from his glass and then handed it back to him.

She had also done her homework:

—I'm told the cook on your plantation is the Hush Puppy Queen!

—Yes, said Wallace with enthusiasm. Her recipe is a . . . closely guarded secret. Kept under . . . lock and key.

Every time Wallace stalled midsentence, she scrunched her nose and gleamed, as if it was just *so* endearing. Well, it was endearing. But she didn't have to make such a fuss about it. So I crashed her little tête-à-tête.

—I hate to interrupt, I said while slipping an arm under Wallace's, but weren't you going to show me the library?

She didn't bat an eye.

—The library *is* splendid, she said, exhibiting her superior familiarity with the Hollingsworths' house. But you can't go in just now. The fireworks are about to start.

Before I could rebut, there was a general movement toward the water. By the time we got to the dock, there must have been a hundred people on it. A few drunken couples had climbed into the Hollingsworths' catboats and set themselves adrift. More people came from behind and pushed us toward the diving board.

There was a loud whistle as the first rocket shot from a raft offshore.

It wasn't the sort of pennywhistle that had accompanied the teenage rockets from the neighboring yard. This sounded more like a piece of artillery. It climbed a long ribbon of smoke, seemed to expire, and then exploded in a white distending sphere. Its sparks broke apart and fell slowly toward the earth like the seedlings blown from a dandelion. Everybody cheered. Four rockets followed in quick succession creating a chain of red stars concluding with a terrific clap. Even more people jostled onto the dock and, apparently, I shoved a little too closely to my neighbor's hip. She tumbled into the drink, furs and all. Another rocket burst overhead. From the water came a thrash and a gasp as she resurfaced in the blue hydrangea light with entangled hair, looking like the Countess of Kelp.

Dicky found me on the terrace as everyone was heading up from the fireworks. Naturally, he knew Wallace—though indirectly, through Wallace's youngest sister. The differential in age seemed to temper Dicky. When Wallace asked him about his ambitions, Dicky lowered his voice an octave and mentioned some nonsense about applying to law school. Wallace excused himself politely and Dicky led me to the bar where the others were waiting. In Dicky's absence, Roberto had apparently gotten sick in the bushes, prompting Helen to wonder if it wasn't time to go home.

Though we had taken the Williamsburg Bridge out of Manhattan, Dicky took the Triborough back. This would make it most practical for him to drop everyone off before me. So soon enough, it was just the two of us headed downtown.

—Land ho, Dicky said as we approached the Plaza. How about a nightcap?

—I'm done in, Dicky.

Seeing his disappointment, I added that I had work tomorrow.

—But it's Saturday.

—Not at my office, it isn't.

When I got out of the car on Eleventh Street he looked glum.

—We never had a chance to dance, he said.

His tone of voice suggested a certain resignation, as if through inattention and a little bad luck he had missed an opportunity that might not present itself again. I had to smile at his boyish concern. Though, of course, he was more subtle than I gave him credit for, and more prescient too.

I gave his forearm a reassuring squeeze.

—Goodnight, Dicky.

As I climbed out of the car he grabbed my wrist.

—*When shall we two meet again? In thunder, lightning, or in rain?*

I leaned back into the roadster and lay my lips against the whorls of his ear.

—*When the hurlyburly's done. When the battle's lost and won.*

CHAPTER FOURTEEN

Honeymoon Bridge

On Sunday afternoon, Wallace and I headed out to the North Fork of Long Island in a dark green convertible.

The promise that he had wanted to keep was to take me shooting—which was pretty much a doozy, no matter how long he took to get around to it. When I asked him what I should wear, he suggested something comfortable. So, I dressed as I thought Anne Grandyn would: in khaki pants and a white button-down shirt with the sleeves rolled up. I figured if it didn't work out as my gun-shooting outfit, it could always serve as my Amelia-Earhart-getting-lost-over-the-Pacific-never-to-be-heard-from-again outfit. He wore a blue V-neck sweater trimmed in yellow with holes in the sleeves.

—I think your hair is . . . super, he said.

—Super?!

—Sorry. Was that . . . unflattering?

—Super's not bad. But I also answer to gorgeous and glamorous.

—How about . . . gorgerous?

—That's the ticket.

It was a bright summer day, and at Wallace's suggestion I took a pair of tinted glasses from the glove compartment. I leaned back and watched the sunshine dappling the leaves over the parkway, feeling like a cross between an Egyptian queen and a Hollywood starlet.

—Have you heard from . . . Tinker and Eve? Wallace asked.

It was the normal sort of common grounding used by an acquaintance to fend off silence.

—I'll tell you what, Wallace. If you don't feel the need to talk about Tinker and Eve, I won't feel the need to either.

Wallace laughed.

—Then how will we . . . explain knowing one another?

—We'll tell people that you caught me picking your pocket on the observation deck of the Empire State Building.

—All right. But only if . . . we make it you who caught me.

Wallace's hunt club was surprisingly run-down in appearance. Outside there was a low portico and slim white pillars that made it look like a sorry excuse for a Southern mansion. Inside, the pine floors were uneven, the rugs frayed, and the Audubon prints slightly askew, as if victims of a distant earthquake. But like the moth-eaten sweater, the worn aspect of the club seemed to put Wallace at relative ease.

At a diminutive desk by a sizable trophy case sat a well-groomed attendant in a polo shirt and slacks.

—Good afternoon, Mr. Wolcott, he said. We're all set for you downstairs. We've laid out the Remington, the Colt and the Luger. But a Browning Automatic came in yesterday and I thought you might like to take a look at her as well.

—Terrific, John. Thanks.

Wallace led me down to the cellar where a series of narrow alleys were separated by white clapboard walls. At the end of each alley, a paper bull's-eye was pinned to a stack of hay bales. Beside a small table, a young man was loading the firearms.

—That's fine, Tony. I'll . . . take care of it. We'll see you at the . . . trout pond.

—Yes sir, Mr. Wolcott.

I took up a position at a respectful distance. Wallace looked back and smiled.

—Why don't you . . . come a little closer.

Tony had laid out the guns with their barrels pointing in the same direction. With a polished silver finish and a bone handle, the revolver looked like a pretty fancy sidearm, but the other guns were a no-nonsense gray. Wallace pointed to the smaller of two rifles.

—That's a . . . Remington Model 8. It's a good target rifle. That's a . . . Colt 45. And that's a . . . Luger. A German officer's pistol. My father brought it . . . home from the war.

—And this?

I picked up the big gun. It was so heavy it hurt my wrists just to balance it in the air.

—That's the Browning. It's a . . . machine gun. It's the one that . . . Bonnie and Clyde used.

—Really?

—It's also the . . . gun that killed them.

I put it down gently.

—Shall we start with the Remington? he suggested.

—Yes sir, Mr. Wolcott.

We approached one of the alleys. He broke open the breach and loaded the rifle. Then he introduced me to the various parts: the action and bolt; the barrel and muzzle; the front and rear sights. I must have been making a bewildered face.

—It sounds . . . more complicated than it is, he said. The Remington has only fourteen parts.

—An eggbeater has only four. But I can't figure out how that works either.

—Okay, he said with a smile. Then watch me first. You rest the butt against your . . . shoulder, the way you would a . . . violin. Hold the barrel with your left hand here. Don't grip. Just . . . balance it. Square your feet. Sight the target. Take a breath. Exhale.

Pow!

I jumped. And maybe shouted.

—I'm sorry, Wallace said. I didn't mean to . . . startle you.

—I thought we were still in discussion mode.

Wallace laughed.

—No. Discussion mode . . . is over.

He handed me the rifle. Suddenly the alley looked much longer than before, as if the target was receding. I felt like Alice after she Drank Me, or Ate Me, or whichever ingestion made her become diminutive. I raised the rifle as if it were a salmon and tucked it in my shoulder like a watermelon. Wallace stepped closer and tried to coach, ineffectively.

—I'm sorry, he said. It's a little like trying to teach someone to . . . tie a bow tie. It's easier if . . . May I?

—Please!

He pulled up the sleeves of his sweater and came up behind me. He placed his right arm along my right arm, his left along my left. I could feel his breath, even and rhythmic, at the back of my ear. In a quiet voice, as if live game was grazing at the end of the alley, he gave me a few instructions and a few encouragements. We steadied the barrel. We sighted the target. We took a breath and exhaled. And when we pulled the trigger, I could feel his shoulder helping mine absorb the recoil.

He let me shoot fifteen rounds. Then the Colt. Then the Luger. Then we took a few turns with the Browning Automatic and I gave those bastards who killed Clyde Barrow something to think about.

Around four o'clock we walked through a pine glade behind the club. As we came into a clearing at the edge of a pond a woman my age came marching toward us. She was wearing jodhpurs and riding boots and had sandy hair drawn back in barrettes. She had a shotgun open at the breach hanging on the crook of her arm.

—Well hello, Hawkeye, she said with a muckraking smile. I haven't caught you on a date, have I?

Wallace blushed a little.

—Bitsy Houghton, she said to me with her hand extended—more stating the fact of her existence than clearing up the matter of her name.

—Katey Kontent, I said straightening my posture.

—Is . . . Jack here? Wallace asked after giving her an awkward kiss.

—No. He's in town. I was just riding over at The Stables and figured it was a good chance to swing by and hammer out a few. Keep myself in form. Not all of us are born to it like you are.

Wallace blushed again, though Bitsy didn't seem to notice. She turned back to me.

—You look like a beginner.

—Is it that obvious?

—Of course. But you'll have a good go of it with this old Indian. And it's a crackerjack day to shoot. Anyway. I'm off. Nice to meet you Kate. See you round Wally.

She gave Wallace a teasing wink and then barreled on.

—Wow, I said.

—Yes, said Wallace watching her go.

—Is she an old friend?

—Her brother and I have . . . been friends since we were boys. She was a . . . bit of a hanger-on.

—Not anymore, I suspect.

—No, said Wallace with something of a laugh. Not . . . for a long time.

The pond was about half the size of a city block and surrounded by trees. Patches of algae drifted here and there like continents on the surface of the globe. Passing a little dock where a rowboat was tethered, we followed a path to a small wooden pulpit hidden by the trees. Tony greeted us, exchanged a few words with Wallace and then disappeared into the woods. On a bench a new gun lay on its canvas case.

—This is a shotgun, Wallace said. It's a hunting gun. It carries a bigger charge. You're going to . . . feel it more.

The gun had elaborate tooling on the barrel, like a piece of Victorian silver. And the stock looked as fine as the leg of a Chippendale. Wallace picked up the shotgun and explained where the skeet would come from and how one should track it with the bead at the end of the barrel, aiming just ahead of its trajectory. Then he raised the gun to his shoulder.

—Pull.

The skeet materialized from the brush and hovered for an instant over the surface of the pond.

BOOM!

The pigeon shattered and the pieces rained down over the water like the fireworks at Whileaway.

I missed the first three pigeons, but then I began to get the hang of it. I hit four of the next six.

In the shooting range, the sound of the Remington had seemed somehow constrained, clipped, confined, and it got a little under your skin like the sound of someone biting on the blade of a knife. But here on the trout pond, the shotgun was resonant. It boomed like a ship's cannon and the sound lingered for a full beat. It seemed to give shape to the open air, or rather to reveal the hidden architecture that was there all along—the invisible cathedral that vaulted over the surface of the pond—known to sparrows and dragonflies but invisible to the human eye.

Relative to the rifle, the shotgun also felt more like an extension of yourself. When the bullet from the Remington flitted through the bull's-eye at the far end of the shooting range, the sound seemed independent of your finger pulling the trigger. But when the skeet shattered there was no question that you had commanded it so. Standing at the pulpit, peering down the barrel into the open air, you suddenly had the power of a Gorgon—the ability to influence matter at a distance merely by meeting it with your gaze. And the feeling didn't dissipate with the sound of the shot. It lingered. It permeated your limbs and sharpened your senses—adding a certain self-possession to your swagger, or a swagger to your self-possession. Either way, for a minute or so, it made you feel like a Bitsy Houghton.

If only someone had told me about the confidence-boosting nature of guns, I'd have been shooting them all my life.

Dinner consisted of club sandwiches at six on a bluestone patio overlooking a salt marsh. But for a few men scattered among the cast-iron tables, the patio was empty. It was decidedly unglamorous, but not without its charms.

—Will you be having anything to drink with your sandwiches, Mr. Wolcott? the young waiter was asking.

—Just some iced tea for me, Wilbur. But feel free to . . . have a cocktail, Katey.

—Iced tea sounds perfect.

The waiter navigated the tangle of tables back toward the clubhouse.

—So, do you know everyone's first name? I asked.

—Everyone's first name?

—The front desk guy, the gun guy, the waiter. . . .

—Is that unusual?

—My postman comes twice a day and I don't know *his* name.

Wallace looked bashful.

—Mine's . . . Thomas.

—I've obviously got to pay more attention.

—I suspect you pay plenty.

Wallace was absently polishing his spoon with his napkin and looking around the patio. He had a serene gaze. He put the spoon back in its proper place.

—You don't mind, do you? That . . . we're having dinner here?

—Not at all.

—It's part of the fun for me. It's like when I . . . was a kid and we spent Christmas at our camp in the Adirondacks. When the lake was frozen, we'd skate all afternoon; and then the caretaker, an old Dubliner, would serve us cocoa from a zinc canister. My sisters would sit in the main room with their feet by the fire. But my grandfather and I, we'd sit in these big green rockers on the porch and watch the day draw to a close.

He paused and looked out on the salt marsh, pinning down a detail in his memory.

—The cocoa was so hot that when you got outside in the cold air a skin would form on its surface. It floated there a shade darker than the cocoa and it would come up in a single piece at the touch of your finger. . . .

He gestured toward the whole patio.

—The cocoa was sort of like this.

—A little reward that you've earned?

—Yes. Does that seem silly?

—Not to me.

The sandwiches came and we ate without talking. I began to understand that with Wallace there were no awkward silences. He felt unusually at ease when nothing needed to be said. Occasionally ducks flew from over the trees and settled on the marsh with a flapping of wings and outstretched feet.

Perhaps Wallace was feeling relaxed in the run-down environment of his club—having exhibited his mastery of firearms and earned his iced tea. Or perhaps it was his memories of his grandfather and the Adirondack dusk. Perhaps he was just getting comfortable with me. Whatever the reason, as Wallace reminisced, the stall in his sentences had all but disappeared.

Back in Manhattan, when we were leaving Wallace's garage and I thanked him for a terrific afternoon, he hesitated. I think he was weighing whether to ask me back to his apartment, but he didn't. Maybe he was concerned that by asking, he might somehow spoil the day. So he gave me a kiss on the cheek like a friend of a friend. We exchanged good-byes and he began to walk away.

—Hey Wallace, I called.

He stopped and turned.

—What was the name of the old Irishman? The one who poured the hot chocolate.

—It was Fallon, he said with a smile. *Mr.* Fallon.

The next day at a little shop on Bleecker Street I bought a postcard of Annie Oakley. She was in full western regalia—a deerskin shirt, white-fringed boots, and two pearl-handled six-shooters. On the back, I wrote: *Thanks Pardner.* In Thursday's four o'clock post, I received a note saying: *Meet me tomorrow on the steps of the Metropolitan Museum at High Noon.* It was signed *Wyatt Earp.*

◆　◆　◆

Wallace skipped up the museum steps dressed in a pale gray suit with a white cotton handkerchief peeking squarely from his breast pocket.

—I hope you're not trying to woo me by taking me to see some paintings, I said.

—Definitely not! I wouldn't . . . know where to start.

Instead, he took me to the museum's collection of guns.

In the dim light, we drifted shoulder to shoulder from case to case. Naturally, these were guns that were famous for their design or provenance rather than for their firepower. Many had elaborate engravings or were fashioned from precious metals. You could almost forget that they were designed to kill people. Wallace probably knew every last thing there was to know about the guns, but he didn't overdo it. He shared some colorful arcana and a little bit of lore. Then he suggested we go to lunch exactly five minutes before the novelty of the experience was due to wear off.

When we came out of the museum, the brown Bentley was waiting at the bottom of the steps.

—Hello, Michael, I said, congratulating myself on remembering his name.

—Hello, Miss Kontent.

Once in the car, Wallace asked where I'd like to have lunch. I suggested that he treat me like an out-of-towner and take me to his favorite spot. So we went to the Park, a restaurant on the ground floor of a prominent midtown office tower. In the modern style it had high ceilings and walls without ornamentation. Most of the tables were occupied by men in suits.

—Is your office close to here? I asked innocently.

Wallace looked embarrassed.

—It's in the building.

—What a stroke of luck! That your favorite restaurant is in the same building as your office!

We ordered martinis from a waiter named Mitchell and reviewed the menus. To begin, Wallace ordered aspic, of all things, and I had the house salad—a terrific concoction of iceberg greens, cold blue cheese and warm red bacon. If I were a country, I would have made it my flag.

While we waited for Dover sole, Wallace began drawing a circle on the tablecloth with his dessert spoon, and for the first time I noticed his wristwatch. It had the inverse of the usual design—white numbers on a black dial.

—Sorry, he said putting down the spoon. It's an old habit.

—Actually, I was just admiring your watch.

—Oh. It's . . . an officer's watch. It had a black face so that at night it would be less likely to . . . draw fire. It was my father's.

Wallace was quiet for a moment. I was about to ask him a little more about his father when a tall, balding gentleman came to our table. Wallace pushed his chair back and stood.

—Avery!

—Wallace, the gentleman said warmly.

Having been introduced to me, the gentleman asked if I could spare Wallace a moment. Then he led him to his own table where another older man waited. From their demeanors, it was plain that they were seeking Wallace's counsel. When they finished talking, Wallace asked a few questions and then began making observations. You could tell there was no stall in his speech now either.

When I had looked at Wallace's watch it was almost two. Alley had agreed to cover me until our daily three o'clock with Mr. Tate. If I skipped dessert, I still had time to taxi back and switch into a longer skirt.

—This looks very *entre nous.*

Slipping into Wallace's chair was the horse-riding, gun-toting Bitsy Houghton.

—We don't have more than a minute, Kate, she said conspiratorially. We'd better get to it. How do you know Wally?

—I met him through Tinker Grey.

—That good-looking banker? Isn't he the one who got in the car wreck with his girl?

—Yes. She's an old friend of mine. Actually, we were all in it together.

Bitsy looked impressed.

—I've never been in a car wreck.

Though from the way she said it, you got the sense she had been in other kinds of wrecks—like in an airplane or motorcycle or submarine.

—So, she continued, is your friend as ambitious as the girls claim?

(As ambitious as the girls claim?)

—No more so than most, I said. But she has got spunk.

—Well, they'll hate her for that. Anyway. I dislike meddlers more than cats. But can I give you a tip?

—Sure.

—Wally is grander than Mount Rushmore, but he's twice as shy. Don't wait for him to smooch you first.

And before I could speak, she was halfway across the room.

◆ ◆ ◆

The next night, as I was doubling myself on a four-heart bid, there was a knock at my door. It was Wallace with a bottle of wine in one hand and a briefcase in the other. He said he had just had dinner with his attorney in the neighborhood—an explanation that must have required a rather generous definition of neighborhood. I closed the door and we shared one of Wallace's unawkward silences.

—You've got a . . . lot of books, he said at last.

—It's a sickness.

—Are you . . . seeing anyone for it?

—I'm afraid it's untreatable.

He put his briefcase and the wine on my father's easy chair and began circling the room with a tilted head.

—Is this the . . . Dewey decimal system?

—No. But it's based on similar principles. Those are the British novelists. The French are in the kitchen. Homer, Virgil and the other epics are there by the tub.

Wallace wandered toward one of the windowsills and plucked *Leaves of Grass* off a teetering stack.

—I take it the . . . transcendentalists do better in sunlight.

—Exactly.

—Do they need much water?

—Not as much as you'd think. But lots of pruning.

He pointed the volume toward a pile of books under my bed.

—And the . . . mushrooms?

—The Russians.

—Ah.

Wallace carefully returned Whitman to his perch. He wandered over to the card table and circled it the way one circles an architectural model.

—Who's winning?

—Not me.

Wallace took the chair opposite the dummy. I picked up the bottle.

—Will you stay for a drink? I asked.

—I'd . . . love to.

The wine was older than me. When I came back to the table, he had taken up the south hand and was rearranging the cards.

—Where's the . . . bidding?

—I just bid four hearts.

—Did they double?

I plucked the cards out of his hand and swept up the deck. We sat for a minute saying nothing and he drank to the bottom of his glass. I sensed that he was about to go. I tried to think of something captivating to say.

—By any chance, he asked, do you know how to play honeymoon bridge?

It was an ingenious little game. Wallace had played it with his grandfather on rainy days in the Adirondacks. Here's how it works: You place the shuffled deck on the table. Your opponent draws the top card and then has two options: He can keep the card, look at the second one, and discard *it* facedown; or he can discard the first card and *keep* the second one. Then it's your turn. The two of you go back and forth in this manner until the deck is exhausted, at which point you each hold thirteen cards, having discarded thirteen—giving the game an unusually elegant balance between intention and chance.

As we played, we talked about Clark Gable and Claudette Colbert, about the Dodgers and the Yankees. We had a lot of laughs. After I won a small slam in spades, I took Bitsy's advice and leaned forward to kiss him on the mouth, but he was just about to say something and we ended up clacking our teeth. When I leaned back, he was trying to put a hand around my shoulder and he almost fell out of his chair.

We both sat back and laughed. We laughed because somehow we suddenly knew exactly where we stood. Ever since the visit to the hunt club, a small uncertainty had buzzed between us. It was a sense of chemistry that had been a little elusive, a little imprecise. Until now.

Maybe it was because we found being in each other's company so effortless. Maybe it had something to do with the fact that he had clearly been in love with Bitsy Houghton since he was a kid (star-crossed romance being the spoiler that it is). Either way, we knew that our feelings for each other weren't urgent, or impassioned, or prone to deception. They were friendly and fond and sincere.

It was like the honeymoon bridge.

The romantic interplay that we were having wasn't the real game—it was a modified version of the game. It was a version invented for two friends so that they can get some practice and pass the time divertingly while they wait in the station for their train to arrive.

CHAPTER FIFTEEN

The Pursuit of Perfection

August 26, 98°. As if by design, the glass of Mason Tate's office was just thick enough so you could hear him raising his voice without gleaning the specifics. At this particular juncture, he was articulating some nuance of dissatisfaction to Vitters, the staff photographer, while pointing a commanding finger in the direction of New Jersey.

Judging from a distance, most people probably assumed that Mason Tate was insufferable. Certainly, he seemed to care about his little glamour magazine to an irrational degree: *That rumor is too well founded. This blue too cerulean. That comma too early. This colon too late.* But it was precisely his nit-picking mania that lent a sense of purpose to the rest of us.

With Tate at the helm, the work of *Gotham* wasn't some vague agrarian battle with the seasons in which the outcomes of one's efforts were held hostage to time and temperature; it wasn't the drudgery of the firetrap seamstress needling the same loop over and over until it's one's sanity that's being stitched into a seam; nor was it the life of the seafarer exposed to the elements for years at a time, returning like Odysseus older, weaker, nearly forgotten—unrecognizable to all but one's dog. Ours was the work of the demolition expert. Having carefully studied the architecture of a building, we were to install an array of charges around its foundation set to go off in an orchestrated sequence such that the building would collapse under the weight of its own infrastructure—simultaneously inspiring gawkers with awe and clearing the way for something new.

But in exchange for this heightened sense of purpose, you kept your hands on the wheel or got them whacked with a ruler.

As Vitters sprinted back to the safety of his darkroom, Tate buzzed me three times in quick succession: *Get. In. Here.* I smoothed my skirt and picked up a steno pad. He turned from the drafting table looking especially imperious.

—Does the color of my tie look more accommodating than usual?

—No, Mr. Tate.

—What about my new haircut. Does it seem more encouraging?

—No, sir.

—Is there *anything* about me today which would suggest that I want an unasked-for opinion more than I did yesterday?

—Not in the least.

—Well, that's a relief.

He turned back to the drafting table and leaned against it with both arms. On it were ten different candids of Bette Davis: Bette in a restaurant; Bette at a Yankees game; Bette strolling down Fifth Avenue, putting the window treatments to shame. He isolated four pictures that had been taken within minutes of each other. They showed Bette, her husband, and a younger couple seated in a booth at a supper club. On the table were full ashtrays and empty glasses. The only food left was a candle-lit slice of cake sitting in front of the starlet.

Tate waved at the pictures.

—Which is your favorite?

One of them had been penciled by Vitters to suggest how the photo might be cropped. In it, the candle was freshly lit and the two couples smiled at the camera like smokers on a billboard. But in one from a little later in the evening, Bette offers the last bite of cake to the young man at her side as his wife looks on with the narrowed eyes of a Harpy.

I pulled it from the pile.

Mr. Tate nodded sympathetically.

—It's funny about photography, isn't it? The entire medium is founded on the instant. If you allow the shutter to be open for even a few seconds, the image goes black. We think of our lives as a sequence of actions, an accumulation of accomplishments, a fluid articulation of style and opinion. And yet, in that one sixteenth of a second, a photograph can wreak such havoc.

He looked at his watch and waved me toward a chair.

—I've got ten minutes. Take a letter.

It was addressed to Davis's agent. It referenced Mr. Tate's respect for the actress and his fondness for her husband and the lovely birthday dinner they must have had at El Morocco. After an aside about an upcoming contract negotiation with Warner Brothers and a parenthetical about the little seaside town where he thought he saw Davis in the off-season, he requested an interview. He told me to leave the letter on his desk, grabbed his briefcase, and left for a vacation that apparently no one else had earned. Maybe Mr. Tate was still irked at Vitters, or maybe it was our faulty air-conditioning; whatever the reason, the letter was a paragraph too long, a verb too insistent, and an adjective too obvious.

When Alley and I came out of the building fifteen minutes later, it was so hot even she didn't want a slice of cake. We wished each other well and parted company at the corner. Then it was back to the girls' room at the automat, where this time I donned a black velvet dress and a bright red ribbon for my hair.

◆ ◆ ◆

That first night Wallace and I played cards in my apartment, he confessed that he had been seeing his attorney in order to put his assets in trust. Why? Because on the twenty-seventh of August, he was going to Spain to join up with the Republican forces.

And he wasn't kidding.

I guess I shouldn't have been that surprised. All sorts of interesting young men were joining the fray—some spurred by fashion, some by a love of risk, most by a healthy dose of misplaced idealism. For Wallace, there was also the small matter of having been given too much.

Born in a brownstone on the Upper East Side with an Adirondack summer house and hunting plantation waiting in the wings, Wallace had gone to his father's prep school, his father's college, and taken over the family business when his father had died—inheriting not only his father's desk and car but the secretary and driver that went with them. To his credit, Wallace doubled the business, he established a scholarship in his grandfather's name, he earned the respect of his peers. But all the while, he suspected that the life he was living so reliably was not his own. Those seven years he had just spent becoming a captain of industry and a deacon of the church were his father's fifties. His reckless twenties had eluded him altogether.

But not for much longer.

In a single stroke, he was going to shed every aspect of his life that was sensible, familiar, and secure. And in the month before he left, rather than review the disadvantages of his decision with friends and family, he opted for the company of an amiable stranger.

We were both working long hours, so midweek we would meet Bitsy and Jack for a late supper and a few rounds of bridge. Née Van Heuys, Bitsy was Pennsylvania landed-wealth and she was tougher and shrewder than she needed to be given her looks. What solidified our relationship was her discovery that I had a head for cards. By the second date, we were playing the boys for money and fronting them points. Then when the night was over, Wallace would give me a friendly kiss at the curb, put me in a cab, and we'd head home to our respective apartments for a good night's sleep. But the weekends, Wallace and I spent those side by side celebrating the doldrums of Manhattan.

On any given Saturday, if there was a party on the water in Westport or Oyster Bay, Wallace Wolcott was probably invited. But the first time he spread a selection of invitations on the table for my consideration, I could tell that his heart wasn't in it. Pressed, he admitted that these sprawling affairs made him feel a little out of place. Lord knows, if they made *him* feel out of place, I wasn't going to be much help. So we regretted. We told the Hamlins and the Kirklands and the Gibsons that we would not be able to attend.

Instead, on Saturday afternoons we ran Wallace's errands in the Bentley: *To Brooks Brothers, Michael, to pick up the new khaki shirts; to Twenty-third Street to get the pistols cleaned; then on to Brentano's for a Spanish phrase book.*

Olé!

Maybe it was my exposure to Mason Tate, but as we tackled these simple tasks, I found I had a burgeoning taste for flawlessness. Just a few weeks before, no detail of my life had been big enough to merit my attention. The Chinese laundress could have ironed a hole in my skirt and I would have tossed a nickel on the drum, thanked her kindly, and worn it to the church social. After all, where I came from the mission was to pay as little as one could without stealing, so on those rare occasions when you got home and discovered you had the unbruised melon, you had good reason to suspect you didn't deserve it.

But Wallace deserved it. At least, as far as I was concerned.

So, if the color of a new sweater clashed with the color of his eyes, I sent it back. If the first four shaving soaps smelled too flowery, I told the girl at Bergdorf's to bring four more. And if the porterhouse steak wasn't thick enough, I stood right there at the counter and watched Mr. Otto-manelli swing his cleaver until he got it right. Taking care of someone else's life—that may have been what Wallace Wolcott was running away from, but I found it suited me just fine. Then, with our errands behind us (having "earned" it), we'd cocktail at an empty hotel bar, dine at a nice restaurant without a reservation, and stroll back up Fifth Avenue to his apartment, where we could trade novels and divvy up Hershey bars.

One night in early August while having a late supper at the Grove— where the potted ficus were hung with little white lights—Wallace observed wistfully that he wouldn't be home for Christmas.

Apparently, Christmas was a big holiday for the Wolcotts. On Christmas Eve, three generations spent the night at the Adirondack camp, and while they attended the midnight service, Mrs. Wolcott would put a pair of matching pajamas on every pillow. So in the morning, they all came down to the freshly cut spruce in matching red and white stripes or a tartan plaid. Wallace didn't particularly enjoy shopping for himself, but he took pride in finding that perfect gift for his nephews and nieces, especially his young namesake, Wallace Martin. But this year he wasn't going to make it back in time.

—Why don't we shop for them now? I suggested. We can wrap the gifts, tag them with a *Don't Open Til Xmas*, and drop them off at your mother's.

—Better yet, I could give them to . . . my attorney. With instructions to deliver on Christmas Eve.

—Better yet.

So we shoved aside our plates and sketched a plan of action identifying each recipient, their relation to Wallace, their age, their character, and a potential gift. In addition to Wallace's sisters, brothers-in-law, nieces, and nephews, the list included Wallace's secretary, the chauffeur Michael, and a few others to whom he felt indebted. It was like a cheat sheet on the entire Wolcott family. What the girls in Oyster Bay wouldn't have paid to get a look at it.

We spent a weekend shopping, then two nights before Wallace was to set sail, we planned a dinner for two at his apartment so we could wrap. As I looked through my closet that morning, my first thought was to wear my polka-dot dress. But somehow, it didn't seem to strike the right note. So I dug in the back of the closet and found a black velvet dress that I hadn't worn in a century. Then I rummaged in my sewing kit for a length of ribbon as red as a poinsettia.

◆ ◆ ◆

When Wallace opened the door to his apartment, I curtsied.

—Ho, ho . . . ho, he said.

In the living room, carols were playing on the phonograph and a bottle of champagne was wreathed in evergreens. We toasted St. Nick and Jack Frost and rapid returns from bold adventures. Then we sat on the carpet with scissors and adhesive tape and went about our work.

As the Wolcotts were in the paper business, they had access to every kind of wrapping paper on earth: forest greens patterned with candy canes; velvety reds with pipe-smoking Santas in sleighs. But the family tradition was to wrap everything in a heavy white stock that was delivered to the house by the roll. Then they dressed the gifts with a different-colored ribbon for each member of the clan.

For ten-year-old Joel, I wrapped a miniature baseball field with a spring-released bat that knocked ball bearings around the bases—and then tied it with a ribbon of blue. I wrapped and finished in yellow ribbon a pair of stuffed lizards for fourteen-year-old Penelope, a Madame Curie in the making who frowned on most amusements, including candy. As the pile grew smaller, I kept an eye out for Little Wallace's gift. When we had gone shopping, Big Wallace had said he had something special in mind for his godson, but in taking a quick inventory, I couldn't identify it. The mystery was solved when, with the last of the presents wrapped, Wallace cut a small rectangle of paper and then took his father's black-dialed watch from his wrist.

With the job complete, we passed into the kitchen, where the air smelled of slow-roasting potatoes. After checking the oven, Wallace wrapped an apron around his waist and seared the lamb chops that I had carefully selected the day before. Then he removed the chops and deglazed the pan with mint jelly and cognac.

—Wallace, I asked as he handed me my plate, if I declared war on America, would you stay and fight with me?

When dinner was over, I helped Wallace carry the gifts to the back pantry. Lining the hallway were photographs of family members smiling in enviable locales. There were grandparents on a dock, an uncle on skis, sisters riding sidesaddle. At the time it seemed a little odd, this back hall gallery; but running into a similar setup in similar hallways over the years, I eventually came to see it as endearingly WASPy. Because it's an outward expression of that reserved sentimentality (for places as much as kin) that quietly permeates their version of existence. In Brighton Beach or on the Lower East Side, you were more apt to find a single portrait propped on a mantel behind dried flowers, a burning candle, and a generation of genuflection. In our households, nostalgia played a distant fiddle to acknowledgment of the sacrifices made by forebears on your behalf.

One of the pictures was of a few hundred boys in coat and tie.

—Is that St. George's?

—Yes. From my . . . senior year.

I leaned a little closer, trying to find Wallace. He pointed to a sweet, unassuming face, which I had already passed over. Wallace was just the sort who blends into the background of the school photo (or the greeting line at the cotillion) but who, with the passage of time, increasingly stands out against the lapses in character around him.

—This is the whole school? I asked after another moment of scanning the boys' faces.

—You're . . . looking for Tinker?

—Yes, I admitted.

—He's here.

Wallace pointed to the left side of the photograph where our mutual friend stood alone at the outskirts of the assembly. Given another minute, I would certainly have identified Tinker. He looked just as you'd expect him to look at the age of fourteen—his hair a little tussled, his jacket a little wrinkled, his eyes trained on the camera as if he were ready to spring.

Then Wallace smiled and moved his finger across the photograph to its opposite edge.

—And he's here.

Sure enough, at the far right of the assembly was another figure, slightly blurred, but unmistakably him.

In order to have the whole school in focus, Wallace explained, they used the old box cameras on stilts where an aperture is slowly pulled across a large negative, exposing one part of the assembly at a time. This allows someone on the far side to sprint behind the student body and appear in the photograph twice—but only if he times it well and runs like the devil. Every year a few freshmen tried the stunt, but Tinker was the only one Wallace remembered succeeding. And from the wide smile on the second Tinker's face, you sensed that he knew it.

Wallace and I had been reasonably true to our promise of leaving Tinker and Eve out of our conversations. But there was something nice for the both of us in seeing Tinker's Puckish self at play. We lingered, giving the stunt its due.

—Can I ask you something? I said after a moment.

—Sure.

—That night we all had dinner at the Beresford—when we were riding down in the elevator, Bucky made a crack about Tinker rising like a phoenix from the ashes.

—Bucky is . . . a bit of a boor.

—Even so. What was he talking about?

Wallace was silent.

—Is it that bad? I prodded.

Wallace smiled softly.

—No. It's . . . not bad, per se. Tinker came from an old Fall River family. But I gather his . . . father had a run of rotten luck. I think he . . . lost just about everything.

—In the Crash?

—No.

Wallace pointed to the photograph.

—It was around then, when Tinker was a freshman. I remember, because I was a . . . prefect. The trustees met to discuss what they should do given the . . . change in his circumstances.

—Did they give him a scholarship?

Wallace gave a slow shake of the head.

—They asked him to leave. He finished high school in Fall River and . . . put himself through Providence College. Then he got a job as a clerk at a . . . trust company and began working his way back up.

Born in the Back Bay, attended Brown, and worked at his grandfather's bank. That had been my smug assessment of Tinker ten minutes after we'd met.

I took a second look at the photo of this boy with his curly hair and friendly smile and for the first time in months, I wanted to see him. Not to hash anything out. I didn't need to talk about Eve or what had or hadn't or might have happened. I just wanted a second shot at a first impression—to have him walk into The Hotspot and sit at the neighboring table and watch the band—so that when the soloist began to bray and Tinker gave me that bewildered smile, I could take him in without assumptions. For this little piece of information from Wallace told me something that I should have known all along—that as Tinker and I had come of age, we hadn't been on opposite sides of a threshold; we'd been standing side by side.

Wallace looked back and forth across the photograph with a probing gaze—as if the very moment that it had been taken was when Mr. Grey had lost the last of the family fortune—and the two Tinkers on either side of the assembly represented the end of one life and the beginning of another.

—Most people remember the phoenix for being born from the ashes, he said. But they forget its other feature.

—What's that? I asked.

—That it lives five hundred years.

◆ ◆ ◆

The next day, Wallace shipped out.

Well, not exactly.

In 1917, they "shipped out." Young men in pressed uniforms with fair hair and red cheeks gathered in battalions on the docks of the Brooklyn shipyards. With their duffel bags on their shoulders, they marched up the gangplanks of the great gray cruisers gamely singing choruses of "Over There, Over There." And when the whistle finally blew, they competed to hang over the railings so that they could blow kisses at their sweethearts or wave to their mothers, who presciently wept in the background.

But if you were a well-to-do young man in 1938 off to fight in the Spanish Civil War, there wasn't much fare to fan. You bought a first-class ticket on the *Queen Mary* and showed up on the docks after a leisurely lunch. Passing among the tourists who were already thumbing through phrase books, you politely made your way up the gangplank and headed to your cabin on the upper deck where your luggage, which had been sent ahead, was being carefully unpacked by a steward.

Ever since the League of Nations prohibited the volunteering of extra-nationals in the conflict, it had been bad form to discuss that you were headed there while you dined at the captain's table (seated in between the Philadelphia Morgans and the Breezewood sisters in the company of their aunt). You certainly couldn't say it to the immigration officials in Southampton. Instead, you'd say you were on your way to Paris to see some school chums and purchase a painting or two. Then you'd take the train to Dover, the boat to Calais, and a car to the south of France, where you could either hike over the Pyrenees or hire a fishing trawler to run you down the coast.

—See you Mike, Wallace said at the gangplank.

—Good luck, Mr. Wolcott.

When he turned to me, I observed that I wouldn't know what to do with my Saturdays anymore.

—Maybe I could run some errands for your mother? I suggested.

—Kate, he said. You shouldn't . . . be running someone's errands. Not mine. Not my mother's. Not Mason Tate's.

When Michael and I were driving back from the dock, it was pretty mournful in the car—for the both of us. As we crossed the bridge into Manhattan I broke the silence.

—Do you think he'll be careful, Michael?

—Being that it's a war, Miss, that would sort of defeat the purpose.

—Yes. I suppose it would.

Through the windows of the car, I saw city hall float past. In Chinatown, miniature old women crowded around street carts laden with ungodly fish.

—Shall I take you home, Miss?

—Yes, Michael.

—To Eleventh Street?

It was sweet of him to ask. If I had given Wallace's address, I think he would have taken me there. After pulling up to the curb, he would have opened the door to the backseat, Billy would have opened the door to the building, and Jackson would have brought me in the elevator up to the eleventh floor, where for a few weeks more I could fend off my future. But with a pile of presents waiting patiently in a law firm's file room, Michael would soon be covering the brown Bentley in tarpaulin even as John and Tony dismantled the Remington and the Colt and stowed them in a locker. Maybe it was time for my brush with perfection to be dismantled and stowed away too.

On the Thursday after Wallace left, I wandered over to Fifth Avenue after work to see the windows at Bergdorf's. A few days before, I'd noticed that they'd been curtained for the installation of the new displays.

Winter, Spring, Summer, Fall, I always looked forward to the unveiling of the new seasons at Bergdorf's. Standing before the windows, you felt like a tsarina receiving one of those jeweled eggs in which an elaborate scene in miniature has been painstakingly assembled. With one eye closed you spy inside, losing all sense of time as you marvel at every transporting detail.

And *transporting* was the right word. For the Bergdorf's windows weren't advertising unsold inventory at 30% off. They were designed to change the lives of women up and down the avenue—offering envy to some, self-satisfaction to others, but a glimpse of possibility to all. And for the Fall season of 1938, my Fifth Avenue Fabergé did not disappoint.

The theme of the windows was fairy tales, drawing on the well-known works of the Brothers Grimm and Hans Christian Andersen; but in each set piece the "princess" had been replaced with the figure of a man, and the "prince" with one of us.

In the first window, a young lord with raven hair and flawless skin lay in state under a flowering arbor, his delicate hands folded on his chest. But at his side stood a dashing young woman (in a red bolero jacket by Schiaperelli), her hair cut short for battle, her sword tucked neatly through her belt, and the reins of her faithful horse in hand. With an expression at once worldly and compassionate she looked down upon the prince in no apparent rush to rouse him with a kiss.

In the next window, with the renaissance trickery of an opera set, one hundred marble steps descended from a palace door to a cobbled court, where four mice hid in the shadow of a pumpkin. On the periphery, the diminishing figure of a golden-haired stepson turned the corner at a sprint, while front and center knelt a princess (in a fitted black dress by Chanel) looking with determination at a Derby shoe made of glass. From her expression you could just tell that she was ready to call her kingdom into action—from the footmen to the chamberlains—and have them scour the countryside from dawn to dusk for the boy who fit that shoe.

—It's Katey, isn't it?

I turned to find a prim brunette at my side—Wyss from the little state of Connecticut. If I had been asked to speculate on Wisteria's style for an afternoon in August, I would have guessed Garden Club of America; but I would have been wrong. She was dressed in perfect elegance with a cobalt blue short-sleeved dress and a matching asymmetric hat.

At Tinker and Eve's dinner party, we hadn't exactly hit it off, so I was a little surprised that she'd bothered to approach me. As we exchanged pleasantries, her demeanor was welcoming and her eyes almost twinkled. Naturally, the conversation turned quickly to their European holiday. I asked how it went.

—Lovely, she said. *Perfectly* lovely. Have you ever been? No? Well, the weather in July in the south of France is *ravissant*, and the food is not to be believed. But it was such an added pleasure to be with Tinker and Evelyn. Tinker speaks such beautiful French. And being a foursome provides that extra spark to every hour: the early morning swims on the strand . . . and the long lunches overlooking the sea . . . and the late night jaunts into town . . . Though of course (*light laugh*), Tinker adds a little more spark to the early morning swim and Eve to the late night jaunt.

I was beginning to understand why she had approached me, after all.

That night at the Beresford, she had been the odd girl out. But like a seasoned evangelist, she'd put up with the fast talk and the occasional wisecracks at her expense, confident that the Good Lord would one day reward her for her patience. And here it was: redemption day. The Rapture. The unexpected chance for a little table turning. Because when it came to the south of France, we both knew exactly who was the odd one out.

—Well, I said, winding down the conversation. It's good to have you all back.

—Oh, we didn't come back *together*. . . .

She stayed me with the gentle touch of two fingers on my arm.

I could see that the color of her fingernail polish matched the color of her lipstick precisely.

—We intended to, of course. Then just before we were scheduled to sail, Tinker said he had to stop in Paris on business. Eve said she just wanted to go home. So he bribed her (*conspiratorial smile*) with a promise of dinner on the Eiffel Tower.

(*Conspiratorial smile returned.*)

—But, you see, continued Wyss, Tinker wasn't going to Paris on business at all.

?

—He was going to see Cartier!

To Wyss's credit, I could feel a slight burning sensation on my cheeks.

—Before they left for Paris, Tinker pulled me aside. He was in an absolute state. Some men are hopeless when it comes to these things. Ruby bracelet, sapphire brooch, *sautoir de perles*. He didn't know what he should get.

Naturally, I wasn't going to ask. But it didn't make a difference. She was already extending her left hand languidly to show a diamond the size of a grape.

—I just told him to get her one of these.

When I got back downtown, still reeling a bit from my encounter with Wyss, I finally went to the grocer to restock the pantry of my routines: a new deck of cards, a jar of peanut butter, a bottle of second-grade gin. Trudging up the stairs, I was a little stunned to smell that the bride in 3B had already perfected her mother's Bolognese, maybe even improved upon it. I turned the key while balancing the groceries in the crook of my arm, crossed the threshold, and almost stepped on a letter that had been slipped under my door. I set the bag down on the table and picked the letter up.

It was in an ivory envelope embossed with a scallop shell. On the front, there was no stamp, but it was addressed in perfect calligraphy. I don't think I had ever seen my name so beautifully inscribed. Each of the Ks stood an inch tall, their legs sweeping elegantly under the other letters, curling at the end like the toe of an Arabian shoe.

Inside, there was a card edged in gold. It was so thick I had to rip the envelope to set it free. At the top was the same image of the scallop, while below were the time and date and the requesting of the honor of my company. It was an invitation to the Hollingsworths' sprawling Labor Day affair. From a few hundred miles at sea, another act of grace by the right fine Wallace Wolcott.

CHAPTER SIXTEEN

Fortunes of War

This time when I arrived at Whileaway, I didn't have to take a detour through the garden—I got to go right through the front door with the rest of the invited guests. But having let Fran convince me to buy a dress from the Macy's bargain bin that looked better on her figure than mine, I couldn't shake that nagging feeling that I should have been pushing my way through the hedge. As if to make the point, two college boys brushed past me at the door. They sloughed off their coats into the hands of a footman and took glasses of champagne from a waiter—making eye contact with neither. With no achievements behind them, they already looked as self-assured as the flyboys would at the end of the Second World War.

At the entrance to the great room, exactly where you couldn't avoid them, representatives of the Hollingsworth family had formed an impromptu receiving line: Mr. & Mrs., two of the boys, one of the wives. When I gave my name, Mr. Hollingsworth welcomed me with the polite smile of one who has long since quit keeping track of his children's acquaintances. But one of the older sons leaned over.

—She's Wallace's friend, Pop.

—The young lady he called about? Why of course, he said—adding quasi-confidentially: That call caused quite a stir, young lady.

—Devlin, chastened Mrs. Hollingsworth.

—Yes, yes. Well, I've known Wallace since the day he was born. So if there's anything you'd like to know about him that he wouldn't tell you himself, come and find me. In the meantime, make yourself at home.

Outside on the terrace, the breeze was temperate and wild. Though the sun had yet to set, the house was lit from stem to stern as if to assure arriving guests that should the weather take a turn for the worst, we could all stay the night. Men in black tie conversed casually with the rubied and the sapphired and the *sautoir de perles*-ed. It was the same sort of familiar elegance that I had seen in July, only now it spanned three generations: Alongside the silver-haired titans kissing the cheeks of glamorous goddaughters were young rakes scandalizing aunts with wry remarks sotto voce. A few stragglers from the beach with towels on their shoulders were making their way toward the house looking fit and friendly and not the least ill at ease for running late. Their shadows stretched across the grass in long, attenuated stripes.

A table at the edge of the terrace supported one of those pyramids where overflowing champagne from the uppermost glass cascades down the stems until all of the glasses are filled. So as not to spoil the effect, the engineer of this thousand-dollar parlor trick produced a fresh glass from under the table and filled it for me.

Whatever Mr. Hollingsworth's encouragements, there wasn't going to be much chance of my feeling at home. But Wallace had made such an effort, I was just going to have to splash some water on my face, trade up to gin, and throw myself into the mix.

Inquiring for a powder room, I was directed up the main staircase, past a portrait of a horse, down a wainscoted hall to the end of the east wing. The ladies' dressing room was a pale yellow parlor overlooking a rose garden. It had pale yellow wallpaper, pale yellow chairs, a pale yellow chaise.

There were two women already there. Sitting in front of a mirror I pretended to tinker with an earring as I watched them in the reflection. The first, a tall brunette with short hair and a cool expression, had just come up from the dock. Her bathing suit was at her feet and she was drying her naked body unself-consciously. The other, in teal taffetta, was sitting at a well-lit vanity trying to repair mascara after a bout of tears. Every thirty seconds or so she let out a whimper. The swimmer wasn't showing her much sympathy. I tried not to show her any either.

Uncomforted, the girl gave a sniff and left.

—Good riddance, the swimmer said blandly.

She gave her hair a final rub with the towel and tossed it in a pile. She had an athlete's body and a backless dress that she was going to wear to great advantage. As she moved her arms you could see her muscles articulate around her shoulder blades. She didn't bother to sit when she put on her shoes. She slipped her feet into them and wiggled her heels until they wedged their way in. Then she extended her long thin arm over her shoulder and zipped her own dress.

In the mirror, I saw a glimmer on the carpet under the settee where her shoes had been stowed. Crossing the room, I got down on my knees and reached for the object. It was a diamond earring.

The brunette was watching me now.

—Is this yours? I asked, knowing it wasn't.

She took it in hand.

—No, she said. But it's quite a piece.

She looked around the room indifferently.

—These normally travel in pairs.

As I checked under the settee, she shook the wet towels. We looked around for a minute more and then she handed the earring back.

—A fortune of war, she said.

The swimmer was more right than she knew. Because I was fairly certain that this particular earring—with its baguette-cut diamonds and its clasp in white gold—was one of the pair that Eve had found in Tinker's bedside table.

Descending the curved front stair I felt off my balance, as if the one glass of champagne had gone straight to my head. Whatever news Tinker and Eve were bringing home from Paris, I wasn't ready to hear it—not in a setting like this. I slowed my pace and shifted to the outer edge of the staircase, where the steps were widest and the banister was close at hand.

Crowding the lobby was a parade of new arrivals—more flyboys and self-zipping brunettes. Jolly glad to see one another, they were blocking the exit with their fashionable lateness. But if Tinker and Eve were at Whileaway, they wouldn't be stuck in the lobby; they'd be adding sparks to the hour in the company of friendly foursomes. As I reached the bottom stair I figured it was twenty steps to the door and half a mile to the train.

—Katey!

A woman marching out of the great room caught me off guard. But I should have known who it was from the pace of her approach.

—Bitsy . . .

—Jack and I are positively rotten about Wally rushing off to Spain.

She had two glasses of champagne and thrust one in my hand.

—I know he's been saying for months he intended to join up, but no one thought he'd go through with it. Especially after you came along. Are you beside yourself?

—I'm doing all right.

—Of course you are. Have you heard from him?

—Not yet.

—Then no one has. Let's figure out when we can lunch. You and I are going to be fast friends this fall. That's a promise. But come say hi to Jack.

At the entrance to the great room Jack was having a good laugh with a girl named Generous, who appeared anything but. Even at ten feet you could tell she was spinning a yarn at a friend's expense. As Jack introduced me, I wondered how long I'd have to chat before I could extricate myself politely.

—Go back to the beginning, Jack told Generous. It's priceless!

—All right, she said with expert weariness—as if boredom had been invented the day she was born. Do you know Tinker and Evelyn?

—She was in the car wreck with them, Bitsy said.

—Then you're definitely going to want to hear this.

Freshly back from the Continent, Generous explained, Tinker and Eve were spending the weekend at Whileaway in one of the guesthouses. And that morning, while everyone was having a dip, Tinker had admired *Splendide*.

—That's Holly's yawl, Jack explained.

—His *baby*, Generous corrected. He leaves it bobbing on its buoy so everyone can ooh and aah. Anyhow. Your friend was going on and on about the boat and just like that, all nonchalant, Holly says, *Why don't you two take her for a spin?* Well, you could have burned us to the ground like Atlanta—Holly lending his boat! But he and Tinker had planned the whole thing, you see—the swim on the dock, the on and on, the nonchalance. There was even a bottle of bubbly and a stuffed chicken stowed on board.

—What does that tell you? asked Jack.

—That someone's thrown in the towel, said Bitsy.

There it was again. That slight stinging sensation of the cheeks. It's our body's light-speed response to the world showing us up; and it's one of life's most unpleasant feelings—leaving one to wonder what evolutionary purpose it could possibly serve.

Jack held up an imaginary trumpet and gave it a *bah bup bup baah* as everyone laughed.

—But here comes the best part, said Jack, egging Generous on.

—Holly assumed they'd be out for an hour or two. Six hours later, they still hadn't come back. Holly began worrying they'd made a run for Mexico. When up to the dock come two brats in a dory. They say they came across *Splendide*—run aground on a sandbar. And the man on board promised them twenty dollars if they could find him a tow.

—God save us from romantics, said Bitsy.

Someone ran up wild-eyed, choking with laughter.

—They're coming in. Towed by a lobster boat!

—We've got to see this, said Jack.

Everyone made for the terrace. I made for the front door.

I suppose I was in a state of modified shock; though God knows why. Anne had seen it coming for months. Wyss too. The whole crowd at Whileaway seemed prepped and ready to gather on the dock for the impromptu celebration.

Waiting for my coat, I looked back toward the great room. It was emptying out as the last gawkers made for the French doors. A man a little older than me in a white dinner jacket stood in front of the bar. With his hands in his pockets, he seemed lost in sober reflection. Cutting in front of him, a celebrant grabbed a magnum by the neck and then knocked over an urn filled with hydrangea while heading back outside. The dinner-jacketed man watched with an expression of moral disappointment.

The footman returned with my coat and I said thanks, conscious a

moment too late that like the college boys at the beginning of the evening, I hadn't looked him in the eye either.

—You're not leaving us so soon!

It was old Mr. Hollingsworth coming in from the driveway.

—The party's lovely, Mr. Hollingsworth. And you were so kind to
invite me. But I'm afraid I'm feeling a bit under the weather.

—Oh. I'm sorry to hear that. Are you staying nearby?

—I took the train in from the city. I was just going to ask someone
to call me a cab.

—My dear, that's out of the question.

He looked back toward the great room.

—Valentine!

The young man in the white dinner jacket turned. With his fair-
haired good looks and serious mien, he seemed like a cross between an
aviator and a judge. He took his hands out of his pockets and walked
quickly across the lobby.

—Yes, father.

—You remember Miss Kontent. Wallace's friend. She's not feeling
well and is headed back to the city. Can you take her to the station?

—Of course.

—Why don't you take the Spider.

Outside, the Labor Day wind was scattering leaves to the ground.
You could just tell it was going to pour. The rest of the weekend would
have to be cribbage and tea to the tune of a banging screen door. The
casinos would be shuttered, the tennis nets lowered, and the dinghies,
like the dreams of teenage girls, would be dragged ashore.

We crossed the white gravel drive to a six-bay garage. The Spider was
a two-seater, fire engine red. Valentine passed it, opting for the 1936
Cadillac, bulky and black.

Along the drive there must have been a hundred cars parked on the
grass. One had its lights on, its doors open, its radio playing. On the hood
lay a man and woman smoking side by side. Valentine gave them the same
look of moral disappointment that he had given the magnum grabber. At
the end of the drive, he turned right heading toward the Post Road.

—Isn't the station in the other direction?

—I'll take you in, he said.

—You don't have to do that.

—I've got to head back anyway; I've got a meeting first thing.

I doubted he really had a meeting; but it wasn't a ploy to spend time with me. As he drove, he didn't look over or bother to make conversation. Which was just as well. To get out of that party, we both would have volunteered to walk a rabid dog.

After a few miles he asked me to check the glove compartment for a pad and pen. He balanced the pad on the dash and wrote some notes to himself. He tore the top sheet off and stuffed it in his jacket pocket.

—Thanks, he said, handing back the pad.

To stave off any chatter, he switched on the radio. It was tuned to a station playing swing. He turned the dial. He passed over a ballad, paused on a speech by Roosevelt, and then turned back to the ballad. It was Billie Holiday singing "Autumn in New York."

Autumn in New York,
Why does it seem so inviting?
Autumn in New York,
It spells the thrill of first-nighting.

Written by a Belarusian immigrant named Vernon Duke, "Autumn in New York" practically debuted as a jazz standard. Within fifteen years of its first being played, Charlie Parker, Sarah Vaughn, Louis Armstrong, and Ella Fitzgerald had all explored its sentimental bounds. Within twenty-five, there would be interpretations of the interpretations by Chet Baker, Sonny Stitt, Frank Sinatra, Bud Powell, and Oscar Peterson. The very question that the song asks of us about autumn, we could ask ourselves of the song: *Why does it seem so inviting?*

Presumably, one factor is that each city has its own romantic season. Once a year, a city's architectural, cultural, and horticultural variables come into alignment with the solar course in such a way that men and women passing each other on the thoroughfares feel an unusual sense of romantic promise. Like Christmastime in Vienna, or April in Paris.

That's the way we New Yorkers feel about fall. Come September, despite the waning hours, despite the leaves succumbing to the weight of gray autumnal rains, there is a certain relief to having the long days of summer behind us; and there's a paradoxical sense of rejuvenation in the air.

Glittering crowds
And shimmering clouds
In canyons of steel—
They're making me feel
I'm home.

It's autumn in New York
That brings the promise of new love.

Yes, in the autumn of 1938 tens of thousands of New Yorkers would be falling under the spell of that song. Sitting in the jazz bars or the supper clubs, the worn and the well-to-do would be nodding their heads in smiling acknowledgment that the Belarusian immigrant had it right: that somehow, despite the coming of winter, autumn in New York promises an effervescent romance which makes one look to the Manhattan skyline with fresh eyes and feel: *It's good to live it again.*

But still, you have to ask yourself: If it's such an uplifting song, then why did Billie Holiday sing it so well?

♦   ♦   ♦

When I got on the elevator early Tuesday morning, I found that like Mason Tate's desk, it was made of glass. A story below me, stainless steel gears turned like the works of a drawbridge while thirty stories overhead was a square of clear blue sky. On the panel in front of me were two silver buttons. One that said Now and one that said Never.

It was seven o'clock and the bullpen was empty. On my desk sat the letter to Bette Davis's agent, its flaws faithfully transcribed and carefully proofed. I read the letter one more time, then I put a fresh piece of stationery in the typewriter and fixed it. I left both versions on Mr. Tate's desk with a handwritten cover note indicating that given his time constraints, I had taken the liberty of preparing a second draft.

Mr. Tate didn't buzz until the end of the day. When I went in, he had the two versions of the letter sitting side by side on his desk, both of them unsigned. He didn't invite me to sit. He looked me over like a model student who's been caught slipping out of the dorm after curfew. Which in a way is just what I was.

—Tell me about your personal situation, Kontent, he said at last.

—I'm sorry, Mr. Tate. What is it you would like to know?

He leaned back in his chair.

—I can see you're unmarried. But do you like men? Do you have children stashed away? Siblings you're raising?

—Yes, no, and no.

Mr. Tate smiled coolly.

—How would you describe your ambitions?

—They're evolving.

He nodded his head. He pointed to the draft of an article that was on his desk.

—This is something of a profile by Mr. Cabot. Have you read any of his pieces?

—A few.

—How would you characterize them? Stylistically, I mean.

Despite its wordiness, I could tell that Mr. Tate generally appreciated Cabot's work. Cabot had a good instinct for the intersection of gossip and history and he seemed to be an unusually effective interviewer—charming people into answering questions that were better left unanswered.

—I think he's read too much Henry James, I said.

Tate nodded for a second. Then he handed me the draft.

—See if you can make him sound a little more like Hemingway.

CHAPTER SEVENTEEN

Read All About It

Two nights later, an unseasonal snow fell in my dreams. Ashlike and serene, it settled over a city block lined with tenements and Coney Island amusements and the brightly colored minarets of the church where my grandparents were wed. Standing on the steps of the church, I reached out to touch the doors—so blue they could have been fashioned from planks of heaven. While somewhere on the periphery, all of twenty-two, her hair in barrettes, a safecracker's satchel in hand, my mother looked left and looked right and then turned the corner at a sprint. I reached out to knock on the door, but it knocked first.

—Police, a weary voice called. Open up.

. . .

The clock read two in the morning. I put on a robe and cracked the door. In the stairwell stood a top-heavy cop in a plain brown suit.

—Sorry to wake you, he said not sounding it. I'm Sergeant Finneran. This here's Detective Tilson.

It must have taken me a while to hear them, because Tilson was sitting on the stairs interrogating his nails.

—Do you mind if we come in?

—Yes.

—Do you know a Katherine Kontent?

—Sure, I said.

—Does she live here?

I pulled my robe tighter.

—Yes.

—Is she your roommate?

—No . . . I'm she.

Finneran looked back at Tilson and the detective looked up from his nails as if I'd finally roused his interest.

—Hey, I said. What's this all about?

The station house was quiet. Tilson and Finneran led me down a back stair into a narrow passage. A young cop opened a steel door that led to the holding cells where the air smelled of mold and ammonia. Eve was laid out like a rag doll on a cot without a blanket. Over a little black dress, she was wearing my flapper's jacket, the same one that she'd worn the night of the accident.

According to Tilson, she had passed out drunk in an alley off Bleecker Street. When one of the beat cops found her, she didn't have a purse or a wallet, but in the pocket of the coat they found—believe it or not—my library card.

—Is that her? Tilson asked.

—That's her.

—You said she lives uptown. What do you figure she was doing around Bleecker Street?

—She likes jazz.

—Don't we all, said Finneran.

I stood by the door waiting for Tilson to open the cell.

—Sergeant, he said, get a matron to put her in the showers. Miss Kontent, why don't you come with me.

Tilson took me back upstairs into a little room with a table, chairs, no windows. It was obviously an interrogation room. Once we both had a paper cup of coffee in front of us, he leaned back in his chair.

—So, how do you know this . . .

—Eve.

—Right. Evelyn Ross.

—We were roommates.

—Is that right. When was that?

—Until January.

Finneran came in. He nodded at Tilson and then supported the wall.

—So when Officer Mackey roused your friend in the alley, Tilson continued, she wouldn't tell him her name. Why do you think that was?

—Maybe he didn't ask nicely.

Tilson smiled.

—What does your friend do?

—She's not working right now.

—How about you?

—I'm a secretary.

Tilson put his fingers in the air and pretended to type.

—That's it.

—So what happened to her?

—Happened?

—You know. The scars.

—She was in a car accident.

—She must have been going pretty fast.

—We were hit from behind. She went through the windshield.

—You were in the accident too!

—That's right.

—What if I were to say the name Billy Bowers. Mean anything to you?

—No. Should it?

—How about Geronimo Schaffer?

—No.

—Okay, Kathy. Can I call you Kathy?

—Anything but Kathy.

—Okay then, Kate. You seem smart.

—Thanks.

—It's not the first time I've seen a girl end up like your friend.

—Drunk?

—Sometimes they get battered about. Sometimes it's a broken nose. Sometimes . . .

He let his voice drift off for emphasis. I smiled.

—You're way off the page on this one, Detective.

—Maybe. But a girl can get in over her head. I understand that. All she wants is to make a living. Like any of us. It's not how she thought she was going to end up. But then who ends up like they thought they would? They call em dreams for a reason, right?

Finneran grunted in appreciation of Tilson's turn of phrase.

When they brought me back to the front of the station house, Eve was there slumped on a bench. The matron stood by in full uniform. She helped me get Eve into the back of a cab while Tilson and Finneran looked on, hands in pockets. As we drove away, Eve with eyes closed began mimicking the sound of a trumpet.

—Evey. What's going on?

She gave a girlish laugh.

—Extra! Extra! Read all about it!

Then she leaned on my shoulder and purred herself to sleep.

She looked done in, all right. I stroked her hair like she was a little kid. It was still wet from the precinct showers.

At Eleventh Street, I gave the cabby an extra buck to help me get her up the stairs. We dumped her on my bed with her legs dangling off the mattress. I called the apartment at the Beresford but no one answered. So I got a pot of warm water from the kitchen and washed her feet. Then I took off her dress and tucked her in bed in a camisole that cost more than my entire outfit, shoes included.

Back at the station house, after the desk sergeant got me to sign for Eve's belongings, he had poured a single item from a large manila envelope. It fell on the desk with a delicate clunk. It was an engagement ring and it had a diamond you could skate on. From the second I picked it up, it made my palms sweat. So I took it from my pocket now and put it on the kitchen table. The flapper's jacket, I threw that in the trash.

Looking at Eve asleep, I wondered what the hell was going on. How did she end up drunk in an alley? What happened to her shoes? And where was Tinker? Whatever their story, Eve was breathing easy now—for the moment forgetful, vulnerable, at peace.

It's a purposeful irony of life, I suppose, that we never get to see ourselves in that state. We can only pay witness to our waking reflection, which to one degree or another is always fretting or afraid. Maybe that's why young parents find it so beguiling to spy on their children when they're fast asleep.

———

In the morning as we drank coffee and ate fried eggs with Tabasco, Eve was her chipper self—telling me what a bore the south of France had been with its moldy buildings and crowded beaches and Wyss making a scene over every von This and von That. If it weren't for the croissant and casinos, she said, she would have walked all the way home.

I let her chatter on for a while, but when she asked me how work was going, I pushed the ring across the table.

—Oh, she said. We're talking about that.

—I think so.

She nodded a second and then shrugged.

—Tinker proposed.

—That's great, Eve. Congrats.

She made a startled face.

—Are you kidding? For Christ's sake, Katey. I didn't accept.

Then she brought me up-to-date. It was just like Generous had said: Tinker had taken her out on the yawl with the bubbly and the chicken. After lunch they went for a swim, toweled off, then he got down on one knee and plucked the ring from the saltcellar. She turned him down on the spot. Actually, her exact words were: *Why don't you just drive me into another lamppost?*

When Tinker presented the ring, she wouldn't even touch it. He had to close it in her palm and insist she think it over. But she didn't need to. She slept like a baby. Then she got up at dawn, stuffed an overnight bag, and slipped out the back door while Tinker was sound asleep.

Ambitious, determined, no-nonsense, whatever you wanted to call her, Eve never ceased to surprise. I thought of Eve six months earlier dressed in white, draped across the couch in Tinker's apartment dissolving barbiturates in tepid gin. From that lotus-eating repose, she had roused herself to run the city ragged as the rest of us watched with varying degrees of admiration, envy, and contempt, convinced she was angling for a proposal. And all the time, she was laying in wait for everyone's smug assessments like a cat in the barnyard grass.

—I wish you'd been there, she said with a nostalgic smile. You would've peed in your pants. I mean, he takes a week to engineer this song and dance and as soon as I tell him no, he sails his buddy's yacht right into the ground. He didn't know what to do with himself. He must have gone in and out of that cabin a hundred times looking for a flare gun. He trimmed the sails. Climbed the mast. He even got out and pushed.

—What were you doing?

—I just lay there on the deck with the rest of the champagne. I was listening to the whistle of the breeze, the flap of the sails, the lap of the waves.

Eve buttered a piece of toast as she recalled it, her expression almost dreamy.

—It was the first three hours of peace I'd had in half a year, she said.

Then she stuck the knife in the butter like it was a banderilla in the back of a bull.

—The irony, of course, is that we don't even like each other.

—Come on.

—You know what I mean. We've had some fun. But mostly, it's he says po-tay-to and I say po-tah-to.

—You think that's the way he saw it?

—Only more so.

—Then why'd he propose?

She took a sip of her coffee and scowled at the cup.

—What do you say we liven these up?

—Suit yourself. But I've got work in thirty minutes.

She found a fifth of whiskey in a cabinet and Irished her cup. When she sat back down, she tried to change the subject.

—Where the hell did all the books come from?

—Not so fast, Sis. I'm serious. If the two of you were so po-tay-to po-tah-to, why did he propose?

She shrugged and put her coffee down.

—It was my mistake. I got pregnant and I told him so when we got to England. I should have kept my trap shut. If he was a pain in the neck when I came out of the hospital, you can just imagine what he was like after that.

Eve lit a cigarette. She tilted her head back and shot the smoke toward the ceiling. Then she shook her head.

—Watch out for boys who think they owe you something. They'll drive you the craziest.

—So what are you going to do?

—With my life?

—No. With the baby.

—Oh. I took care of that in Paris. I just hadn't got around to telling him. I was going to find some way to cushion it. But in the end, I had to let him have it.

We were quiet for a moment. I stood to clear the plates.

—I had no choice, Eve explained. He'd cornered me. We were a mile at sea.

I turned on the tap.

—Katey. If you start washing those dishes like my mother, I'm going to throw myself out the window.

I came back to my seat. She reached across the table and squeezed my hand.

—Don't look so disappointed in me. I can't bear it—not from you.

—You're just catching me off guard.

—I can see that. But you've got to understand. I was brought up to raise children, pigs & corn and to thank the Good Lord for the privilege. But I've learned a thing or two since the accident. And I like it just fine on this side of the windshield.

It was like she'd said all along: She was willing to be under anything, as long as it wasn't somebody's thumb.

She tilted her head to study my expression more carefully.

—Are you going to be okay with this?

—Sure.

—I mean, I'm the fucking Catholic, right?

I laughed.

—Yeah. You're the fucking Catholic.

She tamped out her cigarette and pulled back the lid on the pack. There was one more left. She lit it and threw the match over her shoulder; then she held it out to me like an Indian chief. I took a drag and handed it back. We were both silent, trading the tobacco.

—What are you going to do now? I finally asked.

—I don't know. I've got the Beresford to myself for a bit, but I'm not going to stay. My parents have been hounding me to come home. Maybe I'll pay them a visit.

—What's Tinker going to do?

—He said he might go back to Europe.

—To fight the Fascists in Spain?

Eve looked at me in disbelief and then laughed.

—Shit, Sis. He's going to fight the waves on the Côte d'Azur.

♦   ♦   ♦

Three nights later, while I was undressing for bed, the telephone rang.

Ever since seeing Eve, I'd been expecting it—a call late at night, when New York was in shadows and the sun was rising a thousand miles away over a cobalt sea. It was a phone call that but for a patch of ice on Park Avenue might have come six months, or a lifetime, before. I felt my heart race a little. I slipped my shirt back over my head and answered the phone.

—Hello?

But it was a weary patrician voice.

—Is this Katherine?

— . . . Mr. Ross?

—I'm sorry to bother you so late, Katherine. I just wanted to find out if by any chance . . .

There was silence on the other end of the line. I could hear twenty years of upbringing and a few hundred miles of Indiana trying to contain his emotions.

—Mr. Ross?

—I'm sorry. I should explain. Apparently Eve's relationship with this Tinker fellow has come to an end.

—Yes. I saw Eve a few days ago and she told me.

—Ah. Well. I . . . That is, Sarah and I . . . received a cable from her saying that she was coming home. But when we went to meet her train, she wasn't there. At first, we thought we had simply missed her on the platform. But we couldn't find her in the restaurant or the waiting room. So we went to the stationmaster to see if she was on the manifest. He didn't want to tell us. It's against their policy and what have you. But eventually, he confirmed that she had boarded the train in New York. So you see, it wasn't that she wasn't on the train. She just didn't get off.

It took us a few days to get the conductor on the phone. By that time he was in Denver headed back east. But he remembered her—because of the scar. And he said that when the train was approaching Chicago, she had paid to extend her ticket. To Los Angeles.

Mr. Ross was quiet for a moment, collecting himself.

—So you can see, Katherine, that we're quite confused. I tried to reach Tinker, but it seems he's gone abroad.

—Mr. Ross, I don't know what to tell you.

—Katherine, I wouldn't ask you to betray a confidence. If Eve doesn't want us to know where she is, I accept that. She's a grown woman. She's free to chart her course. It's just that we're parents. You'll understand one day. We don't want to meddle. We just want to make sure that she's all right.

—Mr. Ross, if I knew where Eve was, I'd tell you—even if she'd sworn me to silence.

Mr. Ross gave a truncated sigh, the more heartbreaking for its brevity.

What a scene that must have been: Having gotten up at dawn to make the journey to Chicago, the Rosses probably drove with the radio off, exchanging only the occasional word—not because they were some cliché of a married couple that time has turned into strangers but because in that closest of emotional alignments they were dwelling in the bitter-turned-sweet sense that their daughter, prone to self-reliance, bruised by New York, was at long last coming home. Through the revolving doors they walked, dressed as for a Sunday service, making their way through the democratic melee of the arriving and departing, a little anxious but on the whole exhilarated to be fulfilling this mission essential not simply to their parenthood but to their species. How devastating it must have been—that first inkling that their daughter wasn't going to be there, after all.

Meanwhile, in another railway station over a thousand miles away—one filled with color and light, its architecture reflecting the optimistic modern style of the West rather than the brooding industry of America's great nineteenth-century depots—Eve would disembark. Without a trunk to pick up from the porter, she would limp out onto a palm-lined street with no particular destination in mind, looking like a starlet from a rougher, more unforgiving land.

I felt a great wave of sympathy for Mr. Ross.

—I'm considering hiring a Pinkerton to look for her, he said, obviously unsure of whether this was the appropriate step. Does she know anybody in Los Angeles?

—No, Mr. Ross. I don't think she knows a soul in California.

But if Mr. Ross were to hire a detective, I thought to myself, then I'd have some advice for him. I'd tell him to go to all the hock shops within ten blocks of the train station looking for a skateable engagement ring and a chandelier earring missing its pair—because that's where the future of Evelyn Ross had just commenced.

The next night, Mr. Ross called again. This time, he didn't ask any questions. He was calling to give me an update: Earlier that day he had talked to a few of the girls at Mrs. Martingale's—none of them had heard from Eve. He had contacted the Missing Persons Bureau in L.A., but as soon as they learned that Eve was of age and had bought her ticket, they explained that she did not meet the legal definition of missing. To comfort Mrs. Ross, he had also checked the hospitals and emergency rooms.

How was Mrs. Ross bearing up? She was like someone in mourning, only worse. When a mother loses a daughter, she grieves over the future that her daughter will never have, but she can take solace in memories of close-knit days. But when your daughter runs away, it is the fond memories that have been laid to rest; and your daughter's future, alive and well, recedes from you like a wave drawing out to sea.

The third time Mr. Ross called, he didn't have much of an update. He said that while going through some of Eve's letters (in search of mentioned friends who might be of help) he had come across the one in which Eve described meeting me for the first time: *Last night, I spilled a plate of noodles on one of the girls; and she's turned out to be a real jim dandy.* Mr. Ross and I shared a good laugh over it.

—I had forgotten that Eve was in a single when she first moved in, he said. When did you two become roommates?

And I could see the problem I had gotten myself into.

Mr. Ross was in mourning too, but he had to be strong for his wife. So he was looking for someone he could reminisce with, someone who knew Eve well but who was safely in the distance. And I fit the bill just perfectly.

I didn't want to be uncharitable, and having this little chat wasn't such an inconvenience, but how many chats would follow? For all I knew, he was a slow mender. Or worse, he was someone who would savor his grief rather than let it go. How was I going to extricate myself when the time came? I wasn't going to stop answering my phone. Was I going to have to start sounding mildly rude, until he got the message?

When the phone rang a few nights later, I adopted the voice of a girl with one hand on her key chain and the other through the sleeve of her coat.

—Hello!
—Katey?
. . .
—Tinker?
—For a second I thought I had the wrong number, he said. It's good to hear your voice.
. . .
—I saw Eve, I said.
. . .
—I thought you might have.
He gave a halfhearted laugh.
—I've sure made a hash of it in 1938.
—You and the rest of the world.
—No. I get special credit for this one. Since the first week of January, every decision I've made has been wrong. I think Eve has been fed up with me for months.

As a rueful parable, he told me how in France he had taken to going to bed early and rising with the sun for a swim. Dawn was so beautiful, he said, and in such a different way from the sunset, that he had asked Eve to watch it with him. In response, she started wearing eyeshades and slept every day until lunch. Then, on the last night, when Tinker was climbing into bed, she went off to a casino by herself and played roulette until five in the morning—coming up the drive, shoes in hand, just in time to join him on the beach.

Tinker related this as if it was somewhat embarrassing for the both of them; but I didn't see it that way. Whatever the limitations of Tinker and Eve's relationship, however expedient or imperfect or tenuous it had been, neither of them had reason to be humbled by that little tale. As far as I was concerned, the notion of Tinker rising alone for a sunrise that he wanted to share, and of Eve showing up at the very last minute from the other side of a night on the town, spoke to the very best in both of them.

In each of the various phone conversations that I had imagined having with Tinker, he had sounded different. In one he had sounded broken. In another confounded. In another contrite. But in all of them he had sounded unsettled, having come full speed through a ringer of his own design. Yet, now that I had him on the phone, he didn't sound unsettled at all. Though obviously chastened, Tinker's voice was also even and at ease. It had an ineffable almost enviable quality to it. It took me a moment to realize that it was the sound of relief. He sounded like one who is sitting on the curb in a strange city in the aftermath of a hotel fire, having nearly lost nothing but his life.

But broken, confounded, relaxed, or relieved—however his voice sounded, it wasn't coming from across the sea. It was as clear as a radio broadcast.

—Tinker, where are you?

He was alone at the Wolcotts' camp in the Adirondacks. He had spent the week walking in the woods and rowing on the lake thinking about the past six months, but now he was worried that if he didn't talk to someone he might go a little crazy. So he was wondering if I'd be interested in coming up for the day. Or I could take the train on Friday after work and spend the weekend. He said the house was amazing and the lake was lovely and

—Tinker, I said. You don't have to give me reasons.

After hanging up the phone, I stood for a while looking out my window wondering if I should have told him no. In the doleful court behind my building a patchwork of windows was all that separated me from a hundred muted lives being led without mystery or menace or magic. In point of fact, I suppose I didn't know Tinker Grey much better than I knew any of them; and yet, somehow, I felt like I'd known him all my life.

I crossed the room.

From a pile of British authors, I pulled out *Great Expectations*. There, tucked among the pages of the twentieth chapter was Tinker's letter describing the little church across the sea, with its mariner's widow, its berry-toting wrestler, its schoolgirls laughing like seagulls—and its implicit celebration of the commonplace. I tried to smooth the wrinkles in the tissuelike paper. Then I sat down and read it for the umpteenth time.

CHAPTER EIGHTEEN

The Now and Here

The Wolcotts' "camp" was a two-story mansion in the Arts & Crafts style. At one in the morning, it loomed from the shadows like an elegant beast come to the water's edge to drink.

We went up the lazy wooden steps of the porch into a sprawling family room with a stone fireplace that you could stand in. The floors were knotty pine and they were covered with Navajo rugs woven in every imaginable shade of red. Sturdy wooden chairs were arranged in groups of two and four so that in high season the different generations of Wolcotts could play cards or read books or assemble jigsaw puzzles partly in private and partly in kin. All was cast in the warm yellow light of mica-shaded lamps. I remembered Wallace saying that though he spent just a few weeks a year in the Adirondacks, it always felt like home—and it wasn't hard to see why. You could just imagine where the Christmas tree would go come December.

Tinker began giving an enthusiastic history of the place. He mentioned something about the Indians in the region and the aesthetic schooling of the architect. But I had started the day at six and put in ten hours at *Gotham*. So with the smell of smoke in the air and the rumble of thunder in the distance, my eyelids rose and fell like the bow of a boat on its mooring.

—I'm sorry, he said with a smile. I'm just excited to see you. We'll catch up in the morning.

He grabbed my bag and led me up the stairs to the second floor, where the hallway was lined with doors. The house must have slept twenty or more.

—Why don't you take this one, he said, stepping into a little room with a pair of twin beds.

He placed my bag on the bureau beside a porcelain washbasin. Though the old gas lamps on the wall glowed with electricity, he lit a kerosene lantern on the bedside table.

—There's fresh water in the pitcher. I'm at the other end of the hall, if you need anything.

He gave me a squeeze of the hands and an *I'm so glad you came.* Then he retreated into the hall.

As I unpacked my things, I could hear him going back down the stairs to the family room, securing the front door, scattering the embers in the hearth, clicking off lights. Then, from the far end of the house there was the heavy thunk of a switch being thrown. The remote rumbling that I had thought was thunder ceased and all the lights in the house went out. Tinker's steps bounded back up the stairs and headed down the opposite hall.

I undressed in the nineteenth-century lamplight. My shadow on the wall went through the motions of folding my blouse and brushing my hair. I put my book on the bedside table with no intention of reading it and climbed under the covers. The bed must have been built when Americans were smaller because my feet went straight to the baseboard. It was surprisingly cold, so I unfolded the patchwork quilt that graced the foot of the bed. Then I opened my book, after all.

Walking into Penn Station earlier that evening, I had realized I had nothing to read; so at a newsstand I surveyed the paperback fare (romance novels, westerns, adventure stories) and settled on an Agatha Christie. At the time, I hadn't read many mystery novels. Call it snobbery. But once on the train, after staring out the window to my limit, I waded into Mrs. Christie's world and was pleasantly surprised by how diverting it was. This particular crime was set on a British estate and the heroine was a foxhunting heiress who by page 45 had already had two brushes with disaster.

I turned to chapter eight. Several mildly suspicious people were having tea in a parlor. They were talking about a young local who had gone to fight in the Boer War and never returned. There were daylilies from a secret admirer in a vase on the piano. The whole scene was just remote enough in time and place that I had to go back to the beginning of the seventh paragraph a second time, then a third. After a fourth try, I turned down the wick and the room went dark.

With the heaviness of the quilt weighing on my chest, I could feel every beat of my heart—as if it was still keeping time, measuring the days like a metronome set somewhere on the finely graduated scale between impatience and serenity. For a while, I lay there listening to the house, to the wind outside, to the hoot of what must have been an owl. Then I finally fell asleep, listening for the footsteps that weren't going to come.

◆ ◆ ◆

—Rise and shine.

Tinker was standing in the doorway.

—What time is it? I asked.

—Eight.

—Is the house on fire?

—This is late for camp living.

He threw me a towel.

—I've got breakfast cooking. Come on down when you're ready.

I got up and splashed water on my face. Looking out the window, you could tell it was going to be a cold, bright, cusp-of-fall kind of day. So I put on my best foxhunting heiress outfit and took my book in hand, assuming the morning would be spent before a fire.

In the hallway, family photos hung from floor to ceiling just like in Wallace's apartment. It took me a few minutes, but I finally found pictures of Wallace as a boy: The first was an unfortunate snapshot of him at six in a French sailor's suit; but the second was Wallace at ten or eleven in a birch bark canoe with his grandfather, showing off the catch of the day. From the expressions on their faces, you would have thought they were holding up the world by the gills.

Drawn by other photographs, I continued past the staircase to the western end of the hall. The very last room was the one that Tinker had claimed. He was sleeping in the bottom of a bunk bed! There was a book on his bedside table too. With Hercule Poirot whispering in my ear, I ventured quietly in and picked it up. It was *Walden*. A five of clubs marked the reader's progress—though from the colors of the underlinings you could tell it was at least a second reading.

> Simplicity, simplicity, simplicity! I say, let your affairs be as two or three, and not a hundred or a thousand; instead of a million count half a dozen, and keep your accounts on your thumbnail. In the midst of this chopping sea of civilized life, such are the clouds and storms and quicksands and thousand-and-one items to be allowed for, that a man has to live, if he would not founder and go to the bottom and not make his port at all, by dead reckoning, and he must be a great calculator indeed who succeeds. . . .

The ghost of Henry David Thoreau frowned upon me, as well he should. I returned the book, tiptoed to the landing, and headed down the stairs.

I found Tinker in the kitchen frying ham and eggs in a big black skillet. Two places were set at a small kitchen table with a white enamel top. Somewhere in the house there must have been an oak table for twelve, because this little one couldn't handle more than a cook, a governess, and three of the Wolcotts' grandchildren.

Tinker's outfit was embarrassingly similar to my own—khaki pants and a white shirt—though he was wearing heavy leather boots. After serving up the plates, he poured the coffee and sat across from me. He looked well. His skin had lost the pampered tan of the Mediterranean, taking on a rougher hue, and his hair had curled with the humidity of summer. The fact that his beard was a week old was to his advantage—having outgrown the appearance of a hangover but having yet to reach that of a Hatfield or McCoy. His demeanor reflected that same unhurried state that I had heard on the phone. He grinned at me as I ate.

—What? I said finally.

—I was just trying to picture you as a redhead.

—Sorry, I laughed. My redhead days have come and gone.

—It's my loss. What was it like?

—I think it brought out the Mata Hari in me.

—We'll have to lure her back.

Once we'd finished, cleared, and cleaned, Tinker slapped his hands together.

—What do you say we go for a hike?

—I'm not the hiking sort.

—Oh, I think that's exactly what you are. You just don't know it yet. And the view of the lake from Pinyon Peak is breathtaking.

—I hope you're not going to be this insufferably upbeat all weekend.

Tinker laughed.

—There's a risk of it.

—Besides, I said, I didn't bring any boots.

—Ah! So that's it, is it?

On the other side of the family room, he led me down a hall past a billiard room and swung open a door with a flourish. Inside was a muck room with slickers on pegs and hats on shelves and boots of all shapes and sizes lined along the baseboard. From Tinker's expression you would have thought he was Ali Baba revealing the riches of the forty thieves.

◆ ◆ ◆

A trail behind the house led through a grove of pines into a deeper wood of oaks or elms or some other towering American timber. For the first hour, it was a gradual incline and we walked shoulder to shoulder through the shade at an easy pace, conversing like friends from youth for whom every exchange is an extension of the last, regardless of the passage of time.

We talked about Wallace, echoing each other's affection for him. We also talked about Eve. I told him about her escape to California, and with a friendly laugh he said the news was surprising right up until the moment you heard it. He said that Hollywood had no idea what it was in for, and that within the year Eve would be either a movie star or a studio chief.

To hear him talk about Eve's future you wouldn't have had an inkling of what had just transpired between them. You would have assumed they were old familiars with a fond and unspoiled camaraderie. And maybe that was just about right. Maybe for Tinker their relationship had been reset to January third. Maybe for him the last half a year had been snipped from the chain of events like a poorly scripted scene in a film.

As we walked farther, our conversation became intermittent like the sunlight through the woods. Squirrels scattered before us among the tree trunks and yellow-tailed birds zipped from branch to branch. The air smelled of sumac and sassafras and other sweet-sounding words. And I began to think that maybe Tinker was right: Maybe I was a hiker.

But the slope began to grow steep, then steeper, and steeper still until it was the pitch of a staircase. We were climbing single file in silence. An hour went by, maybe four. My boots became a size too small and my left heel felt like I had stepped on a frying pan. I fell twice, scuffing my foxhunting khakis, and I had long since sweat through my heiress's shirt. I found myself wondering if I had enough self-control to ask *How much farther?* in a casual, disinterested, offhand sort of way. But then the trees started thinning and the grade mellowed, and suddenly we were on a rocky peak exposed to the open sky with a view to the horizon unmarked by man.

Far below us, a mile wide and five miles long, the lake looked like a giant black reptile crawling across the wilds of New York.

—There, he said. You see?

And I could see. I could see why Tinker, feeling that his life was in disarray, had chosen to come here.

—Just as it looked to Natty Bumppo, I said, taking a seat on the hard stone.

Tinker smiled that I remembered who he had wanted to be for a day.

—Not far from it, he agreed, pulling sandwiches and a canteen from his knapsack.

Then he sat down a few feet away—at a gentleman's distance.

As we ate, he reminisced about when his family had spent Julys in Maine and he and his brother had hiked the Appalachian Trail for days at a time—outfitted with the tent and compasses and jackknives that their mother had given them for Christmas and that they had waited six long months to put to use.

We still hadn't spoken about St. George's or the change in Tinker's circumstances as a youth. I certainly wasn't going to bring it up. But when he talked about hiking in Maine with his brother, he was making it clear in his own way that those were halcyon days preceding less fortunate times.

When we finished lunch, I lay down with Tinker's pack under my head and he broke sticks and tried to toss them onto a small bed of moss twenty feet in the distance, in the manner of a schoolboy for whom no walk home is without its world championship. His sleeves were rolled up and he had freckles on his forearms from exposure to the summer sun.

—So were you a Fenimore Cooper fan in general? I asked.

—Oh, I must have read *Last of the Mohicans* and *Deerslayer* three different times. But then, I loved all the adventure books: *Treasure Island* . . . *20,000 Leagues Under the Sea* . . . *The Call of the Wild* . . .

—*Robinson Crusoe*.

He smiled.

—You know, I actually picked up *Walden* after you said you'd want to be marooned with it.

—What did you think? I asked.

—Well, at first I wasn't sure I was going to make it. Four hundred pages of a man alone in a cabin philosophizing on human history, trying to strip life to its essentials . . .

—But what did you think in the end?

Tinker stopped breaking sticks and looked into the distance.

—In the end—I thought it was the greatest adventure of them all.

At around three, a bank of blue gray clouds appeared in the distance and the temperature began to drop. So Tinker gave me an Irish sweater from his pack and we headed back down the trail, trying to keep a few strides ahead of the weather. We had just gotten to the grove of trees when it began to sprinkle, and we were vaulting up the steps of the house with the first clap of thunder.

Tinker built a fire in the great fireplace and we settled down on the Navajo rug at the edge of the hearthstone. The warmth began to bring out the starburst blushes on his cheeks as he cooked pork and beans and coffee right over the embers. I pulled his sweater off over my head and the wet wool gave off a warm, earthy smell that recalled another hour. It took me a moment to realize it was that snowy night when we had snuck into the Capitol Theatre and I had found myself in the embrace of Tinker's shearling coat.

As I was drinking a second cup of coffee, Tinker poked at the fire with a stick dislodging sparks.

—Tell me something that no one knows about *you*, I said.

He laughed, as if I was kidding; but then he seemed to think about it.

—All right, he said, turning a little toward me. You know that day we bumped into each other at that diner across from Trinity Church?

—Yes . . .

—I followed you there.

I slugged him in the shoulder like Fran would have.

—You did not!

—I know, he said. It's terrible. But it's true! Eve had mentioned the name of your firm, so just before noon I went across from your building and hid behind a newsstand to see if I could catch you going to lunch. I was waiting for forty minutes and it was freezing.

I laughed, remembering the bright red tips of his ears.

—What prompted you to do that?

—I couldn't stop thinking about you.

—Blah, I said.

—No, I'm serious.

He looked at me with a gentle smile.

—Right from the first, I could see a calmness in you—that sort of inner tranquility that they write about in books, but that almost no one seems to possess. I was wondering to myself: *How does she do that?* And I figured it could only come from having no regrets—from having made choices with . . . such poise and purpose. It stopped me in my tracks a little. And I just couldn't wait to see it again.

By the time we went upstairs, having turned off the lights and scattered the embers, we both looked ready for a good night's sleep. On the steps, our shadows swung back and forth with the movement of the lanterns in our hands. As we reached the landing, we bumped into each other and he apologized. We stood awkwardly for a second, then after giving me a friendly kiss, he went west and I went east. We closed our doors and undressed. We climbed into our little beds and read a few aimless pages before dousing our lights.

In the dark, as I pulled up the quilt I became conscious of the wind. Rolling down from Pinyon Peak it was shaking the trees and the windowpanes as if it too was restless for resolution.

There is an oft-quoted passage in *Walden,* in which Thoreau exhorts us to find our pole star and to follow it unwaveringly as would a sailor or a fugitive slave. It's a thrilling sentiment—one so obviously worthy of our aspirations. But even if you had the discipline to maintain the true course, the real problem, it has always seemed to me, is how to know in which part of the heavens your star resides.

But there is another passage in *Walden* that has stayed with me as well. In it, Thoreau says that men mistakenly think of truth as being remote—behind the farthest star, before Adam and after the reckoning. When in fact, *all these times and places and occasions are now and here.* In a way, this celebration of the now and here seems to contradict the exhortation to follow one's star. But it is equally persuasive. And oh so much more attainable.

I pulled Tinker's sweater back on over my head, tiptoed down the hall, and stopped outside his room.

I listened to the creaking of the house, to the rain on the roof, to the breathing on the other side of the door. Careful not to make a sound, I put a hand on the knob. In sixty seconds it was going to be the midpoint between the beginning and the end of time. And in that moment, there would be a chance to witness, to partake in, to succumb to the now and here.

In exactly sixty seconds.

Fifty. Forty. Thirty.

On your mark

Get set

Go

◆ ◆ ◆

On Sunday afternoon when Tinker took me to the depot, I didn't know when I would be seeing him again. Over breakfast he said he was going to spend a little more time at the Wolcotts' to sort things out. He didn't mention how long that would take and I didn't ask. I wasn't a schoolgirl.

I boarded the train, walked a few cars ahead, and sat on the wooded side of the tracks so that we wouldn't have to go through the motions of waving. Once the train was under way, I lit a cigarette and dug in my bag for the Agatha Christie. I hadn't gotten much further than the seventh paragraph of chapter VIII and I was looking forward to pressing on. But as I pulled the book out of my bag, I saw something jutting from between the pages. It was a playing card torn in two—the ace of hearts. On the face of the card was written: *Mata—Meet me at the Stork Club on Monday the 26th at 9PM. And come alone.*

After memorizing its contents, I held the message over an ashtray and lit it on fire.

CHAPTER NINETEEN

The Road to Kent

On Monday the 26th of September, I phoned in sick.

The previous week had been unrelenting. On the twentieth, the drafts of four features vying for our first cover were delivered and Mason Tate hated them all. He threw the pages over the bullpen the way the Russians used to shoot the body parts of interlopers out of the Kremlin cannons back in the direction of their homelands. To better express his dissatisfaction, the next three nights he kept the entire staff at the office until after ten. Alley and I put in half the Sabbath to boot.

So, having dialed in sick, a wise young woman would have climbed right back in bed. But in as much as the skies were sunny, the air was brisk, and this particular September day promised to be a long one, I aimed to squander every last minute of it.

Showered and dressed, I went to a café in the Village and drank three cups of Italian coffee topped with steamed milk and shaved chocolate. I drew & quartered a pastry and read the paper cover to cover. I completed the crossword square to square.

What a transcendent diversion the crossword can be. A four-letter word for *solo* beginning and ending in A. A four-letter word for *sword* beginning and ending in E. A four-letter word for *miscellany* beginning and ending in O. ARIA, EPEE, OLIO—no matter how vestigial these words are in the body of common English, watching them fit so neatly into the puzzle's machinery, one feels as the archaeologist must feel when assembling a skeleton—the end of the thighbone fitting so precisely into the socket of the hip bone that it simply has to confirm the existence of an orderly universe, if not a divine intention.

The last squares to be filled in the puzzle were ECLAT—a five-letter word for a *brilliant success or ostentatious display*. Taking this as a favorable omen, I left the café and went around the corner to Isabella's hair salon.

—How would you like it? the new girl Luella asked.

—Like a movie star.

—Turner or Garbo?

—Anyone you like. As long as she's a redhead.

Historically, once in the hands of a hairdresser, I had done whatever necessary to stymie conversation: grimacing; sleeping; staring blankly into the mirror; once I even feigned ignorance of English. I just wasn't much of a small-talker. But today, when Luella started rattling on about Hollywood romances inaccurately, I found myself setting her straight. Carole Lombard wasn't back with William Powell; she was still with Clark Gable. And Marlene Dietrich didn't call Gloria Swanson a has-been; it was the other way around. I was surprising the both of us with the extent of my knowledge. It must have seemed like I had followed the celebrity papers for years. But they were just tidbits I had unintentionally absorbed during the workday. When proofreading, these nuts and bolts of the Hollywood conveyer belt didn't seem so titillating. But they were titillating to Luella. At one point she even called over two of the other girls so I could tell them about Katharine Hepburn and Howard Hughes—since they'd never believe it if they didn't hear it straight from the horse's mouth. It was the first time in my life I'd been called the horse's mouth and it didn't seem so bad. I began to think that maybe I was a small-talker after all. A hiker and a talker! It was a season of personal discovery.

Once I was under the dryer, I pulled Agatha Christie out of my bag and proceeded unhurriedly toward the dénouement.

Poirot had risen unusually early. He had gone to the third floor of the manor and entered the old nursery. Having run his gloved fingertip along the sills, he opened the westernmost window, took a brass paperweight from his jacket (which he had pocketed in the library in chapter fourteen), and shot it laterally across the slate roof up over the adjoining dormer. Like the ball in a Chinese lottery, the paperweight caromed off the far side of the dormer and rattled down a story until it hit the dormer of the master bedroom, where it then angled off over the living room, spilled onto the eaves of the conservatory, and disappeared into the garden.

Why Poirot would pursue such an experiment one could only imagine.

Unless . . .

Unless he suspected that someone, having shot the heiress's fiancé, had run up the stairs to the nursery and propelled the gun from the window over the adjacent dormer so that it would career across the west wing and into the garden, prompting everyone to think that the gunmen had dropped it there during his escape. This would allow the killer to come down the stairs from the opposite end of the house asking demurely what all the commotion was about.

But to accomplish this, one would probably have had to experiment with the angles of the roof—as a child would with a ball. And the only one who had come down the stairs after the shooting was . . . our heroine the heiress?

Uh, oh.

—Let's take a gander, said Luella.

Coming out of Isabella's, I remembered Bitsy's promise to be fast friends and decided to give her a buzz.

—Can you meet for lunch?

—Where are you calling from? she whispered instinctively.

—A phone booth in the Village.

—Are you playing hooky?

—More or less.

—Then of course I can.

Getting right into the spirit of things, she suggested we meet in Chinatown at Chinoiserie.

—I can be there in twenty minutes, she promised gamely from the Upper East Side.

I figured it would take her thirty and me ten. So to give her a sporting chance, I stepped into a used bookshop a few doors from the salon.

The shop was aptly named Calypso's. It was a little sunlit storefront with narrow aisles and crooked shelves and a shuffling proprietor who looked like he'd been marooned on MacDougal Street for fifty years. He returned my greeting reluctantly and gestured at the books with an annoyed wave as if to say: *Peruse, if you must.*

I picked an aisle at random and walked far enough into it that I would be out of his line of sight. The shelves held highfalutin books with broken spines and ragged covers—the usual secondhand, bohemian fare. In this aisle there were biographies, letters, and other works of historical nonfiction. At first it seemed as if they had been stuffed on the shelves willy-nilly, since neither the authors nor the subjects appeared to be in alphabetical order, until I realized that they had been shelved chronologically. (Of course they had.) To my left were Roman senators and early saints. To my right the Civil War generals and latter-day Napoleons. Looking straight ahead, I found myself smack dab in the middle of the Enlightenment. Voltaire, Rousseau, Locke, Hume. I tilted my head to read their rational spines. A Treatise on this. A Discourse on that. Enquiries and Inquiries.

Do you believe in fate? I never have. God knows that Voltaire, Rousseau, Locke, and Hume didn't. But there at eye level on the very next shelf, as the mid-eighteenth century gave way to the late, was a small volume in red leather with a gold star embossed on the spine. I pulled it out thinking maybe it was my pole star—and lo and behold, it turned out to be *Assorted Writings by the Father of Our Republic.* Turning past the title page, right after the Contents came his adolescent maxims, all 110 of them. I bought it from the old proprietor for fifteen cents, and he looked as pained to part with it as I was pleased to acquire it.

◆　◆　◆

Chinoiserie was a restaurant in Chinatown which had recently come into vogue. The interior was a fantasy of soon-to-be-clichéd Oriental fixtures: large porcelain urns, brass Buddhas, red lanterns, and the stiff-postured silent deference of an Oriental waitstaff (the last servile ethnicity of America's nineteenth-century immigrant classes). At the back of the dining room two wide zinc doors swung to and fro, giving the clientele a direct view into the kitchen. It was so hectic it looked more like a village market than a commissary—complete with burlap sacks of rice piled on the floor and cleaver-wielding cooks holding live chickens by the throat. The well-to-do of New York were in love with the place.

The front of the restaurant was partly offset from the dining room by a large crimson screen swirling with dragons. In front of me a broad-shouldered man with the twang of an oil-producing state was trying to communicate with the maitre d', an impeccably groomed Chinaman in a tuxedo. Though both men could travel the normal distance from their accents to the neutral ear of the educated New Yorker, they were finding the distance between their respective homelands difficult to traverse.

The maitre d' was explaining politely that without a reservation he would not be able to seat the gentleman's party. The Texan was trying to explain that whatever table he had would do just fine. The maitre d' suggested that perhaps a table later in the week would suffice. The Texan replied that no table was *too* close to the kitchen. The Chinaman stared at the Texan for a characteristically inscrutable moment. So the Texan stepped forward and characteristically put a ten-dollar bill into the maitre d's palm.

—Confusion say, the Texan observed, you scratchee my back, I scratchee yours.

The maitre d', who seemed to get the gist of the remark, would have raised an eyebrow had he had one. Instead, with a sort of grim we-invented-paper-a-thousand-years-ago resignation, he gestured stiffly toward the dining room and led the Texans in.

As I waited for the maitre d' to return, there was Bitsy handing her jacket to the coat-check girl. To have gotten here this fast, she must have walked. We greeted each other and turned toward the dining room.

That was when I saw Anne Grandyn. She was sitting alone in a booth with empty dishes scattered around the tabletop. She looked typically at ease. Her hair was short, her outfit sharp. On her earlobes she wore her emeralds. She didn't notice me because she had her eyes trained toward the hallway that led to the washrooms, from which Tinker then appeared.

He looked beautiful. He was back in one of his tailored suits—a tan affair with narrow lapels. He wore a crisp white shirt and a cornflower tie, having (thankfully) put his open-collar days behind him. He had shaved off his beard and gotten a trim, reassuming the elegant and understated appearance of the Manhattan success story.

I stepped back behind the screen.

My assignation with Tinker wasn't until 9:00 at the Stork Club. My plan was to arrive at 8:30 and hide behind a pair of tinted glasses and my new red hair. I didn't want to spoil the fun. Bitsy was still standing in front of the dining room. If Tinker saw her, my cover might be blown.

—Psst, I said.

—What? she whispered.

I pointed toward the booth.

—Tinker's here with his godmother. I don't want them to see me.

Bitsy looked perplexed. So I grabbed her by the arm and pulled her behind the screen.

—Are you talking about Anne Grandyn? she asked.

—Yes!

—Isn't he her banker?

I looked at Bitsy for a moment. Then I pushed her farther behind the screen and leaned around it. A waiter was just pulling back the table so that Tinker could take his seat. Tinker eased into the booth beside Anne. And in the moment before the waiter tucked the table back, I could see Anne sliding her hand discreetly along Tinker's thigh.

Tinker nodded to the maitre d', who was standing nearby, signaling that they were ready for the check. But when the maitre d' put the small red-lacquered tray on the table, it was Anne who raised her hand to retrieve it. And Tinker didn't flinch.

Anne glanced over the check as Tinker drank every last drop of his drink. Then she reached into her bag and pulled out a money clip with a familiar fold of freshly minted bills. The clip was sterling silver and in the shape of a high-heel shoe—smithed, no doubt, by a maker

of whimsical martini shakers, cigarette caddies, and other fine accessories. Like the Texan said: You scratchee my back, I scratchee yours.

Once she had paid in full, Anne looked up and saw me standing at
the front of the restaurant. Ever plucky, she waved. She wasn't hiding
behind an Oriental screen or a potted palm.

Tinker followed Anne's gaze to the front of the restaurant. When he
saw me, his charms collapsed from the inside out. His face grew gray.
His muscles sagged. Nature's way of letting you see someone a little more
clearly for what they are.

The only consolation in being humiliated is having the presence of mind
to leave immediately. Without saying a word to Bitsy, I went through
the lobby and out the crimson doors into the autumn air. Across the
street, a single cloud was anchored like a zeppelin to the top of a savings
& loan. Before it had the chance to cast off, Tinker was at my side.

—Katey . . .

—You freak.

He reached for my elbow. I yanked it away and my purse fell to the
ground, spilling its contents. He said my name again. I knelt to sweep
up the mess. He got down and tried to help.

—Stop!

We both stood up.

—Katey . . .

—This is what I've been waiting for? I said.

Or maybe shouted.

Something fell from my jawbone to the back of my hand. It was a
teardrop of all things. So I slapped him.

That helped. It restored my composure. And unsettled his.

—Katey, he pleaded one more time without showing much imagination.

—Off with your head, I said.

I was halfway up the block when Bitsy caught me. She was uncharacteristically breathless.

—What was that all about?

—I'm sorry, I said. I was feeling a little light-headed.

—Tinker's the one feeling light-headed.

—Oh. Did you see that?

—No. But I saw a handprint on his face and it looked about your size. What's afoot?

—It's stupid. It was nothing. It was just a misunderstanding.

—The Civil War was a misunderstanding. That was a lovers' quarrel.

Bitsy's dress was sleeveless and goose bumps were visible on her arms.

—Where's your coat? I asked.

—You ran off so fast that I had to leave it in the restaurant.

—We can go back.

—No way.

—We should get it.

—Quit worrying about the coat. It'll find *me*. That's why I leave my wallet in the pocket in the first place. Now what's the fuss?

—It's a long story.

—Leviticus long? Or Deuteronomy long?

—Old Testament long.

—Don't say another word.

She turned to the street and raised a hand. A cab materialized instantaneously, as if she had powers over their domain.

—Driver, she commanded, find Madison Avenue and start driving up it.

Bitsy sat back and was silent. I could tell that I was supposed to do the same. It was sort of like when Dr. Watson kept quiet so that Sherlock Holmes could deduct. At Fifty-second Street she told the driver to pull over.

—Don't move a muscle, she told me.

She jumped out and ran into the Chase Manhattan Bank. When she came out ten minutes later she had a sweater over her shoulders and an envelope in her hands. The envelope was filled with cash.

—Where'd you get the sweater?

—They'll do anything for me at Chase.

She leaned forward.

—Driver, take us to the Ritz.

Nearly empty, the dining room of the Ritz looked like a half-witted room at Versailles. So we went back across the lobby to the bar. It was darker, smaller, less Louis Quatorze. Bitsy nodded.

—That's more like it.

Bitsy sequestered us in a booth at the back, ordered hamburgers, French fries, and bourbons. Then she looked at me expectantly.

—I probably shouldn't tell you this, I said.

—Kay-Kay, those are my six favorite words in the English language. So I told her.

I told her how Evey and I had met Tinker at The Hotspot on New Year's Eve and how the three of us had bandied about—to the Capitol Theatre and Chernoff's. I told her about Anne Grandyn and how she'd introduced herself at the 21 Club as Tinker's godmother. I told her about the car crash and Eve's recovery and the night with the closed-kitchen eggs and the star-crossed kiss at the elevator door. I told her about the steamer to Europe and the letter from Brixham. I told her how I'd talked my way into a new job and insinuated myself into the glamorous lives of Dicky Vanderwhile and Wallace Wolcott and Bitsy Houghton née Van Heuys.

And, at long last, I told her about the late night call that I'd received after Eve disappeared and how with my overnight bag in hand I'd skipped to Penn Station like a schoolgirl so that I could catch the Montrealer and take it to a hoot owl and a hearthstone and a can of pork and beans.

Bitsy emptied her glass.

—That's a Grand Canyon of a tale, she said. A mile deep and two miles wide.

The metaphor was apt. A million years of social behavior had worn away this chasm and now you had to pack a mule to get to the bottom of it.

I suppose I suspected that some display of sororal sympathy was in order; or if not that, then outrage. But Bitsy exhibited neither. Like a seasoned lecturer, she seemed satisfied that we had covered the necessary ground for the day. She signaled the waiter and paid the bill.

When we were outside, parting ways, I couldn't resist but ask:

—So . . . ?

—So, what?

—So, what do you think I should do?

She looked a little surprised.

—Do? Why, keep it up!

◆ ◆ ◆

When I got back to my place it was after five. In the apartment next door, I could hear the Zimmers sharpening their sarcasm. Over an early dinner, they chipped away at each other like little Michelangelos, placing every stroke of the mallet with care and devotion.

I kicked my shoes at the icebox, poured a glass of gin, and dropped into a chair. The rehash with Bitsy had helped me regain some perspective, even more than the crack I'd taken at Tinker. It had left me in a scientific mood, a mood of morbid fascination—the way a pathologist must feel when looking at a viral rupture on the surface of his own skin.

There's an old parlor game called On the Road to Kent in which someone describes a walk he has taken on the road to Kent and all of the things that he witnessed along the way: the various tradesmen; the wagons and carriages; the heath and heather; the whip-poor-will; the windmill; and the gold sovereign dropped by the abbot in the ditch. When the traveler finishes, he describes the journey a second time, leaving out some items, adding others, rearranging a few, and the game is to identify as many of the changes as possible. Sitting there in my apartment, I found myself playing a version of this game in which the road was the one that I had traveled with Tinker from New Year's Eve to the present.

This is a game that is won through powers of visualization more than memory. The best player puts herself in the traveler's shoes as the journey unfolds, using her mind's eye to see exactly what the traveler has seen, so that when she walks the route a second time the differences will draw attention to themselves. So as I took a second pass at 1938, setting out from The Hotspot and proceeding through the pageant that is day-by-day Manhattan, I immersed myself in the landscape and reobserved the little details, the offhand remarks, the actions on the periphery—all through the new lens of Tinker's relationship with Anne. And many fascinating changes did I discover there. . . .

I remembered the night that Tinker called me to the Beresford—and how he had come home from the office after midnight with his hair combed and his twice-shaven cheeks and his crisp Windsor knot. But, of course, he hadn't been to the office at all. Once he had poured me that warm martini and backed apologetically out the door, he had taken a taxi to the Plaza Hotel—where after exertions of one form or another, he had freshened up in Anne's convenient little bath.

And the night at the Irish bar on Seventh Street—when I ran into Hank and he referred to *that manipulative cunt*—he wasn't referring to Eve. He probably didn't even know Eve. He was referring to Anne, the hidden hand that made all things Tinker come to life.

And you better believe I remembered how subtle a partner Tinker had been in the Adirondacks—how clever; how inventive; how he had surprised me; how he had folded me; reversed me; explored me. Sweet Jesus. I wasn't even close to being born yesterday, but not for one minute had I let myself dwell on the obvious—that he had learned all of that from someone else; someone a little more bold, a little more experienced, a little less subject to shame.

And all the time, the outward appearance so artfully maintained was that of a gentleman: well mannered, well spoken, well dressed—well honed.

I got up and went to my purse. I pulled out the little volume of Washingtonia that fate had dropped in my lap. I opened it and began skimming through young George's aspirations:

1st Every Action done in Company, ought to be with Some Sign of Respect, to those that are Present.

15th Keep your Nails clean and Short, also your Hands and Teeth Clean yet without Shewing any great Concern for them.

19th Let your Countenance be pleasant but in Serious Matters Somewhat grave.

25th Superfluous Complements and all Affectation of Ceremonie are to be avoided, yet where due they are not to be Neglected.

Suddenly, I could see this for what it was too. For Tinker Grey, this little book wasn't a series of moral aspirations—it was a primer on social advancement. A do-it-yourself charm school. A sort of *How to Win Friends and Influence People* 150 years ahead of its time.

I shook my head like a midwestern grandma.

What a rube Katherine Kontent had been.

Teddy to Tinker, Eve to Evelyn, Katya to Kate: In New York City, these sorts of alterations come free of charge—or so I had thought to myself as the year began. But what circumstances should have brought to mind were the two versions of *The Thief of Baghdad*.

In the original version, an impoverished Douglas Fairbanks, enamored of the caliph's daughter, disguises himself as a prince to gain access to the palace. While in the Technicolor remake, the lead played a prince who, bored by the pomp of the throne, disguises himself as a peasant so that he can sample the splendors of the bazaar.

Masquerades such as these don't require much imagination to initiate or comprehend; they happen every day. But to assume that they will enhance one's chances at a happy ending, this requires the one suspension of disbelief that the two versions of *The Thief of Baghdad* share: that carpets can fly.

The telephone rang.

—Yeah?

—Katey.

I had to laugh.

—Guess what I have in front of me?

—Katey.

—Go ahead and guess. You'll never believe it.

. . .

—The *Rules of Civility & Decent Behaviour*! Remember those? Wait. Let me find one.

I fumbled with the phone.

—Here we go! *Mock not nor Jest at any thing of Importance.* That's a good one. Or how about this? Number Sixty-six: *Be not forward but friendly and Courteous.* Why, that's you in spades!

—Katey.

I hung up. I sat back down and began reading Mr. Washington's list a little more closely. You had to give that precocious colonial kid credit. Some of them made a lot of sense.

The phone began ringing again. It rang and rang and rang and then fell silent.

As an adolescent, I had mixed feelings about my long legs. Like the

legs on a newborn foal they seemed engineered for collapse. Billy Bogadoni, who lived around the corner with his eight siblings, used to call
me Cricket, and he didn't mean it in the complimentary sense. But as it
goes with such things, I eventually grew into my legs and ultimately
prized them. I found I liked being taller than the other girls. By seven-
teen, I was taller than Billy Bogadoni. When I first moved into Mrs.
Martingale's she used to say in her saccharine manner that I really
shouldn't wear heels because boys didn't like to dance with girls who
were taller than them. Perhaps because of those very remarks, my heels
were half an inch higher when I left Mrs. Martingale's than when I'd
arrived.

Well, here was another advantage of being long-legged. I could lean
back in my father's easy chair, extend my foot with my toes pointed
forward, and tip my new coffee table so that the telephone slid overboard
like a deck chair on the *Titanic*.

I read on without interruption. As I have mentioned before, there
were 110, which might have led you to believe the list was a little overdone. But Mr. Washington had saved the best for last:

**110th Labour to keep alive in your Breast that Little Spark of Celes-
tial fire Called Conscience.**

Obviously, Tinker had read many of the Rules on Mr. Washington's
list quite closely. Maybe he had just never gotten this far.

On Tuesday morning, I woke early and walked all the way to work at
a Bitsy Houghton pace. The sky was autumn blue and the streets bustled
with honest men on their way to earn an honest wage. The Fifth Avenue
high-rises shimmered to the envy of the outer boroughs. On the corner
of Forty-second Street I gave the whistling newsie two bits for the *Times*
(keep the change, kid) and then the Condé Nast elevator whisked me
up twenty-five floors faster than it would have taken to fall them.

As I walked across the bullpen with my paper under my arm (and
the newsie's whistle on my lips), I noticed out of the corner of my eye
that singing-telegrammed Fesindorf stood when I passed. Then Cabot

and Spindler did the same. Across the room I could see Alley at her desk typing at full clip. She caught my eye with a hint of caution. Through the glass walls of his office, I could see Mason Tate dipping his chocolate into his coffee.

At my desk, in place of my chair, I found a wheelchair with a red cross emblazoned on the back.

As he crossed First Avenue, he made eye contact with two Caribbean girls in the light of a street lamp. They stopped talking so that they could smile at him professionally. By way of response, he shook his head. He looked farther along Twenty-second Street and quickened his pace. They picked up where they'd left off.

It started to rain again.

He took off his hat and tucked it under his jacket, counting the numbers of the tenement houses. No. 242. No. 244. No. 246.

When he had spoken to his brother on the telephone, his brother had been unwilling to meet uptown, to meet in a restaurant, to meet at a reasonable hour. He had insisted they meet in the Gashouse district at eleven o'clock where he had some business to attend to. He found him sitting on the stoop of No. 254 smoking a cigarette, looking as pale as a miner.

—Hey Hank.

—Hello Teddy.

—How are you?

Hank didn't bother to answer or get up or ask him how he was. Hank had stopped asking how he was a long time ago.

—What have you got there? Hank said, nodding his head at the lump under his jacket. The head of John the Baptist?

He took out the hat.

—It's a Panama hat.

Hank nodded with a wry smile.

—Panama!

—It shrinks in the rain, he explained.

—Of course it does.

—How's the work going? he asked Hank, changing the subject.

—Everything I imagined and more.

—*Are you still working on the marquee paintings?*

—*Didn't you hear? I sold the lot of them to the Museum of Modern Art. Just in time to stave off eviction.*

—*Actually, that's one of the reasons I wanted to see you. I just got a bit of a windfall. And I don't know when I'll get another. You could put some of it toward the rent. . . .*

He took the envelope out of his jacket pocket.

Hank's expression soured at the sight of it.

A car pulled up in front of the stoop. It was a police car. Before turning fully around, he put the envelope back in his pocket.

The officer in the passenger seat rolled down his window. He had dark eyebrows and olive skin.

—*Everything all right? the patrolman asked helpfully.*

—*Yes, officer. Thanks for stopping.*

—*Okay, he said. But watch out for yourselves. This is a nigger block.*

—*Sure thing, officer, Hank called over his shoulder. And you watch out on Mott Street. That's a wop block.*

Both officers got out of the car. The driver already had his baton in hand. Hank stood up, ready to meet them at the curb.

He had to step in between his brother and the officers. He put both hands up in front of his chest and spoke in a quiet, apologetic voice.

—*He didn't mean it, officers. He's been drinking. He's my brother. I'm taking him home right now.*

The officers studied him. They studied his suit and his haircut.

—*All right, the passenger-seat cop said. But don't let us find him here later.*

—*Or ever, the driver-seat cop said.*

They got back in the car and drove away.

He turned to Hank shaking his head.

—*What were you thinking?*

—*What was I thinking? I was thinking, why don't you mind your own fucking business?*

It was all going wrong. He reached into his pocket and took out the envelope again anyway. They were standing face-to-face now.

—*Here, he said with his best conciliatory tone. Take it. Then let's get out of here. We can go get a drink.*

Hank didn't look at the money.

—I don't want it.

—Take it Hank.

—You earned it. You keep it.

—Come on, Hank. I earned it for the both of us.

As soon as he said it, he knew he shouldn't have.

Here it comes, he thought. He watched Hank's torso rotate and his arm extending from the shoulder. It knocked him off his feet.

It began to rain more heavily.

Hank always had a good cross, he thought to himself, tasting the iron on his lips.

Hank leaned over him, but it wasn't to give him a hand. It was to tell him off.

—Don't you put that money on me. I didn't tell you to make it. I'm not living on Central Park. That's your business, brother.

He sat upright and wiped the blood from his lips.

Hank stepped away and bent over to pick something up. He assumed it was the money, which had spilled from the envelope. But it wasn't the money. It was the hat.

Hank walked away, leaving him on Twenty-second Street, sitting on the cement in the pouring rain with the Panama hat shrinking on his head.

FALL

CHAPTER TWENTY

Hell Hath No Fury

I read a lot of Agatha Christies that fall of 1938—maybe all of them. The Hercule Poirots, the Miss Marples. *Death on the Nile. The Mysterious Affair at Styles.* Murders . . . *on the Links,* . . . *at the Vicarage,* and, . . . *on the Orient Express.* I read them on the subway, at the deli, and in my bed alone.

You can make what claims you will about the psychological nuance of Proust or the narrative scope of Tolstoy, but you can't argue that Mrs. Christie fails to please. Her books are tremendously satisfying.

Yes, they're formulaic. But that's one of the reasons they are so satisfying. With every character, every room, every murder weapon feeling at once newly crafted and familiar as rote (the role of the postimperialist uncle from India here being played by the spinster from South Wales, and the mismatched bookends standing in for the jar of fox poison on the upper shelf of the gardener's shed), Mrs. Christie doles out her little surprises at the carefully calibrated pace of a nanny dispensing sweets to the children in her care.

But I think there is another reason they please—a reason that is at least as important, if not more so—and that is that in Agatha Christie's universe everyone eventually gets what they deserve.

Inheritance or penury, love or loss, a blow to the head or the hangman's noose, in the pages of Agatha Christie's books men and women, whatever their ages, whatever their caste, are ultimately brought face-to-face with a destiny that suits them. Poirot and Marple are not really central characters in the traditional sense. They are simply the agencies of an intricate moral equilibrium that was established by the Primary Mover at the dawn of time.

For the most part, in the course of our daily lives we abide the abundant evidence that no such universal justice exists. Like a cart horse, we plod along the cobblestones dragging our masters' wares with our heads down and our blinders in place, waiting patiently for the next cube of sugar. But there are certain times when chance suddenly provides the justice that Agatha Christies promise. We look around at the characters cast in our own lives—our heiresses and gardeners, our vicars and nannies, our late-arriving guests who are not exactly what they seem—and discover that before the end of the weekend all assembled will get their just deserts.

But when we do so, we rarely remember to count ourselves among their company.

◆ ◆ ◆

That Tuesday morning in September, when Mason Tate showed his concerns for my health, I didn't bother trying to apologize. I certainly didn't bother trying to explain. I just sat down in my wheelchair and started typing. Because I could tell exactly where I stood—about three feet from the trapdoor in the floorboards.

In Mason Tate's world, there was no room for extenuating circumstances or divided loyalties; so, there wasn't going to be much patience with displays of jauntiness or wit or other signals of the self-assured. I was just going to have to shoulder the yoke and accept whatever additional humiliations the boss had in store for me, until I had earned my way back into his good graces.

So that's what I did. I arrived a little earlier. I avoided the watercooler. I listened to Mr. Tate's critiques of others without a smirk. And Friday evening when Alley went to the automat, like any good penitent from the Middle Ages I went home and copied out rules of grammar and usage:

> · *When you are reluctant to do something, you are* **loath** *to do it, not* **loathe**.

- *Of toward and towards, the former is preferred in America, the latter in the UK.*
- *With possessives, the apostrophe s is used in all proper names ending in s other than Moses and Jesus.*
- *Use colons and the impersonal passive sparingly.*

As if on cue: *There was a knock at my door.*

It was three succinct raps, too precious to be Detective Tilson or the Western Union boy. I opened the door to find Anne Grandyn's secretary standing in the hall. He was wearing a three-piece suit, every button buttoned.

—Good evening, Miss *Kontent.*

—Kon*tent.*

—Yes. Of course. Kon*tent.*

Though as disciplined as a Prussian soldier, Bryce couldn't resist eyeing my apartment over my shoulder. The sum of what little he saw lent a hint of satisfaction to his terse little smile.

—Yes? I prompted.

—I apologize for bothering you at *home* . . .

He added a sort of grave inflection to the word *home* to indicate his sympathies.

—But Mrs. Grandyn wanted you to have this as soon as possible.

He flicked two fingers forward revealing a small envelope. I plucked it free and weighed it in the air.

—Too important to trust to the post office?

—Mrs. Grandyn was hoping for an immediate response.

—She couldn't phone?

—On the contrary. We tried telephoning. Many times. But it seems . . .

Bryce gestured to where the unhooked phone still sat on the floor.

—Ah.

I opened the envelope. Inside was a handwritten note. *Please come and see me tomorrow at four. I think it's important that we speak.* She signed it, *Respectfully, A. Grandyn,* and concluded with the postscript: *I've ordered olives.*

—Can I tell Mrs. Grandyn to expect you? Bryce asked.

—I'm afraid that I shall have to think on it.

—If I may be so bold, Miss Kontent, how long might *that* take?

—Overnight. But you are welcome to wait.

Naturally, I should have thrown Anne's summons in the trash. Almost all summons merit an ignominious end. As Anne was a woman of intelligence and will, a summons from her should have been looked upon with particular distrust. And on top of all that was her presumption that I should go to see her! *The gall*, as they say in all places other than New York.

I tore the letter into a thousand pieces and hurled them at the spot on the wall where a fireplace should have been. Then I carefully considered what I should wear.

For what was the point of standing on ceremony now? Hadn't we sailed a few hundred nautical miles beyond grandstanding? Hercule Poirot certainly wouldn't have turned her down. He would have been hoping for such a summons—practically counting on one—as the unforeseen development that would speed the plow of justice.

Besides, I could never resist the sign-off *Respectfully*; or those who remembered my cocktail preferences with such exactitude.

The bell at suite 1801 was answered at 4:15 by Bryce with a smarmy grin.

—Hello Bryce, I said, holding the sibilant just long enough, so that it would hiss.

—Miss Kon-*tent*, he said punching back. We've been ex-*pect*-ing you.

He gestured toward the foyer. I walked past him into the living room.

Anne was sitting at her desk. She was wearing glasses, the half-frame sort that prudish women wear—a nice touch. She looked up from her correspondence and raised an eyebrow to acknowledge that I had dispensed with the normal formalities. To even the score she gestured toward her couch and continued writing. I walked past her desk to one of the windows.

Along Central Park West, the taller apartment buildings jutted over the trees in solitary fashion like commuters on a railroad platform in the hours before the morning rush. The sky was Tiepolo blue. After a week of sudden cold, the leaves had turned, creating a bright orange canopy that stretched all the way to Harlem. It was almost as if the park was a jewel box and the sky was the lid. You had to give Olmstead credit: He was perfectly right to have bulldozed the poor to make way for it.

Behind me, I could hear Anne folding the letter, sealing the envelope, scratching the address with the nib of her pen. Another summons, no doubt.

—Thank you, Bryce, she said handing him the letter. That will be all.

I turned around as Bryce left the room. Anne offered me a benign smile. She looked opulent, unabashed, as arresting as ever.

—Your secretary's a bit of a prig, I observed, taking a seat on the couch.

—Who, Bryce? I suppose so. But he's quite capable, and really more of a protégé.

—A protégé. Wow. In what? Faustian bargains?

Anne raised an ironic eyebrow and moved to the bar.

—You're rather well read for a working-class girl, she said with her back to me.

—Really? I've found that *all* my well-read friends are from the working classes.

—Oh my. Why do you think that is? The purity of poverty?

—No. It's just that reading is the cheapest form of entertainment.

—Sex is the cheapest form of entertainment.

—Not in this house.

Anne laughed like a sailor and turned around with two martinis. She sat in the chair catty-corner to me and plunked the drinks down. In the center of the table was a bowl of fruits so well-to-do that half of them I'd never seen before. There was a small green furry sphere. A yellow succulent that looked like a miniature football. To get to Anne's table, they must have traveled farther than I had traveled in my entire life.

Laying in wait beside the fruit bowl was the dish of promised olives. She picked up the dish and poured half of them into my glass. They were piled so high that they broke the surface of the gin like a volcanic island.

—Kate, she said. Let's dispense with the catfight. I know it's a temptation, and a sweet one. But it's beneath us.

She raised her glass and extended it toward me.

—Truce?

—Sure, I said.

I clinked her glass and we drank.

—So. Why don't you just tell me why you asked me here.

—That's the spirit, she said.

She reached forward and plucked the olive off the apex of my island. She put it in her mouth and chewed thoughtfully. Then she shook her head with a laugh.

—You'll find this funny; but I hadn't the slightest suspicion about you and Tinker. So when you stormed out of Chinoiserie, for a second I actually thought that you were scandalized. The older woman and the younger man, or what have you. It was only when I saw Tinker's expression that I put it together.

—Life is full of misleading signals.

She smiled conspiratorially.

—Yes. Rebuses and labyrinths. We rarely know exactly where we stand in relation to someone else, and we never know where two confederates stand in relation to each other. But the sum of the angles of a triangle is always 180 degrees—isn't it.

—Well, I think I understand a little better how you and Tinker stand in relation to one another.

—I'm glad of that, Katey. Why shouldn't you? I had my little game for a while. But our relationship isn't really a secret. And it's not that complicated. It's nowhere near as complicated as your relationship with him or my relationship with you. Between Tinker and me the understanding is as straight as the line in a ledger.

Anne put her thumb and finger together and drew an imaginary pencil across the air to emphasize the linear perfection of the accountant's underscore.

—There's a pretty clear difference between physical and emotional needs, she continued. Women like you and I understand this. Most women don't. Or they're unwilling to admit it. When it comes to love, most women insist that the emotional and physical aspects of a relationship be inextricably intertwined. To suggest to them otherwise is like trying to convince them that their children might not love them one day. Their very survival depends upon believing otherwise, no matter what history suggests to the contrary. Of course, there are plenty of women who turn a blind eye to their husbands' indiscretions, but most of them are miserable about it. They perceive it as a tear in the fabric of their lives. But if one of those women were to look coolly into herself, when her husband comes into a restaurant a half an hour late smelling of Chanel No. 5, she's probably more angry about being kept waiting than about the perfume on his collar. But as I say—I think we see eye to eye on all this. And that's why I asked you here instead of Tinker. I think that you and I may come to an understanding that serves Tinker well. An understanding in which we *all* get what we want.

To emphasize the spirit of cooperation, Anne leaned forward and took another olive off of my stack. I put three fingers in my drink, scooped out half the olives, and dumped them in her glass.

—I'm not sure that I'm as good as you are at using people, I said.

—Is that what you think I'm doing?

Anne took an apple from the fruit bowl and held it up as if it were a crystal ball.

—You see this apple? Sweet. Crisp. Ruby red. It wasn't always like that, you know. The first apples in America were mottled and too bitter to eat. But after generations of grafting, now they're all like this one. Most people think this is man's victory over nature. But it's not. In evolutionary terms, it's the apple's victory.

She gestured disdainfully toward the exotics in the bowl.

—It's the apple's victory over hundreds of other species competing for the same resources—the same sunlight, water and soil. By appealing to the senses and physical needs of humans—we beasts who happen to have the axes and oxen—the apple has been spreading across the globe at what in evolutionary terms is a breakneck pace.

Anne leaned forward to put the apple back.

—I'm not using Tinker, Katherine. Tinker is the apple. He has ensured his survival while others have languished by learning how to appeal to the likes of you and me. And probably to some who went before us.

Some people called me Katey, some Kate, some Katherine. Anne cycled between the options as if she was comfortable with all my incarnations. She sat back in her chair adopting an almost academic pose.

—I'm not saying this to Tinker's discredit, you understand. Tinker is an extraordinary person. Perhaps more than you know. And I'm not angry with him either. I assume that the two of you have slept together and that you might well be in love. But that doesn't instill in me jealousy or spite. I don't view you as a rival. I knew from the beginning that he would eventually find someone. I don't mean a firefly like your friend. I mean someone as sharp and urbane as me but a little more contemporary. So, the two of you should know that with me it is nowhere near all or nothing. It's quite happily some or something. All I ask is that he be on time.

As Anne was elaborating, I finally got it—the reason that I had been summoned: She thought Tinker was with me. He must have walked out on her, and she had leapt to the conclusion that I had him stashed away. For a brief moment, I considered playing along just to spoil her afternoon.

—I don't know where he is, I said. If Tinker's stopped answering to your whistle, it's got nothing to do with me.

Anne eyed me cautiously.

—I see, she said.

Buying time, she walked casually to the bar and poured gin into the shaker. Unlike Bryce, she didn't bother with the silver tongs. She put her hand in the bucket, took up a fistful of ice, and dumped it in the booze. Rattling the shaker lightly in one hand, she came back and sat at the edge of her seat. She seemed immersed in thought, weighing possibilities, recalibrating—uncharacteristically unsure of herself.

—Would you like another? she asked.

—I'm fine.

She began filling her own glass but stopped halfway. She looked disappointed with the gin, as if it weren't translucent enough.

—Every time I drink before five, she said, I remember why I don't.

I stood up.

—Thanks for the drink, Anne.

She didn't protest. She followed me to the door. But when she shook my hand at the threshold, she held it for a moment longer than is normally polite.

—Keep in mind what I've said, Katey. About the understanding that we could reach.

—Anne . . .

—I know. You don't know where he is. But something tells me you're going to hear from him before I do.

She let go and I turned toward the elevator. Its doors were open and the elevator boy briefly met my eye. It was the same friendly young man who had elevated me and the unnewlyweds back in June.

—Kate.

—Yes? I asked, turning back.

—Most people have more needs than wants. That's why they live the lives they do. But the world is run by those whose wants outstrip their needs.

I mulled this over for a moment. It led me to one conclusion:

—You're very good with the closing remark, Anne.

—Yes, she said. It's one of my specialties.

Then she softly shut the door.

◆　◆　◆

When I left the Plaza, again the doorman nodded to me without signaling a cab. Conceding the point, I began walking down Sixth Avenue. In no mood to go home, I slipped into a Marlene Dietrich picture at the Ambassador. The picture was an hour under way, so I watched the second half and then stayed for the first. Like most movies, things looked dire at the midpoint and were happily resolved at the end. Watching it my way made it seem a little truer to life.

Outside the theater I hailed a cab in order to teach the doorman a lesson, retroactively. As we drove downtown, I debated what I should get drunk on once I was home. Red wine? White wine? Whiskey? Gin? Like people in the world of Mason Tate, they each had their virtues and vices. Maybe I'd leave it to chance. Maybe I'd blindfold myself, spin around, and pin the tail on the bottle. Just the thought of such a game lifted my spirits. But when I got out of the cab at Eleventh Street, who should appear but Theodore Grey. He emerged from a doorway like a fugitive. Except that he was wearing a clean white shirt and a peacoat that had never set eyes on the sea.

As a quick aside, let me observe that in moments of high emotion—whether they're triggered by anger or envy, humiliation or resentment—if the next thing you're going to say makes you feel better, then it's probably the wrong thing to say. This is one of the finer maxims that I've discovered in life. And you can have it, since it's been of no use to me.

—Hello, Teddy.

—Katey, I need to talk to you.

—I'm late for a date.

He winced.

—Can't you give me five minutes?

—All right. Shoot.

He looked around the street.

—Isn't there a place where we can sit down?

I took him to the coffee shop on the corner of Twelfth and Second. The place was one hundred feet long and ten feet wide. A cop at the counter was building the Empire State Building out of sugar cubes and two Italian boys sat at the back eating steak and eggs. We took the booth near the front. When the waitress asked if we were ready to order, Tinker looked up as if he didn't understand the question.

—Why don't you bring us coffee, I said.

The waitress rolled her eyes.

Tinker watched her walk away. Then he dragged his gaze back to me as if it took an act of will. He had a satisfying grayness to the skin and rings under the eyes as if he hadn't been sleeping or eating well. It made his clothes look borrowed, which in a way, I suppose they were.

—I want to explain, he said.

—What's to explain?

—You've got every reason to be angry.

—I'm not angry.

—But I didn't seek out my situation with Anne.

First Anne wants to explain her situation with Tinker. Now Tinker wants to explain his situation with Anne. I guess there are two sides to every story. And, as usual, they were both excuses.

—I've got a great little anecdote for you, I said, interrupting him. You'll think it's a hoot. But before I get to that, let me ask you a few things.

He looked up with grim resignation.

—Was Anne actually an old friend of your mother's?

. . .

—No. I was at Providence Trust when we met. The head of the bank invited me to a party in Newport. . . .

—And this exclusive arrangement you have—this concession to sell the shares of a railroad—those are her holdings?

. . .

—Yes.

—Were you her banker before or after your *situation*?

. . .

—I don't know. When we met, I told her I wanted to move to New York. She offered to introduce me to some people. To help me get on my feet.

I whistled.

—Wow.

I shook my head in appreciation.

—The apartment?

. . .

—It's hers.

—Nice coat by the way. Where *do* you keep them all? Now what was I about to tell you? Oh yeah. I think you'll find this funny. A few nights after Eve bounced you, she threw herself such a celebration that she passed out in an alley. The cops found my name in her pocket and they picked me up to identify her. But before they let us go, a nice detective sat me down with a cup of coffee and tried to get us to change our ways. Because he thought we were prostitutes. Given Evey's scars, he assumed she'd been roughed up on the job.

I raised my eyebrows and toasted Tinker with my coffee cup.

—Now, how ironic is *that*!

—That's unfair.

—Is it?

I took a sip of coffee. He didn't bother to defend himself, so I barreled ahead.

—Did Eve know? About you and Anne, I mean.

He shook his head wanly. The very definition of wanly. The apotheosis of wanly.

—I think she suspected there might be another woman. But I doubt she realized it was Anne.

I looked out the window. A fire truck rolled to a stop at the traffic light with all the firemen standing on the runners, hanging from the hooks and ladders, dressed for a fire. A boy on the corner holding his mother's hand waved and all the firemen waved back—God bless them.

—Please, Katey. It's over between Anne and me. I came back from Wallace's to tell her. That's why we were having lunch.

I turned back to Tinker thinking out loud.

—I wonder if Wallace knew?

Tinker winced again. He just couldn't shake that wounded look. It was suddenly inconceivable that he had seemed so attractive. In retrospect, he was so obviously a fiction—with his monogrammed this and his monogrammed that. Like that silver flask in its leather sheath, which he must have topped off in his spotless kitchen with a tiny little funnel—despite the fact that on every other street corner in Manhattan you can buy whiskey in a bottle that's sized for your pocket.

When you thought of Wallace in his simple gray suit giving quiet counsel to the silver-haired friends of his father, Tinker seemed a vaudeville performer by comparison. I suppose we don't rely on comparison enough to tell us whom it is that we are talking to. We give people the liberty of fashioning themselves in the moment—a span of time that is so much more manageable, stageable, controllable than is a lifetime.

Funny. I had looked upon this encounter with such dread. But now that it was here, I was finding it kind of interesting; helpful; even encouraging.

—Katey, he said, or rather implored. I'm trying to tell you. That part of my life is over.

—Same here.

—Please, don't say that.

—Hey! I said cheerfully, cutting him off again. Here's one for you: Have you ever been camping? I mean, actually camping in the woods? With the jackknives and the compasses?

This seemed to strike a chord. I could see his jaw muscles tense.

—You're going too far, Katey.

—Really? I've never been there. What's it like?

He looked down at his hands.

—Boy, I said. If your mother could only see you now.

Tinker rose abruptly. He banged his thigh into the corner of the table, disturbing the tranquility of the cream in its pitcher. He laid a five-dollar bill by the sugar, showing appropriate consideration for our waitress.

—Coffee's on Anne? I asked.

He staggered to the door like a drunk.

—Is *this* too far? I called after him. It doesn't seem so bad!

I put another five dollars on the table and got up. As I walked toward the door I staggered a little too. I looked up and down Second Avenue like a wolf that's escaped from its cage. I checked my watch. The hands were splayed between the nine and the three, like two duelers back-to-back who have counted off paces and are about to turn and fire.

The night was young.

◆ ◆ ◆

It took Dicky five minutes to answer the banging on his door. We hadn't seen each other since we crashed the party at Whileaway.

—Katey! What a terrific surprise. Terrific and . . . hieroglyphic.

He was dressed in tuxedo pants and a formal shirt. He must have been tying his tie when I began knocking because it was hanging freely from his collar. It made him look dashing in an untied-black-tie kind of way.

—May I?

—Absolutely!

When I had gotten off the subway uptown, I had stopped for a drink or two at an Irish bar on Lexington. So I slid past him into the living room a little like a will-o'-the-wisp. I had only been in Dicky's place when it was crowded with people. Empty, I could see how orderly Dicky was under his gay exterior. *Everything* was in its proper place. The chairs were arranged in alignment with the cocktail table. The books in the bookcases were organized by author. The freestanding ashtray was just to the right of the reading chair and the nickel-plated architect's lamp just to the left.

Dicky was staring at me.

—You're a redhead again!

—Not for long. How about a drink?

Obviously expected elsewhere, Dicky pointed toward the front door and opened his mouth. I raised my left eyebrow.

—Why, yes, he conceded. A drink is just the thing.

He went to a fine Macassar cabinet along the wall. The front panel came down like the writing surface of a secretary.

—Whiskey?

—Your pleasure is mine, I said.

He poured us both a dram and we clinked glasses. I emptied mine and held it out in the air. He opened his mouth again as if he was going to speak but emptied his glass instead. Then he poured us both more suitable portions. I took a swig and spun around once as if to get my bearings.

—It's a lovely place, I said. But I don't think I've seen the whole thing.

—Of course, of course. Where are my manners? Right this way!

He gestured through a door. It led into a little dining room lit by taper-style sconces. The colonial table had probably been in the family since New York was a colony.

—Here lies the refectory. The table's designed for six, but seats fourteen in a pinch.

At the other end of the dining room was a swinging door with a porthole. We went through it into a kitchen that was as clean and white as heaven.

—The kitchen, he said turning his hand in the air.

We went through another door and down a hallway, passing a guest room that was obviously unused. On the bed were summer clothes neatly folded, ready to be stowed for the winter. The next room was his bedroom. The bed was neatly made. The only loose piece of clothing was his tuxedo jacket, which hung over a chair in front of a little writing desk.

—And what's in here? I asked, pushing open a door.

—Uhm. The lavatorium?

—Ah!

Dicky seemed sweetly reluctant to include it on the tour; but it was a work of art. Wide white tiles with a heavy glaze ran from floor to ceiling. It had the luxury of two windows: one over the radiator and one over the tub. The tub was a freestanding porcelain number six feet long with claw feet and nickel plumbing rising from the floor. On the wall a long glass shelf was lined with what appeared to be lotions, hair tonics, colognes.

—My sister has an affinity for Christmas gifts from the salon, Dicky explained.

I ran my hand along the rim of the tub as one would along the hood of a car.

—What a beauty.

—Cleanliness is next to godliness, Dicky said.

I emptied my drink and put the glass on the windowsill.

—Let's give it a spin.

—What's that?

I lifted my dress up over my head and kicked off my shoes.

Dicky looked as wide-eyed as a teenager. He emptied his drink in a gulp and put it teetering on the edge of the sink. He began talking excitedly.

—You'll not find a finer tub in all New York.

I turned on the water.

—Its porcelain was fired in Amsterdam. Its feet were cast in París. They were fashioned after the paws of Marie Antoinette's pet panther.

Dicky ripped off his shirt. A mother-of-pearl stud skittered across the black-and-white tiles of the floor. He pulled off his right shoe with a tug, but he couldn't get the left one off. He hopped up and down a few times and stumbled against the sink. His whiskey glass slipped from its perch and shattered against the drain. He held the shoe up in the air with a victorious expression.

I was naked now and about to climb in.

—Suds! he shouted.

He went to the shelf of Christmas gifts and studied it frenetically. He couldn't decide which of the soaps he should choose. So he grabbed two jars, stepped to the rim of the tub, and dumped them both in. He stuck his hands in the water and whisked it into a froth. The rising steam gave off a heady smell of lavender and lemon.

I slipped in under the bubbles. He jumped in after me like a truant jumping in a watering hole. He was in such a rush that he didn't realize he was still in his socks. He took them off and slung them against the wall with a splat. He reached behind his back and produced a brush.

—Shall we?

I took the brush and tossed it onto the bathroom floor. I slid my legs around his waist. I put my hands on the rim of the tub and lowered myself onto his lap.

—*I'm* next to godliness, I said.

CHAPTER TWENTY-ONE

Your Tired, Your Poor, Your Tempest-Tost

On Monday morning, I was in the back of a limousine with Mason Tate on our way to interview a grande dame on the Upper West Side. He was in a foul mood. He still didn't have a cover story for the premier issue, and every week that passed without one seemed to lower his threshold for dissatisfaction. Proceeding up Madison Avenue, his coffee had been too cold, the air too warm, the driver too slow. To make matters worse, as far as Tate was concerned this interview, set up by the publisher, was a colossal waste of time. The doyenne's upbringing was too good, he said, her intelligence too dull and her eyesight too dim to promise any skinny of interest. So if being asked to accompany Mr. Tate on an interview was normally a compliment, today it was a form of punishment. I wasn't out of the doghouse yet.

We turned onto Fifty-ninth Street in silence. On the steps of the Plaza stood the hotel's officious captains dressed in long red coats with big brass buttons. Half a block away, the epauletted officers of the Essex House wore a sharply contrasting shade of blue. This would no doubt make things so much easier should the two hotels ever go to war.

We turned onto Central Park West, and having passed the doormen of the Dakota and the San Remo, we came to a stop at Seventy-ninth Street in front of the Museum of Natural History. From there I could see the canopy of the Beresford where Pete was opening the back door of a cab. He offered his hand to the rider, much as he had offered it to me in the past—like the night in March when Tinker had needed to go to the "office," or the night in June when I had cadged a ride from the Dorans in my misbegotten dots.

And a thought occurred to me.

My better judgment told me to keep my mouth shut. This probably isn't the place, she said, and it certainly isn't the time. He's *persona furiosa* and you are *non grata*. But on the marble pedestal towering over the museum's steps, Teddy Roosevelt reared on his bronze horse and shouted, *Charge!*

—Mr. Tate.

—Yes? (*annoyed*)

—You know the piece you've been trying to find for the premier issue?

—Yes, yes? (*impatient*)

—What if instead of the doyennes, you were to interview the doormen?

—What's that?

—None of them have the upbringing, as it were, most have the intelligence, and they see *everything*.

Mason Tate stared straight ahead for a moment. Then he rolled down his window and threw his coffee out into traffic. He turned to me for the first time in fifteen blocks.

—Why would they talk to us? If we printed something they told us, it would come back to bite them in a day.

—What if we spoke to ex-employees—the ones who have quit or been fired?

—How would we find them?

—We could run an ad in the papers offering high pay for doormen and elevator boys with at least one year's experience at five of the most exclusive apartment buildings in the city.

Mason Tate looked out his window. He produced a chocolate bar from his jacket pocket. He broke off two squares and began chewing slowly, methodically, as if his goal was to grind the flavor out of them.

—If I let you place this ad, you really think you would find something of interest?

—I'd stake a month's pay on it, I said coolly.

He nodded his head.

—Make it your career and you've got a deal.

♦   ♦   ♦

On Friday, I walked to work a little early.

The advertisement had run for three days in the *New York Times*, the *Daily News*, and the *Post Dispatch* instructing applicants to come to the Condé Nast building today at 9:00 A.M. Word of my "wager" with Tate had circulated quickly, and a few of the boys in the bullpen had taken to whistling taps whenever I passed. Under the circumstances, you could hardly blame them.

At the time, the buildings along Fifth Avenue still looked like they had sprung from the ground overnight—disappearing into the clouds like beanstalks.

In 1936, the great French architect Le Corbusier published a little book called *When the Cathedrals Were White* detailing his first trip to New York. In it, he describes the thrill of seeing the city for the first time. Like Walt Whitman he sings of the humanity and the tempo, but he also sings of skyscrapers and elevators and air-conditioning, of polished steel and reflective glass. *New York has such courage and enthusiasm*, he writes, *that everything can be begun again, sent back to the building yard and made into something still greater. . . .*

After reading that book, when you walked along Fifth Avenue and you looked up at those towers, you felt like any one of them might lead you to the hen that laid the golden eggs.

But earlier that summer, another visitor who came to the city had a slightly different take. He was a young man named John William Warde. Around 11:30 in the morning, he climbed out on a ledge of the seventeenth floor of the Gotham Hotel. He was promptly observed and a sizable crowd assembled below. Men paused, hanging their coats over their shoulders on the hook of their fingers. Women fanned themselves with their hats. Newspaper reporters gathered quotations and the police kept the sidewalk clear, sensing that at any moment . . .

But Warde just stood there on the ledge trying the patience of the reporters, the police, and the populous alike, prompting skeptics in the crowd to say that he neither had the courage to live with nor end his misery. At least, that's what they said until he jumped at 10:38 P.M.

So I guess the New York City skyline inspires a little of that too.

The Condé Nast lobby was still empty, promising a quick and anonymous ascent. But as I crossed to the elevator bank, Tony at the security desk waved me over.

—Hey Tony. What's up?

He gestured with his head to the side of the lobby. On a chrome-and-leather bench sat two ragged men, hats in hand. Unshaven and downcast, they looked like the god-forgotten sorts who listen to sermons in the Bowery missions just to get the soup. They looked like they wouldn't know skinny if it was wrapped in cellophane and sold at the five-and-dime. What sort of groveling, I wondered, would I have to do to convince Miss Markham to take me back?

—They were waiting outside when we opened up, Tony said, adding out of the side of his mouth: The one on the left there sort of smells.

—Thanks Tony. I'll take them up with me.

—Okay, Miss K. Sure thing. But what do you want me to do with the rest?

—The rest?

Tony stepped from around his desk and opened the stairwell door. It was crowded with men of every size and shape. Some, like the two on the bench, looked like they had ridden into Manhattan on the back of a freight car, but there were others who looked more like British man-servants in retirement. There were Irish, Italians, and Negroes looking sly or sophisticated, brutish or aim-to-please. They sat on the stairs winding two by two up to the turn at the second floor and out of sight.

Upon seeing me, a tall, well-dressed man on the first step stood to attention like I was a commanding officer entering a barracks. A moment later, every man on the stair was on his feet.

CHAPTER TWENTY-TWO

Neverland

It was a Saturday night in mid-November. Dicky, Susie, Wellie, and I had come to the Village to meet the others at a jazz club called The Lean-To. Dicky had heard through the grapevine that downtown musicians gathered there late at night to play impromptu sets, and he figured if the musicians were going, it was a reliable sign that the place had yet to be spoiled by blue bloods. The truth of the matter was that the owner was an old Jew with a thick heart and a thin skin who lent money to musicians without interest. They would have gathered at The Lean-To if it swallowed the *Social Register* whole. But the end result was the same: If you stayed late enough, you got to hear something that was fresh and unfiltered.

The club was a little fancier than when Eve and I had frequented it. There was a coat-check girl now and little red-shaded lamps on the tables. But then, I was getting a little fancier too. I was wearing a choker with a one-carat diamond that Dicky had wheedled off his mother in honor of our three-week anniversary. I don't think Dicky's mother particularly liked me, but for his entire life Dicky had been carefully fashioning a persona that was surprisingly hard to say no to. In general, he was fun loving and free of spite, but when you replied yes to even the smallest of his requests (*Do you want to go for a walk? Do you want to get an ice-cream cone? Can I sit next to you?*), for a moment he would light up like a bingo winner. I doubt Mrs. Vanderwhile had said the word *no* to him more than three times in his life. I wasn't finding it so easy to say myself.

The eight of us were gathered around two four-tops that Dicky had pushed together with the help of the hostess. As we waited for another round, Dicky conducted the conversation with an olive spear filched from my martini. The topic: hidden talents.

Dicky: Wellie! You're next.
Wellie: I'm unusually buoyant.
Dicky: Of course you are. Doesn't count.
Wellie: I'm ambidextrous?
Dicky: Closer.
Wellie: Uhm. On occasion . . .
Dicky: Yes? Yes?
Wellie: I sing in a choir.
Gasps.
Dicky: Touché, Wellie!
TJ: It's not true, is it?
Helen: I've seen him. In the back row at Saint Barth's.
Dicky: You'd best explain yourself, young man.
Wellie: I sang in the choir as a boy. Occasionally, when they're short
    a baritone, the choirmaster gives me a call.
Helen: How sweet!
Me: Will you give us a sample, Howard?
Wellie (*uprightly*):

Most Holy Spirit! Who didst brood
Upon the chaos dark and rude,
And bid its angry tumult cease
And give, for wild confusion, peace
Oh hear us when we cry to thee
For those in peril on the sea.

Awe and applause.

Dicky: You scoundrel! Look at the girls. They're weeping. In ecstasy.
    It's a dirty trick. (*Turning to me*) And you, my love? Hidden talents?
Me: What about you, Dicky?
All: Yes. What about you!
Susie: Don't you know?
Me: I don't think so.
Susie: Go on, Dicky. Tell them.
Dicky looked at me and blushed.
Dicky: Paper airplanes.
Me: Great Caesar's ghost.

As if to bail him out, the drummer wrapped up a Krupa-like solo with six booms on the kettle and then the whole band was swinging. It was like the drummer had jimmied open the door and the others were stealing everything in the house. Dicky was the one who was ecstatic now. When the vibraphonist began playing in triple time, Dicky swung around in his chair and his feet ran in place. His head did a few quick rotations, as if he couldn't decide whether he should be shaking or nodding it. Then he goosed me.

Some people are born with the ability to appreciate serene and formally structured music like Bach and Handel. They can sense the abstract beauty of the music's mathematical relationships, its symmetries and motifs. But Dicky wasn't one of them.

Two weeks before, to impress me, he had taken me to Carnegie Hall to hear some Mozart piano concertos. The first was a pastoral designed to let the spirit flower in a nocturnal breeze. Dicky fidgeted like a sophomore in summer school. At the end of the second, when the crowd began applauding and the old couple in front of us stood, Dicky practically leapt from his seat. He clapped with wild enthusiasm and then grabbed his coat. When I told him it was just the intermission, he looked so crestfallen that I had to take him immediately to Third Avenue for a burger and a beer. It was a little place I knew where the owner played jazz piano accompanied by a stand-up bass and a high school snare.

This low-rent introduction to small group jazz was a revelation for Dicky. The improvisational nature of it was grasped by him instinctively.

Unplanned, disorderly, unself-conscious, it was practically an extension of his personality. It was everything he liked about the world: You could smoke to it, drink to it, chatter to it. And it didn't make you feel guilty for not giving it your full attention. In the nights that followed, Dicky had a gay old time in the company of small group jazz and he gave me credit for it—not always in public, but when it mattered, and often.

—Will we ever go to the moon? he asked, as the vibraphonist acknowledged applause with a tilt of the head. It would be so marvelous to set foot on another planet.

—Isn't the moon a satellite? asked Helen with her innately unsure erudition.

—I should like to go, Dicky confirmed to no one in particular.

He sat on his hands and reflected on the possibility. Then he leaned sideways and kissed me on the cheek.

— . . . And I should like you to come.

At some point, Dicky shifted to the other side of the table to talk with TJ and Helen. It was a sweet display of self-confidence, as he no longer felt the need to entertain me or to advertise his claim on my attentions. It goes to show that even a man who craves constant approval can attain self-assurance through a little hanky-panky.

As I returned one of Dicky's winks, I saw a ragtag crowd of WPA types collecting around the table behind him. In their company was Henry Grey. It took a moment for me to recognize him because he was ill shaven and had lost some weight. But he didn't have trouble recognizing me. He came right over and leaned on the back of Dicky's empty chair.

—You're Teddy's friend. Right? The one with the opinions.

—That's right. Katey. How's the pursuit of beauty coming?

—Rotten.

—Sorry to hear that.

He shrugged.

—Nothing to say and no way to say it.

Hank turned to watch the band for a moment. He nodded his head more in agreement with the music than in time with it.

—Got any cigarettes? he asked.

I pulled a pack from my purse and held it out. He took two cigarettes handing one back to me. He tapped his ten times against the tabletop and then tucked it behind an ear. The room was hot and he was beginning to sweat.

—Listen. What do you say we go outside?

—Sure, I said. But give me a second.

I went around the table to Dicky.

—That's the brother of an old friend. We're just going out for a smoke. All right?

—Of course, of course, he said, showing off his burgeoning self-confidence.

Though just to be on the safe side, he draped his jacket over my shoulders.

Hank and I went outside and stood under the club's canopy. It wasn't winter yet, but it was plenty brisk. After the cozy quarters of the club, it was just the ticket for me. But not for Hank. He looked as physically uncomfortable as when he had been inside. He lit his well-packed cigarette and inhaled with unapologetic relish. I was getting the picture that Hank's lean and agitated physique might not be a manifestation of his struggles with color and form.

—So, how's my brother? he asked, flinging his match into the street.

I told him I hadn't seen Tinker in two months and that I didn't even know where he was—though I guess my tone was a little sharper than I intended, because Hank took another drag and studied me with interest.

—We had a run-in, I explained.

—Oh?

—Let's just say I finally figured out he wasn't everything he presented himself to be.

—Are you?

—Close enough.

—A rare specimen.

—At least I don't go around implying I went straight from the cradle to the Ivy League.

Hank dropped his cigarette and scuffed it out with a sneer.

—You've got it all wrong, spider. The scandal here isn't that Teddy plays it off like an Ivy Leaguer. The scandal is that that sort of bullshit makes a difference in the first place. Never mind that he speaks five languages and could find his way safely home from Cairo or the Congo. What he's got they can't teach in schools. They can squash it, maybe; but they sure can't teach it.

—And what's that?

—Wonder.

—Wonder!

—That's right. Anyone can buy a car or a night on the town. Most of us shell our days like peanuts. One in a thousand can look at the world with amazement. I don't mean gawking at the Chrysler Building. I'm talking about the wing of a dragonfly. The tale of the shoeshine. Walking through an unsullied hour with an unsullied heart.

—So, he's got the innocence of a kid, I said. Is that it?

He grabbed me by the forearm as if I wasn't getting the point. I could feel the imprint of his fingers on my skin.

—*When I was a child, I spake as a child, I understood as a child, I thought as a child: and when I became a man—*

He let my arm drop.

— . . . More's the pity.

He looked away. For the second time, he reached behind his ear for the cigarette that he'd already smoked.

—So what happened? I asked.

Hank looked at me in his discerning way—always weighing whether he should deign to answer a question.

—What happened? I'll tell you what happened: My old man lost everything we ever had, bit by bit. When Teddy was born, the four of us lived in a house with fourteen rooms. Every year we lost a room—and moved a few blocks closer to the docks. By the time I was fifteen, we were in a boardinghouse that *leaned* over the water.

He held his hand out at a forty-five-degree angle so I could picture it.

—My mother had her heart set on Teddy going to this prep school our great-grandfather went to—before the Boston Tea Party. So she squirreled away some cash and combed his curls and plied his way in. Then, in the middle of Teddy's first year, when she went to the cancer ward, my old man found the stash and that was that.

Hank shook his head. One got the sense that with Hank Grey there was no confusion as to whether one should shake or nod.

—It's like Teddy's been trying to get back in that fucking prep school ever since.

A tall Negro couple was coming down the street. Hank put his hands in his pockets and gestured with his chin toward the man.

—Hey, buddy. You got a smoke?

He said it in his abrupt, unfriendly way. The Negro didn't seem put out. He gave Hank the cigarette and even lit the match, holding his big black hand around the flame. Hank watched the couple walk away with reverence, as if he had newfound hope for the human race. When he turned back to me, he was sweating like he had malaria.

—It's Katey, right? Listen. Do you have any dough?

—I don't know.

I felt in Dicky's blazer pockets and found a money clip with several hundred dollars. I considered giving Hank the whole thing. I gave him two tens instead. As I took the money out of the clip, he unconsciously licked his lips, as if he could already taste what the money would become. When I handed him the bills, he squeezed them in his fist like he was draining a sponge.

—Are you going back inside? I asked, knowing that he wouldn't.

By way of explanation, he gestured toward the East Side. The gesture had an air of finality, like he knew we wouldn't be seeing each other again.

—Five languages? I said before he left.

—Yeah. Five languages. And he can lie to himself in every one of them.

Dicky, the crew, and I stayed well into the night and were rewarded accordingly. Just past the witching hour, musicians began arriving with instruments under their arms. Some of them rotated onto the stage while some propped up the wall. Others sat at the bar, making themselves available to acts of charity. At around one, a group of eight musicians including three trumpets began the beguine.

Later, as we were leaving, the big Negro who had played the saxophone in the ensemble intercepted me at the door. I did my best to hide my surprise.

—Hey, he said in a monastic octave.

But as soon as I heard his voice, I knew who he was. He was the saxophonist we'd seen play at The Hotspot on New Year's Eve.

—You're Evelyn's pal, he said.

—That's right. Katey.

—We haven't seen her round in awhile.

—She moved to L.A.

He nodded his head in heavy understanding, as if by moving out to Los Angeles Eve was somehow ahead of her time. And maybe she was.

—That girl's got an ear.

He said this with the appreciation of the too oft misunderstood.

—If you see her, tell her we miss her.

Then he retreated back to the bar.

It made me laugh and laugh.

For on all those nights in 1937 when we had frequented jazz clubs at Eve's insistence, and she had cornered the musicians to bum cigarettes, I had attributed it to her shallower impulses—her desire to shed her midwestern sensibility and mingle in the Negro's milieu. While all that time, Evelyn Ross was a jazz lover of enough subtlety that the musicians missed her when she was out of town?

I caught up with the others outside, giving a little prayer of thanks to no one in particular. Because when some incident sheds a favorable light on an old and absent friend, that's about as good a gift as chance intends to offer.

◆　◆　◆

Dicky wasn't kidding about the paper airplanes.

Having been out late at The Lean-To, the next night we indulged in that sweetest of New York luxuries: a Sunday night at home with nothing to do. Dicky called down to the kitchen for a plate of tea sandwiches. Instead of gin, he opened a bottle of self-pacing white wine. And as the night was unseasonably warm, we took our little picnic onto his fifty-square-foot terrace overlooking Eighty-third Street and entertained ourselves with a pair of binoculars.

Directly across the street on the twentieth floor of No. 42 East Eighty-third was a stifling dinner party at which know-it-alls in smoking jackets were taking turns making ponderous toasts. Meanwhile, on the eighteenth floor of No. 44, three children, having been put to bed, had quietly turned on their light, built barricades with their mattresses, seized their pillows, and commenced a reenactment of the street fighting in *Les Misérables*. But straight across from us, in the penthouse of No. 46, an obese man in the robe of a geisha was playing a Steinway in a state of rapture. The doors to his terrace were open, and drifting over the faint sounds of Sunday night traffic we could hear the strains of his sentimental melodies: "Blue Moon," "Pennies from Heaven," "Falling in Love with Love." He played with his eyes closed and swayed back and forth, passing his meaty hands one over the other in an elegant progression of octaves and emotions. It was hypnotizing.

I wish he'd play "It's De-Lovely," Dicky said wistfully.

—Why don't you ring his doorman, I suggested, and have him send up a request?

Dicky put a finger in the air indicating a better idea.

He went inside and came out a moment later with a box of fine paper, pens, paper clips, tape, a ruler, and a compass—dumping it on the table with an expression of unusual intent.

I picked up the compass.

—You're kidding, right?

He plucked the compass back from me with a bit of a huff.

—Not in the least.

He sat down and organized his tools in a row like the scalpels on a surgeon's tray.

—Here, he said, giving me a stack of paper.

He bit the eraser of his pencil for a moment and then began to write:

> *Dear Sir,*
>   *If you would be so kind, please play us your interpretation*
> *of "It's De-Lovely." For is it not de-lightful to-nightful?*
>   **Your Moonstruck Neighbors**

In rapid fire we prepared twenty requests. "Just One of Those Things," "The Lady Is a Tramp." And then, starting with "It's De-Lovely," Dicky went to work.

Brushing back his bangs, he leaned forward and stuck the point of the compass into the lower-right-hand corner of the watermarked page. He deftly inscribed an arc, and then, with the precision of a draftsman, spun the compass around on the pencil tip, replanting the needle point in the center of the paper in order to draw a tangential circle. Within moments he had a series of circles and interlinking arcs. Laying his ruler down, he scored diagonal lines the way a ship's navigator sets a course on the bridge. Once the blueprint was complete, he began folding along the various diagonals, using his fingernail to sharpen each crease with a satisfying ssffit.

As Dicky worked, the tip of his tongue pointed through his teeth. In four months, it was probably the longest I had seen him go without talking. It was certainly the longest I had seen him focused on a single endeavor. Part of the joy of Dicky was the ableness with which he flitted from moment to moment and topic to topic like a sparrow in a hurricane of crumbs. But here he displayed an unself-conscious immersion that seemed more suited to a defuser of bombs; and pretty endearing it was. After all, no man in his right mind would make a paper airplane with such care in order to impress a woman.

—*Voila*, he said at last, holding the first plane on both palms.

But if I enjoyed watching Dicky at work, I was none too confident in his aerodynamics. It looked like no plane I had ever seen. Where the planes of the day had smooth titanium noses, rounded bellies, and wings that jutted out of the fuselage like the arms of the cross, Dicky's plane was a cantilevered triangle. It had the nose of a possum and the tail of a peacock and wings that had the pleats of a drape.

Leaning a little over the balcony, he licked his finger and held it in the air.

—Sixty-five degrees; wind at half a knot; two miles of visibility. It's a perfect night for flying.

There was no disputing that.

—Here, he said, handing me the binoculars.

I laughed and left them in my lap. He was too preoccupied to laugh back.

—Away we go, he said.

He took one last look at his engineering, then he stepped forward and extended his arm with a motion akin to a swan extending its neck.

Well, the thing of it is—Dicky's streamlined triangular fuselage may not have mimicked the planes of the day, but it perfectly anticipated the supersonic jets of the future. The plane shot out over Eighty-third Street without a tremble. It sailed through the air for a few seconds at a slight incline, leveled, and then began to drift slowly toward its mark. I scrambled for the binoculars. It took me a moment to sight the plane. It was drifting southward on a prevailing current. Ever so slightly, it began to wobble, and then descend. It disappeared into the shadows of a balcony on the nineteenth floor of No. 50—two addresses west and three floors shy of our target.

—Drat, Dicky said, with enthusiasm.

He turned to me with a touch of paternal concern.

—Don't be discouraged.

—Discouraged?

I stood up and smooched him on the smacker. When I pulled back, he smiled and said:

—Back to work!

Dicky didn't have one paper airplane—he had fifty. There were triple folds, quadruple folds, quintuple folds, some of which were doubled back and reversed in quick succession, creating wing shapes that one wouldn't have thought possible without tearing the paper in two. There were those with a truncated wing and a needle nose, others with condors' wings and narrow submarine-like bodies ballasted with paper clips.

As we sent the requests across Eighty-third Street, I began to slowly understand that Dicky's proficiency lay not simply in the engineering of the planes, but in his launching techniques too. Depending on the plane's structure he would use more or less force, more or less incline, showing the expertise of one who has launched a thousand solo flights across a thousand Eighty-third streets in a thousand weather conditions.

By ten o'clock, the ponderous party had come to an end; the young revolutionaries had fallen asleep with the lights on; and we had landed, unbeknownst to our fat pianist (who had waddled off to brush his teeth), four musical requests on the tiles of his terrace. With the last plane launched, we too decided to pack it in. But when Dicky bent over to pick up the sandwich platter, he found one last piece of stationery. He stood up and looked out over the balcony.

—Wait, he said.

He leaned over and wrote out a message in perfect cursive. Without relying on his tools, he folded it back and forth until he had one of his sharper models. Then he carefully aimed and sailed it out over the street toward the nursery on the eighteenth floor of No. 44. As it traveled it seemed to gather momentum. The lights of the city flickered as if they were supporting it, the way that phosphorescence seems to support a nocturnal swimmer. It went right through their window and landed silently atop a barricade.

Dicky hadn't shown me the note, but I had read it over his shoulder.

> *Our bastions are under attack from all sides.*
> *Our stores of ammunition are low.*
> *Our salvation lies in your hands.*

And, ever so appropriately, he had signed it *Peter Pan*.

CHAPTER TWENTY-THREE

Now You See It

The first wind of the New York winter was sharp and heartless. When-ever it blew, it always made my father a little nostalgic for Russia. He'd break out the samovar and boil black tea and recall some December when there was a lull in conscription and the well wasn't frozen and the harvest hadn't failed. It wouldn't be such a bad place to be born, he'd say, if you never had to live there.

My window overlooking the back court was so crooked you could stick a pencil through the gap where the frame was supposed to meet the sill. I caulked it with an old pair of underpants, set the kettle on the stove, and recalled a few sorry Decembers of my own. I was spared the reminiscing by a knock on the door.

It was Anne, dressed in gray slacks and a baby blue shirt.

—Hello, Katherine.

—Hello, Mrs. Grandyn.

She smiled.

—I suppose I deserve that.

—To what do I owe the pleasure on a Sunday afternoon?

—Well, I hate to admit it—but at any given moment, we're all seek-ing *someone's* forgiveness. And at this particular point, I think I may be seeking yours. I put you in the position of playing the fool, which no woman like me should do to a woman like you.

That's how good she was.

—May I come in?

—Sure, I said.

And why not? When all was said and done, I knew I couldn't bear much of a grudge against Anne. She hadn't abused a trust of mine; nor had she particularly compromised herself. Like any Manhattanite of means, she had identified a need and paid to have it serviced. In its own perverse way, her purchase of a young man's favors was perfectly in keeping with the unapologetic self-possession that made her so impressive. Still, it would have been nice to see her a little more off her axis.

—Would you like a drink? I asked.

—I learned my lesson the last time. But is that tea you're brewing? That might hit the spot.

As I readied the pot she looked around my apartment. She wasn't taking an inventory of my belongings as Bryce had. She seemed more interested in the architectural features: the warped floor, cracked moldings, exposed pipes.

—When I was a girl, she said, I lived in an apartment a lot like this one, not too far from here.

I couldn't hide my surprise.

—Does that shock you?

—I'm not exactly shocked, but I assumed you were born rich.

—Oh. I was. I was raised in a townhouse off Central Park. But when I was six, I lived with a nanny on the Lower East Side. My parents told me some nonsense about my father being sick, but their marriage was probably on the verge of collapse. I gather he was something of a philanderer.

I raised my eyebrows. She smiled.

—Yes, I know. The apple and the tree. What my mother wouldn't have given to have me take after *her* side of the family.

We were both quiet for a moment, providing a natural opportunity for her to change the subject. But she went on. Maybe the first winds of winter make everyone a little nostalgic for the days they're lucky to be rid of.

—I remember the morning my mother brought me downtown. I was dropped in a carriage with a trunkful of clothes—half of which wouldn't do me any good where I was headed. When we got to Fourteenth Street it was crowded with hawkers and saloons and trade wagons. Seeing how excited I was by all the commotion, my mother promised I would be crossing Fourteenth Street every week on my way to visit her. I didn't cross it again for a year.

Anne raised her cup of tea to drink, but paused.

—Come to think of it, she said, I haven't crossed it since.

She started laughing.

And after a moment, I joined in. For better or worse, there are few things so disarming as one who laughs well at her own expense.

—Actually, she continued, crossing Fourteenth Street isn't the only thing I've revisited from my youth because of you.

—What's the other?

—Dickens. Remember that day in June when you were spying on me at the Plaza? You had one of his novels in your bag and it triggered some fond memories. So I dug up an old copy of *Great Expectations*. I hadn't opened the book in thirty years. I read it cover to cover in three days.

—What did you think?

—It was great fun, of course. The characters, the language, the turns of events. But I must admit that this time around, the book struck me as a little like Miss Havesham's dining room: a festive chamber which has been sealed off from time. It's as if Dickens's world was left at the altar.

And so it went. Anne waxed poetically on her preference for the modern novel—for Hemingway and Woolf—and we had two cups of tea, and before she had overstayed her welcome, she rose to go. At my threshold, she took one last look around.

—You know, she said as if the thought had just occurred to her, my apartment at the Beresford is going to waste. Why don't you take it?

—Oh, I couldn't, Anne.

—Why not? Woolf was only half right when she wrote *A Room of One's Own*. There are rooms, and there are rooms. Let me lend it to you for a year. It'll be my way of settling the score.

—Thanks, Anne. But I'm happy where I am.

She reached into her purse and pulled out a key.

—Here.

Ever tasteful, the key was on a silver ring with a leather fob the color of summer skin. She put it on a stack of books just inside my door. Then she held up her hand to stay any protest.

—Just think about it. One day during lunch give it a walk-through. Try it on for size.

I swept up the key in my palm and followed her into the hall.

I had to laugh at the whole thing. Anne Grandyn was as sharp as a harpoon and twice as barbed: An apology followed by childhood memories of the Lower East Side; a tip of the hat to her philandering roots; I wouldn't have been surprised if she'd read the whole works of Dickens just to frost this little éclair.

—You're something else, Anne, I said with a lilt.

She turned back to face me. Her expression was more serious.

—You're the one who's something else, Katherine. Ninety-nine of a hundred women born in your place would be up to their elbows in a washtub by now. I doubt you have the slightest idea of just how unusual you are.

Whatever I'd thought Anne was up to, I wasn't ready for compliments. I found myself looking at the floor. As I looked up again, through the opening in her blouse I could see that the skin of her sternum was pale and smooth; and that she wasn't wearing a bra. I didn't have time to brace myself. When I met her gaze she kissed me. We were both wearing lipstick, so there was an unusual sensation of friction as the waxy surfaces met. She put her right arm around me and pulled me closer. Then she slowly stepped back.

—Come spy on me again sometime, she said.

As she turned to go, I reached for her elbow. I turned her back around and pulled her closer. In many ways, she was the most beautiful woman I had ever known. We were almost nose to nose. She parted her lips. I slipped my hand down her pants and deposited the key.

CHAPTER TWENTY-FOUR

Thy Kingdom Come

It was the second Saturday in December and I was in a six-story walk-up across the East River surrounded by strangers.

The afternoon before, I had run into Fran in the Village and she was full of news. She had finally checked out of Mrs. Martingale's and moved in with Grubb. It was a railroad apartment off Flatbush and from the fire escape you could practically see the Brooklyn Bridge. She had a bag in her arms overflowing with fresh mozzarella and olives and canned tomatoes and other Mott Street fare—because it was Grubb's birthday and she was going to make him Veal Pacelli. She'd even bought a hammer like her nana used to use, so she could pound the cutlets herself. Then tomorrow night they were having a party and I had to promise to come.

She was wearing jeans and a tight-fitting sweater, standing about ten feet tall. A new apartment with Grubb and a scaloppine mallet . . .

—You're on top of the world, I said, and I meant it.

She just laughed and slugged me in the shoulder.

—Cut the crap, Katey.

—I'm serious.

—Sort of, she said with a smile.

Then she got all concerned like she'd offended me.

—Hey. Don't get me wrong. Nicer words were never said. But that doesn't mean they aint crapola! I'm on the top of something, I guess, but it aint the world. We're gonna get hitched and Grubb's gonna paint and I'm gonna give him five kids and sagging tits. And I can't wait! But the top of the world? That's more in your line of work—And I'm counting on you getting there.

The crowd was a mulligan stew of their friends and acquaintances. There were gum-smacking girls from the Catholic stretches of the Jersey shore mixed in among a sampling of Astoria's poets-by-day-watchmen-by-night. There were two big-armed boys from Pacelli Trucking who'd been thrown to the mercy of an up-and-coming Emma Goldman. Everyone was wearing pants. They were crowded in elbow to elbow and ethos to ethos, shrouded in a haze of cigarette smoke. The windows were open and you could see that some of the savvier attendees had spilled onto the fire escape to breathe the late autumn air and take in the almost view of the bridge. That's where our hostess had perched herself. She was seated precariously on the fire escape's railing wearing a beret and a low-hanging cigarette in the manner of Bonnie Parker.

A late arrival from Jersey who came in behind me stopped dead in her tracks when she saw the living room wall. Hung on it from floor to ceiling was a series of Hopperesque portraits of bare-chested coat-check girls. The girls were sitting behind their counters looking aimless and bored but somehow confrontational—as if daring us to be just as aimless and bored as they. Some had their hair pulled back and others had it tucked under a cap, but all were versions of Peaches—right down to her eggplant-colored silver-dollar aureoles. I think the latecomer actually gasped. The fact that her high school chum had posed bare-chested filled her with fear and envy. You could just tell that she had made up her mind to move to New York City the next day; or never.

In the center of the wall, surrounded by Grubb's coat-check girls, hung a painting of a theater marquee on Broadway: a Hank Grey original, with apologies to Stuart Davis. He's probably here, I thought, and I found myself hoping to see his misanthropic silhouette. He was basically a porcupine, but with a sentimental stripe and quills that made you think. Maybe Tinker had been right, after all. Maybe Hank and I *had* hit it off.

True to the working-class tone of the gathering, the only alcohol in attendance appeared to be beer—but all I could find were empty bottles.

Collecting at the feet of the partygoers, they would occasionally get knocked over like ten pins and rattle across the hardwood floor. Then, coming down the crowded hallway from the kitchen, I spied a blonde holding a newly opened bottle in the air like the Statue of Liberty holds its torch.

The kitchen was decidedly less gregarious than the living room. In the middle was a raised tub where a professor and a schoolgirl sat knee to knee sniggering over personal business. I made my way to the icebox, which was along the back wall. Its door was blocked by a tall, blue-chinned bohemian. With his pointed nose and vaguely proprietary air, he recalled the half man half jackals that guarded the tombs of the pharaohs.

—May I?

He studied me for a second as if I'd roused him from a dream-filled sleep. I could see now that he was as high as the Himalayas.

—I've seen you before, he said matter-of-factly.

—Really? From what distance?

—You were a friend of Hank's. I saw you at The Lean-To.

—Oh. Right.

I vaguely remembered him now as one of the WPA types who had sat at the adjacent table.

—Actually, I was kind of looking for Hank, I said. Is he here?

—Here? No . . .

He eyed me up and down. He rubbed his fingers across the stubble on his chin.

—I guess you aint heard.

—Heard what?

He studied me a moment more.

—He's gone.

—Gone?

—Gone for good.

For a moment I was startled. It was that strange sense of surprise that unsettles us, however briefly, in the face of the inevitable.

—When? I asked.

—A week or so.

—What happened?

—That's the twist. After spending months on the dole, he had a windfall. Not nickels, you understand. Real money. Second-chance money. Build yourself a house of bricks money. But Hank, he takes the whole wad and throws himself a riot.

The jackal looked around as if he'd suddenly remembered where he was. He waved his beer bottle at the room with distaste.

—Nothin like this.

The motion seemed to remind him that his bottle was empty. With a rattle, he dumped it in the sink. He took a new one from the icebox, closed the door and leaned back.

—Yeah, he continued. It was somethin. And Hank was ring-leadin the whole thing. He had a pocketful of twenties. He was sendin the boys out for tupelo honey and turpenteen. Dolin out the dough. Then around two in the morning he had everyone drag his paintings to the roof. He dumped em in a pile, doused em with gas and set em on fire.

The jackal smiled, for all of two seconds.

—Then he threw everybody out. And that's the last we saw of him.

He took a drink and shook his head.

—Was it morphine, I asked.

—Was what morphine?

—Did he overdose?

The jackal gave an abrupt laugh and looked at me like I was crazy.

—He *enlisted.*

—Enlisted?

—Joined up. His old outfit. The Thirteenth Field Artillery. Fort Bragg. Cumberland County.

In a bit of a stupor, I turned to go.

—Hey. Didn't you want a beer?

He took a bottle from the refrigerator and handed it to me. I don't know why I took it. I didn't want it anymore.

—See ya round, he said.

Then he leaned against the icebox and closed his eyes.

—Hey, I said rousing him again.

—Yeah?

—Do you know where it came from? The windfall, I mean.

—Sure. He sold a bunch of paintings.

—You've got to be kidding.

—I don't kid.

—If he could sell his paintings, why did he enlist? Why did he burn the rest of them?

—It weren't his paintings he sold. It was some Stuart Davises he come into.

When I opened the door to my apartment, it looked unlived-in. It wasn't empty. I had my fair share of possessions. But for the last few weeks, I had been sleeping at Dicky's, and slowly but surely the place had become orderly and clean. The sink and the garbage cans were empty. The floors were bare. The clothes lay folded in their drawers and the books waited patiently in their piles. It looked like the apartment of a widower a few weeks after he's died, when his children have thrown out the trash but have yet to divvy up the dross.

That night, Dicky and I were supposed to meet for a late supper. Luckily, I caught him before he'd headed out. I told him that I was back at my place and ready to pack it in. It was obvious enough that something had spoiled the evening for me, but he didn't ask what it was.

Dicky was probably the first man I'd dated who was so well raised that he couldn't bring himself to pry. And I must have acquired a taste for the trait—because he was far from the last.

I poured myself a gin that was sized to make my apartment seem less depressing and sat in my father's easy chair.

I think it had surprised the jackal a little that Hank had wasted his windfall on a party. But it wasn't hard to see where Hank was coming from. However newly minted the bills, you couldn't escape the fact that the money from the Stuart Davises was a redistribution of Anne Grandyn's wealth—and Tinker's integrity. Hank had no choice but to treat the money with disregard.

Time has a way of playing tricks on the mind. Looking back, a series of concurrent events can seem to stretch across a year while whole seasons can collapse into a single night.

Maybe time has played such tricks on me. But the way I remember it, I was sitting there thinking about Hank's riot when the telephone rang. It was Bitsy in a halting voice. She was calling with the news that

Wallace Wolcott had been killed. Apparently, he'd been shot near Santa Teresa, where a band of Republicans were defending some little hillside town.

By the time I received the call, he was already three weeks gone. In those days, I guess it took a while for the bodies to be recovered and identified and for the news to travel home.

I thanked her for calling and lay the receiver in its cradle before she'd finished talking.

My glass was empty and I needed a drink, but I couldn't bring myself to pour one. Instead, I turned out the lights and sat on the floor with my back against the door.

◆   ◆   ◆

St. Patrick's on Fifth Avenue and Fiftieth Street is a pretty powerful example of early nineteenth-century American Gothic. Made of white marble quarried from upstate New York, the walls must be four feet thick. The stained-glass windows were made by craftsmen from Chartres. Tiffany designed two of the altars and a Medici designed the third. And the Pietà in the southeast corner is twice the size of Michelangelo's. In fact, the whole place is so well made that as the Good Lord sees about His daily business, He can pass right over St. Patrick's, confident that those inside will take pretty good care of themselves.

On this, the fifteenth of December at 3:00 P.M., it was warm and ascendant. For three nights, I'd been working with Mason on "The Secrets of Central Park West" until two or three in the morning, cabbing home for a few hours sleep, showering, changing, and then heading right back into the office without a moment for reflection—a pace which was suiting me just fine. But today, when he insisted I head home early, I found myself wandering down Fifth Avenue and up the cathedral's steps.

At that time of day, there were 400 pews and 396 of them were empty. I took a seat and tried to let my mind wander; but it wouldn't.

Eve, Hank, Wallace.

Suddenly, all the people of valor were gone. One by one, they had glittered and disappeared, leaving behind those who couldn't free themselves from their wants: like Anne and Tinker and me.

—May I, someone asked genteelly.

I looked up a little annoyed that with all that space someone felt the need to crowd my pew. But it was Dicky.

—What are you doing here? I whispered.

—Repenting?

He slid in beside me and automatically put his hands on his knees like someone who had been well trained as a fidgety child.

—How did you find me? I asked.

He leaned to his right without taking his eyes off the altar.

—I stopped by your office so that I could run into you by chance. When your absence spoiled my plan, a rather tough cookie with cat's-eye glasses suggested I might happen into one of the neighborhood churches instead. She said you occasionally visit them on your coffee break.

You had to give Alley credit. I had never told her that I liked to visit churches and she had never made reference to knowing. But giving Dicky that tip may well have been the first concrete sign that she and I were going to be friends for a long, long time.

—How did you know which church I was in? I asked.

—It stood to reason. Because you weren't in the last three.

I gave Dicky's hand a squeeze and said nothing.

Having studied the sanctuary, Dicky was now looking up into the recesses of the church's ceiling.

—Are you familiar with Galileo? he asked.

—He discovered the world was round.

Dicky looked at me surprised.

—Really? Was that him? We've sure made hay with that discovery!

—Wasn't that who you meant?

—I don't know. What I recall about this Galileo fellow is that he was the one who figured that a pendulum takes the same amount of time to swing two feet or two inches. This, of course, solved the mystery of the grandfather clock. Anyway, apparently he discovered this by watching a chandelier swing back and forth from the ceiling of a church. He would measure the duration of the swings by taking his pulse.

—That's amazing.

—Isn't it? Just by sitting in church. Ever since I learned that as a boy, I've let my mind wander during sermons. But I haven't had a single revelation.

I laughed.

—Shhh, he said.

A canon appeared from one of the side chapels. He knelt, crossed himself, ascended into the sanctuary, and began to light the candles on the altar, preparing for the four o'clock mass. He was dressed in a long black robe. Watching him, Dicky's face lit up as if he had just had his long awaited revelation.

—You're Catholic!

I laughed again.

—No. I'm not particularly religious, but I was born Russian Orthodox.

Dicky whistled. It was loud enough that the canon looked back.

—That sounds formidable, he said.

—I don't know about that. But for Easter, we'd fast all day and eat all night.

Dicky seemed to consider this carefully.

—I think I could do that.

—I think you could.

We were silent for a while. Then he leaned a little to his right.

—I haven't seen you in a few days.

—I know.

—Are you going to tell me what's going on?

We looked at each other now.

—It's a long story, Dicky.

—Let's go outside.

We sat on the cold steps with our forearms on our knees and I told him an abbreviated version of the same story that I had told Bitsy at the Ritz.

With a little more distance, and maybe a little more self-consciousness, I found myself telling it as if it were a Broadway romp. I was making the most of the coincidences and the surprises: Meeting Anne at the track! Eve refusing the proposal! Stumbling on Anne and Tinker at Chinoiserie!

—But this is the funniest part, I said.

Then I told him about discovering Washington's *Rules of Civility* and what a numbskull I had been in not realizing that it was Tinker's playbook. For illustration, I rattled off a few of Washington's maxims with a snappy delivery.

But, whether it was from being on the steps of a church in December or from wisecracking about the father of our country, the humor didn't seem to be coming across. As I hit the final lines, my voice faltered.

—That didn't seem so funny, after all, I said.

—No, said Dicky.

He was suddenly more serious than usual. He clasped his hands and looked down at the steps. He didn't say anything. It began to scare me a little.

—Do you want to get out of here? I asked.

—No. That's all right. Let's stay a moment.

He was silent.

—What are you thinking? I pressed.

He began to tap his feet on the steps in an uncharacteristically unfidgety way.

—What am I thinking? he said to himself. What am I thinking?

Dicky breathed in and exhaled, getting ready.

—I am thinking that maybe you're being a little hard on this Tinker fellow.

He stopped tapping his feet and directed his attention across Fifth Avenue toward the deco-era statue of Atlas that holds up the heavens in front of Rockefeller Center. It was almost as if Dicky couldn't quite look at me yet.

—So this Tinker fellow, he said—in the tone of one wishing to make sure that he's got command of the facts—he was ousted from prep school when his father squandered his tuition. He goes to work and along the way he stumbles onto Lucrezia Borgia who lures him to New York with the promise of a foot in the door. You all meet by chance. And though he seems to have a thing for you, he ends up taking in your friend who's been smashed up by a milk truck, until she brushes him off. Then his brother sort of brushes him off too. . . .

I found myself looking at the ground.

—Is that about it? Dicky asked sympathetically.

—Yes, I said.

—And before you knew all of this, all of this about Anne Grandyn and Fall River and railroad shares and what-have-you, you fell for the bloke.

—Yes.

—So I suppose the question now is—despite the rest of it—are you fallen for him still?

After meeting someone by chance and throwing off a few sparks, can there be any substance to the feeling that you've known each other your whole lives? After those first few hours of conversation, can you really be sure that your connection is so uncommon that it belongs outside the bounds of time and convention? And if so, won't that someone have just as much capacity to upend as to perfect all your hours that follow?

So despite the rest of it, Dicky asked with supernatural remove, are you fallen for him still?

Don't say it, Katey. For God's sake, don't admit it. Get off your ass and kiss this madcapper. Convince him never to discuss it again.

—Yes, I said.

Yes—that word that is supposed to be bliss. *Yes,* said Juliet. *Yes,* said Heloise. *Yes, yes, yes,* said Molly Bloom. The avowal, the affirmation, the sweet permission. But in the context of this conversation, it was poison.

I could almost feel something dying inside him. And what was dying was his self-confident, unquestioning, all-forgiving impression of me.

—Well, he said.

Above me, the black-winged angels circled like desert birds.

— . . . I don't know if this friend of yours genuinely aspired to these Rules, or simply aped them so that he would be better received by his neighbors; but is there really any difference? I mean, Old George didn't make them up. He was marking them down from somewhere and trying to make the most of himself. It strikes me as all rather impressive. I don't think I could live up to more than five or six of them at a time.

We were both looking at the statue now with its exaggerated muscu-lature. Though I'd been in St. Patrick's a thousand times, it had never struck me until that moment how odd it was to have Atlas, of all people, standing on the other side of the avenue. He was situated so directly across from the cathedral that as you were walking out, his towering figure was framed by the doorway, almost as if he was waiting for you.

Could there have been a more contrary statue to place across from one of the largest cathedrals in America? Atlas, who attempted to overthrow the gods on Olympus and was thus condemned to shoulder the celestial spheres for all eternity—the very personification of hubris and brute endurance. While back in the shadows of St. Patrick's was the statue's physical and spiritual antithesis, the Pietà—in which our Savior, having already sacrificed himself to God's will, is represented broken, emaciated, laid out on Mary's lap.

Here they resided, two worldviews separated only by Fifth Avenue, facing off until the end of time or the end of Manhattan, whichever came first.

I must have looked pretty miserable—because Dicky patted me on the knee.

—If we only fell in love with people who were perfect for us, he said, then there wouldn't be so much fuss about love in the first place.

♦ ♦ ♦

I suppose that Anne was right when she observed that at any given moment we're all seeking someone's forgiveness. Either way, as I was walking downtown, I knew whose I was seeking. And after telling people for months that I had no idea where he was, suddenly I knew exactly where to find him.

CHAPTER TWENTY-FIVE

Where He Lived and What He Lived For

Vitelli's was on Gansevoort in the heart of the meatpacking district. Large black trucks crowded the curb at odd angles and the faint smell of soured blood rose from the cobblestones. In some infernal version of Noah's ark, teamsters walked off the trucks onto the loading docks carrying carcasses of different species slung over their shoulders two by two: two calves, two pigs, two lambs. Butchers on break dressed in blood-spattered aprons smoked in the cold December air under the great steer-shaped neon sign that Hank had stylized in his painting. They watched me navigate the cobblestones in high-heel shoes with the same indifference that they watched the meat coming off the trucks.

A hophead in a woman's coat was nodding on the stoop. His nose and chin were scabbed as if he'd broken a fall with his face. After a little prodding, he said that Hank lived in #7, saving me the social studies lesson of rapping on every door. The stairway was narrow and damp. Halfway up the first flight was an old Negro with a cane who could have ascended faster to heaven than he could to the fourth floor. I passed him and climbed to the second landing. The door was ajar.

Given all that had happened, I'd prepared myself to find Tinker at low ebb. Hell, at one point, I'd even hoped to find him that way. But standing there on the banks of his comeuppance, I wasn't so sure I was ready for it.

—Hello? I ventured, easing the apartment door open.

The word apartment hardly applied. Lucky #7 was two hundred

square feet. It had a squat iron bed with a gray mattress—the sort you'd expect to see in a prison cell or barracks. In the corner a coal stove sat by a small but-thank-God-for-it window. But for a few pairs of shoes and an empty gunnysack stowed under the bed, Hank's belongings were gone. Tinker's were on the floor against the wall: a leather suitcase, a flannel blanket tied in a roll, a small stack of books.

—He aint in deh.

I turned to find the old Negro on the landing beside me.

—If you looking for Mr. Henry's brotheh, he aint in deh.

The old Negro pointed his cane toward the ceiling.

—He on da roof.

On the roof. The very place where Hank had built the bonfire of his canvases—before he turned his back on New York City and his brother's way of life.

I found Tinker sitting on a dormant chimney, his arms resting on his knees, his gaze cast downward to the Hudson River where the cold gray freighters were lined along the docks. From the back, he looked as if his life had just set sail on one.

—Hey, I said, stopping a few paces behind him.

At the sound of my voice, he turned and stood—and I could see in an instant that I was wrong again. Dressed in a black sweater, clean shaven and easy, Tinker wasn't close to downcast.

—Katey! he said in pleasant surprise.

Instinctively, he took a step forward, but then stopped as if he'd caught himself—as if he suspected that he'd forfeited the right to the friendly embrace. Which in a way, he had. His smile took on an aspect of knowing contrition, signaling that he was ready to receive, or even welcome, another round of reprobation.

—They killed Wallace, I said, as if I'd just heard the news and couldn't quite believe it.

—I know, he said.

And then I unraveled and his arms were around me.

We ended up spending an hour or two on the roof, sitting on the edge of a skylight. For a while, we just talked about Wallace. And then we were quiet. And then I apologized for how I had acted in the coffee shop, but Tinker shook his head. He said I'd been terrific that day, that I hadn't missed a trick, that it was just what he had needed.

As we sat there, dusk was falling and the lights of the city were coming on one by one in ways that even Edison hadn't imagined. They came on across the great patchwork of office buildings and along the cables of the bridges; then it was the street lamps and the theater marquees, the headlights of the cars and the beacons perched atop the radio towers—each individual lumen testifying to some unhesitant intemperate collective aspiration.

—Hank would spend hours on end up here, Tinker said. I used to try to get him to move, to take an apartment in the Village with a sink. But he wouldn't budge. He said the Village was too bourgeois. But I think he stayed because of the view. It's the same one we grew up with.

A freight horn blew and Tinker pointed to it as if it proved his point. I smiled and nodded.

. . .

—I guess I haven't told you much about my life in Fall River, he said.
—No.
—How does that happen? How do you stop telling people where you're from?
—By inches.

Tinker nodded and looked back over the piers.

—The irony is that I loved that part of my life—when we lived near the shipyards. It was a ragtag neighborhood, and when school let out, we'd all run down to the docks. We didn't know the batting averages; but we knew Morse code and the flags of the big shipping lines and we'd watch the crews coming down the gangplanks with their duffels over their shoulders. That's what we all wanted to be when we grew up: merchant marines. We wanted to set sail on a freighter and make landfall in Amsterdam or Hong Kong or Peru.

You look back with the benefit of age upon the dreams of most children and what makes them seem so endearing is their unattainability— this one wanted to be a pirate, this one a princess, this one president. But from the way Tinker talked you got the sense that his starry-eyed dreams were still within his reach; maybe closer than ever.

———

When it grew dark, we retreated to Hank's room. In the staircase, Tinker asked if I wanted to get a bite. I said I wasn't hungry and he looked relieved. I think we'd both had our fill of restaurants for the year.

Without any chairs on hand, we made do sitting face-to-face on two overturned produce crates: HALLELUJAH ONIONS and AVIATOR LIMES.

—How are things going at the magazine? he asked, enthusiastically.

Up in the Adirondacks, I had told him about Alley and Mason Tate and the search for our first cover story. So now I told him my idea of interviewing the doormen and some of the scuttle we'd dredged up. As I was describing it, for the first time I felt a little squeamish. Somehow, the whole notion seemed more unseemly here in Hank's flophouse than it had in the back of Mason Tate's limousine.

But Tinker loved it. Not in the way that Mason loved it. Not because it was going to peel the New York potato. Tinker just loved the ingenuity of it, the human comedy of it—that all those secrets of adultery and illegitimacy and ill-gotten gains—secrets which had been so closely kept—had all the time been floating freely across the surface of the city unheeded, just like the little boats that boys fold from the headlines and sail across the ponds in Central Park. But most of all, Tinker loved that I had come up with the idea.

—We deserve it, he said with a laugh and a shake of the head, classing himself among the secret keepers.

—You certainly do.

When we both stopped laughing, I began telling him some funny story we'd learned from an elevator boy, but he cut me off.

—I encouraged her, Katey.

I met his gaze.

—From the minute I met Anne, I encouraged her to take me on. I knew exactly what she could do for me. And what it would cost.

—That wasn't the worst of it, Tinker.

—I know. I know. I should have told you at the coffee shop; or upstate. I should have told you everything the night we met.

At some point, Tinker noticed that my arms were wrapped around my torso.

—You're freezing, he said. I'm such an idiot.

He leapt up and looked around the room. He unfurled his blanket and put it over my shoulders.

—I'll be right back.

I heard him trounce down the stairs. The door to the street slammed shut.

With the blanket still on my shoulders, I stamped my feet and wandered in a circle. Hank's painting of the protest on the pier was lying on the center of the gray mattress, suggesting that Tinker had been sleeping on the floor. I stopped in front of Tinker's suitcase. The inside of the lid was lined with blue silk pockets sized for different items—a hairbrush, a shaving brush, a comb—all of which presumably had borne Tinker's initials and all of which were gone.

I knelt to look at the stack of books. They were the reference books from the study at the Beresford and the book of Washingtonia that had been given to him by his mother. But there was also the edition of *Walden* that I'd seen in the Adirondacks. It was a little more scuffed around the edges now, as if it had been carried in a back pocket—up and down the trail to Pinyon Peak, up and down Tenth Avenue, up and down this narrow flophouse stair.

Tinker's footsteps sounded on the landing. I sat on his crate.

He came through the door with two pounds of coal wrapped in newspaper. He got down on his knees in front of the stove and set about lighting the fire, blowing on the flames like a scout.

He always looked his best, I thought to myself, when circumstances called for him to be a boy and a man at the same time.

That night, Tinker borrowed a blanket from a neighbor and laid out two beds on the floor a few feet apart—maintaining the same respectful distance that he had established on the roof when I'd first arrived. I rose early enough so I could get home and shower before work. When I got back in the evening, he leapt up from the HALLELUJAH ONIONS as if he'd been waiting there all day. Then we went across Tenth Avenue to the little diner on the piers with the blue neon sign that read OPEN ALL NIGHT.

———

It's a funny thing about that meal. All these years later, I remember the oysters I ate at the 21 Club. I remember the black bean soup with sherry at the Beresford when Eve and Tinker had returned from Palm Beach. I remember the salad I had with Wallace at the Park with blue cheese and bacon. And, all too well, I remember the truffle-stuffed chicken at La Belle Époque. But I don't remember what we ate that night at Hank's diner.

What I remember is that we had a lot of laughs.

Then at some point, for some stupid reason, I asked him what he was going to do. And he grew serious.

—Mostly, he said, I've been thinking about what I'm not going to do. When I think of the last few years, I've been hounded by regrets for what's already happened and fears for what might. By nostalgia for what I've lost and desire for what I don't have. All this wanting and not wanting. It's worn me out. For once, I'm going to try the present on for size.

—You're going to let your affairs be as two or three, and not a hundred or a thousand?

—That's it, he said. Any interest?

—What'll it cost me?

—According to Thoreau, nearly everything.

—It'd be nice to have everything at least once before giving it up. He smiled.

—I'll give you a call when you've got it.

When we got back to Hank's apartment, Tinker lit a fire and we swapped stories into the night—the details of one circumstance triggering the memory of another and then another in effortless succession. Like two teenagers who've struck up a friendship on a cross-Atlantic steamer, we raced to trade reminiscences and insights and dreams before reaching port.

And when he laid out our bedrolls at the same respectful distance, this time I pushed mine over until there wasn't a breath of space between us.

◆　◆　◆

The next evening, when I returned to Gansevoort Street, he was already gone.

He hadn't taken the fine leather case. It was sitting there empty beside the stack of books, its lid leaning against the wall. In the end, he had stuffed his clothes into his brother's gunnysack. I was surprised at first that he'd left the books behind; but on closer inspection, I saw that he'd taken the little, worn edition of *Walden*.

The stove was cold. On top of it there was a note in Tinker's hand, written on a torn endpaper.

> *Dearest Kate,*
> *You have no idea what it has meant to me to see you these last two nights.*
> *To have left without speaking, without telling you the truth, would have been the only regret I carried away.*
> *I'm so glad that your life is going well. Having made a hash of mine, I know what a fine thing it is to have found your spot.*
> *It was a rotten year of my own making. But even at its worst, you always gave me a glimpse of what might otherwise be.*

I'm not sure where I'm going, he concluded. *But wherever I end up, I'll start every day by saying your name.* As if by doing so, he might remain more true to himself.

Then he signed it: *Tinker Grey 1910 – ?*

I didn't linger. I went down the stairs and into the street. I got as far as Eighth Avenue before turning back. I trudged all the way across Gansevoort, back over the cobblestones, up the narrow stair. And when I got into the room, I grabbed the painting of the dockworkers along with the volume of Washingtonia. One day he would regret having left them behind. I looked forward to being in a position to return them.

Some of you will think this a romantic thing to have done. But at another level, the reason I went back for Tinker's things was to assuage a sense of guilt. For when I had walked in the room and found it empty, even as I was fending off a sense of loss, a slender, vigorous part of myself was feeling a sense of relief.

CHAPTER TWENTY-SIX

A Ghost of Christmas Past

On Friday, the 23rd of December, I was sitting at my kitchen table cutting slices from a ten-pound ham and drinking bourbon from a bottle. Beside my plate was a proof of the premier issue of *Gotham*. Mason had spent a lot of time thinking about the cover. He wanted it to be *Eye-Catching*, *Beautiful*, *Witty*, *Scandalous*, and above all else, a *Surprise*. So only three copies of the mock-up existed: Mason's, the art director's, and mine.

It was a photograph of a naked woman standing behind a five-foot-high model of the San Remo apartment building. Through the windows you could see her skin, but curtains had been drawn selectively to obscure your view of her finer parts.

I had been given one of the mock-ups because the image had been my idea.

Well, sort of.

It was actually a variation on a painting by René Magritte that I had seen at the Modern. Mason had loved the idea and bet me my career that I couldn't find a woman to pose for it. The photograph was framed so that you couldn't see the woman's face, but if the curtains on the fifteenth floor had been open, you would have seen a pair of eggplant-colored silver-dollar aureoles.

That afternoon Mason had called me into his office and asked me to sit—something he hadn't done more than twice since the day he'd hired me. As it turned out, Alley had been on the money with her plan—both of us were going to be held on for another year.

When I stood to go, Mason gave me his congratulations, the proof with the mock-up and, as a bonus, he threw in the honey-baked ham that the mayor had sent him. I knew it came from the mayor because His Honor's warm wishes were written on a golden card in the shape of a star. Lugging the ham under my arm, at the door I turned back to thank Mr. Tate.

—No thanks are necessary, he replied without looking up from his work. You've earned it.

—Then thank you for giving me the opportunity in the first place.

—You should thank your sponsor for that.

—I'll give Mr. Parish a call.

Mason looked up from his desk and eyed me with curiosity.

—You'd better keep a closer eye on who your friends are, Kontent. It wasn't Parish who recommended you. It was Anne Grandyn. She's the one who twisted my arm.

I took another slug of bourbon.

I wasn't much of a bourbon drinker, but I had bought the bottle on the way home thinking it would go well with the ham. And it did. I had bought a little Christmas tree too and set it up by the window. Without decorations it looked a little forlorn, so I pulled the mayor's golden star off the ham and propped it on the highest branch. Then I got myself comfortable and opened *Hercule Poirot's Christmas*, Mrs. Christie's latest. I had bought it back in November and had been saving it for tonight. But before I could get started, there was a knock at the door.

I suppose it's an immutable law of human nature that we sum up the events of the year as we approach its end. Among other things, 1938 had been a year of knockings at my door. There was the Western Union boy who brought Eve's birthday wishes all the way from London; and Wallace with a bottle of wine and the rules of honeymoon bridge. Then Detective Tilson; then Bryce; then Anne.

In the moment, only some of those intrusions seemed welcome; but I guess I should have treasured them all. Because in a few years' time,

I'd be living in a doorman building myself—and once you're in a door-man building, no one comes knocking ever again.

Tonight, the knocker at my door was a heavyset young man dressed in a Herbert Hoover suit. The walk up the stairs had winded him and his brow looked waxy with perspiration.

—Miss Kontent?

—Yes.

—Miss Katherine Kontent?

—That's right.

He was greatly relieved.

—My name is Niles Copperthwaite. I am an attorney with Heavely & Hound.

—You're kidding, I said with a laugh.

He looked taken aback.

—Hardly, Miss Kontent.

—I see. Well. An attorney making house calls on the Friday before Christmas. I hope I'm not in some sort of trouble.

—No, Miss Kontent! You are not in any trouble.

He said this with all the confidence of youth, but a moment later he added:

—At least no trouble of which Heavely & Hound is aware.

—A well-considered qualification, Mr. Copperthwaite. I shall bear it in mind. How can I help you?

—You have helped me already by being home at your previously listed address. I come at the behest of a client.

He reached behind the doorjamb and produced a long object wrapped in heavy white paper. It was tied with a polka-dot ribbon and had a tag that read DON'T OPEN TIL XMAS.

—This is being delivered, he said, as per the instruction of—

—One Wallace Wolcott.

—That's right.

He hesitated.

—It's a little out of the ordinary, as . . .

—As Mr. Wolcott is no longer with us.

We were both silent.

—If you don't mind my saying so, Miss Kontent, I can see that you are surprised. I hope the surprise is not an unpleasant one.

—Mr. Copperthwaite, if there were mistletoe over my door, I would kiss you.

—Well, yes. I mean . . . no.

He stole a glance at the top of the door frame, then straightened his posture and said more formally:

—A Merry Christmas to you, Miss Kontent.

—And a Merry Christmas to you, Mr. Copperthwaite.

I was never the type to wait until Christmas morning to open gifts. If I've got a Christmas present in my grips on the Fourth of July, I'll open it by the light of the fireworks. So I sat down in my easy chair and opened this package that had been waiting so patiently to come knocking at my door.

It was a rifle. I didn't know it then, but it was a Winchester 1894 from a small run overseen by John Moses Browning himself. It had a walnut stock, an ivory sight, and elaborate, floral scrolling on the polished-brass frame. It was a rifle you could have worn to your wedding.

Wallace Wolcott sure had the gift of timing. You had to grant him that.

I balanced the rifle in my palms the way that Wallace had taught me. It probably weighed no more than four pounds. I pulled back the action and looked inside the empty chamber. I closed it again and leveled the gun against my shoulder. Sighting down the barrel, I aimed at the top of my little Christmas tree and then I shot the mayor's star right off the top.

Twenty minutes before the whistle, the foreman circled by and told them to slow the fuck down.

In a long chain, teams of two were relaying sacks of sugar from a Caribbean freighter to a warehouse on the Hell's Kitchen wharf. He and the Negro they called King were at the front of the chain. So when the foreman gave the order, King reset the tempo: one-one-thousand hook, two-one-thousand heft, three-one-thousand turn, four-one-thousand toss.

On the day after Christmas, the union of tugboat engineers had gone on strike without warning or the support of the longshoremen. At the edge of the Lower Bay, somewhere off Sandy Hook and Breezy Point, an armada of cargo ships were drifting, waiting to make landfall. So the word, up and down the line, was to ease it. God willing, the strike would be over before the ships in dock were empty, and they'd be able to keep the crews intact.

As the new man, well he knew that if they began cutting, he'd be the first to go.

But that was just as it should be.

The pace that King had chosen was a good one. It let him feel the strength in his arms and his legs and his back. The strength was moving through him now with every swing of the hook like an electrical charge. It was a feeling that he had lived without for a long time. Like the feeling of hunger before supper, or exhaustion before sleep.

Another good thing about the pace was that it allowed for a little more conversation:

(One-one-thousand hook.)

—So where are you from, King?

—Harlem.

(Two-one-thousand heft.)

—How long have you lived there?

—All my life.

(Three-one-thousand turn.)

—How long have you worked this wharf?

—Even longer.

(Four-one-thousand toss.)

—What's it like?

—Just like heaven: full of fine folk who mind their own business.

He smiled at King and hooked the next sack. Because he understood what King was driving at. It was the same in Fall River. Nobody liked the new guy to begin with. For every man the company hired, there were twenty brothers or uncles or childhood pals who'd been passed over. So the less trouble you made for yourself the better. And that meant carrying your weight and keeping your mouth shut.

When the whistle sounded, King lingered as the other men headed for the Tenth Avenue bars.

He lingered too. He offered King a cigarette and they smoked with their backs against a packing crate, watching the men retreat. They smoked idly without speaking. When they were done with their cigarettes, they tossed the butts off the pier and began walking toward the gates.

Halfway between the freighter and the warehouse, there was a pile of sugar on the ground. One of the men must have torn the burlap of a sack with his hook. King paused over the sugar and shook his head. Then he knelt, took a fistful, and put it in his pocket.

—Come on, he said. You might as well take some too. If you don't, it's just going to the rats.

So he knelt down and took some too. It was amber and crystalline. He almost put it in his right pocket, but remembered in time that the right pocket was the one with the hole, so he put it in his left.

When they got to the gate, he asked King if he wanted to walk a bit. King gestured with his head in the general direction of the elevated. He was headed home to a wife and kids. King had never said as much, but he didn't need to. You could just tell.

The day before, when work let out, he had walked south along the wharf. So today, he walked north.

With nightfall, the air had grown bitter cold and he wished that he had worn his sweater under his coat.

The piers above Fortieth Street reached into the deepest waters of the Hudson and were lined with the largest ships. Bound for Argentina, the one at Pier 75 looked like a fortress, impregnable and gray. He had heard that it was looking for seafaring men, and he might have angled for the job if he had only saved enough money. He was hoping to wander a bit once he'd made port. But there would be other chances on other boats heading to other places.

On Pier 77, there was a Cunard ocean liner stocked for a transatlantic crossing. On Boxing Day, it was blowing its horn and the confetti was falling from the upper decks to the docks—when word of the strike reached the helm. Cunard sent the passengers home, advising them to leave their trunks on board, as the strike was sure to be resolved within the day. Five days later, every stateroom had its share of cocktail dresses and evening gowns, of waistcoats and cummerbunds waiting in a ghostly silence—like the costumes in the attics of an opera house.

On Pier 80, the longest pier on the Hudson, there were no ships in dock. It jutted out into the river like the first leg of a new highway. He walked all the way out to the end. He took another cigarette from the pack and lit it with his lighter. Snapping the lighter shut, he turned and leaned against a piling.

From the end of the pier he could see the city's skyline in its entirety—the whole staggered assembly of townhouses and warehouses and skyscrapers stretching from Washington Heights to the Battery. Nearly every light in every window in every building seemed to be shimmering and tenuous—as if powered by the animal spirits within—by the arguments and endeavors, the whims and elisions. But here and there, scattered across the mosaic, were also the isolated windows that seemed to burn a little brighter and more constant—the windows lit by those few who acted with poise and purpose.

He scuffed out his cigarette and decided to dwell in the cold a little while longer.

For however inhospitable the wind, from this vantage point Manhattan was simply so improbable, so wonderful, so obviously full of promise—that you wanted to approach it for the rest of your life without ever quite arriving.

EPILOGUE

Few Are Chosen

It was the last night of 1940 and the snow was blowing two knots shy of a blizzard. Within the hour there wouldn't be a car moving in all Manhattan. They'd be buried like boulders under the snow. But for now, they crawled along with the weary determination of wayward pioneers.

Eight of us had stumbled out of a dance at the University Club that we hadn't been invited to in the first place. The party had been on the second floor under the great palazzo ceilings. A thirty-piece orchestra dressed in white was ushering in 1941 in the brand-new and already outmoded style of Guy Lombardo. Unbeknownst to us, the party had an ulterior motive—to raise money for refugees from Estonia. When a latter-day Carry Nation stood alongside a dispossessed ambassador to rattle her tin can, we made for the door.

On the way out, Bitsy had somehow come into possession of a trumpet and, as she was making a pretty impressive show of the scales, the rest of us huddled under a street lamp to plan a course of action. A quick look at the roads and we could tell a taxi wouldn't be coming to the rescue. Carter Hill said he knew of a perfect hideaway just around the corner where we could find food and drink, so under his direction we set off westward through the snow. None of the girls were dressed for the weather, but I had the good fortune of being tucked under one wing of Harrison Harcourt's fur-collared coat.

Midway down the block, a rival party coming in the other direction pelted us with snowballs. Bitsy sounded the charge and we counterattacked.

Taking cover behind a newsstand and a mailbox, we drove them off hooting like Indians, but when Jack "mistakenly" toppled Bitsy into a snowbank, the girls turned on the boys. It was as if our New Year's resolution was to act like we were ten.

The thing of it is—1939 may have brought the beginning of the war in Europe, but in America it brought the end of the Depression. While they were annexing and appeasing, we were stoking the steel plants, reassembling the assembly lines, and readying ourselves to meet a world-wide demand for arms and ammunition. In December 1940, with France already fallen and the Luftwaffe bombarding London, back in America Irving Berlin was observing how the treetops glistened and children listened to hear those sleigh bells in the snow. That's how far away *we* were from the Second World War.

Carter's nearby hideaway ended up being a ten-block slog. As we turned onto Broadway, the wind howled down from Harlem blowing the snow against our backs. I had Harry's coat cloaked over my head and was letting myself be steered by an elbow. So when we got to the front of the restaurant I didn't even see what it looked like. Harry ushered me down the steps, pulled back his coat, and *voila*, I was in a sizable midblock joint serving Italian food, Italian wine, and Italian jazz, whatever that was.

Midnight had come and gone so the floor was covered with confetti. Most of the revelers who had spent the countdown in the restaurant had come and gone too.

We didn't wait for their plates to be cleared. We just stomped our shoes, shook off the snow, and commandeered a table for eight opposite the bar. I sat next to Bitsy. Carter slipped into the chair on my right, leaving Harry to find a seat across the table. Jack picked up a wine bottle left by the prior patrons and squinted to see if there were remnants.

—We need wine, he said.

—Indeed we do, said Carter, catching a waiter's eye. Maestro! Three bottles of Chianti!

The waiter, who had the big eyebrows and big hands of Bela Lugosi, opened the bottles with glum attention.

—Not exactly the jovial sort, Carter observed.

But it was hard to tell. Like so many Italians in New York in 1940, maybe his normal joviality was overshadowed by the unfortunate allegiances of the old country.

Carter volunteered to order a few plates for the table, and then made a reasonable stab at launching a conversation by asking people what was the *best* thing they did in 1940. It made me a little nostalgic for Dicky. No one could get a table talking nonsense like Dicky Vanderwhile.

As someone rattled on about a trip to Cuba ("the new Riviera"), Carter leaned toward me and whispered in my ear.

—What's the *worst* thing you did in 1940?

A piece of bread sailed across the table and hit him on the head.

—Hey, Carter said, looking up.

The only way you could tell it was Harry was by his perfect repose and a slight upward turn of his lips. I considered giving him a wink; instead I threw the bread back. He acted aghast. I was about to do the same when a waiter handed me a piece of folded paper. It was an unsigned note scrawled in a rough hand.

SHOULD OLD ACQUAINTANCE BE FORGOT?

When I looked confused, the waiter pointed toward the bar. Seated on one of the stools was a stocky, good-looking soldier. He was grinning a little impolitely. Well groomed as he was, I almost didn't recognize him. But, sure as the shore, it was unwavering Henry Grey.

Should old acquaintance be forgot, and never brought to mind?

Sometimes, it sure seems that's what life intends. After all, it's basically like a centrifuge that spins every few years casting proximate bodies in disparate directions. And when the spinning stops, almost before we can catch our breath, life crowds us with a calendar of new concerns. Even if we wanted to retrace our steps and rekindle our old acquaintances, how could we possibly find the time?

The year 1938 had been one in which four people of great color and character had held welcome sway over my life. And here it was December 31, 1940, and I hadn't seen a single one of them in over a year.

———

Dicky was forcibly uprooted in January 1939.

On the heels of the New York cotillion season, Mr. Vanderwhile finally became fed up with his son's easy ways. So under the auspices of the recovering economy, he sent Dicky to Texas to work on an old friend's oil rigs. Mr. Vanderwhile was convinced that this would make "quite an impression" on Dicky; and it did. Though not in the way Mr. Vanderwhile expected. His friend happened to have an ornery daughter who adopted Dicky as a dance partner when she was home for the Easter break. When she went back to school, Dicky sought to extract some promise of love, only to be rebuffed. While the weeks with Dicky had been great fun, she explained, in the long run she saw herself with someone a little more practical, down to earth, ambitious—that is, of course, someone a little more like her pa. Before long Dicky found himself working extra hours and applying to Harvard Business School.

He would get his degree in 1941, just six months before Pearl Harbor. From there, he enlisted, served with distinction in the Pacific, returned to marry his Texan, had three children, went to work in the State Department, and generally made a hash of everything that anyone had ever said of him.

Eve Ross, she just waltzed away.

The first I heard tell of her after she disappeared to Los Angeles was a clipping that Peaches gave me in March of 1939. It was a photograph from a gossip magazine and it showed a boisterous Olivia de Havilland pushing through a line of photographers outside the Tropicana on Sunset. She was on the arm of a young woman with a good figure, a sleeveless dress, and a scar on her cheek. The photograph was titled *Gone with the Wind* and the caption referred to the scarred woman as de Havilland's "confidante."

The next I heard of Evey was on the first of April, when I received a long-distance call at two in the morning. The man on the other end of the line identified himself as a detective with the Los Angeles Police Department. He said he was sorry for disturbing me, he knew it was late, but he had no alternative. A young woman had been discovered unconscious on the lawn of the Beverly Hills Hotel and my telephone number had been found in her pocket.

I was stunned.

Then I heard Eve in the background.

—Did she bite?

—Of course she did, said the detective, betraying an English accent. Like a trout to a fly.

—Give me that!

—Wait!

The two were wrestling for the phone.

—April fools, the man shouted.

Then the receiver was plucked away.

—Did we get you, Sis?

—Did you ever.

Evey howled with laughter.

It was good to hear. For half an hour, we back-and-forthed, bringing each other up-to-date and paying tribute to the fine times we'd had in New York City. But when I asked if she might be coming back east any time soon, she said as far as she was concerned, the Rockies weren't high enough.

Wallace, of course, was stolen from the living.

But in one of life's little ironies, of the four with whom I'd spent 1938, it was Wallace who maintained the greatest influence on my daily life. For in the spring of 1939, I received a second visit from the perspiring Niles Copperthwaite. This time he brought the extraordinary news that Wallace Wolcott had written me into his will. Specifically, he had directed that the dividends from a generation-skipping trust be diverted to me for the remainder of my life. This was to bring me an annual income of eight hundred dollars. Eight hundred dollars may not have been a fortune, not even in 1939, but it was enough to ensure that I could think twice before accepting the advances of any man; which, come to think of it, for a girl in Manhattan entering her late twenties, was fortune enough.

And Tinker Grey?

I didn't know where Tinker was. But in a sense, I knew what had become of him. Having cut himself adrift, Tinker had finally found his way to unfettered terrain. Whether trekking the snows of the Yukon or sailing the seas of Polynesia, Tinker was where the view to the horizon was unimpeded, the crickets commanded the stillness, the present was paramount, and there was absolutely no need for the *Rules of Civility*.

Should old acquaintance be forgot and never brought to mind? If so, then only at our peril. I crossed to the bar.

—Katey, right?

—Hello, Hank. You look well.

And he did. Better than anyone in their right mind would have expected. The demands of army life had filled out his features and his build. And the stripes on his crisp khaki uniform advertised the rank of sergeant.

I acknowledged his stripes with a figurative tip of the hat.

—Don't bother, he said with an easy smile. They won't last.

But I wasn't so sure. He looked like the army had yet to see the best of him.

He nodded toward our table.

—I see you've found yourself a new circle of friends.

—Several.

—I'll bet. I think I owe you one. Let me buy you a drink.

He ordered beer for himself and a martini for me, as if he'd known all along that that was my drink. We clinked glasses and wished each other a Happy 1941.

—Have you seen my brother around?

—No, I admitted. I haven't seen him in two years.

—Yeah. I suppose that makes some sense.

—Have you heard from him?

—On and off. When I get leave, sometimes I come up to New York and we get together.

I wasn't expecting that.

I took a drink of my gin.

He eyed me with a sly smile.

—You're surprised, he said.

—I didn't know that he was in New York.

—Where would he be?

—I don't know. I just figured that when he quit, he'd left town.

—No. He stuck around. He got a job working on the Hell's Kitchen docks for a while. After that, he drifted around the boroughs and we lost touch. Then last spring I ran into him on the street in Red Hook.

—Where was he living? I asked.

—I'm not sure. One of the flophouses by the Navy Yards, I suppose. We were both silent for a moment.

—How was he? I asked.

—You know. A little scruffy. A little lean.

—No. I mean how was he?

—Oh, Hank said with a smile. You mean how was he on the *inside*. Hank didn't need to consider.

—He was happy.

◆ ◆ ◆

The snows of the Yukon . . . the seas of Polynesia . . . the footpaths of the Mohicans . . . These were the sorts of terrain that I had imagined Tinker wandering for the last two years. And all the time, he had been right here in New York City.

Why had I assumed that Tinker was so far afield? I'd like to say it was because the unsettled landscapes of London and Stevenson and Cooper had suited his romantic sensibility since he was a boy. But as soon as Hank said that Tinker was in New York, I knew that I had pictured him far afield because it was easier for me to accept his willingness to leave, if it was to travel alone in the wilds.

So it was with mixed feelings that I received this news. Picturing Tinker wandering among the crowds of Manhattan, poor in all but spirit, I felt regret and envy; but a touch of pride too; and a little bit of hope.

For wasn't it just a matter of time before we crossed each other's path? Despite all the hoopla, wasn't Manhattan just ten miles long and a mile or two wide?

So in the days that followed, I kept an eye out. I looked for his figure on the street corners and in the coffee shops. I imagined coming home and having him emerge once more from the doorway across the street.

But as the weeks turned into months, and the months into years, this sense of anticipation waned, and slowly, but surely, I stopped expecting to see him in a crowd. Swept along by the currents of my own ambitions and commitments, my daily life laid the groundwork for the grace of forgetting—until, that is, I finally ran into him, after all, in the Museum of Modern Art in 1966.

+ + +

Val and I took a taxi back to our apartment on Fifth Avenue. The cook had left us a little dinner on the stove, so we warmed it and opened a Bordeaux and ate standing in the kitchen.

I suppose that for most, the image of a husband and wife eating reheated food at their counter at nine o'clock would lack a certain romance; but for Valentine and me, who dined out formally so often, eating alone on our feet in our own kitchen was the highlight of the week.

As Val rinsed the plates, I walked down the hallway toward our bedroom. Along the wall were photographs hung from floor to ceiling. Normally, I ignored them as I passed, but on this night I found myself considering them one by one.

Unlike the photographs on Wallace's walls, these were not from four generations. They were all from the last twenty years. The earliest was of Val and me at a black-tie affair in 1947 looking a little awkward. A mutual acquaintance had just tried to introduce us, but Val had cut him short, explaining that we had already met—on Long Island in 1938— when he had given me a ride into the city to the tune of "Autumn in New York."

Among the photographs of friends, and of vacations in Paris and Venice and London, were a few with a professional bent: There was the cover of the February 1955 issue of *Gotham*—the first that I was to edit, and there was a picture of Val shaking the hand of a president. But my favorite was the picture of the two of us at our wedding with our arms around old Mr. Hollingsworth, his wife already gone and he soon to follow.

Having poured the last of the wine, Val found me in the hall surveying the photographs.

—Something tells me you're going to stay up a little longer, he said, handing me my glass. Do you want company?

—No. You go ahead. I won't be long.

With a wink and a smile, he tapped a picture taken on the beach in Southampton shortly after I had cut my hair an inch too short. Then he gave me a kiss and went into the bedroom. I went back to the living room and out onto the terrace. The air was cool and the lights of the city shimmered. The little planes no longer circled the Empire State Building, but it was still a view that practically conjugated hope: *I have hoped; I am hoping; I will hope.*

I lit a cigarette and then I threw the match over my shoulder for good luck thinking: *Doesn't New York just turn you inside out.*

It is a bit of a cliché to characterize life as a rambling journey on which we can alter our course at any given time—by the slightest turn of the wheel, the wisdom goes, we influence the chain of events and thus recast our destiny with new cohorts, circumstances, and discoveries. But for the most of us, life is nothing like that. Instead, we have a few brief periods when we are offered a handful of discrete options. Do I take this job or that job? In Chicago or New York? Do I join this circle of friends or that one, and with whom do I go home at the end of the night? And does one make time for children now? Or later? Or later still?

In that sense, life is less like a journey than it is a game of honeymoon bridge. In our twenties, when there is still so much time ahead of us, time that seems ample for a hundred indecisions, for a hundred visions and revisions—we draw a card, and we must decide right then and there whether to keep that card and discard the next, or discard the first card and keep the second. And before we know it, the deck has been played out and the decisions we have just made will shape our lives for decades to come.

Maybe that sounds bleaker than I intended.

Life doesn't have to provide you any options at all. It can easily define your course from the outset and keep you in check through all manner of rough and subtle mechanics. To have even one year when you're presented with choices that can alter your circumstances, your character, your course—that's by the grace of God alone. And it shouldn't come without a price.

I love Val. I love my job and my New York. I have no doubt that they were the right choices for me. And at the same time, I know that right choices by definition are the means by which life crystallizes loss.

◆　◆　◆

Back in December 1938, alone in that little room on Gansevoort Street, having already cast my lot with Mason Tate and the Upper East Side, I stood beside Tinker's empty suitcase and his cold coal stove and I read his promise to start every day by saying my name.

For a while, I guess I had done the same—I had started the days saying his. And just as he had imagined, it had helped me maintain some sense of direction, some sort of unerring course over seas tempest-tost.

But like so much else, that habit had been elbowed aside by life— becoming first intermittent, then rare, then lost to time.

Standing on my balcony overlooking Central Park almost thirty years later, I didn't punish myself for having let the practice lapse. I knew too well the nature of life's distractions and enticements—how the piecemeal progress of our hopes and ambitions commands our undivided attention, reshaping the ethereal into the tangible, and commitments into compromises.

No. I wasn't too hard on myself for all those years that had passed without my saying Tinker's name. But on the following morning, I woke with it on my lips. And so I have on so many mornings since.

APPENDIX

The Young George Washington's
*Rules of Civility & Decent Behaviour in
Company and Conversation*

1st   Every Action done in Company, ought to be with Some Sign of Respect, to those that are Present.

2nd   When in Company, put not your Hands to any Part of the Body, not usually Discovered.

3rd   Shew Nothing to your Freind that may affright him.

4th   In the Presence of Others Sing not to yourself with a humming Noise, nor Drum with your Fingers or Feet.

5th   If You Cough, Sneeze, Sigh, or Yawn, do it not Loud but Privately; and Speak not in your Yawning, but put Your handkercheif or Hand before your face and turn aside.

6th   Sleep not when others Speak, Sit not when others stand, Speak not when you Should hold your Peace, walk not on when others Stop.

7th   Put not off your Cloths in the presence of Others, nor go out your Chamber half Drest.

8th   At Play and at Fire its Good manners to Give Place to the last Commer, and affect not to Speak Louder than Ordinary.

9th   Spit not in the Fire, nor Stoop low before it neither Put your Hands into the Flames to warm them, nor Set your Feet upon the Fire especially if there be meat before it.

10th   When you Sit down, Keep your Feet firm and Even, without putting one on the other or Crossing them.

11th   Shift not yourself in the Sight of others nor Gnaw your nails.

12th   Shake not the head, Feet, or Legs rowl not the Eys lift not one eyebrow higher than the other wry not the mouth, and bedew no mans face with your Spittle, by approaching too near him when you Speak.

13th   Kill no Vermin as Fleas, lice ticks &c in the Sight of Others, if you See any filth or thick Spittle put your foot Dexteriously upon it if it be upon the Cloths of your Companions, Put it off privately, and if it be upon your own Cloths return Thanks to him who puts it off.

14th   Turn not your Back to others especially in Speaking, Jog not the Table or Desk on which Another reads or writes, lean not upon any one.

15th   Keep your Nails clean and Short, also your Hands and Teeth Clean yet without Shewing any great Concern for them.

16th   Do not Puff up the Cheeks, Loll not out the tongue rub the Hands, or beard, thrust out the lips, or bite them or keep the Lips too open or too Close.

17th   Be no Flatterer, neither Play with any that delights not to be Play'd Withal.

18th   Read no Letters, Books, or Papers in Company but when there is a Necessity for the doing of it you must ask leave: come not near the Books or Writings of Another so as to read them unless desired or give your opinion of them unask'd also look not nigh when another is writing a Letter.

19th   Let your Countenance be pleasant but in Serious Matters Somewhat grave.

20th   The Gestures of the Body must be Suited to the discourse you are upon.

21st   Reproach none for the Infirmaties of Nature, nor Delight to Put them that have in mind thereof.

22nd   Shew not yourself glad at the Misfortune of another though he were your enemy.

23nd   When you see a Crime punished, you may be inwardly Pleased; but always shew Pity to the Suffering Offender.

24th   Do not laugh too loud or too much at any Publick Spectacle.

25th   Superfluous Complements and all Affectation of Ceremonie are to be avoided, yet where due they are not to be Neglected.

26th   In Pulling off your Hat to Persons of Distinction, as Noblemen, Justices, Churchmen &c make a Reverence, bowing more or less according to the Custom of the Better Bred, and Quality of the Person. Amongst your equals expect not always that they Should begin with you first, but to Pull off the Hat when there is no need is Affectation, in the Manner of Saluting and resaluting in words keep to the most usual Custom.

27th Tis ill manners to bid one more eminent than yourself be covered as well as not to do it to whom it's due Likewise he that makes too much haste to Put on his hat does not well, yet he ought to Put it on at the first, or at most the Second time of being ask'd; now what is herein Spoken, of Qualification in behaviour in Saluting, ought also to be observed in taking of Place, and Sitting down for ceremonies without Bounds is troublesome.

28th If any one come to Speak to you while you are are Sitting Stand up tho he be your Inferiour, and when you Present Seats let it be to every one according to his Degree.

29th When you meet with one of Greater Quality than yourself, Stop, and retire especially if it be at a Door or any Straight place to give way for him to Pass.

30th In walking the highest Place in most Countrys Seems to be on the right hand therefore Place yourself on the left of him whom you desire to Honour: but if three walk together the middest Place is the most Honourable the wall is usually given to the most worthy if two walk together.

31st If any one far Surpasses others, either in age, Estate, or Merit yet would give Place to a meaner than himself in his own lodging or elsewhere the one ought not to except it, So he on the other part should not use much earnestness nor offer it above once or twice.

32nd To one that is your equal, or not much inferior you are to give the cheif Place in your Lodging and he to who 'tis offered ought at the first to refuse it but at the Second to accept though not without acknowledging his own unworthiness.

33rd They that are in Dignity or in office have in all places Preceedency but whilst they are Young they ought to respect those that are their equals in Birth or other Qualitys, though they have no Publick charge.

34th It is good Manners to prefer them to whom we Speak before ourselves especially if they be above us with whom in no Sort we ought to begin.

35th Let your Discourse with Men of Business be Short and Comprehensive.

36th Artificers & Persons of low Degree ought not to use many ceremonies to Lords, or Others of high Degree but Respect and highly Honour them, and those of high Degree ought to treat them with affibility & Courtesie, without Arrogancy.

37th In Speaking to men of Quality do not lean nor Look them full in the Face, nor approach too near them at lest Keep a full Pace from them.

38th In visiting the Sick, do not Presently play the Physicion if you be not Knowing therein.

39th In writing or Speaking, give to every Person his due Title According to his Degree & the Custom of the Place.

40th Strive not with your Superiers in argument, but always Submit your Judgment to others with Modesty.

41st Undertake not to Teach your equal in the art himself Professes; it Savours of arrogancy.

42nd Let thy ceremonies in Courtesy be proper to the Dignity of his place with whom thou conversest for it is absurd to act the same with a Clown and a Prince.

43rd Do not express Joy before one sick or in pain for that contrary Passion will aggravate his Misery.

44th When a man does all he can though it Succeeds not well blame not him that did it.

45th Being to advise or reprehend any one, consider whether it ought to be in publick or in Private; presently, or at Some other time in what terms to do it & in reproving Shew no Sign of Cholar but do it with all Sweetness and Mildness.

46th Take all Admonitions thankfully in what Time or Place Soever given but afterwards not being culpable take a Time & Place convenient to let him him know it that gave them.

47th Mock not nor Jest at any thing of Importance break no Jest that are Sharp Biting and if you Deliver any thing witty and Pleasant abstain from Laughing there at yourself.

48th   Wherein you reprove Another be unblameable yourself; for example is more prevalent than Precepts.

49th   Use no Reproachfull Language against any one neither Curse nor Revile.

50th   Be not hasty to beleive flying Reports to the Disparagement of any.

51st   Wear not your Cloths, foul, unript or Dusty but See they be Brush'd once every day at least and take heed that you approach not to any Uncleaness.

52nd   In your Apparel be Modest and endeavour to accomodate Nature, rather than to procure Admiration keep to the Fashion of your equals Such as are Civil and orderly with respect to Times and Places.

53rd   Run not in the Streets, neither go too slowly nor with Mouth open go not Shaking yr Arms kick not the earth with yr feet, go not upon the Toes, nor in a Dancing fashion.

54th   Play not the Peacock, looking every where about you, to See if you be well Deck't, if your Shoes fit well if your Stockings sit neatly, and Cloths handsomely.

55th   Eat not in the Streets, nor in the House, out of Season.

56th   Associate yourself with Men of good Quality if you Esteem your own Reputation; for 'tis better to be alone than in bad Company.

57th   In walking up and Down in a House, only with One in Company if he be Greater than yourself, at the first give him the Right hand and Stop not till he does and be not the first that turns, and when you do turn let it be with your face towards him, if he be a Man of Great Quality, walk not with him Cheek by Joul but Somewhat behind him; but yet in Such a Manner that he may easily Speak to you.

58th   Let your Conversation be without Malice or Envy, for 'tis a Sign of a Tractable and Commendable Nature: And in all Causes of Passion admit Reason to Govern.

59th   Never express anything unbecoming, nor Act agst the Rules Moral before your inferiours.

60th   Be not immodest in urging your Friends to Discover a Secret.

61st   Utter not base and frivolous things amongst grave and Learn'd Men nor very Difficult Questians or Subjects, among the Ignorant or things hard to be believed, Stuff not your Discourse with Sentences amongst your Betters nor Equals.

62nd   Speak not of doleful Things in a Time of Mirth or at the Table; Speak not of Melancholy Things as Death and Wounds, and if others Mention them Change if you can the Discourse tell not your Dreams, but to your intimate Friend.

63rd   A Man ought not to value himself of his Atchievements, or rare Qualities of wit; much less of his riches Virtue or Kindred.

64th   Break not a Jest where none take pleasure in mirth Laugh not aloud, nor at all without Occasion, deride no mans Misfortune, tho' there Seem to be Some cause.

65th   Speak not injurious Words neither in Jest nor Earnest Scoff at none although they give Occasion.

66th   Be not forward but friendly and Courteous; the first to Salute hear and answer & be not Pensive when it's a time to Converse.

67th   Detract not from others neither be excessive in Commanding.

68th   Go not thither, where you know not, whether you Shall be Welcome or not. Give not Advice without being Ask'd & when desired do it briefly.

69th   If two contend together take not the part of either unconstrained; and be not obstinate in your own Opinion, in Things indifferent be of the Major Side.

70th   Reprehend not the imperfections of others for that belongs to Parents Masters and Superiours.

71st   Gaze not on the marks or blemishes of Others and ask not how they came. What you may Speak in Secret to your Friend deliver not before others.

72nd   Speak not in an unknown Tongue in Company but in your own Language and that as those of Quality do and not as the Vulgar; Sublime matters treat Seriously.

73rd   Think before you Speak pronounce not imperfectly nor bring out your Words too hastily but orderly & distinctly.

74th   When Another Speaks be attentive your Self and disturb not the Audience if any hesitate in his Words help him not nor Prompt him without desired, Interrupt him not, nor Answer him till his Speech be ended.

75th   In the midst of Discourse ask not of what one treateth but if you Perceive any Stop because of your coming you may well intreat him gently to Proceed: If a Person of Quality comes in while your Conversing it's handsome to Repeat what was said before.

76th   While you are talking, Point not with your Finger at him of Whom you Discourse nor Approach too near him to whom you talk especially to his face.

77th   Treat with men at fit Times about Business & Whisper not in the Company of Others.

78th   Make no Comparisons and if any of the Company be Commended for any brave act of Vertue, commend not another for the Same.

79th   Be not apt to relate News if you know not the truth thereof. In Discoursing of things you Have heard Name not your Author always A Secret Discover not.

80th   Be not Tedious in Discourse or in reading unless you find the Company pleased therewith.

81st   Be not Curious to Know the Affairs of Others neither approach those that Speak in Private.

82nd   Undertake not what you cannot Perform but be Carefull to keep your Promise.

83rd   When you deliver a matter do it without Passion & with Discretion, however mean the Person be you do it too.

84th   When your Superiours talk to any Body hearken not neither Speak nor Laugh.

85th   In Company of these of Higher Quality than yourself Speak not til you are ask'd a Question then Stand upright put of your Hat & Answer in few words.

86th   In Disputes, be not So Desirous to Overcome as not to give Liberty to each one to deliver his Opinion and Submit to the Judgment of the Major Part especially if they are Judges of the Dispute.

87th   Let thy carriage be such as becomes a Man Grave Settled and attentive to that which is spoken. Contradict not at every turn what others Say.

88th   Be not tedious in Discourse, make not many Digressigns, nor repeat often the Same manner of Discourse.

89th   Speak not Evil of the absent for it is unjust.

90th   Being Set at meat Scratch not neither Spit Cough or blow your Nose except there's a Necessity for it.

91st   Make no Shew of taking great Delight in your Victuals, Feed not with Greediness; cut your Bread with a Knife, lean not on the Table neither find fault with what you Eat.

92nd   Take no Salt or cut Bread with your Knife Greasy.

93rd   Entertaining any one at the table it is decent to present him wt. meat; Undertake not to help others undesired by the Master.

94th   If you Soak bread in the Sauce let it be no more than what you put in your Mouth at a time and blow not your broth at Table but Stay till Cools of it Self.

95th   Put not your meat to your Mouth with your Knife in your hand neither Spit forth the Stones of any fruit Pye upon a Dish nor Cast anything under the table.

96th   It's unbecoming to Stoop much to ones Meat Keep your Fingers clean & when foul wipe them on a Corner of your Table Napkin.

97th   Put not another bit into your Mouth til the former be Swallowed let not your Morsels be too big for the Gowls.

98th   Drink not nor talk with your mouth full neither Gaze about you while you are a Drinking.

99th   Drink not too leisurely nor yet too hastily. Before and after Drinking wipe your Lips; breath not then or Ever with too Great a Noise, for its uncivil.

100th   Cleanse not your teeth with the Table Cloth Napkin Fork or Knife but if Others do it let it be done wt. a Pick Tooth.

101st   Rince not your Mouth in the Presence of Others.

102nd   It is out of use to call upon the Company often to Eat nor need you Drink to others every Time you Drink.

103rd In Company of your Betters be not longer in eating than they are lay not your Arm but only your hand upon the table.

104th It belongs to the Chiefest in Company to unfold his Napkin and fall to Meat first, But he ought then to Begin in time & to Dispatch with Dexterity that the Slowest may have time allowed him.

105th Be not Angry at Table whatever happens & if you have reason to be so, shew it not but on a Cheerfull Countenance especially if there be Strangers for Good Humour makes one Dish of Meat a Feast.

106th Set not yourself at the upper of the Table but if it Be your Due or that the Master of the house will have it So, Contend not, least you Should Trouble the Company.

107th If others talk at Table be attentive but talk not with Meat in your Mouth.

108th When you Speak of God or his Atributes, let it be Seriously & wt. Reverence. Honour & Obey your Natural Parents altho they be Poor.

109th Let your Recreations be Manfull not Sinfull.

110th Labour to keep alive in your Breast that Little Spark of Celestial fire Called Conscience.

Finis

Acknowledgments

Foremost, I thank my wife and children along with my parents, siblings, and in-laws, for providing me with endless hours of joy and support. I thank Messrs. Arndt, Britton, Loening, and Seirer for being such extraordinary colleagues and friends over the last fifteen plus years. I thank my close companions and fellow readers Ann Brashares, Dave Gilbert & Hilary Reyl, as well as Sarah Burnes, Pete McCabe, and Jeremy Mindich, who all gave valuable feedback. Special thanks to Jennifer Walsh, Dorian Karchmar & the team at William Morris, Paul Slovak & the team at Viking, and Jocasta Hamilton at Sceptre who helped bring this work out into the world. And thanks to all the excellent purveyors of coffee from Canal Street to Union Square as well as to the Danny Meyer and Keith McNally organizations for providing such terrific stomping grounds.

Looking further back, I want to thank my grandmothers who had such poise and verve; Peter Matthiessen, whose early confidence made all the difference; Dick Baker, who remains my paragon of intellectual curiosity and discipline; Bob Dylan for creating several lifetimes' worth of inspiration; and Chance for landing me so unexpectedly in New York.